Born in Brisbane, Al Campbell is a mother and full-time carer. Long ago she studied a bit, acted a bit, and pulled a lot of beers. Her first-ever publication was in *Overland* in 2020, followed by a story in *Signs of Life – an anthology*. *The Keepers* all but begged her to write it, given it is about issues – and people – that matter to her more than anything.

Book club notes are available at www.uqp.com.au

THE KEEPERS

AL CAMPBELL

First published 2022 by University of Queensland Press
PO Box 6042, St Lucia, Queensland 4067 Australia

University of Queensland Press (UQP) acknowledges the Traditional Owners and
their custodianship of the lands on which UQP operates. We pay our respects to their
Ancestors and their descendants, who continue cultural and spiritual connections to
Country. We recognise their valuable contributions to Australian and global society.

uqp.com.au
reception@uqp.com.au

Cover design by Laura Thomas
Cover artwork *For the Love of My Son* by Tanya Darl
Typeset in 11.5/16 pt Bembo Std by Post Pre-press Group, Brisbane
Printed in Australia by McPherson's Printing Group

University of Queensland Press is assisted
by the Australian Government through
the Australia Council, its arts funding and
advisory body.

A catalogue record for this book is available from the National Library of Australia.

ISBN 978 0 7022 6548 8 (pbk)
ISBN 978 0 7022 6667 6 (epdf)
ISBN 978 0 7022 6668 3 (epub)
ISBN 978 0 7022 6669 0 (kindle)

University of Queensland Press uses papers that are natural, renewable and
recyclable products made from wood grown in well-managed forests and other
controlled sources. The logging and manufacturing processes conform to the
environmental regulations of the country of origin.

For Rupert and Frazer

Nothing is performed by demons; there are no demons.

– *Siddhartha*, Hermann Hesse

Special needs group pays tribute to 11yo Sydney boy with autism killed by train after escaping from respite care

A disability care service provider says it is cooperating with a police investigation into the death of a young boy with severe autism who was hit and killed by a train in Sydney's south.

The 11-year-old boy died after he escaped from a respite care facility at Oatley just after 7:00pm yesterday.

His carers alerted authorities and a police search was set up involving Polair and the dog squad.

The boy's body was found at the Oatley train station two hours later.

Police confirmed on Monday morning that the child, who was non-verbal, was hit by a train.

Civic Disability Services Limited confirmed the child was from its short-term accommodation facility for children and young people.

It said family members had been informed of the details, but due to the sensitive nature, and out of respect for the family, it would be inappropriate to release any more details.

'This is a tragic and distressing incident and our deepest sympathies and thoughts go out to the child's family', Civic CEO Annie Doyle said.

'Counselling and assistance services have been made available to our staff and others who have been affected.'

The Sydney Friendship Circle, a support group for families of children with special needs, posted tributes to the 11-year-old on social media, saying he was a treasured son, grandson, brother and friend.

Monday, 2:06 am

'What about shock treatment?' I say, the scissors and I pausing.

He looks at me, the way he does. Thinks I'm being flippant. But he doesn't speak, too busy being *enigmatic*, so it's up to me.

'Is it still called that?' I ask. 'Shock treatment?'

I finish trimming two newspaper clippings. 'As you'd expect,' I say, 'I've not kept up. Only discovered what a Fortnite is the other day, courtesy of Frank. Not a typo after all.'

And now, the printout of the online article. 'Either way,' I say, the horror on the page a thing of thorns in my hand.

Eleven years old, dead at the end of a night-time street.

'Regardless of what it's called …'

Struck by a train. Some mother's child sniffed out by dogs.

Frank and I would have been watching television, having a laugh, Teddy behind us at the dining table, headphones on, YouTubing.

'It couldn't hurt, could it? Another go couldn't hurt.'

I drop the scraps into the bin, return the scissors to the desk drawer, fish about for the glue. Scrapbook #12 lies open before me, almost full. He observes my night's work. Patient. Bemused.

'Well, I'm supposed to want something, aren't I?' I say, pasting, blowing on the page.

'"What do *you* want, Jay?" they all ask – the doctors, the therapists. "What's your happy ending?"' Am I provoking him or, by his vivid quiet, is it the other way around? 'Problem is, the only thing I want I can't have, can I? *Happy ending?* Christ. Because we all get one of those. Right, Keeper?'

His head tilts back impossibly far, until all I see are shoulders and the latched spindle of his neck. I half-expect to hear a thud – a bloodless cartoon bonce wheeling around the bedroom floor. But of course I don't. His movements are controlled, measured – everything on his terms. He has all the time in the world – time being, for him, an idly whistled tune. He can kick it up on a whim, suspend and resume it at will. A trinket in his pocket. His magic act.

'Besides, isn't that why it's called ECT? Electro*convivial* therapy?' I set the scrapbook on the pile of earlier volumes under my desk. 'How many ba*ZING*s this time do you think? Six? Ten? Like … microdermabrasion? Perhaps I ought to consider that instead.'

Through the small-pane windows is the dark gully of our street, its lone plucky lamppost gooned by wanton whacks of lightning. Keep's reflection gutters like a flame.

'So, what do you say?' I turn to face him. 'Hit the dim switch for a bit?'

Finally, a response: *You don't need shock treatment.* At times, his voice is very beautiful.

'Shucks.' My shoulders heave, concede. 'You say the sweetest things.'

I lean forward, inspecting his latest incarnation. Bald as bone and mouthless. No breath, of course. Without ears. His nose the vaguest squinch. No need of slots or slits to speak or hear. A waist worked so thin I could circle it with my hands, gnawed like the core of an apple. And that face – I want to touch it, whatever it might be. Some ancient mica, colourless and brittle? Or fossilised hoof, unclean and before time? Next visit it might be something else. His appearance is rarely the same.

'It might stop the things I see, for a while at least,' I suggest. 'The things I hear.'

4

With him, I might as well be mouthless too.

'It's like a twenty-four-hour test pattern inside my head.'

Words are formed – I know they are. Lips part, brush together. Tongue taps teeth.

'Are they still a thing, test patterns?'

Yet we have never been overheard, not once in more than forty years.

'My very own catastrophe channel. Warning! Warning!'

I know I'll be irritating him.

'Evacuate! Abort! *RUN!*'

He hates it when I whinge.

'It never stops. Can you imagine?'

Still as a statue, one of his self-preening poses – elbow on armrest, fingers a pensive claw like some famous auteur being interviewed. He speaks: *Any supply of baZINGs would soon be exhausted.*

'You know, sarcasm makes you common.'

Ah-ha, ah-ha. He laughs, a tweezered whistle. *Hardly.*

We sit listening to the storm, and I press a palm to the window. I long to be cold. Frozen eyelashes cold.

'East Antarctic Plateau,' I confide to the glass. 'Coldest recorded temperature – minus eighty-nine point two degrees Celsius, Vostok Station, 1983.'

Frozen organs cold.

But I have never seen so much as a single snowflake, no winter-famous geographies with their peaks and fjords, rivers and ruins. Though I have seen other things. Things less celebrated. Things infrequently discussed.

Closing my eyes, it looms – my big cold, a great wolfing white, ripped from the Earth's frozen rimrock-edge, survived by none. So terrible, so darkly fabled it cannot be named. It chances upon us yet knows us, takes us with it, the three of us: me, Teddy, Frank.

Takes you where? he asks, no thought safe from him.

'The rest of the way.'

But this world I'm in steams. No hoarfrost here. This window that cannot be opened, stuck for years, is like sheeted heat. Four dead flies lie forever between it and the wire screen. My hand drops, disappointed, into my lap. This town's usual clamminess, grimy and mope-sunk, is the best a March night can do.

Next to my bed is a bookcase, a set of unnested matryoshka dolls hip-to-hip along its middle shelf. I imagine what they might say were their painted lips ever to open and speak. Given all they have witnessed, their stories must weigh like millstone.

You still have them, he remarks, watching me just as intently.

'As you well know.'

I pick up the smallest, tip her gently, hear her quiet rattle.

And there she is, the tiny facsimile.

'She's nothing of the sort.' And she isn't. No raven curls for her, no rosy cheeks. She is blonde but plain. And stern – none of the others' self-delight.

'She is—'

Forever boxed in? A mise en abyme?

I give him a sour look. 'The end of the line.'

Outside, a mosh of trees like go-go girls, squid-limbed and wild, all beat and buck and peril. He knows how much I love rainy nights. Rainy days. Rain. Perhaps the drear and squall are only rabbits in a hat, carnival tricks to enchant and distract, when what's really out there is only ever the same: grass dry as rusted tin, trees like stone markers.

'Is this from you?' I ask him. 'This tempest?'

It can all be from me if you like.

'You've been saying that forever,' I say. 'And I still don't know what it means.' I pause, giving him a chance to respond. He doesn't. Not that it matters. Perhaps this part is a dream.

'Shock treatment,' I say, back on message. 'It started the crazy.'

Did it?

'Another go might take it away.'

Would it?

'Fry the junk.'

Fry it?

'Reset me.'

Reset you to what?

He's got me there.

'Never mind,' I say later, much later. I'm exhausted. Perhaps I did drift off. 'I'll tell you what I want. Since you asked.'

I don't believe I did.

'Certainty.'

You all want that.

'But I deserve it.'

You all think that.

'Not for me,' I say, looking over at Teddy. 'For him.' My son, my roommate these past fifteen years, finally asleep. 'And for his twin,' I add, heart heavy. 'Who knows where Frank will land?'

So many years the three of us in here together, both boys terrified of the night, of sleep itself. Three single beds abreast – me in the middle; Frank on my left, finger-doodles on my arm; Teddy ever-watchful on my right. Close enough to save each other, close enough to all perish at once. Jerrik upstairs in his own quarters, his 'suite', as he calls it, the top floor where the walls have been cut away and the rooms tunnelled through, offering both grand space and an even grander semblance of being somewhere else, someone else.

Jerrik the ~~husband~~ lodger. The bloke one floor up more than he is father, the boys' Danish *far*. Posing no risk but liable for no rescue. Oblivious to us, to his sons' small below-stairs triumphs. Frank's first night in his own room across the hall, making it through till breakfast. And the grudge-grey afternoon when a hollow-eyed

Teddy watched me prise our beds apart, first by mere inches – holding hands still a nightly protocol – then, weeks later, by the vast expanse of a standing lamp. The hours we lay in them, facing one another, practising our separation, just to make sure that a shifted bed didn't also shift the world in its turning.

'I need to know they'll be alright, Keep,' I say, tears lurking, eager for opportunity. 'That's it. The only thing I'll ever want.' Always my undoing, these words.

All around us slump toys that once stood, dolls that once sang. Against the walls, teetering stacks of life, plastic-crated. Trains, cars, blocks, green crocodiles and pink-suede pigs, things that spun and hopped and flew. Not done with; decommissioned. Momentarily relieved of active service. Waiting to be loved again.

'Without it,' I say, 'there's no point to anything.' Teddy flutters in his sleep, left side, right side. 'Without certainty,' I continue, 'I may as well opt for nothing.'

Keep's eyes, those two black voids, follow mine around the cramped, broken-down room. *Option actioned.*

'Don't mock,' I say, defiant. 'Not everyone finds it, Keep. Their yellow-brick road. Their "fabulous yellow".'

Oh my, is that the time? he says, feigning a look at his twiggish wrist, at a watch he isn't wearing. *Kerouac o'clock?*

'Most people don't even look,' I persist. 'But I looked, didn't I? Got close, once or twice.'

Yes, you looked. And then you looked away.

My turn now for silence.

Bringing us here.

I nod. 'Bringing us here.' Those tears seizing their moment.

An index finger ascends from his lap – a deliberate, showy movement – points to where a right eye might be, then arcs slowly down his narrow drag of a face. His meagre shoulders flag theatrically. A black line draws itself just above his chin, then splits

8

wide, freezing into a mute scream. Inside it sit all the screams of the world. He is Melpomene's tragic mask, miming tears.

Ho hum, says the frozen hole.

In a blink, no more mouth. No more tragedy.

Ho hum.

'Up yours,' I say, drying my face with my sleeve. Even after all these years, I can still misread his mood, a visit's underlying motive. He has come to be cruel, tell me what's what. He does that sometimes.

Keep does not approve of my scrapbooks. *Morbid, pointless,* he says of them.

Urgent, essential, I reply in their defence.

Can you not move past it? he says of them. To which I say, No, I cannot get past it. I won't. I'm the one who doesn't.

But we're not saying that tonight. Tonight I say, 'The only people for me are the mad ones. Who burn, burn, burn, like fabulous yellow Roman candles exploding like spiders across the stars.'

I don't know why I recite Kerouac's words. Maybe to prove I still can. Maybe to see if that part of me is still there, deep inside those plastic crates, mad to live, mad to be saved, spinning and flying.

Awww, he says. Auteur again, back to regarding his lordly claw – long and hairless and gecko-pink.

'I'm frightened, Keep.'

His dead eyes flare once, twice. Quite a feat given he's forgotten eyelids. *I know,* he replies.

'All the time.'

I hear him sigh. *You are.*

His stalked fingers hover in front of my face. It is how he reads – pages, heads; how he sees – anyone, in any place, at any time. Before we come to be, long after we are unchained and gone. Those thin places from which we slip, to which we randomly return. His hovering hands showing him all. Not always a comfort to see those

9

bogey digits up and about, eavesdropping the brute asides of my mind.

I decided on you when you were four, you know.

'Why?'

A long, slow, tidal shrug.

Twelve fingers but not one nail, just hooked flesh, smooth as plastic. No prints. Those hands truly are reptilian, more like some loch creature's feet, slimy pads for trawling through murk and silt.

Because you needed me, Spider.

I remember the first time I saw him, less horrified than a child probably should have been.

'What was wrong with me?'

What wasn't? What isn't?

His tentacle-arms, so thin and flat, resettle along the armrests of his chair. But they unfurl, spilling, spooling along the floor, coming to rest at my feet.

'Time to wake up now,' I tell myself.

You're not asleep.

'I am.'

You're too busy to sleep, Spider. A busy little bitie with her busybody books, a-wincing a-watching the world go by.

'Busybody? Keep, it's—'

The quailing in the back of your mind all you hear, the slant in the corner of your eye all you see, everywhere you look. No fool more blinkered.

I cross my arms. 'You're in a mood.'

WHO'S in a mood? His voice a barrelling blast of light. It swallows me, spins me in its tight white throat, time chunked and pitched like jump cuts in a film. My bed is made, the sheets tucked smooth, now unmade, made again. The scrapbooks, piled neatly under the desk, fly open, scatter, then close, spines aligned. Clothes are strewn about on the floor, heaped in corners, then hanging as they were. Heaped, hanging. My hair is a long, thick braid, then loose and sweeping over my shoulder, a braid again until I can't remember how it had been to start with.

Party tricks. Keep's cabaret.

'Too tired, Keep. Enough now.'

Awww! I'm tired, Keep. I'm frightened, Keep. Woe, woe, woe is me, Keep. Using my own voice to mock me.

No longer four dead flies in the windowsill. Now there are fifty, a hundred, each one alive and ulcerating into ten more, the size of toads, their faces rubbery against the glass, their twitching eyes-within-eyes all turned on me.

'Are these from you?' I ask.

It can all be from me if you like.

'Okay ... enough!' The flies, a seething pile-on, all squirm as one, watch as one. 'Take your posturing and your God complex and piss off.'

The toad-flies startle. I worry the window will shatter. If they get in, I will never get them out. They will join forces with the rest – the Other Things. So many of them already, crouching in corners, behind, in, under everything.

His voice is as it was – a cool current. *My God complex?* The voice of the upper hand. *Could I not allege the same, Spider?*

'Me?' I say, a sharp laugh. 'No, no, I'm no god. I'm a mother. Far more powerful. I could tell the boys that night is day, up is down, good is bad, that *they* are bad – and they'd believe every word, play out every vile prophecy. You of all people know there's nothing about a child that its mother can't fuck up. Turn its life into grey rags and burnt sticks.'

The darkness of the room is all at once too large, too absolute, outside the law of things. It locks over us like a lidded box.

Everything stops, the wind and rain, the grumbling glass panes. Only the sound of Teddy's breathing, exploding my heart.

11

Thursday, 1:14 am

Another sleepless night. Technically, morning. A Thursday, I think.

Teddy, full of wriggle and fidget. I stroke his face (slightly flushed), his jaw, apply deep pressure to his elbows and knees, trying to stir them, remove the blindfolds from his sluggy neurons and proprioceptors. Only when his body wakes up can it remember how to relax, register its need for rest. I know how it is meant to be done, how it is meant to work. But tonight, both the theory and its practitioner are failing badly. Teddy's body is lost, and I cannot marshal it home. All I unshutter is a romping hilarity – convulsant laughter, hiccups nerve-deep flipping him inside out. And before long Teddy is out of bed, a spark pogoing from one impulse to the next – the piano, the computer, book corner, the bathtub-cum-ball pit, the front porch hammock. Me a creak in his wake, begging quiet.

2:02 am

Plan B: a decampment to the downstairs laundry.

Narrow and windowless, black as tar after sunset. Arctic air conditioning.

A salt lamp offers us a milky mauve welcome and the rack of drying laundry pastels the air, blossomy and biscuit-sweet. Teddy, a thin dart, aims himself at our makeshift bed – a downy bolthole on the floor slotted below an old desk. At the urging of a sleep specialist, a storyboard of Teddy's 'ideal bedtime routine' was once velcroed to its underside:

brush teeth 😄 → into bed 🛏 → story time 📖 → sleepy rub 🧸 →
kiss kiss 😘 → night light 💡 → sleep tight 🌙
HAPPY MORNING FACES! 😁 🧍

And, as urged, Teddy would point to each picture in the sequence as though ticking off the steps, my job to nod with enthusiasm. Our ritual of faith.

None of it did a jot for Teddy's sleep. 'Zero jots,' as Frank would say. We replaced the storyboard long ago with pictures of meerkats and miniature donkeys, the 2000 Essendon dream team. Also worth zero jots in terms of a sleep dividend, but better to snug up in happy cheer than be stared down by dud allied-health alchemy. Awake either way.

Almost bespoke, our Plan B bower is tailored to Teddy's needs: ordered, unchanging, close. It is our last-chance saloon – our final hope of resetting the night's clock. If sleep doesn't find us here, it doesn't find us at all.

It was by accident, so often the way, that we discovered the witching of the washing machine – its operatic, soothing predictability. The filling tub – a trickling overture. The to-ing and fro-ing recitatives of the wash cycle – *swish-a slosh, swish-a slosh*. The crescendo whir of its finale. Cradlesong, for Teddy at least. Before commando-crawling in beside him, I sacrifice a basket of frowzy bath towels to the machine's paddled maw – an offering to our personal god of sleep.

In the pale-lilac glow, Teddy's fingers skim my face, barely there taps across my nose, my cheeks. He is counting my freckles and I have no doubt he will calculate their precise number. As he does this, he lies listening to his pillow, its covert life. A warble of feathers under his head? The stretch and yawn of the freshly washed cotton slip, its breath raincloud-clean? Microbial cooties? I drag a summer blanket up to his chest. The back of his hand circles lightly over the fabric's weave – four circles, ten circles, minutes of circles, his head tilted, his ear tuning. The blanket itself may not be the thing, the stimming circles merely a grounding, enabling focus, a shift closer to whatever it is he hears – signals, transmissions, a rock's slow rusting, the travails of a worm – for it will be something, far from here yet far from silent.

Could it be that those restless feathers tickle up this: a ripple that soon becomes a king tide?

Feathers … birds ducks geese … two legs that paddle two legs that swim … swimming … beach trip car—

no legs on a car … tyres on a car … black tyres black car black seat black dog black—

dogs bark don't quack … bark on a dog bark on a tree … tree timber wood—

wood this desk … four legs this desk four legs like a dog not like a dog—

second-hand this desk

not seconds on a clock

second-hand (why hands?) … no hands on a desk no hands on a duck no hands on a goose …

And on it goes, a rocket ride in seconds as the rest of us plod on. A rocket ride of roundabouts and ring roads, intersections, flyovers, curlicues of hyperconnections swerving beyond his control. Possibly sublime, possibly maddening.

Then again, it may be nothing like this at all.

For here's what I know (but can never hope to understand) about Teddy: everything is somehow connected, everything a purposeful fit. Nothing is ever nothing.

Also this: the spike of an old-style fluorescent tube makes him flinch as though struck, flee the room, shielding his ears – hence our predilection for lamplight. He *feels* light as surely as he does the growth of his hair, scissors an insult to each and every strand, haircuts long abandoned. The colour yellow possesses terrors that turn him to stone. Despite never speaking, not a single word in fifteen years, Teddy can sing like an angel, in Latin, Italian, French, for precisely sixty seconds. And he's yet to meet a stranger whose birthday month he can't predict. Anyone, anywhere. A perfect score.

And here's what I *think* I know about Teddy: unmapped terrain is his surest footing – hearing the unvoiced, seeing the just-beyond, drawn always to the underside of the leaf than to the fanfare of the bloom. There is more than just us in this room, in this world, more than what we know and transact and applaud. A world more beaten track and borderland to Teddy than paved lanes and centred lines. A *more-than* beyond the grapplings of most. But the shy lodgers with their dark-corner dialects, Teddy observes them all, observes them best. Out of the shadows come the rumoured and the remnant, their hands held out, palms open, inviting him into a wayside world that Teddy, willingly or not, seems to be part of.

Who could blame him for not wanting to sleep through all that – an endless carnival of discovery? But what a weight of care and affection. How exhausting.

Teddy reaches out, picks up my hand. We lace our fingers. He squeezes, I squeeze, back and forth we go. This takes as long as it takes, until my turn goes unanswered, and he sleeps.

2:54 am

Some people count backwards when they can't sleep. Instead, I do this:

Canada – population thirty-five million, capital Ottawa, coldest recorded temperature -63.0°C, Yukon, 1947.

Iceland – population three hundred and seventy-one thousand, capital Reykjavík, coldest recorded temperature -38.0°C, 1918.

It started when I was a child. The five coldest countries, then ten, then twenty. Though I refresh population statistics with every census, I ran out of countries long ago. I include cold cities now. Hot places are forever ineligible.

And now my mind travels through time, as minds in the dark often do, to nights of another life.

And to last night. *Dimension Unknown*, season finale. Frank's favourite show.

Frank: 'Most other pare ... most other pare ... most other parents make their k- ... make their k- ... make their ... k-*KIDS* watch ... watch the news. But we never wa- ... we never do.'

'No, darling, we don't.'

'I'm gl- ... I'm gl- ... I'm gl-*GLAD* you're not like most parents, Mum.'

'I'm glad you're not like most kids, Franko.'

Our hero, Commander Noah Hay, wrestling an ailing shuttle, low fuel, oxygen fast running out. *Do you read? Do you read, over?* Tense music swells.

Frank leaning across, whispering, 'If I was a magish- ... magish- ... magician, Mummy, I'd ... I'd make ... I'd make ... I'd make C- ... I'd make C- ... C-*COMMANDER* ... I'd make Commander Hay marry you.'

Frank, make-believing (for his sake or for mine?) that I'm not still technically married to his father. To Jerrik, who may be sleeping upstairs in his suite or, more likely, who may be sleeping with Cassie or Mia or Yumi.

'Sweet,' I tell him. 'However ... *Jay Hay?*'

'Hey ... Hey ... Hey Jay.' Frank chuckles. 'Hey, Jay Hay.'

'Hey, Frank Hay.'

When we stop laughing, Frank says that if he were a magician, he'd make Commander Noah Hay come around and hold my hand whenever I get sad.

'Not the c- ... not the c- ... not the ... c-*CHARACTER*. The actor. I kn-know … I kn-know … We all know how much you like him. Almost as much as Daniel Craig.'

'What a lovely thought,' I say.

3:10 am

Teddy in deep sleep. I curl and shift around him (his body a little warmer than I think it should be), trying to ease the ache in my hip, recalling the many attempts to set him up in his own room like his brother. Losing sleep so as to devour books on sleep, on the evils of bed-sharing. The popular parenting paradigms just couldn't be made to fit. Nor will the 'family life cycle theory' – the idea of a family as a system moving through time. Stage 1: single young adult, living independently. I got to Stage 1, somehow. For Jerrik, no stage exists beyond it. Much of what I do aims to put Stage 1 within Frank's reach, to have him grow some feathers, ready him for short-burst flights from the nest. He may or may not get there. But there is no cycle theory for Teddy and me, so we have fashioned our own. Single-phase. And this is it.

Russia – population one hundred and forty-six million, capital Moscow, coldest recorded temperature -67.7°C, Oymyakon, 1933.

It isn't a nervous tic. Not an obsessive-compulsive ritual though, if it were, I wouldn't fight it because these are also facts. No-one could deny them, not even my mother, who to this day denies everything. No claiming, *There's no such place, Jay.* All in your head, those three-point-three-million wind-chapped Mongolians. Havens of frost, blizzarding and creaturely, cold enough to ice over hell and all its spiv spruikers. Ghosts self-destruct in snow. Mine would, at least.

Scotland – population five point three million, capital Edinburgh, coldest recorded temperature -27.2°C, Aberdeenshire, 1895/1982, and Altnaharra, 1995.

No more ridiculous than counting sheep.

Teddy's chest rising and falling. The Whirlpool muscling through the rinse cycle.

Cradlesong for Teddy.

Agitato for me.

Not just her voice now, the lady herself. My mother, Lenore, though none ever called her that. She was Lonnie, Cyclone Lonnie, and here she is centrestage, her natural place, the corner of my eye (Keep, you bastard) as brightly lit as a stadium.

I am eight when she brings home our tea.

And I am twelve as she throws it onto the kitchen table.

Seven and ten and fourteen I am, when she tears open the Charcoal Charlie's silver bag, shredding its jolly comic-book flames, its conga line of jubilant hens. Our *tea*; never our dinner. Dinner was for upstarts, what la-di-das ate. Our tea – headless and oozing, scummed in half-jellied slime. In ruins to start with. Night after night. Year after year.

Her handbag still over her shoulder as she mauls the mangled chicken, long nails slick with grease, sucking on the parson's nose, undressing at the same time, screaming at me in her petticoat and Razzamatazz: *Tomato! Lettuce! Why the HELL haven't you buttered the bread!*

But it's 6:04 pm. Mike has started without her.

Mike Hilton, moustache heavy. The last word in newsreaders, according to my mother. Mike's six o'clock news, less observed than worshipped. If so much as the first half-minute of Mike's broadcast is missed, it all has to be missed, the dial smacked *OFF* in fury. But missing the start means she has to deny herself the end – the cherished sign-off.

'Now I won't see Mike's "Goodnight and God bless!"' A catastrophe. 'You know how much I love it. "Goodnight and God bless! Goodnight and God bless!" Is that too much to ask out of life? *Christ all-bloody-mighty!*'

18

On such nights, those first few seconds lost, I can see she does her best to get past it, counselling herself as though she is two people: *It doesn't matter, Lon, it really doesn't.* Fingers fussing at the cloth mat under her plate. *Eat your tea. Waste not, want not. A sin, wasting food.* But missing Mike's opening – his handsome, *trust-me-Lonnie* face looking up from his paper copy directly into my mother's adoring eyes – clamps a hand over her mouth. She can't breathe. She can't think or listen to the rest of what Mike has to tell her. Panic rises in her like a killing flood. Eating tea and watching the news, all the news, go hand in hand. She and Mike, hand in hand. It's as though she is letting him down.

On Missing Mike nights, our plates fly like frisbees, our TV trays upended like Jesus in the temple with his cleansing whip of cords, making a mess of everything. Baked beans and fried eggs skitter down the walls, smear the curtains. Tinned soup and buttered toast sog up the carpet.

At least on this night we haven't made it past the kitchen, because tonight is different. Tonight is worse. Someone has obviously done something in the chicken shop or at work, said wounding words on the phone, treated her like the office junior (*that little tart*) when she's a *secretary, for God's sake! A private bloody secretary!* Her rage a slow, day-long simmer. And into the steaming pot have fallen other remembered slights – ancient insults, outstanding offences – a Lenore-long simmer now, an endless one, congealing the hell-broth until it boils up and over, too much for the pot to hold.

I know what happens next. This show's been running for years.

Flinging open the fridge, she goes to put the remains of the chicken away, the chicken that is no longer our ~~dinner~~ tea. But she stops. No. Storing it away, that chicken, to become leftovers, everyday leftovers, will not do. Why, that would be getting on with things when my mother is in pain – pain *good and proper* – and when Lonnie is in pain things *cannot must not will not* simply be gotten on with!

Laying waste now to that fridge.

Teeth clenched, fists thrashing side to side, the length and breadth of every shelf, motoring over cling-filmed corn, tinned fish, fruit salad. The milk and juice cartons spew and gush, the lettuce that falls to her feet booted into the hall. Like a dog digging a hole, she scrapes and scratches – everything in must be out, everything up must be down, everything whole, crushed. It ends when she flies to her room and slams the door, sobbing on the other side of it.

'I'll do better, Jay. I promise. Tomorrow I'll be really good. Just you watch.'

Her bedroom light off, so suddenly, as though the room itself has passed out.

3:28 am

Eyes closing, and Frank is back: *But we never watch the news.*

I think of the eleven-year-old struck by the train and all the headlines I never want us to become.

'No, darling,' I say into the dark, 'we don't.'

Friday, 6:45 am

My long, mean pinch of a kitchen – a strip of old verandah, converted by someone circa 1973. Lime green. Slime green, according to Frank. Knotty pine panelling. Overhead cupboards only the boys can reach. Under-bench cupboards whose doors fell off years ago, still waiting for repair like the holes in the bathroom wall. In a previous life, this house had been 'emergency accommodation'. How I laughed when the agent told us this. Made to order, I remember thinking, hands on my swollen belly. A low-rent hostel for homeless men – straight out of prison or some medically ordered incarceration. Men well accustomed to disappointment – feeling it, being it – grateful for somewhere to sleep and eat and wash, even here. A rabbit warren of uselessly small rooms and warping passageways, long walls and steep shadows. What the near-bys (who've rarely come near) call the 'dip-down house', sitting as it does in the frown of two sharp hills. A 'renovator' when we bought it – a 'detonator' now.

Leaning against the sink, I sip black coffee, trying to escape the reek of fried egg and animal. Jerrik's late-night, post-a-couple-of-reds-with-the-boys fry-up. Surfaces feel tacky and the air like something bittered and hurriedly spittooned.

Friday again. April again.

My tongue probes the inside of my cheek, trying to assess whether my latest mouth ulcer (named Lenore – they're all named after my mother) has become any less ferocious overnight.

Bad things happen in April.

Eliot agreed – it is the cruellest month. ANZAC Cove. Hitler was born. Shakespeare died. Jerrik and I got married in the hottest April for a century. His mother fainted during the ceremony. Poor Mette. We could only assume it was the heat.

Doctor Alastair Jones, another Friday morning, ten Aprils ago: 'Apologies if my candour has caught you off guard. But you've got to know what you're in for, what you're up against.'

What we were up against? Our own child?

'In all my thirty-three years of practice, I've never seen anyone so severe, so affected, ever get any better. Teddy has no hope, and nor do you if you keep him.'

April words. April fools.

'So, I definitely ... I definitely ... So I definitely don't have to g- ... don't have to g- ... don't have to ... *attend*, Mum?'

The third time this morning Frank has asked this. A school camp, he can think of nothing else.

'Thank ... thank you, Mum,' he says, panting, sucking back on his inhaler, one puff. 'Thank you. Because ... because Mad- ... because Madison ... because Madison F- ... F- ... because Madison F- ... F- ... F-*FOX* is going.'

I spoon warmed baked beans into a bowl, slide it to him. 'I thought we'd taken care of the feculent Miss Fox. I distinctly recall strangling her with my own fair hands. Oh no! That *was* Madison, wasn't it? Or did I suit up and slay the wrong little villain?'

'They're every- ... they're every- ... they're every-... everywh- *WHERE*, Mum,' says Frank, his voice leaden. 'Like Butch ... like ... like Butch ... like Butch and Sun-Sundance. We're surrounded.'

I smile grimly, my doomed-cowboy smile. 'We are indeed, kid.'

'Bach's Brandenburg concerto no. 2.'

That's Teddy, from the other end of the breakfast bar.

'In F-major. First movement.'

Or, rather, they are the words selected by Teddy on his iPad and spoken by Siri. The familiar music begins.

'Here w-we ... here we g-go,' says Frank miserably.

Teddy plays the first movement every morning, at around the same time. He often announces his online searches this way, as though sharing them, taking us with him live-to-air as he squirrels about, one obscure curio to the next.

I try to slot a nugget of dry, untouched cereal between his zip-locked lips. 'Not hungry, Teddy Bear?'

Or maybe it's just that Teddy likes to hear the words he cannot speak himself.

'Not even this teeny one?' I coax again, but Teddy only tilts his face away. He looks thinner to me, but I can't know for sure – he won't stand still on a scale.

It also could be that having Siri speak on his behalf has nothing to do with communicating; just something Teddy happened to do one day and has been doing ever since. Another ritual.

'Not peckish?' I rest the back of my hand against his forehead. 'Who are you, imposter? And what have you done with my sugarholic kid?'

But I prefer option one – that my non-verbal son, the one without hope, the denounced 'hope wrecker', is intentionally engaging with us – and I proceed according to its possibilities.

Next to Teddy sits a wicker basket crammed with drinking straws, most of their plastic centres chewed flat and colourless. Teddy inventories his supply, isolates a straw still largely intact, bends it into a V, bites it several times in its middle until it is just the right kind of malleable and begins an elaborate, rapid-fire flicking.

'*Hey!*' Frank protests. 'He's fl- ... he's fl- ... he's flick- ... fl-*FLICKING* spit right into my bean-beanos!'

'Not at all,' I say. 'Not at all.'

'Track five, disc one, Voyager Golden Record.' Siri again as the straw-flicking continues, Teddy's DJ-ing hands always so adept at performing multiple unrelated tasks at once.

'Now I've g- ... Now I've g- ... I have to eat his s-spit.'

'Frank, there's no spit,' I say, as I do most mornings, aware that his breakfast is likely to be swimming in it.

'Ted's straws look ... look like ... look like ... look like spiders' legs,' says Frank.

'Finish your beanos, come along.'

Frank eats his spitty-beans while I drink my lousy coffee.

Teddy and Siri: 'The goliath bird-eating tarantula is the biggest arachnid on the planet, larger than the average dinner plate.'

'I know ... I know ... I've heard about those!' adds Frank. 'They're as big ... they're as big ... they're as big as your f-face!'

I won't make Frank go to camp. I did, once, four years ago. Other kids, different school. They hid his bag. A harmless prank. Frank the Fretter, as one of his teachers once unhelpfully labelled him, always losing his belongings and weeping over it. A gag, a bit of fun to watch the big dunce lose everything in one go. They didn't understand, the little demi-brutes, the potential for ruin – of the bag and its contents, buried for days under forest muck, picked over by insects, birds, possums, brewed by rain and hinterland sun. And of Frank, without the comfort of his things – the scraps and colours of home that breathe for him when he cannot. His seamless socks, gone. His soft T-shirts, print and pain-free against his skin. The loose elastic waists. Gone and gone. His inhaler, teeming with roaches. The remains of Morris Elephant in his arms – bed-buddy since birth, a secret stowaway – a wet polka-dot rag. An asthma attack. Frank's face blue in the back of an ambulance. So many seeds of mockery sown that day. A merciless, ongoing reaping.

Because a head cut off a Hydra is soon replaced by two more.

'F- ... f- ... f-fat lezzo, Madison c-calls me,' says Frank, the hard blinks setting in. 'She says not even Hog- ... not even

Hog- ... not even Hog-*WARTS* had ... had a ... had ... had a ...'

We've heard all the names before.

'A talking twat.'

I spoke to the school; school spoke to the parents. An afternoon of bulk-bought diocesan tea and restorative justice. An exercise, in its turn, promptly doused in teenage scorn and set alight. And on we roll.

'Yesterday ... yesterday ... yesterday ... someone ... someone put hand ... hand soap all over my pencils. Madison yells out, "*Yuck!* G- ... g- ... g- ... g- ... G-*GUTS* G-Gundersen's jizzed in his pencil ... in his pencil c- ... in his pencil c- ... c-*CASE!*" Everyone laughed. I don't even ... I don't even ... I don't ... She says things I don't understand.'

Though not identical, Frank and Teddy once shared the same physique: tall like their father but stick-thin, all bony elbows, chicken legs and clown feet. Toothpicks with heads. But then Frank exploded: a beanstalk ballooning into a giant whiskery gourd, Teddy suddenly his 'little' brother. More than a growth spurt – a metabolic imbalance, stippling Frank's body with wine-red stretch marks neck to knee. 'Guts Gundersen' at school ever since.

'On 25 August 2012,' Teddy tells us, 'Voyager 1 entered interstellar space.'

'Thank you, Ted,' I say, again offering food – toast this time. Again a refusal.

I go to Frank, hug him hard the way he likes. I know the wise, consoling words: *It's all about her, love, not about you.* Festooned vessels I wave on by. Their cargo has no currency here.

Instead, I say, 'If only we had one of those spiders. Face-size, for eating faces.'

A brief staccato giggle from Teddy.

25

'That would be funny, wouldn't it, Ted?'

'Ted- ... Teddy wasn't laughing at ... at that,' says Frank.

'I think he was,' I say.

'He w- ... he w-wasn't.'

Teddy: 'Upon hearing Voyager's classical tracks and folksongs, extra-terrestrials are believed to have contacted Earth: *Would. Have. Preferred. Beatles ...*'

'See?' says Frank.

I catch Frank's eye just in time to see baked beans slip from his spoon and skid down the front of his singlet. He looks down at himself, back up at me, defeated. We've conquered shoelaces, more or less, and flossing, buttons. Toast remains a work in progress, more often stabbed to pieces on its way to being spread. And while Frank can draw and paint, his handwriting itself a work of art, spoons and forks may always have the better of him.

I pluck a bean from a fold in the fabric, eat it. 'Delete. Delete.'

Frank laughs. 'Cybermum.'

Yellow crumbling scurf peppers Frank's hair. His scalp smells like a blocked drain. 'You know we're visiting Doctor Ling again soon?'

'Mum, did ... did you know the Cybermen ... the Cybermen ... the Cybermen w-were number two on the all ... on the all-time ... on the all-time top ten *Doctor ... Doctor Who* villains?'

'No, Franko, I didn't, but—'

'No way are the Cybermen- ... the Cybermen scarier than the W- ... W- ... than the W- ... W-*WEEPING* Angels.'

'Frank—'

'Or the Silence. And they w- ... w- ... and they w-were number *six*. C- ... C- ... Do you believe that?'

'Frank. *First* Doctor Ling,' I say, holding up my left hand. '*Then Doctor Who*,' holding up my right.

He shakes his head, rocks back on his chair, pulling at his chest.

'This singlet … this singlet … this singlet is cr- … is cr- … this singlet is cr-*CRUSHING* me.'

'Oh, darling—'

'It's like Mary … It's like Mary … It's like Mary Qu- … Mary Qu- … Mary Qu-*QUEEN* of Scots' g- … g- … g-*GIRDLE*,' he says, wrenching the singlet over his head. 'It's always … it's always … it's always so hot, Mum.'

Tight-fitting clothes, wet heat. Tools of torture for Frank.

'Doctor Ling told us what to do and we haven't done it, have we?' I say this as gently as I can, rinsing the singlet in the sink.

'Mum, please, *please* don't say … say I … don't say I … have to shave … don't say I have to shave my hair off. *Please.*'

The dermatologist has read us the riot act more than once. Frank has too much hair for the psoriasis creams to work. Immunosuppressants will be next, with all their attendant risks and side effects. He may lose his hair regardless.

'Mum … Mum … they w- … they w- … w- … they'll never let up. I'll be even more ugly.'

'Your hair will grow back,' I say. 'And you could never be ugly, my darling. You're the most beautiful sweet potato I know.'

'I hate sweet potato,' says Frank, sounding old and tired. At times, the stammer also fatigues.

'I know you do,' I say. 'But I love them. They take such a long time to grow, but when they do.' I pop my lips. 'Ahh, such talent. Virtuosic. There's nothing like them. No substitutes, no equal.'

I retrieve two apples from the fridge, peel and dice one for Teddy, take a bite from the other and hand it to Frank. The same fruit, like so much else, approached so differently. As Frank eats, I stroke his hair, a foamy frizz, and begin braiding it for school. Frank's hair is his trademark, that part of him he wants the world to see – the Zeppelin guy, the Ronnie James Dio look-alike, the hard-rock pilgrim. The artist who thinks his own way. He worries he will be a fright without hair, and he has good reason. Already he couldn't be more of a target at school if he had a vestigial tail. Bald, he will be crucified.

'Down to business,' I say, still braiding. 'Since school plays hard about its camps, we'll have to get a little ... creative. You in?'

'What we've got here is failure to communicate,' says Frank, quoting a song that quotes a film. Frank never stammers when he is someone else.

'Listening ears on?'

Frank pats his ears. 'C- ... c- ... c-copy that. Over.'

'At the last minute you'll –' I curl two fingers into air quotes '– "come down with something". Flu. Tonsillitis. Haemorrhoids. We'll sort out the details later. Until then, we play possum.' Still holding Frank's plait, I lean over, tap twice on Teddy's water cup. 'Drink, Teddy Bear.'

Teddy mimics my two taps on the cup's lid, but doesn't drink.

'*Hemm*aroids?' echoes Frank. 'W- ... w- ... w-what's hemm—?'

'Piles, love. Nothing for you to worry about.'

'Piles of w-what?'

'Nothing, love. Just a silly joke.'

Spittle from Teddy's straw hits the side of Frank's face.

'Stop fl- ... stop fl- ... stop fl-*FLICKING*, *Tedward*!'

'Frank.'

'Edward *Spitterhands*!'

Teddy, typically cryptic: 'Red-footed boobies, rats and goats roamed the rocky isle of Redonda for over a century.' Flicking with renewed zeal.

'Your brother had a bad night,' I say. 'You know he gets scatty when he's tired.' Shadows like dirty moths have settled under Teddy's eyes – made darker by his too-pale skin.

'Scat- ... *scatty*?' says Frank.

'The Tennessee Fainting Goat does not in fact faint but suffers a transitory muscle stiffness when startled.'

Frank talks over Teddy's goat facts: 'More ... more like ... more ... more like annoying as *hell*—'

'As for Doctor Ling,' I cut in. Teddy waggles his cup above his head. 'We'll work it out. Together, Franko. You'll see.'

I finish Frank's braid then go to Teddy, pick up his iPad, lean into his space. He's skipped to a *7:30 Report* clip from 2004. 'Looking at Mum,' I say, lightly guiding his face – mellow, expressionless – from Kerry O'Brien's to mine. '*First* talk, *then* YouTube,' I tell him. 'Use your words, Ted. Tell me what you want.'

Opening his communication app, Teddy's fingers dart across the screen, the touch of a safecracker. 'I, want, more, water, please, Mummy,' says Liam, the app's pre-programmed 'young male Australian' voice. Teddy places the iPad in his lap, threads his fingers through mine. He squeezes, I squeeze back, before his focus returns to the YouTube search pane and I am dismissed. He types *The Mikado*.

'Good talking, Teddy boy,' I say, looking at his still full cup. 'Though you're not drinking what you already have.' I gift the unsatisfactory contents to the African violet by the window and open the fridge, refill the cup.

'Thank you,' says Liam, Teddy adding, 'Jump jump,' as he scrolls through related searches for Gilbert and Sullivan. 'Jump jump.' Teddy-speak for 'Thank you,' or 'What a great idea,' or 'Sure, why not?'

I tell Frank to finish up, wash his hands. 'Time to get dressed.'

'An- ... an-android. Asteroid.'

'Frank, did you hear me? First hands, then uniform.'

'Cyl- ... Cylindroid. Droid.'

'Frank? First hands—'

'*Hemma*roid.'

'Frank!'

Breezing into the kitchen – freshly showered, fizzing with blue-chip cologne – Jerrik ruffles Teddy's ringlets. 'Egghead. Sleep well?'

I was pulling beers on weekends when I met Jerrik. When he staggered in, brutally inebriated, looking for someone to marry so he could stay in the country. Of all the meat markets, he had to eenie-meanie mine. Behind the bar we shook our heads when he produced an actual ring, and watched, amused, as he got down on bended knee before only the most delicate-boned beauties.

'Well, we didn't end up in the laundry,' I say, swilling the dregs of my UlcerEase Blister Blend. 'So, there's that.'

Jerrik offers me a cursory glance and a Horse & Hound–worthy toss of his damp Nordic-blond hair. For Frank he performs a little hip swivel. 'Lemme B. Frank,' he says, as he usually does. Irresistible.

Irresistible as he thought he was that Sunday afternoon, knocking back thumps of tequila with a ruler-thin brunette – eyes cyborg-wide, super-model eyes – who whispered long and close in his ear. He suddenly needed a pen. He needed her to have a pen. Neither did. I unclipped a Sharpie from the waistband of my apron, and as I offered it to him he clamped his hand over mine, taking in my freckles, my unruly plaits. I pulled my hand away, but he only smiled, pleased with himself, displaying for me his large blue-ribbon teeth.

'W- ... W- ... W- ... W-*WASTOID*,' says Frank, pushing back in his chair and sock-sliding to his room.

'What did I say about those hands?' I implore the ceiling. 'Franko?'

'Doing it!'

The cyborg, also sway-drunk, looped her number along his forearm. Jerrik the Dane did not return my pen.

'What did he call me?' Jerrik asks, pouty.

'It's a line, Jerrik, from a show. And he wasn't saying it to you. He was just saying it. It's what Frank does.'

A systems engineer (still not entirely certain what that is), barely holding on to his visa-sponsoring job, Jerrik the Dane's hierarchy of needs appeared to be only these: a wife-not-wife to do him a favour, frequent sex (not necessarily with the favour purveyor) and room to run. A wife-not-wife to share a residence and a cover story, but not a life. It hadn't seemed impossible.

'Wastoid,' muses Jerrik. 'Wastoid?'

A hedonist with a potholed attention span, but one with an EU passport, unrestricted access to kingdoms of ice and snow. My ticket out of town. (Denmark – population five point eight million, capital Copenhagen, coldest recorded temperature -31.2°C, Hørsted, 1982.) *No, not impossible nor necessarily a long-term undertaking. He watched the cyborg and her chums head to the loo, fingers sliding through his marvellous mane, confident he was onto something.*

He wanted to make a fresh start someplace new. That, I could understand.

'Oh, I get it,' Jerrik snorts, displaying his impressively whitened incisors. 'Good one, *Francis*.'

'Only you, Jerrik, would weaponise your own son's name against him.'

'He started it,' says Jerrik.

'Oh, that's alright then.'

I slid around the bar, snatched my pen from his fingers, scribbled my details on my order book. He looked down at me, ice-blue eyes bulging as I shoved the torn-off page into his pants pocket. 'In case you dip out, sport,' I said, half-hoping he wouldn't understand the idiom.

Teddy looks up from his iPad, grabs his father's hand, runs the back of it gently under his chin, back and forth, relaxed and tender. Affection to us; *stimming* to an occupational therapist.

Half an hour later Jerrik trotted off, arm in arm with the cyborg. But he turned back to me as they were leaving, a shrug of his lovingly bench-pressed shoulders, something almost equine about his blockish, handsome head.

Easier, most days, just to see him as a horse.

'Uniform in five,' I tell Teddy, holding up my hand, fingers splayed.

As Teddy caresses one of his father's buckskin ears, I ask Jerrik, 'Do you think he feels warm?'

Jerrik retrieves his hand from Teddy's chin-stim, begins Windsor-knotting his Tom Ford tie. 'Warm?' he asks with no more or less than his usual lack of interest.

'Yes, warm. Feverish? Shall I repeat the question? Do you think he feels *warm?*'

Hands falling to his side, Jerrik gives me one of his I-don't-know-what-you-want-me-to-do looks. 'Take his temperature if you are worried,' he tells the tie. 'I'm late already.'

He called three weeks later. The cyborg hadn't worked out.

'No little accidents,' he said. 'My only condition, if you are to be my Viking Wife.' So blunt. 'When are you coming over?' he demanded. 'I need you to help me move my things.'

And he cared not a jot for romance – not then or since, that ball of string whose end, he argues, is inevitable, implicit in itself. Merely a matter of how long you take to unravel it, irk it into a narky tangle of twine to trip you down the stairs.

'Do you have a car? I will need a car.'

His needs, his wants. A sound so familiar.

'Does your apartment have a balcony? My body needs sun.'

Cold as the North Sea. And so very well qualified to be my new next of kin.

'Time for uniform, Teddy Bear,' I say.

Teddy leaps balletically down the hallway, appearing anything but ill. 'Jump jump,' says Liam. 'Jump jump jump jump jump jump.'

'Good listening, Nureyev,' I call after him, stomping my feet. 'Better watch out! I'm coming to get you.'

'You're gonna get got, Ted,' yells Frank, demon-voiced from beyond. 'You're gonna get so got!' Frank never stammers when he's demonic.

Teddy's screams and giggles fade as he slams the bedroom door behind him. He will be waiting for me under the covers of his bed. He always gets got on school mornings.

Jerrik, from the doorway of the kitchen. 'Ah, Queenie. Missouri's run into trouble, so I'm needed in St Louis by the end of the week.'

My queen. His name for me when all the boys' therapies started.

'Missouri? Go Cardinals,' I say limply.

Because a Warrior Queen was more useful than a Viking Wife, someone to pilot the swelling ranks of care professionals.

'Then home a few days, before that conference I mentioned. Cardiff.'

And when the scale of the boys' needs first dwarfed us, four wan specks in its monster shadow. One of us had to pick up the hammer, take a swing, level a mountain or two.

'Cardiff,' scoffs Jerrik. 'Wet dump.'

Warrior Queen when the war began, Teddy vs Sleep, every night a hopeless crusade, Jerrik working ever longer hours, his career a suddenly prioritised mission.

I rinse out Frank's bowl, slot Teddy's lunch box into his schoolbag. 'We could always swap, Jerrik,' I say. 'You stay here and I'll fly business class to your Cardiff conference. A comfy hotel instead of the laundry floor. A G&T and a hot meal every night.'

Jerrik barely waits for me to finish. 'And then there's the new gig in—'

'Gig?' I say. Like he's a jobbing actor or in a band. Hair metal would be Frank's suggestion.

'The new *project* in Bangalore,' continues Jerrik. 'There's a team of us going out there. Could wipe out most of May. But you'll be okay, right?' Jerrik wears his trying-hard-not-to grin. 'Warrior Mother, pushing the planet.' The same grin I see when the dinner burns and I have to start over, when my football team is thrashed. I also see it when he talks about his girlfriends. His lovers.

Sponging over the breakfast bar, I begin to remove my apron. Jerrik's fingers fiddle with the knotted ties behind my waist and I spring away as I might from a killer bee. From a talking palomino. He raises his hands in surrender.

'Yes, yes,' I say, a wave of my apron. 'A few days, a few months. Off you go.'

I look up at him, impassive. He fills the doorway – a man who looks a lot right now like a smirking teenage boy wanting to borrow the car, a six-pack of beer and a girl stashed somewhere, waiting on him as he waits on me, the formidable bonneted matron, holding the keys.

'A new *project*, you say? Let me see? Project Didi, is it? Kiki? Project Loulou? I know I'm getting close.'

Jerrik's show-pony ears prick forward, the smirk gone, whipped off his face as though by a switch. 'Minnie,' he clarifies.

'Goodness. Up to the M's already?' Though in truth, this is Jerrik's second run through the alphabet.

As he turns and finally trots away, I bite into the apple Frank didn't finish, crunching down hard.

Ow! A smiting of blood on my tongue.

Lenore.

Ferocious as ever.

Tuesday, 8:04 am

'And make sure you eat your lunch, okay? Art tonight, so a late dinner.'

'Gaht it,' says Frank, hauling his bag out of the back seat. We're parked outside his small, inner-city, 'learner-centred' high school, engine idling. A puzzling claim to fame for a school – what else might its efforts be centred on? Beside me, Teddy enjoys a 1994 production of *Pirates of Penzance* playing on his iPad.

'Hey, Ma,' says Frank, grinning. 'D'jav breakfast? D'jeet?'

He is practising his New Jersey accent, and feeding candy to the stutter. Frank never stammers when he's a Russian, a Bostonian, Cletus Spuckler, Ozzy Osbourne.

'Yes, thank you, darling. I did have breakfast. I did eat.'

'Yeet breakfast awf-ten?'

'Yes,' I reply, amused. 'I eat breakfast often.'

'So, Ma? Ma?' he continues. 'Wad yeeting for lunch? A seal? Or a madda-baby?'

'A seal or a matter-baby?' I repeat. 'What's a matter-baby?'

'Nuttin',' replies Frank. 'What's a madda w'jou, baby?'

Frank's smile is the same today as it was when he was three years old, three months old. A charm so potent and so precious it warrants a glass case and key. But perhaps that's only me, a still-swooning mother, overly sentimental. I doubt Jerrik has ever noticed it. Even as a newborn, Frank failed to impress his father.

'There's something wrong with this one's face.' Jerrik's first words that morning as Frank slid from my body. 'But the other one looks alright,' giving Ted the once-over.

Surprising even myself, I'd suggested Gene as a middle name for both boys.

'*Gene?* Don't you think this one's got trouble enough?' Jerrik tutted, openly appalled by Frank's jaundiced eyes and skin. 'Where has this *Gene* come from?'

Jerrik wasn't pleased. Jerrik hadn't been pleased for months. When my pregnancy was confirmed, he fled home, forgetting that Mette and his sister, Pia, are also mothers. They sent him back before he'd even had time to unpack. Compounding the outrage, I announced that *a* baby wasn't on the way, but two. 'My coupé is not for carry capsules, *wife*,' he said, protective of his new French convertible. 'You will need a station wagon next.' He'd actually winced. 'A people mover. Let me guess, a *Toyota*?' Like a curse proclaimed.

The boys arrived that morning just before six. Metal plate covers grizzled as breakfast was delivered to the ward. The chokey smell of powdered egg. I remember looking down at my sons and vowing they would never have to clean a yolk off a wall as long as they lived.

'Francis is already a girl name,' Jerrik said, defeated. 'The yellow one would have two girl names.'

But nothing Jerrik said could deflate my delirium.

'He won't be yellow for long,' I assured him. 'And, well, yes, it was my grandmother's name, though more than a few chaps have been Genes. Roddenberry, Wilder, Kelly. The bloke with the tongue from Kiss.' I couldn't stop grinning. 'Bacon and Sinatra. Coppola. Scott Fitzgerald—'

'A talking donkey.'

'A talking mule.' I laughed. 'I thought you liked Francis.'

'Well, I have changed my mind. Frank is okay. But people will know it is Francis. Francis *Gene* Gundersen? F.G.G. They will call him fag.'

'Who will?'

'Little shits at school. Big shits at work. Look at the favours my name has done me. "Delivery for Gundersen? Jerk?" Fucking autocorrect.'

'He has your family name, Jerrik. Boys can be named after their mothers too.'

'Fine. Francis Murphy Gundersen. In fact ... Murphy. I like it.'

'No, not Murphy,' I said, delirium flatlining. 'Anyway, we can talk about it later. Daddy.'

'*Far*,' Jerrik snapped. 'Not Daddy. They will call me *far*. Let me have something to say in all this.'

So I let it go, no more bargaining over what they would be called and by whom. Just Francis and Edward. Frank and Teddy. Solid names to give them, I'd hoped, a solid start. I put my face to Teddy's, a composed baby whose relaxed look seemed to say, *Finally, here we all are.* I breathed in his newborn smell, touched my fingers to Frank's entirely perfect skin.

'You will know love,' I swore to them. 'We will know it together.'

At the school gate, Frank turns, waves, just as a stick-thin boy in a junior-school uniform dashes past him.

'Mornin', Guts!' the boy yaps, casting a snip of a look over his shoulder. *Catch me if you can.*

Guts Gundersen.

Cut one head off the Hydra ...

I prepare to pull away from the kerb. Next stop: Teddy's school, a half-hour south. Frank, still waving, blinking too hard, too often. *We're surrounded,* mouth his lips, and we exchange our doomed-cowboy smiles. I know he will be trying not to cry.

I see the skinny kid scooting off to meet his mates, to blithe impunity. He'll have forgotten it already, but the moment will live on in Frank, thieving his sleep, spoiling his food. 'Guts Gundersen' he will call himself when he drops something or when he catches his reflection. And his scalp will boil and he will scratch and scratch until his fingernails bog up bloody with his own skin. And I will nag. And we will buy more creams, visit the specialist, the OT, the whole pantheon of therapists if we must, all because of two cruel little words let loose this April morning.

In the passenger seat, Teddy is full of growl, his straw flaying the window like a cudgel. Spittle sprays the dashboard and the side of my face.

'I couldn't agree more, bear cub.'

Traffic is gridlocked and I worry Teddy will be late. My old high school, Mercy Grammar, looms over the approach to the river bridge. Still as proud and dramatic as an old showgirl, despite a new-century spit and polish. A place where I could just be, if only between eight-thirty and three, instead of what my mother would have me be. Her backstage pass to fame and fortune. A star. A fantasy. All of her fantasies.

My jaw clenches as Teddy and I inch along, and I indulge in some fantasies of my own.

I fantasise about a world where all the skinny kids leave the fat ones alone. Where Frank wouldn't spend his breaks talking to the librarian's pug or talking to himself, afraid and hiding in an empty art room. Where a kindly teacher might arrive just in time to save Frank from today's 'sack whacking'. Where a genuinely progressive, compassionate generation would be far beyond such puerile taunts as *Look out, it's Guts Gundersen! Fat fag alert! Fat fag alert!*

And when you compare our two fantasies like that, side by side, it is hard to believe it's my mother who is considered the mad one.

Wednesday, 8:35 am

Almost two weeks since Teddy's temperature began its game of now you see me, now you don't: 37.9. 36.7. 38.5. 37.4. 38.1 … The thermometer lives in my handbag. At 38.9 I called the GP who was, of course, booked for the week. We were added to his cancellation list, but four hours later it was 36.3. Normal. Wide-eyed, circling its toes in the dirt normal, as it was when we set out this morning. But here in the queue at his school's Kiss-and-Drop zone, playing our game of squeeze, his skin again feels warmer than it should. We have a conversation on his iPad.

'Do you feel sick, Teddy?'

The app takes us to a new page I have set up, offering only three replies: a green yes button, a red no, and a bold white-on-black I don't know.

Teddy chooses all three: 'yes, no, I don't know.'

The question, of course, is too vague. Sick? Sick could mean anything.

The line of cars creeps forward. I try to drill down.

'Does your body feel bad?'

'Yes, no, I don't know.'

Bad? As nebulous a notion as sick.

'Is your body sore?'

'Yes, no, I don't know.'

'Are you sleepy?'

'Yes, no, I don't know.'

Three cars pull away from the front of the queue, and as we stop and start and stop again, I delete the I don't know option from the page.

'Does your tummy hurt?'

'Yes, no.'

Teddy and I aren't used to this. Unlike Frank with his asthma and chronically troubled skin, Teddy is rarely unwell with anything more than a sniffle. I try a few test questions.

'Is it Wednesday today?'

'Yes.'

'Do you like brownie?'

'Yes.

'Did you have brownie for breakfast?'

'No.'

Self-reporting is bafflingly difficult for people like Teddy. I know this, everyone in our world knows this, and yet no-one knows why. Teddy can Google-search Bavarian bear sightings in perfect German but can't reliably tell me he has a headache. I suppose if he could, he wouldn't be Teddy.

At the front of the queue now, and Teddy unbuckles his seatbelt. I walk around to his side of the car, help him load up his backpack. Now, our ~~slow~~ quick goodbye, our ~~quick~~ slow dance. My cheek rests for a moment on his chest. I will call later in the day, make sure all is well. A long, thin arm curls around my head, checking the alignment of my ears, tucking my hair primly behind them. My fifteen-year-old personal stylist. Teddy completes his inspection by surveying my hands – for bandaids, of which he does not approve – before our noses kiss, the bridge of his held to mine.

'Have a big day, big Ted,' I always say.

And always, 'Jump jump,' is the reply.

Speech pathology after school today. 'Xander this afternoon,' I remind him as he heads in. Xander first brought the app to our world, and Liam, Teddy's voice. She works from her home and as we are her final appointment of the day, lets us swim in her pool after the session. '*First* Xander, *then* swim.'

And tomorrow afternoon, occupational therapy. Martha stretched Teddy's diet from a featherweight six foods to a kaleidoscopic fifteen. She stopped Frank throwing up with every new smell and texture by suggesting an art class. She saw he liked to draw – might getting messy with paint and clay, adjusting to their alien cling, chip into that resistance, break it down? As with Teddy's hypersensitive palate, it was a long play that eventually paid off.

'Good morning, buddy,' says a teacher aide at the first gate. 'Hello, handsome,' says the next, stationed further along the race. Holding up a pump bottle of hand sanitiser, she says gently, 'Clean hands, Teddy?'

He holds out his hands, jumping a little at each cold, sticky squirt, before rubbing them together. Some of the kids don't like the feel of the gel, the odour. Teddy couldn't cope with it either, at first. Teddy couldn't cope with a lot of things. Five weeks to submit to the uniform. Five weeks of eyeballing the grey shorts and maroon collared shirt, risking only the odd shove and rub of their miscreant cloth. And eight weeks of attending school with him, side by side in the classroom, until he could bear a single minute without me, then two, then five, though he could see me through the glass door, a big bold stopwatch on his iPad counting down the seconds until my return.

Teddy watches me as he walks, waving when I wave, returning my kisses in that funny way of his. Only he and I know how brave he is, how accomplished, walking himself to class. Nothing so special to a heedless heart. Only we know what it has taken to achieve just this, these small steps – the uniform and the hand gel and attending school on his own – the inchingly slow road we've travelled to get here, shoulder-to-shoulder, bumping along, the sideways stumbles, the landslides. So many drills – 'Good boy, Teddy, again. Good boy, Teddy, again. Again. Again. Again' – until we were told that drills were no longer the thing, picture exchange no longer the thing, auditory integration therapy no longer the thing, that the next thing would be the thing, and the thing that would come after that. Lines drawn through the years and under my eyes.

Life drilled is a backbreaker. A life therapied-to-fit, a pitiful heap. Heedless hearts don't know how heavy it is, dragging it around all day, all night, like a legless dog.

Poorly slept today. Not up to much today. Not a day napper, the best I can do is keep busy. Difficult, when the first victim of exhaustion is purpose. Fatigue simmers deep inside, steaming me undone, paring me down to an outline, to a dotted trail of myself left behind as I walk. Yet I *am* walking – I look down, see feet moving. I have no idea how.

Sometimes I envy Teddy – his hours mapped out, broken down into steps: *First* breakfast, *then* uniform; *after* lunch comes this, *before* bath comes that. Every place, person, activity and possible contingency photographed and scheduled in an app. Anything is made possible, just as anything can be ruled out. Teddy lives and breathes by it.

Today I could use a visual aid too, something to hold me in place and compass-point my day because as I drive away from here, from Teddy, I feel myself getting smaller, my shrinking legs too short to reach the pedals, a steering wheel I have no hope of seeing over. I don't know how the car gets to where it is going. Alone, I can't always be sure I am even awake. Alone and still and unslept, I seem to vanish.

Friday, 3:58 pm

Airbrakes and impatient engines. The city streets – a chaos-cauldron of jangle and screech and chronic construction. Jerrik unmoored in the midst of it, his voice in shreds on the other end of the line.

'Where are you exactly?' I ask, putting him on speaker as the bathtub fills.

'On a park bench,' he replies. 'In the gardens. Looking at ducks. I think they are ducks. All of them ugly. One chased me.'

I think he's been drinking. He has been in a foul mood since the St Louis trip. 'Jerrik?'

'They told me to get out of the building.'

'Who, the ducks?'

'"Clear my head." De kan skride ad helvede til ... Fuck dem ... Det er fandme ikke fair ...' The rest of Jerrik's rant only he can understand, though 'asshole' sounds the same in both languages.

'What happened?' I leave off the 'this time'.

'*What happened?*' says Jerrik. '*De kan rende mig!* Where to begin, my Queen? Okay, for starts ...' Always *starts*, never starters. 'There is the new department head ...'

I could tell Jerrik that I am on my knees soaping Teddy. That he discovered the liquid paper in the desk drawer and that, no doubt curious in a repulsed kind of way, he emptied both bottles over himself.

'... Treats me like a graduate ... *Dumme svin!* ...'

44

And that the itchy, siccative sensation of it on his skin brought up his lunch and afternoon tea.

'... An *under*graduate ...'

I could confer with Jerrik in his capacity as the boys' father – can we be sure it was the white-out that made Teddy sick? Should we be worried? How worried?

As though reading my thoughts, Teddy surveys his forearms, his fingernails, verifying he is free of all referenced vomit and chalky residue.

'... *Røvhul* ...'

The three of us had been watering the lettuce and nasturtiums and tomatoes and parsley, creating the 'incidental and anecdotal engagement' that the books tell us to do, that the therapists are paid, year after year, to tell us we must do with our children.

'... And then they go and promote a *graduate* over *me* ...'

But Jerrik never reads the books, or the OT's notes, or the speechie's, not even the bits I highlight with him in mind.

'... *Det gamle røvhul!* ... *Hold kæft* ...'

I could bullet-point what happened if I thought it might hold Jerrik's attention:

- Frank and I watering, pulling weeds
- Teddy wafting away towards the house
- liquid paper encounter
- Teddy's senses in uproar, seeks comfort in refrigerator
- Teddy eats entire packet of Tim Tams, still in uproar
- copious spew

'... I am so tired of ...'

But I don't confer with Jerrik, and keep my bullet points to myself.

'... So tired of being sold under.'

I want to believe it was a sensory thing, the vomiting. But Teddy has gorged on pilfered sweets before and never been sick.

'Sold under, yes? Under-sold?'

When Teddy cools down after the bath, I will take his temperature again. The elevated readings seem to be lasting longer. We are permanently parked on our GP's next available appointment list.

'You don't understand how hard it is for me, Jay …'

I don't share any of what has taken place this afternoon. Nor do I confess that my superpowers have let me down today, and that for a moment I failed to be omnipresent.

'Always so much pressure …'

The bathroom floor's unfinished concrete digs into my knees. Above the drip-stained basin there were once glass-fronted cabinets. To the right, an oval mirror used to hang. I try to remember how they broke or when they fell, and wonder why we didn't replace them, why we are okay with warped walls sprayed with wounds, like bullet groupings, made by long-ago nails and screws.

'Never a moment to think …'

Sugar ants live behind the walls now. Jerrik squirts insecticide into the punctures and watches as hundreds, possibly thousands, of the honey-coloured pests gush out, tumbling in horde-heaps around the toothpaste and shaving cream, a deathbed choreography, sticking to the cloth I use to wipe them away. The bathroom is tiny and the stink of killing chemical lingers. I tell Jerrik not to use it. He fires back with, 'What would you have me do, *wife*,' before storming off in that high-stepping, dressage prance of his.

'Never a moment to relax …'

From the bath, Teddy grabs my hand, pushes it towards the crumpled book at my knees – *Upsy Down Town*. He wants me to read it again. We've been reading it for fifteen years.

'You could never understand what I go through here, *Queenie*,' Jerrik continues. 'Because I work, and you don't.'

I open the book. 'In Upsy Down Town,' I begin.

Monday, 12:30 pm

'I don't think you need shock treatment.'

I think, *Too late*, but I say, 'That's a relief.'

I sit across from Doctor Zelda Penelope Crasno. With both feet on the floor and my back a ramrod, I still manage to feel like a tangle, something poorly knitted. I rarely sit comfortably in a chair I don't know, especially one in a squinty bright, minimally furnished psychiatrist's office. First visit.

I did my research, chose this woman specifically – a specialist in treating children with developmental conditions (and their parents). Then took my place on her eleven-month waiting list. If I am to see another shrink – and I am not persuaded that I will for long (it's not like I'm being forced this time) – I don't want to have to start at the subatomic particle level of my life, recalling events from my personal Big Bang. I haven't got the energy to work with someone who would require me to decode concepts like perseveration, proprioception, generalisation, stimming, speech disfluency, low registration, sensory hypersensitivity. I need someone who speaks my language.

'Why shock treatment?'

To offset my uneasy sit, I hug a throw cushion, quietly de-snarling the threads of its rubber-duck-yellow fringe. 'Because it would just be … easier, I think.'

'Easier than what?'

Teddy would hate this yellow throw cushion. Out of loyalty, I decide to hate it too, and set it aside with a shove.

'Easier than you spending an hour deciding that what I really need is time to myself. Easier than me sitting here for that hour having to resent hearing that; thinking instead of what I need to defrost for dinner. Because that's everyone's advice, isn't it? Every doctor, every therapist, every well-meaning soul in the post office, the pharmacy, the supermarket, the other mums at school. Everywhere we go, the boys and I, all anyone wants to tell me is how much I need some *me* time – a trip away, time at a spa or a health resort, like I'm Adele or something.'

Doctor Zelda's face, well moisturised and lovely, seems to say, *I see.*

'And then you'd ask if I have respite, surely I'm getting some respite, right? Because, you know, the streets are littered with top-shelf support workers – a committed, caring workforce that sweeps into our homes and looks after our children as well as if not better than we do ourselves. And then ... when I say, *Don't start me on the whole respite issue ...* You'd look aghast and think I'm terribly disagreeable and then you'd be reaching for the prescription pad so that I could commence the antidepressant merry-go-round because we all know the first one we try is never quite right and the first dose we try is never quite right but we must commence on something so we can come off it and then have a go at something else.'

Another, *I see.*

'And then you'd say, *I'm afraid we've run out of time,* and then I'd make another appointment with your receptionist to come back and say the same things to you all over again until you move to Byron or Milford Sound or the Lake District and I opt out of therapy for another seventeen years. Or I could just take a shot at ECT and see if it resets me a bit. I've heard it works that way for some.'

'Resets you to what?'

Keep in my head. *She's got you there, Spider.*

'Something else,' I say. 'Just … something less afraid. Less cynical.'

'Cynicism is mostly a form of defence. A way of deflecting fear, hopelessness.'

'The sophistry of the sook?' I say, not meaning to sound so hostile. 'I prefer world-weary wag.'

Zelda Crasno takes a moment. We both do. Though my mobile is muted, I've positioned it in front of me on the curling, multi-tiered entrail of wood I assume is a coffee table. Teddy's temperature is still erratic and I don't want to miss any calls from school.

Doctor Crasno removes her glasses and slowly folds in the arms, careful not to touch the lenses. 'I need for us to go back a bit, if we can?'

Oh, super, I think. 'Sure,' I reply.

'Also,' she says, 'just a bit of housekeeping. Do you prefer Jay or Rory? You've printed one and signed the other.'

'Take your pick. I answer to anything.'

I sound testy. Nothing's coming out right.

'For the moment,' says the doctor. 'Let's focus on you. Just Jay. You've talked about the boys, about your husband—'

'The boys' father,' I leap in, correcting her. 'Jerrik is my husband but not my partner, in the accepted sense of the word. He never really was, and that's not a criticism of him.'

A frowning smile opposite.

'And there is no Just Jay. I know what you mean but there simply isn't.'

'Is that why you believe you need shock treatment, Jay? To get back in touch with you? Is that what needs resetting?'

I take a very deep breath, possibly my first since entering this room. 'Not exactly.'

'Can you help me to understand?'

'A friend,' I say, meaning Keep, 'thinks I worry too much about

49

the past. *And* the future. Trying to stay out in front of both, while not spending enough time in the here and now.'

Doctor Zelda nods. 'A concerned friend,' she says, to which I reply, 'That's one way to describe him.'

She gives me time to elaborate on this, which I don't.

'A preoccupation with the future I think I can understand, especially as a parent in your position. The boys' future care needs, I'm assuming?'

'Yes. First thought on waking, last one as I go to sleep. If I go to sleep. The horror stories never end of what happens to kids like mine when mothers like me die.'

'They don't, sadly,' she agrees, rather too casually. 'But staying out in front of the past. You're afraid of it somehow catching up to you?'

'Catching up to me? You mean, I'm meant to have outrun it by now? Gosh, I've really been doing this wrong.'

'Your parents?' asks Doctor Crasno. 'Are they still alive?'

'Mother, yes. Father, wouldn't know. I never met him.'

Another of Doctor Crasno's little nods. *She sees.*

'And how is Mum? Are you close?'

'Erm,' I say, searching for the right words, deciding instead to run with the wrong ones. 'She signed me in to Harriet's when I was seventeen. Didn't even let me finish school.'

Doctor Crasno, very still, stares hard at me. 'Harriet House?'

'Involuntary treatment order.'

'And ... when was this exactly?'

'Two years before the royal commission closed it down and handed me back to her.'

Doctor Crasno's eyes look to the floor, blink twice, then return to me. She inhales, long and steady.

'So, Mother and I?' I say, replying to her earlier question. 'Not close.'

It is a crowded, all-stops elevator odyssey to return to the double-B basement where I've parked the car, some twenty-seven storeys below Doctor Crasno's office. Three of the elevators are not in use; *Closed for Maintenance DO NOT ENTER* signage across their doors. I stand to the rear of our transport cube and stare at backs, all taller than mine, trying not to consider whether this tin can we are in, our continued existence entirely reliant on the functioning health of its cables and pulleys, is also due for service. I can't help but picture Teddy's face at the school gate. No app in the world could adequately explain my failure to show up, nor why the world had suddenly turned against him.

Heilongjiang province – population thirty-one million eight hundred and fifty thousand, coldest recorded temperature -52.3°C, Mohe City, 1962.

This massive building had started life in the late 1980s when the notion of the multifunction polis took hold of the state. We would live, work, eat and be entertained all in a single monolith. Fewer cars, less pollution and time wasted on commuting. An idea considered so scarily futuristic by a quick-to-spook constituency it was soon aborted. This provincial town – still more given to public celebrations of woodchopping and herding dogs than to dreams of electric sheep – thought better, in the end, of innovation and of standard-setting and of getting ahead of itself. Now the Regatta Towers are just a skyscraping ubiquity of sweat-shop retail and eyebrow kiosks, scratch-tickets and food courts, everything smelling of deep-fry.

The Otis Elevator Company faithfully delivers me to the airless underground. I sit a while in the car. So many layers of concrete above, Doctor Crasno will have moved on to her next patient. Tomorrow someone else will slide out the aluminium name plaque outside her office and replace it with their own, as Doctor Crasno works elsewhere on Tuesdays. I feel both heavy and empty – a husk, light enough to jag a breeze, but a sackweight too, sunk to the lowest depths. Gone either way. I'd stay here in this dug-out dinge if it wasn't almost time to collect Teddy, and if it wasn't so steamy, my sweat already starting to bead and run. I turn over the motor, crank the air conditioning, grind my way up and out of the concrete bilge, into the crackle and squint of the eastern seaboard sun.

If I visit Doctor Crasno again, I will ask her to close the blinds during our session. Shrinks' offices should at least be cosy if not downright confessional – all lamplight, clarets and cobalts. Comrade colours as worn down as you, as accustomed to a kicking.

Then again, perhaps all I'm looking for is the opposite of Doctor Alastair Jones, 'that famous psychologist', who worked out of rooms as white as an igloo.

White concrete blockwork.

White ceiling fans, white leather chairs.

Pallid watercolours, framed in white.

Everything hospital white. Dug-up bones white.

White walls reflect it all back, share none of the load. Let it fall at your feet in dry, dirty flakes.

That very last Friday we visited Doctor Jones, the boys were only five years old. We'd been seeing him most of their lives. Yet that final Friday Doctor Jones never once looked at my children. He spoke around them, over and through them, never to them, as though their presence made him cross, displeased.

'Apologies if my candour has caught you off guard,' he said at our final visit, nostrils flexing like a tiny plane's even tinier wing flaps. 'But you've got to know what you're up against ...'

He meant Teddy.

'I urge you to choose.'

'Choose?' Jerrik had repeated. '*Choose?*' Jerrik, confused and offended, unaccustomed to confusion and offence.

Somewhat elvish, Doctor Jones, with his pointy ears, pointy nose. A surlier elf, for sure, than at our previous visit, when all had been 'on track', when we were 'doing so well', when the boys were 'progressing nicely'.

'Choose, Mr Gundersen. It's too much for the two of you. Jay has had to give up work. You say you're struggling, no-one can sleep. I'm worried for you.'

'Give him away?' Jerrik, so put out. Nothing to do with Jerrik, surely, could be as bad as all that.

'Frank has his issues, I don't deny,' continued British-born Doctor Jones, 'but he's a doddle compared to Teddy. You've a right to live your lives. No-one would blame you.'

Doctor Jones laughed when he said the word *doddle*. Laughed.

'Give him to who?' said Jerrik, his face invaded by all the white in the room. 'Where?'

'Foster care,' replied Alastair Jones, developmental psychologist deluxe. 'It's the only option you have in this country.'

That morning the boys and I had watched *Playschool*: *There's a boy in here*, I wanted to shout at the celebrated Doctor Jones. *With stories to tell.*

Teddy kept me moving – in my lap, out of my lap, on the floor, stacking, lining up, adjusting my hair, my ears, levelling my eyebrows, removing all the books from all the very white bookcases.

What about a massage – elbows, knees?

What about a song – 'Ten Little Candles', 'Here is the Beehive', all the actions we'd learnt in music therapy, as Doctor Elf chittered on, as The Aggrieved Father bemoaned the variables and contingencies that had beset his life since the day our 'little accidents' arrived, our 'twin troubles'. The boys right there, every accusation leaching through their skin like an airborne bane, distorting the pretty defaults all children are born with. A deep, cell-level mangling only a parent can inflict.

Bad things happen in April.

As usual, I felt like I was in the wrong place. An incongruity in a black shirt and jeans. A person who'd walked into the wrong meeting, on the wrong floor, in the wrong building. Soon Jerrik and the doctor would look up.

Can we help you? they'd ask.

No, they could not, because I'd come to wonder why we were there. Had I thought Doctor Jones possessed a 'cure'? A magical formula for an 'ordinary' life? What the hell did I know about ordinary? Had I wanted a way to stop Frank being Frank, to cure Teddy of himself? Would I know them if they suddenly woke up one day not as they are? Would they know me? Is that how I had defined a cure – finding different children in their beds?

What do you want, Jay? What would be your happy ending?

At some point, Frank pulled our crumpled copy of *Robert the Rose Horse* from my bag, dragged a little chair alongside mine and commenced to read. Only he wasn't, he couldn't. I'd read it to the boys so many times that Frank could recite it word-for-word, knew exactly when to turn each page, mimicking the wobbly Scottish brogue I'd use for the horse's doctor. It was quite something, a glimpse of talents to come.

'In all my thirty-three years of practice …'

Not thirty-three years, thirty-three *yars*.

'In all my thirty-three *yars* of practice … I've never seen anyone so severe, so affected, ever get any better.'

How much more substantial Doctor Alastair Jones – world authority on the condition, *the* authority, according to his website and book jackets – looks on television. Yes, his Sunday night prime-time self is far more imposing. That very week of our visit he'd been trotted out to discuss the case of a nine-year-old autistic boy, driven to a lake by his mother, held under until he stopped breathing. Until he died. Mum heading to the shops, filling the boot with groceries, ice cream, fresh bread and toothpaste, before jumping off the roof of the car park.

A headline. A sad, sorry time-slot triumph.

Someone had called to let me know. 'That famous psychologist's on!'

Someone from the sob squad who phones with such news.

Who insists you try craniosacral therapy and camel milk.

Who sends you links to stem cell research and chelation and Temple Grandin's website. 'Seen the movie? Claire Danes – OMG!'

Who wants you to join their church. 'He's not your child, anyway. He's God's.'

'What about respite?' they all ask. 'Are you getting any respite?'

'Korean kimchi,' they urge, such wisdom. 'It's all in the gut.'

Get him a dog. 'Though a horse would be better.'

'What about respite? *Are you getting any respite?*'

'Move to England.' (In a whispery voice:) 'They have residential schools.'

'Respite? Respite? *RESPITE!*'

The sob squad delivering casseroles and carrot cakes to your door. The flavours of loss, as though someone has passed away.

So I tuned in, as the camera cut to:

Doctor Alastair lamenting the lack of services and the woman's 'failure' to reach out, presumably to those services he'd only just lamented as lacking.

As the camera cut to:

Doctor Alastair consoling the boy's father. 'He was my best mate,' grieving dad said as he wept in close-up. 'I miss him every day.' Even though Dad had left his best mate, years earlier, in Mum's care, to start a new life, in a new state, with a new wife, new kids.

He wasn't in a good mood, the famous psychologist, that day in April.

In all my thirty-three yars ... 'Teddy has no hope, and nor do you if you keep him.'

I don't think Doctor Jones wanted to be on telly for a while.

55

Not a good look – ~~murderous~~ suicidal mothers, drowned sons. Waiting lists could have swung either way: longer, because things were so grim they were jumping off roofs. Shorter, because they were jumping off roofs.

A doddle compared to Teddy.

Perhaps Doctor Alastair thought we looked like the drowning-leaping kind, hence our revised prognosis: no longer on track. That track was history. Submerged, cratered, fucked. Don't even bother.

He was drafting us a detour, leading us through dense, gloomy scrub.

Come along, he wheedled, little nostrils flaring. *I've taken you this far, haven't I? My dust jackets don't lie.* A devious fey shortcut, an easy out: get rid of him. *No-one would blame you.* The world authority telling us our kid was officially *too much,* for ~~all of us~~ everyone.

It was like the teacher telling us it's okay to cheat. A kindly nun in full habit blowing smoke rings.

A doddle compared to Teddy. No-one would blame you.

Because only *doddles* have the right to stay with their families. The rest should be given away.

Clock on the wall. White plastic, of course.

It was time for us to leave, and never go back.

April words. April fool.

May begins next week, I realise with relief, shouldering my way onto the south-bound freeway. Edging closer to winter, such as it is here, my favourite season. Even bad days are better in the cold.

11:54 pm

Tonight he is barely there, a voice mostly. A shadow, if you look very hard, seated by the bay window.

I sit at my desk, finishing up a scrapbook entry. 'Why are you always so different?' I ask him.

Am I?

'You know you are. Do I always look the same to you?'

Do you always look the same to yourself?

'God, you're worse than a psychiatrist,' I reply, 'answering questions with questions. It's hard to say. Whenever I think of myself, I am always me, but I can only see myself from behind, the back of my head, and my hair is short and colourless and slept on. Like another woman's head altogether. And I'm old. Always old. Even when I recall myself as a child, or as a young woman, in my memories I'm never young.'

He says nothing, but the edges of him twinkle as though he is stitched with fairy lights. He glimmers, jewelled.

'Remember my flat?' I ask him. 'The one above the Cash Converters and the Indian takeaway?'

And the laundrette.

'Do you miss it?'

Do you miss your flat?

'I miss my glass bead curtains.'

Of course. So tasteful.

Wednesday through Saturday I was a librarian at the Fryer Library. On Sundays I pulled beers at Purple Pie Pete's where I met Jerrik. I loved my jobs and the smells of my flat. I lived there for almost nine years. It was my first place, my first time on my own. After mother, after what was done.

'Do you remember the day Jerrik moved in?' I laugh.

How could I forget?

'I lost you for a couple of weeks. You disappeared.'

Not I who was lost.

The visa Jerrik applied for required us to marry within nine months. I said we could get it done just as soon as a date became available at the wedding registry, but Jerrik was happy to leave off until the last possible moment. I knew he was giving himself a chance to find someone better to marry. Someone younger (he is five years my junior). Someone else.

I ask Keep, 'Do you remember the little notes around my bathroom mirror?'

Your affirmations?

'I am strong. I am smart. I am worthy. I am enough. Good Lord, did I ever really believe that?'

Are you not strong, Spider?

I remember how the ball of Blu Tack behind each note was breaking down, leaking, a greasy blotch that bled through the affirmation's very core.

You can be smart, on occasion.

'Yes, Keeper, yes. But only in ways that don't seem to matter much.'

I remember too how Jerrik said he wanted to wait for a bit before having sex with me, as a show of respect.

Sure. Respect.

'I am worthy.' Uncertain if I say this aloud.

'There are laser treatments for freckles now,' Jerrik had told me. 'Not that they bother me, the freckles.'

My voice, a will of its own. 'I am worthy.'

'Only … it's such a shame,' Jerrik had added. 'When the rest of you is so gorgeous.'

'I am worthy.'

We'd been driving when he jabbed at my knee, pointed to a motel up ahead. 'Pull in there,' he said. 'I want to be naked.' The Adeline Lodge, international terminal nearby.

'I am worthy.'

He had to use the toilet first. I lay under the covers, jumbo jets booming overhead.

'I am worthy.'

I thought it was so he could freshen up – finger-brush his teeth.

'I am worthy.'

The Adequate Lodge, as I remember it. Adequate tea- and coffee-making facilities, adequate parking and breakfast buffet.

'I am worthy.'

Of course we didn't stay till morning, back in the car straight after. And so small, that room, it stunk all the way through the sex.

'I am worthy.'

Jerrik didn't seem to notice.

'I am worthy.'

I couldn't notice anything else.

'I am enough.'

Jerrik had me drop him off someplace, and I went home, back to my flat, and peeled all the affirmations off the mirror, wadding them up. They fell, surprisingly heavily, into the bin. I told myself I'd rewrite them.

Across the room, Keep's spectral hands rise up, waterweed fingers bending and swaying, so slowly, back and forth. *Is this what you discussed, you and your new doctor? Your abandoned attempts to self-heal?*

'Abandoned, are they?'

He is silent.

'So that's why you've shown up. You want to know if I talked about you?'

And did you?

I try to picture my own face, turn that aged, short-haired head in my mind. But I can't do it.

'We discuss my problems, what's wrong with me,' I say. 'What needs to change.'

His hands resettle calmly in his lap. He glitters, brighter than I thought possible. The whole room sings with a light-not-light – the light of all that isn't yet, and all the light that was. Lighting up the either side. A light not meant for here.

'Why would I mention you, Keeper?'

SA Police investigating death of woman in 'disgusting and degrading circumstances'

Police are investigating how an Adelaide woman with cerebral palsy was allowed to die in 'disgusting and degrading circumstances', and have declared her death a major crime.

They say Ann Marie Smith died on April 6 of severe septic shock, multi-organ failure, severe pressure sores, malnutrition and issues connected with her cerebral palsy after being stuck in a cane chair for 24 hours a day in her Kensington Park home for more than a year.

The 54-year-old lived alone in Adelaide's eastern suburbs and relied on a carer for all of her needs.

Police have now opened a manslaughter investigation alongside a coronial inquiry.

Detective Superintendent Des Bray said her death had been declared a major crime.

'Unable to care for herself, she was living her days and sleeping at night in the same woven cane chair in a lounge room for over a year with extremely poor personal hygiene,' he said.

'That chair had also become her toilet.'

Police last week searched offices of the company providing care for her and seized records.

Superintendent Bray said the carer attended Ms Smith's home on April 5 and called an ambulance after discovering her in a 'semi-conscious state'.

She was taken to the Royal Adelaide Hospital, where she had major surgery to remove rotting flesh from severe pressure sores on her body.

She then went into palliative care and died the next day, Superintendent Bray said.

He said Ms Smith lived in a nice home in one of Adelaide's premier suburbs.

'The outside of the house gives no indication as to the horrors that were perhaps occurring within it,' he said.

'This is a tragic case.'

5 years old, early spring

A sore throat, and a day off from school. The midday movie playing on my grandmother's television.

I am working my way through a box of *new* old books Grandma has collected for me. Books left at the Methodist hall where she goes to have her chest X-rayed. I open each one, turn their pages. Mine now – these places, their stories. During the commercials, she reads me all their titles (I don't let her know I can already read most of them myself). *Aircraft of the Great War, Woodwork and Joinery, The History of Croquet, Remarkable Raspberries, Great Steamers of Scotland, Homes of Tangier, Yosemite National Park, Whiteoaks of Jalna, Tender Is the Night*. Enough for a whole new stack under my bedroom window. I hold them against my face, breathe them in. The best smell in all the world.

Between the end of the film and the start of my grandmother's afternoon shows – her 'American Plays' she calls them, during which there must always be silence – there will be *Crusader Rabbit, Popeye*, maybe *Casper the Friendly Ghost*. Anything, please, but *Mr Magoo*. A mean old man, always blaming people for things he has done himself. His bald head and big nose remind me of my grandfather. JG is at the track, the midweek races in Ipswich town.

During the cartoons Grandma will make us lunch. Sometimes a jam sandwich – apple and raspberry that comes in a tin. Usually though, I'm handed two pieces of hand-cut bread with sliced meat. I prefer the jam, but I know better than to say this. *Seen and not heard*, says my mother. *All good children should be seen and not heard.* When my grandmother isn't looking, I slide out the meat and shove it in my pocket or under the waistband of my pants. After eating the heavily buttered bread, I say I'm going outside to pat Paddy.

'One pat,' Grandma warns, settling back in front of the screen. 'One pat, then back inside, out of the wind. Girls with sore throats stay indoors. Grandma's rules.'

Before I go outside I use the toilet, my pee a stop-start dribble so Grandma can't hear me, like I always hear her and JG. This place was a farm once, not a good one by all accounts, too steep, and the toilet was an outhouse for its workers. It was all they owned to start with, my grandparents, building the cottage around it, adding rooms when they could: ten steps up to a kitchen, a sitting room that lists right, two small bedrooms, a bathroom by the front door only Grandma and I use. JG washes outside, behind the rainwater tank. No hallways, no verandahs, no radio or records – only rooms, each tacked to the next and all of it perched over a toilet stall with a shoulder-high door but no roof, sound and smell creeping up and over its weatherboard walls.

Paddy waits for me on the other side of the screen door, the ugly wooden yoke JG makes him wear tugging his head low. He follows me around the corner of the house where I feed him the secret meat. He swallows my crimes gladly and without chewing. Down the hill, on the other side of JG's busy garden and through a sticky metal gate is the 'front house', where I live with my mother. Grandma's tiny sloping hut on the hill is where we call 'up the back'.

Run this up the back, says Mother. ~~Alex Phil~~ *Thommo's coming over. Go up the back for a bit.*

I don't mind. I get to play with Paddy, talk to José and Lucia next door. José is teaching me Spanish. Hola! Buenos dias! ~~Terry Don~~ *Jim's dropping something off. Piss off up the back!* Stuey, Dennis,

Ian 'Hooksy' Hooks, Neville who sells cars – my mother's favourite, I think, though he's not been around for a while. Brian, who calls me Jazzy Jay because of my sequinned pantsuit, brings me armloads of books he finds at the dump. *I'll bring you some more, Jazzy, next trip.* But Mum always says, *Don't you go spoiling her,* laughing with her lips, telling me to *get lost quick* with her eyes. She's better when the men are around. Her hair's always nice and she sings along with the radio and boops my nose and says, *Snooks!* I wish the men would come more often, stay longer. But they don't.

After work, Mother will collect me, take me to the doctor's. We have a five-thirty appointment. I go to the doctor's often. *Bloody flu,* says Mother. *Kid's always got the bloody flu.* But I know she loves it, the drama of it – sweeping in, talking so loudly to the nurse receptionist that everyone in the waiting room can hear what a trouble I am, how she, a poor single mother, never has a moment's peace from having to worry about me.

Doctor Timothy has trouble keeping my patient file open, so many index cards clipped together.

'Say *ahh*,' and then 'No, I don't think it's flu.' He never thinks it is flu.

'Gastric?' my mother will prompt. 'Glandular fever? Epiglottomy? That famous actor, his kid died-a that.' The thrill of a dash to hospital, like a TV show.

'No, not epiglottitis either.'

I am never sick enough, and she will look at me, disappointed.

Doctor Timothy sometimes asks me if I feel worried, nervous. Then my mother's face burns itch-pink and she asks, 'What the bloody hell's she got to be nervous about?'

When Doctor Timothy won't write a prescription, my mother tells Grandma to hand over some of her pills, that she needs something to settle her nerves. Then she grinds them up between two spoons, mixes in some honey, and makes me swallow it. 'There you go,' she says. 'Off to sleep, everybody's nerves sorted.' And then, 'But not a word to your grandmother, you hear me? Not one bloody word.'

But I know this already. She doesn't need to remind me anymore.

The last time we went to see Doctor Timothy, he got angry with Mother about my face, my freckles. When he discovered she was bleaching them, he told her to stop. 'As of now,' he said in a voice I'd never heard him use, that stopped up my mother's lips and dried out her tongue.

Back inside, it's the break between *General Hospital* and *The Young and the Restless*. Grandma warms milk on the stove. 'What about you stay with me this Saturday night,' she says, mixing up a custard powder paste, pouring it into the milk. 'Soft on your tonsils.' She smiles at me, turns back to the pot. There is a rhythm to her stirring – slow, calm. I watch her thin back, her shoulders so sharp, bony, one so much higher than the other, bits of her collapsing, barely held in place by her princely black cardigan.

'Can't,' I say to her. 'Got to go to Mummy's friends, Mummy says.'

My grandmother shakes her head. 'But you're sick, Rory Jay.'

That's the name my grandmother gave me. Rory after her brother who died in the war, and after her mother, Molly Josephine O'Cassidy, or Molly Jay as everyone knew her. My mother had wanted a boy, and when she saw I wasn't one she was too upset to think about names. Too upset for months. 'Call her whatever you like.' So Grandma did. A couple of years later, Mum decided she did care after all, that Rory was a boy's name, that Jay was too, but less so. A girl with a boy's name would get picked on, she said, so she's called me Jay ever since. I am never to go by my first name. 'Never ever,' she says. Only Grandma calls me Rory, mostly when no-one's about.

66

As the custard thickens, Grandma peers through the small kitchen window, eyes left, right, low, then behind us, over my head, down the kitchen steps. My grandfather can be like Casper too, appearing out of nowhere when you least expect him. Not so friendly though. 'And you know Pop won't be here,' she says, voice a whisper. 'He's off to the course early on Saturdays, and straight from there to the dogs or Albion Park. Wherever there's a drink and a place to lose his money, he's there till closing. Gone all day. We'll be asleep well before he gets home.' She says she will make us scones for our tea. That we'll have them with jam and cream. 'Real cream,' she adds, eyebrows high and hopeful. 'Lucy next door gets it in for me, keeps it in her fridge. Pop doesn't know a thing about it. He also doesn't know I bring Paddy into the house on a Saturday night.' She winks. 'He lies on the settee and we watch the movies together.'

My grandmother's secret life. I want so much to be a part of it.

'I don't want you going to those people, Rory. I never have. Your mum told us they had other children, that you were going there to play. But Pop asked around, found out that isn't so.' She turns off the gas, the blue flame snuffed. 'What on Earth is she thinking, sending you off to strangers?'

The custard lazily unfolds itself from the pot, thick waves gliding into my bowl. My favourite food in all the world, with or without a sore throat.

'Some sense is about to be talked into her, I'd say,' says Grandma, laying slices of banana across the top. My mouth waters. 'If there's one thing Pop's good at,' she says, not quite looking at me, 'it's keeping us all in line.'

5 years old, summer

Another day at the beach. You don't know it yet, Spider, but I am here with you now. All day, all night. Keeping the darkness at our heels.

'Aren't you a lucky girl?' they all ask.

You become a gulp, you do not become a smile.

'Excited, Missy?'

Full of dread.

'Stand still,' your mother grumbles, smearing the lotion up and down your arms, across your face and chest. You skitter forward, shuffle back, a doll, a toy, powered by your mother's rough hands.

Let's play pretend.

Let us pretend you are a paper girl, a girl made of paper, waxy and brown – a lunch-bag balloon. Push you a little, you swoosh up and away, pull you too close and you'll crush – *pop!* Dip you in water, in enough of this beach butter, and soon you'll dissolve into nothing.

Go ahead! Are you swooshing?

Are you swooshing and popping?

Are you gone?

'Are you sure she'll be no trouble?' Your mother asks this each time.

Coppertone, reads the bottle. Distinctive, sweet. Like the coconut ice Marjorie sometimes makes just for you.

'Jay? Trouble?' says Marjorie, easing back into your mother's front verandah settee. 'I'll be the one in trouble if Lord William doesn't see his little princess.'

You look down through the iron railings onto a car's blue roof. Inside the car, Billy is waiting. Lord Billy.

'You know how much Bill loves this one.' Marjorie looks like she wants to say more but smiles instead when she catches you watching her.

Marjorie and your mother worked together at Coles, in the meat section. You remember the butchers – orange-haired Glen and big-bellied Colin – but not Marjorie herself who sells dresses now in a shop, a boutique. Sometimes she brings your mother a pretty new frock. 'A return,' she calls it, with a wink. 'A return,' replies your mother, a tap at the side of her nose.

These are the only times Marjorie ever comes to the house, to take you away for one of their weekends. She never drops by for a cup of tea, never calls to say hello. She appears only to drop off and collect, make an exchange – a dress for a child.

'Besides,' Marjorie says to your mother, 'you deserve some time to yourself, Lon,' adding, 'or … with Dennis?'

Your mother inhales through the thin, straight rod of her nose, a wounded shake of her head.

Dennis knocked on the door one day selling encyclopaedias. Doubleday Dennis. Didn't sell you a page but stayed for tea. A week's worth of teas. She still has the two-volume dictionary he left behind. 'Hostages,' your mother calls them, though Doubleday Dennis never did risk a return for their rescue.

'Brian?' quizzes Marjorie.

Book Brian, your favourite. Brian with his treasures from the tip.

'Nev,' Mother says quietly, quickly. 'He's taking me to the Pasadena Room.'

A spill of silence, only the sticky licks of Coppertone on your skin, before Marjorie drops her face into her hands. 'Neville *Creasy*?' She slaps her knees. 'Greasy Creasy?' Marjorie is in fits.

'Oh, come on,' says your mother, not laughing. 'He's not that bad.'

'Oh, Lonnie, he is! Even his wife can't stand him!'

Billy always behind the wheel, Marjorie snuggling beside him on the bench seat, her hand on his thigh, her head on his shoulder, you in the back – and baby makes three. People often think that, that Marjorie and Billy are your parents, and they just let it pass, never bothering to set things straight.

They especially don't go on to say that your father is dead, as your mother does at every opportunity. That the man she claims to have married – so briefly she'd no time even to change her name – died years ago and is *dead I tell you, dead good and proper*, make no mistake about it.

Dropped dead at the track, she insists.

They never know where to look, the people to whom she says this.

Last race of the day.

It makes them uncomfortable.

The Get-Out Stakes they call it.

Everyone knows that is why she tells it.

Got out alright. Got right *out.*

Nervous and quiet, you are, in the back seat, and while Billy's car isn't all that large, your feet don't touch the floor. You prop yourself up, trying to see through the windows, but there is nothing of interest – only roofs, the sky, its scrunches of cloud. *Cloud schmoud*, you've never been one for the outdoors. Your mother smacked from your hands the book you tried to bring. You feel too small, an ant on a crumb, or like you've come along by mistake. You worry that Billy might look in his rear-view mirror and say, Hey, Marj. Did y'know there's some kid in the back? and pull over, leave you by the side of the road. Outside the car, inside it too – you have no idea where you are.

Your fingertips worry away at a tear in the upholstery. The car seat is damaged, no longer lovely. You mustn't make it worse, you tell yourself. You mustn't make that tear any bigger.

Billy and Marjorie arrive early on Saturday mornings, take you for long drives to parks, to waterfalls with picnic tables. Marjorie says she loves kids' movies more than grown-up ones, and she makes sure you see them all – *Bambi, 101 Dalmatians, The Love Bug, Fantasia*. Afterwards, Billy takes 'his girls' to a café in town where you eat cheese sandwiches toasted flat as cardboard, cups of jelly with peach cubes inside. Billy and Marjorie don't mind that you can never finish everything. You never once hear them say, Waste not want not, Missy.

But today, the beach – the worst of all places, not that you would ever say as much. Seen and not heard, says Mother. Blindingly bright, no shade. So much sand, a furnace underfoot, the sun with the bite of a buzz-saw.

In the water, Billy sits you on his shoulders. With his hands locked around your ankles, he plunges you both into the barrelling waves. They fly at you, the waves – roaring, hateful things, fast as ghouls, heavy as felled mountains – the breath punched from you as though by a fist. Colliding with the ocean is a game – you see how other children do it. Saving yourself from its false depths, its dragging and grabbing, is weekend fun. You know you are meant to enjoy this.

You fall asleep in the back of the car, then wake, hot and stiff. Marjorie sits close to the passenger door, looking out, too far away to put her hand on Billy's knee.

'I spy with my little eye …' she begins.

You wait for her to say 'L'.

'Something beginning with … um … let, me, think.' Marjorie raises her chin, eyes narrowed in thought.

'L' is always Marjorie's first go, for the haku lei that hangs from the rear-view mirror. A crown of flowers, Marjorie wore it at her

71

wedding to Billy in Hawaii, then dried it, to keep forever. Billy and Marjorie travel often.

'I've got one!' she declares.

Asia last year. You've heard her tell your mother they go to this Asia place a great deal.

'Bet you can't guess, Jay Jay.'

Bet you can.

The windows are open and the wind makes it hard to hear what Marjorie is saying.

You don't know where Asia is. When you get home, you will search for it in one of your books.

'Want a hint?'

She and Billy have been quarrelling. Warm words, your grandmother calls it. 'They're having a few warm words,' she says of the couples tittling and tattling on her television set in the afternoons. Marjorie wants the windows up, the radio down, to turn around and go home.

'L!' Like she's saying, *Surprise!*

Your fingers circle the split in Billy's back seat, skipping from peak to brittle peak of its broken skin. How you want to rip it. 'La la la la … lipstick?'

'Clever guess, hon, but not my "L".'

'La la la … ladybird?'

'Not a ladybird.'

'Lollipop?' It would be a shame to guess Marjorie's word too soon.

'No, silly! We haven't seen any lollipops! But nice try.'

A red light. Billy looks at Marjorie.

Uh-oh.

'Billy's turn,' he says, in a voice that is not playful. He takes a deep breath, his fists opening and closing around the steering wheel. 'Lunatic? Louse? Leper?'

Marjorie ignores him, stares straight ahead.

'No?' he continues. 'How 'bout … laxative?'

When Marjorie says she wants to turn around and go home, you know she means Melbourne.

'Loser?'

She tries to make him agree to the flip of a coin: Heads – we go back; tails – we stay.

'Leech?'

There's no going home, Billy always says. Ever, Marj.

'Lame-duck? Lemon?'

I'm sick of moving around, Bill, Marjorie argues. And always such hot places. Can't you find what you're after in the cold?

'Liar? Lackey? Lout? *Lesbian?*'

You've never heard of half Billy's guesses.

The light changes to green, yet no-one moves.

'Laughing-stock?'

Billy can't find what he is after in the cold. You tell yourself to remember this. Are cold places easier to hide in?

Marjorie's chin quivers, Billy's thumb and forefinger catching quick on the skin of her neck, squeezing it hard like a flea for the killing. Car horns beep beeping. You pick picking at the tear in the seat alongside you.

'Loony? *Lush?*'

You think of 'love' but wouldn't dare say it, the game long since ended.

Wednesday, 1:17 pm

Mrs Redman calls from Teddy's school.

Instant panic.

'Teddy's fine,' she says, 'doing his work, always a lovely boy. Though he looks a little flushed today.'

His temperature had been up slightly over the weekend, but completely normal since. I must have taken it twenty times in the past three days.

'Teddy's rostered on this week to collect everyone's communication books in the morning, and hand them back in the afternoons. Did you know?'

I wonder how in the world I would know this. Via his iPad, Teddy communicates his wry observations and drive-by threads of random information, but his teacher should know he rarely tells us anything about himself and nothing about his day.

'No,' I reply. 'Is he doing his job?'

'Oh, yes! He's doing it wonderfully. But as he collects each book, he's also announcing the kids' birthday months. You know, that thing he does?'

'Yes, I know it.'

'Every single one he got right! Even Laura, the new girl. She only started last week. Pointed to June on his iPad, straight up. Course, he had a feel of her ears first. But even I didn't know Laura's birthdate, had to look her up, so he can't have been reading my mind. You know there's this theory that some of these kids can read minds?'

'Um, yes. I think so—'

'Anyway, the reason I called is, it's lunchtime, and Teddy is just lying on the ground. He's happy enough, just no interest in playing. He could hardly wait for break time, once, always first to the swings. You know how he is about swings.'

'Yes.'

'But he was like this last term too.'

'Last term?' *Last term?* Why has she waited so long to mention this?

'I suppose I thought I'd better let you know. It's so unusual for him,' she says.

'It is,' I say. 'We've actually got an appointment with our doctor after school, but I think I'll come now, just in case.'

Teddy's school is located in a relatively new dormitory suburb, most of it government-owned reserve with so much native fauna it has come to be known as Kangaroo Valley. I pass five of them on the way to collect him – three nibbling by the roadside and two splattered across it.

Once, on a particularly joyless family drive to a park in Byron Bay, Jerrik hit and killed a wallaby. He refused to ever again go with us on a day drive, though I think the scuppered Skippy was mostly a convenient excuse. That was ten years ago. Jerrik, unravelling behind the wheel of the much-resented Toyota sedan. We'd planned to have a sandwich somewhere, some hot chips (Frank's favourite), maybe take a swim, but Teddy had swung for over an hour, the vestibular feedback nectar-sweet. We couldn't persuade him to stop. His was far from an everyday tantrum, more the trapping of a wild youngling. The sounds he made shocked even me and distressed his brother until Frank was tearing in circles, slapping his face, shrieking, what speech he had like barbs in his throat. Two hours to drive to the park, two minutes to clear it – parents swooping on their children, abandoned swings still eerily swinging, roundabouts a ghost ride. Kids called to safety – that being a safe distance from us. Less a park suddenly than an active crime scene and there we were in the centre of it, the danger, swinging a still-bloody axe. Everyone watching. Everyone.

I remapped our routes to everywhere to avoid passing by any parks – circuitous journeys that doubled our travel time. But now and then, unslept, I'd forget. Teddy had only to glimpse a swing through the car window and he'd scream for us to stop, unbuckling himself from his booster seat and trying to wrench open the back door, biting the backs of his hands until they bled. It was as though his life depended on it, as though a swing, once spotted, just had to be swung, that passing one by meant some connection or other was imperilled: Teddy and swings go together; no swing, no Teddy. Once, in a terrifying rage, he got his fingers inside the roof liner of the car, collapsing it on himself and his quivering brother.

I needed to dig in deep beside him, into the wayside, relinquish my own thinking, redesign it in step with Teddy's. Beginnings and endings – what did they mean? Duration? Why should it mean anything? Teaching these concepts was like tending an introduced species in a wholly unsuitable habitat. Like grafting a variant cutting onto old growth, hostile to tampering. Using visual aids, we counted the minutes and seconds of everything we did, day and night, laminated squares in my pocket everywhere we went – Stop and Go traffic lights – to help Teddy understand stopping, starting, transition.

Eventually, recreational reserves were no longer theatres of war.

Nonetheless, we rarely went to them on weekends, at peak play times. Like something endangered, we lurked at the edges of such scenes, slipping in and out as meekly as we could. Still feeling my way as a mother, not yet inured to the stares and dipped-voice dissections of other mothers who weren't like me, whose children weren't like mine, I let us have only what was left over. Better for everyone, I thought.

An hour later: 'Too big for the swings now, aren't you, mate?' says the GP with a poke at Teddy's knee. 'A growing boy.' And another poke. 'Just dropping some puppy fat.'

Teddy wipes the unexpected touch from his skin.

'So you agree, he looks thinner?'

'Perfectly fine at this age.'

'Don't you want to weigh him?' I ask. 'He can be a bit wiggly but—'

'Temperature?'

'It hovers – high thirty-sevens, low thirty-eights. Comes and goes, like his appetite.'

'Body pain?'

This GP has treated the boys for the past eleven years. 'Well, that's the problem, isn't it?' I say. 'It's so hard for us to know.'

'Probably nothing.' He smiles, a comforting pat on my arm. 'Baby Panadol if you think he needs it.'

'Teddy won't take Baby Panadol, remember? He won't take any pain relief. It's the thick texture that—'

'Well, I'm sure it'll pass,' he says with annoying calm. 'Keep an eye on things but come back in three weeks if he doesn't improve.'

'*Three weeks?*'

Last term. Three weeks. What's the rush?

2:04 am

Another night in the last-chance saloon. I use my phone to guide us along the unlit, olive-green hallway, down the flight of uneven stairs that lead to our underground. Our Plan B bower.

We tried to have lights installed. This extended part of the house was a DIY job, said one electrician after another. Shoddy work done by previous owners without council approval. No-one would touch it.

Barely an energetic leap wide, the laundry feels tomb-narrow tonight, its ceiling too low-slung. Teddy throws himself under the desk. He wasn't happy in his own bed, wasn't happy to be moved, and clearly isn't happy to be here. Tonight, he just isn't happy.

With his temperature reset to the top end of normal, there had been all the indicators of a looming all-nighter: raucous sprints down the hallways, violent rocking at the dinner table and, worse, the noise. The relentless, savage sounds that jackboot their way out of him, as though his voice is livid with itself, would rather be destroyed than function as intended. Impossible to believe those sounds don't cause him pain. Frank claims he can feel Teddy's noise in his fingertips, that it makes his skin vibrate. I don't doubt it. He has an exam tomorrow and needs rest. At least Jerrik is in Bangalore. He fares less well than any of us with shattered sleep.

I drop an armload of washing into the top loader, but I know Teddy is hours from settling. So here we are, fingers laced. Teddy's turn to squeeze, my turn.

Squeezed, squeezing. If only it were possible to renovate the laundry, nights down here in the bower might not seem so dismal.

Squeezed, squeezing. Would it be too ridiculous to install a washing machine in our room upstairs?

Squeezed, squeezing. I think of Jerrik, what he would have to say about it. Warm Danish words, no doubt.

Squeezed, squeezing. Jerrik. Joyless Jerrik. They say girls marry their fathers. Do fatherless girls marry their mothers?

Squeezed, squeezing. I certainly seem to have done.

After what happened, after what Lonnie did, I worked as soon as I could, any job I could find, one day a week, then two, then seven, grateful for every hour offered. I had lost my place, had it taken away, and something in me wanted it back. I studied part-time. Day, night, moving, never still. The faster I went, the easier it was to retrace my steps, to follow the faint, fallen-away dots of me like a trail of breadcrumbs until they drifted together; until, from a distance at least, I resembled a whole. Every penny stashed away – my *chilly* fund. One day I would trek my cherished worlds of ice, find one I loved the most and do what I had to do to make myself a home in it. I'd dump this sweaty little town and never look back.

Every year I'd swear to myself: next year, next year we'll be done. Next year, we're off. My passport application all signed, verified, ready to go. I even got as far as the doors of the lodgement office. Twice.

But then, how smoothly would come the second-guessing, the capital-D Doubt, sidling up behind, pulling my head to the broad bones of its carcass chest, ~~devil-got~~ honey-pot words in my ear. *What's another year?* it would whisper. *It's tough out there. What if they don't want you either?* A pock-white hand so protective on my hip. *Is it so bad, what we have here?* Its other arm, its cords of vulture-neck muscle, steadying my aim. *Better the devil you know.* Showing me how to squeeze the trigger to shoot my plans to hell.

And then came Jerrik and our baby, bubbling into brothers, and Jerrik said if only we had a house, a house would make it easier, with a home of his own he might see it through. So I let the ice melt in my hand (*It wouldn't have wanted you anyway*, Doubt soothed, stroking my hair) and put down a deposit. The dip-down could be renovated, said Jerrik, working up a design before we'd even signed the contract. Oh, it was to be very stylish, his plans shown to me with such pride. But then Frank, silent as a blink, didn't clap or wave or point, and at thirteen months Teddy stopped looking at us, started shuffling about on his toes and the house has been fracturing ever since, struggling to bear us up.

Teddy lies on his side, his back to me, headphones on, his ears brimful of the *Crucifixus*. His own noise surges and ebbs as he listens, its discordant jabs and blasts slowly tamed by Lotti's plaintive lines. I begin to feel hopeful that sleep may yet come. I rub his back through his pyjama shirt. When I stop, he wriggles – *more, more*. He flips over, left side, right, knees up, knees down, pausing to stroke the ridges and arcs of my ear, the Whirlpool already winding up the rinse cycle.

Eventually, he sets his headphones and iPod beside him and turns to face me, his hands coming to rest over my ears, tenderly, as though they belong to us both, as though cupping my ears will inform and sharpen what he hears. This is how it begins.

Crucifixus: Soprano 1's final minute, note after exquisite note, my breath caught in each and every perfect suspension. I don't know how he does it; I've heard no practice, no false starts. The singing simply began one night here in the laundry, as fine and clear as any Tallis Scholar. Still no words from my wordless son, but music, luminous and sacred. His voice, a minute-long miracle.

I record him on my phone.

In the morning I will play Teddy's song to Frank who will say, 'Nice work, brother,' and to Jerrik when he returns, who might say, 'For all the good,' if he says anything at all.

Saturday, 6:35 am

For years, the boys and I would walk to our local park every Saturday morning. It has generous shade, toilets and multiple adult-sized swings. We'd arrive and be done before anyone else showed up. Teddy could go as high and as long as he needed without disgruntling others. His recent dips of lethargy, despite being random and brief, terrify me. I want to turn back the clock. I want my boy to swing again, see on his face the exhilaration I know lightens the load of his body.

We set off, leaving Frank to have a lie-in. But today we're not early enough.

'I've got a cousin with a boy like him,' says the woman.

Her daughter, six or seven, hangs frozen by her feet from the monkey bars, transfixed by Teddy's chunky gold headphones, the iPod fused to his palm, his Wookiee-like warblings.

I keep my head down, my rhythm going, hoping the woman will lose interest, just go away. She doesn't.

'Blond and six feet?' I say.

A silent rictus laugh, wide-mouthed, like an oversized dead fish. I don't look at her, though I do wait for her to say, *Great to see you haven't lost your sense of humour*, as so many do. No doubt she'll get around to it.

To my delight, Teddy had charged to the swings the second we arrived, but now the fishwoman's daughter drops from her bat-like repose and hits the ground running.

'What's wrong with that boy?' she calls to her mother, pointing at Teddy with her fingers and with her voice, pointing with her laser-beam eyes. 'What's wrong with him?'

It is yet another opportunity for me to be someone else, a 'bigger' someone, generous and pure, someone who thinks, *Aw, kids are just curious.*

But I'm sick of doling out excuses like Halloween candies to strangers' children. They would offer us none. Sick of being guest speaker in some great diversity workshop, my own sons wheeled out as exhibits. It is not Teddy's job to PowerPoint his personal humiliation for the sake of everyone else's growth and education. I am not here to teach anyone else's children anything, their lack of social grace not my responsibility. You exist, and we exist. We come in peace and hope only for incident-free planet-sharing. Now sod off.

'Yes, Cami,' the woman replies, picking dead leaves off a row of agapanthus, using her feet to bustle bark off the pathway and back into the garden. 'He's a special boy, isn't he?' as though Teddy had arrived on a flying carpet or on the back of a chortling mammoth, cranking a hurdy-gurdy.

'So tall,' says the woman. 'Must get that from his daddy?'

I smile as politely as I can though I do not look at her.

'There's a special park, did you know? An *all-inclusive* park,' she corrects herself proudly, 'with special equipment, for ...'

Now I look at her, watch her struggle to finish her sentence.

'For ... all ages ... and that,' she says. 'Down bayside way.'

'Yes,' I reply. 'But the bayside is a very long drive and a very large park, with many people, *special* or otherwise. This is our local park. We can walk here and keep to ourselves.'

'Just something to bear in mind,' she says, pootling off to pick and prune.

I don't doubt this woman means no harm. She claims to

have disability in her family after all – albeit attached by a long exculpating thread – so nudging us in the direction of what she considers a more suitable recreational reserve is, perhaps, her way of helping and supporting. I respect you, she is telling me, I respect the situation. Just take it out of my park, why don't you, because it wasn't expected – my child is not prepared and her exposure to it is making us all uncomfortable, no matter how much, respectfully, I wish it were not.

Teddy suddenly jumps from the swing, breaking into a series of grand jeté leaps towards the climbing fort. Cami outsprints him to be the first to the top. But I know Teddy will only want to lie for a while on the slide, watch a YouTube clip. As with everything else, there is an order that must be observed in play parks, and lying at the very bottom of a slide usually precedes a message on the app: 'I, want, home.'

But Cami doesn't know that and she, Queen of the Castle, wants to keep Teddy, the dirty rascal, in his place. At the top of the fort, she tugs on overhead branches, stripping leaves and snapping twigs.

'You can't come up here,' she decrees, whatever carnage that comes away in her meaty little fists thrown down at him. 'You can't come up here.'

Aw, kids.

Teddy, suddenly so weary-looking, opens the app on his iPod. But I already know what he will be typing. 'I want to go home too, love,' I say, beating Liam to it.

3:30 pm

Late autumn, and still thirty-one degrees. The three of us spend the afternoon in our bathers in the backyard. Frank aims the hose at the sky, his finger over its dribbling flow, showering us. When it gets too hot we run inside, still dripping, swatting flies, and pile into the hammocks on the front verandah. Frank and I sing 'We're

Going on a Bear Hunt', Teddy letting us know when he wants us to stop and when he wants us to start again by pressing on our chins. Then we play one of Frank's favourite games. He recites a line, in character, from a program we've watched together – in some cases multiple times – and I must name both the show and the person who said it.

Frank: '*Not Penny's boat.*'

Me: 'Charlie, *Lost.*'

Frank: 'C-correct. *Is mayonnaise an instrument?*'

Me: 'Too easy. Patrick, *SpongeBob SquarePants.*'

Frank: 'C-correct. *Swing away, Merrill. Merrill? Swing away.*'

I enjoy this game almost as much as Frank does. The stutter gets confused amid the accents, can't keep up with who's who.

Me: 'Um … Mel Gibson! *Signs!*'

Frank: 'Mum … Mum, you know … you know the rules.'

Me: 'Argh! He played the dad … the pastor. Ian? Gordon? No … *Henry*! Do I still get a point?'

Frank: 'G- … G- … G-*GRAHAM* Hesse. Point-adjacent.'

6:07 pm

Bathtime, and the start of the night shift.

While Frank needs supervision with his personal cares – more than he would prefer – I still have to bath Teddy myself, shampoo his hair, brush his teeth. I am not sure he will ever manage his hygiene independently. Small pustules have erupted across his eyebrows, arms and legs. Molluscum contagiosum, according to the GP. I asked our doctor where this might have come from, why Teddy has suddenly developed it when his skin has always been so clear. *Kids get these things*, is all he had to say, along with, *Four to six months, should resolve itself.* Do nothing, in other words – his usual advice. Doctor Google suggests wheatgrass lotion, which I bought online. A generous dollop applied to each one, twice a day.

A lengthy ordeal night and morning. Time to wonder who would do this in my absence?

Teddy is more bewitched by the candle I have lit by the basin than by the stories I read by its light, his eyes in sync with its flicflac-ing flame. But I press on, trying to engage him, doing my best silly voices, pointing to a sheep on a plane, and a sheep in the rain, a big sheep that is close, a tiny sheep that is far.

'*Far*,' says Frank, as he walks by the bathroom.

A sheep on a surfboard, one flying a kite. 'Fabulous lives, these sheep,' I say to Teddy.

'Where is ... where is ... F-Far?' Frank asks.

A question I can't answer. 'India,' I say, though I'm not certain Jerrik ever went there in the first place, or where he's been sleeping since he got back.

'Where is that dang sheep?' I ask Teddy.

I am Mummy, and Jerrik is Far. But who will come after? Who are they? Will they be kind? The boys are fifteen now, an age when such a worry should loom less lethal. Not so, in our case. This question stalks me, hunching about like a hoodlum, all bar-fly eyes and lolling toothpick. I will never outrun it, its shadow slant in the corner of my eye. Who will come after us, after me, because someone will have to?

9:37 pm

At night, the three of us still lie together for a while before lights-out. Sometimes Frank reads stories to his brother, or performs them for us, flexing his accents, his flamboyant impressions, seeing if he can still recall by heart the stories he'd recite when he was young.

Tonight I read *The Paper Bag Princess*, *Happy Birthday Dotty* and two Hairy Maclary books. Teddy lies facing me, picks up my right hand, weaves his fingers with mine. When our game of squeeze ends, I blow him a kiss. He taps an open palm against his mouth, his lips taut and stretched thin – the very opposite of a pucker. I hope it never changes.

Frank sits on the edge of the bed, his fingers drawing invisible figures on my left arm, his touch light and soothing. His unseeable picture is getting larger, more detailed. 'I had ... I had ... I had the dream ag- ... ag-again last night,' he says sleepily. 'So I ... I'm drawing it.'

Frank's dolphin dream. He's been having it since he was old enough to tell me about it.

'You're drawing Teddy?'

'Teddy has ... he has ... he has no legs. But he has a nice ... a nice ... he has a nice tail.'

'Because he's a dolphin,' I say.

'And he saves ... Teddy saves us in the dream. On the ... on the ... on the boat. We're all ... we're all so scared, don't know ... don't know ... we don't know wh-what to do. But he dives and sw-swims and saves us. We all ... we all ch-cheer.'

I see that Teddy's eyes are closed, but on his face, a dawning smile. The hero of his brother's dream. 'What strange and wonderful little people you are,' I whisper, leaning across Teddy to turn the reading lamp off and the salt lamp on.

Getting to his feet, Frank – six feet, five inches – looks down at me. 'Little?' He fixes me with a blank but benign stare. *The owls are not what they seem.*

'Ha! That is a trick question! Almost everybody in *Twin Peaks* says that at some stage. But I'm going to guess you're The Giant.'

'One and the same,' he says, in Carel Struycken's halting Dutch accent before bowing his head and disappearing to his room.

12:02 am

Wide awake, I realise Jerrik is probably having sex with someone.

I never even dream of it, sex. With anyone. I rarely think about it despite it being everywhere, as easy to find as a set of golden arches along a service road. The same old act as it has ever been, yet still so remarkable to many. So much complexity, profundity attached to the rhythmic stimulation of over-congratulated bits and pieces. So much talking up.

Marc's voice out of nowhere.

You have a smile like Meryl Streep.

Marc with a 'c'.

I remember not knowing how to take his comment, so long ago. Compare a girl to Jessica Lange, or a young Jane Fonda, and you knew where you stood. But Meryl?

Turning to him, the look on my face.

I find Meryl rather sexy, he'd said, back-pedalling, comically unconvincing.

Call yourself an actor? I laughed.

I don't dream of sex, but I do dream of love. Of being loved. Love deserves more talking up than it gets.

Soon enough, in the pasty-green dim, he fades in.

On his haunches, his back to us, cloaked in thick layers – pelts, one heaped upon another, bulking him out, savage and invincible. His shoulders push out our four walls, vault our ceiling. Our room becomes a cathedral, our beds whittled to matchsticks. I am small; is this what he is trying to tell me? I am *less-than*.

Hardly, he says, reading my thoughts like a neon sign. *Merely picking up your hammer, Spider. My turn to watch, your turn to rest.*

I look over at Teddy and pray, as I do every night of late, that the new day will bring an end to his strange malaise.

'I'll know if it's the right thing, won't I, Keep? When the time comes?'

Your plan?

'My plan.'

And though he doesn't turn, and shows no sign of even thinking it, were he to touch his hand to mine, a demon hand, burnt or boiled or bone or pustulant, I wouldn't pull away.

The later the hour, the louder self-pity rattles its cage, Spider.

Telling me what's what. He does that sometimes.

'Night, night, Keeper.'

Monday, 9:24 am

The door to her room is a heavy heritage-style, ornate white metal, but with stainless-steel security mesh and a deadlock. She can see through it, down the corridor, the corner of the nurses' station, and she can be observed at all times, save for when using the bathroom. The door has been specially fitted; no-one else in all of the Gardens of Holy Marian Aged Care Home has one. It stays open when anyone enters.

She is dozing in the chair when I arrive, an alarm cushion beneath her.

I sit down opposite, our knees almost touching.

Even in sleep, she is wound tight. Ready for war.

I take a picture of her on my phone just as a young girl with a thick twist of strawberry-cream hair appears at the door. 'Do you think Lenore will want any of that?' she whispers, pointing at the barely touched breakfast tray. 'I could leave the toast. She sometimes eats it cold.' I shake my head, and the girl wisps in, picks up the tray and vanishes. Nobody who knows better ever wants to wake up Lenore.

I visit when I can on a day of my choosing – when the boys don't need me to be doing something else, when I am not too exhausted to anticipate the ambush that is inevitable. As it is, I can't stay long today. I have a midday appointment with Doctor Crasno, my second visit. The timing is serendipitous: an hour with Lonnie – a rich, festering seam of woe for Zelda to dehisce.

Lonnie has a ground-floor room, its generous window looking out over the gardens – of no interest to her – and two tennis courts that are beyond the interest of anyone here. Stage props, surely, for the sake of the brochures.

She shoved a racquet in my hand the moment I was big enough to swing it. Club fixtures on Saturday, Catholic tennis association on Sunday, junior academy squad training three nights a week. We lived on fish-paste sandwiches and grilled cheese to afford my lessons, my gear. A brief reprieve was offered by the winter months when I was expected to conquer all who came before me during the netball season. But tennis was the game the rich kids played and rich is what Lonnie aimed to be by any manner of means. Those means, of course, were mostly me. I was to be a champion, a WTA star. But my hands were soft and quick to blister. When I was eleven, twelve perhaps, she thought she'd lit upon a solution.

It was one of her bad nights. Another meal had been hurled around the kitchen, my hair speckled thick with it. Her job to storm to her room, my job to clean up the mess. The way of us. I didn't expect her to surface until morning, and was leaning over the sink, sponging café curtains, when she suddenly reappeared.

'How're those blisters?' she asked, yawning.

My mother's questions were often dangerous, and I couldn't see down all the half-lit lanes this one may lead. 'Okay,' I replied, approaching with extreme caution.

'Well, I gotta pee,' she said. 'May as well put it to good use.'

She had heard that a famous player treated his blisters by peeing on his hands, that something in urine toughened the skin. My racquet turned just as I would strike the ball. The jarring burnt, opened my skin early in a match. I played with my right palm bandaged. Some flaw in my grip. *In your head more like*, Mother would say. No coach could remedy it.

'Well?' she barked. 'Don't just stand there looking at me with your big dumb googs.'

She'd taken to peeing in a plastic container and had me soak my hands in it. She had instructed me to pee on myself. I did it once or twice. I told her I did it still.

'But … aren't you going to—'

'Oh, for Christ's sake, Mutt!' she yelled, so viper-quick to turn. 'Too much messing around with the bucket. It's late and I'm buggered. Some of us have been at work all day.'

So I followed her into the toilet and knelt in front of the bowl. Turning my face to the side, I inspected the peeling wallpaper while she pissed on my hands. Fixing me. I risked a quiet, 'Thank you,' as the front of my nightie was splashed.

'All be worth it when you win Wimbledon,' she said, wiping herself.

She went back to bed and, once my hands were dry, I finished up in the kitchen, putting the flung-about remains in the freezer so they wouldn't stink up the bin.

As though she knows the hour is almost up, and with it her window to launch an attack, her eyes blink open. My mother sizes me up and I can hear it, her approach – dreadful, like a club dragging over so many blunt-struck skulls.

I don't say anything.

Wait instead for the net to drop.

Trapping me, hogtied.

She wears the woollen socks I brought her the last time, a trim of ulcerated skin at their tops. I doubt they have been changed in a month.

'There's geysers all over my stomach.'

She points at herself, her nails thin blades. The nurses once tried to trim them as she slept, but she had woken, and they never tried again. All over, her flesh is a chew of stains – choked reds, burnt blacks, veins of worm-blue. A wreckage of time-stomped skin. It should move me more than it does.

'Springs. Big tall spurts-a water. See? Like the fountain in town. In the square.'

She forgets how long I spent behind the scenes, her craven understudy. I'd know the smell of greasepaint anywhere.

'You don't have them in your belly, do you?'

I don't need to shake my head.

'Only rotten eggs in your belly.'

One day, a long-ago visit, I'd been low. Some sorrow with the boys. My hide tender, my heart clutching, opening up to that make-believe mother who would sometimes play me at poker and almost let me win, who once came home with a marked-down Rolling Stones cassette. There were no songs on it I liked, but she had bought it just for me, to show she meant what she said. *Promised I'd do better, didn't I?*

'How are the r-r-r-r-rotten eggs these days?'

A hide that is tender should just go home, keep her fool mouth shut.

Holding my phone to her face, I take another shot.

Beyond the grey-white caul of her hair, and the browning leaf that is the rest of her, my mother has little in common with the others behind the doors of this place – those who sit all day because it is all they remember how to do, and those who lie, past remembering how to sit. She has yielded to no softening, no crimpling of her machine-cut edges. No renewed, kitten-like wonder of the world for her, and certainly none of the artless indulgence of the old and unmendable.

A blonde woman pushing a cart appears in the doorway. 'Magazine? Crossword? Caramello Koalas today.'

Lenore flicks a regal 'No thank you' to the woman, sharing with me her who-the-hell-does-this-tart-think-she-is look.

'She'd love one,' I say, perky. The daughter, her only visitor. 'Wouldn't you, Mother?'

A *Woman's Day*, a *Take 5*, and the children's chocolate are hurriedly set on the end of Lonnie's bed, the woman exiting quickly without turning her back. I mouth a *Thank you* as she retreats.

I hold up my phone, show her one of the shots I've taken. 'Here's what you look like now.'

She jerks her head back to get a better view.

'Just thought you'd like to know.'

Lonnie hasn't been allowed any mirrors since she smashed one four years ago. *How else was I s'posed to get rid of him?* is what she said of the Home's chaplain who'd required eighteen stitches in his forearm. *He wasn't taking the hint.*

She regards her picture. 'What rot,' she says. 'What rot.' With a fed-up *pfft*, she reaches over to snatch at the gossip rag. 'Hey! What happened to my toast?' she demands, indignant.

I tell her I ate it and that it was delicious.

'You're a piece,' she replies. 'Why do you even show up here?'

Lonnie's sunken eyes are spongy from crying, which she does often. One of the geriatricians mooted Sundown Syndrome, but he doesn't know my mother. She always was a crier, an actress – an exponent of the grand classical technique, surely; one face as easy as any other, as good as any other so long as it profited her. Tears came easily – to sidestep, disarm, to sway, to conquer. When things went her way and when they didn't. Another's happiness routinely brought on a gush – because for Lonnie, happiness was a communal pie, someone else's share of it always a risk to her own portion. And like any good actress, she knows how to hold a moment, milk it for all it's worth, as she is now, eyes puffy and pity-pink, luring succour, sympathy. Every outburst – *Everything was fine until you came along! It's on you, these things I do!* – was rounded off by waterworks, my responsibility as her audience to fully appreciate her suffering, accepting always its sovereignty over my own. Not so much begging my forgiveness as stealing it, as parents so easily do from their children. It was all about Lonnie. She was the centre of the world and the only rightful licensee of all its emotions. Things didn't matter unless they affected her, and what affected her stopped the tides.

'Why?' she demands again, eyes looping side to side. Plotting eyes. 'It's not like you *want* to spend your time with your mother.' Tears pooling on cue, giving her all to the role of meek old lady. 'Do you? Do you, Jay?'

Two male nurses pass by, surveilling, as they do. Admirers of her work.

Cue: a dainty sob. A dainty sob as though I have upset her, expertly delivered by the still dainty 'o' of my mother's mouth. 'Why don't you just ... *go*?' Trying to hide that sobbing, trying not to hide it too. Making it, in fact, the main event. A coy one. It's quite a skill, and she's still got it.

Why do I come here?

On my way out, my mother shoots bullets into my back. 'Off she goes, Lady Muck!'

Why do I come here?

I let one of the nurses know about the sores on my mother's legs—

'I'm not done with you, *Mutt*! You hear me?'

—that they'll need to be looked at, and that there's blood and excrement on her dressing-gown—

'Back then, that night, all of it, it's ...'

—which will not do—

'*all in her HEAD!*'

—that I'll bring her a clean one—

'The whole bloody thing.'

—on my next visit.

'Why won't anyone *believe* me?'

But she is wrong. Someone does believe her. Me. Every visit. She is still that good.

I hear the door to my mother's room being closed and locked, but the ward's long corridor plays tricks — becomes an endless enfilade of architraves and columns that look like hallways within hallways, doors within doors. The faster I go, the further the end draws away. I feel very small again, helpless again. The carpet splinters, lifts from the floor like a startle of flies. Paintings melt from walls that dissolve away too. And then it all explodes, the tumbling corridor a sewer, everything blasted to lumps and bits. I flush like waste as I walk.

Tonight, Keep will find what is left of me. Whatever I need he will know it, secure it — a hireling devil, *my* devil, my poultice and protector, destroyer of others. When I sink with exhaustion he will crouch down, beckon me to climb the great knots of his back, hoop my arms around his neck. Between his gargoyle shoulders, I will sleep the sleep of the truly loved while he, at his post, will guard the dread night, his hundred hunting eyes lit arrows, turning all raiders to red mist.

Disability Royal Commission hears teenager was left with severe disability after being given psychotropic medication

Oliver McGowan was a school prefect, played representative football and athletics and was training to become a Paralympian.

But the Royal Commission into Disability on Tuesday heard how that all changed.

His mother gave evidence about how her teenaged son, who lived with autism, focal partial epilepsy and an intellectual disability, was told by a neurologist he had full life expectancy and would eventually live independently.

But Oliver's quality of life drastically deteriorated after he was prescribed a drug he and his parents begged doctors not to give him.

After suffering seizures in December 2015, the hearing was told Oliver was given psychotropic drug Olanzapine in a UK hospital, despite not having been diagnosed with psychosis or a mental illness.

His mother, Paula McGowan, who now lives in Newcastle [...] told the commission the effect of the drugs on Oliver was catastrophic.

'We were told by the doctors that Oliver's brain was so badly swollen it was bulging out the base of his skull ... Oliver was now profoundly disabled,' she said.

'The doctors told us that Oliver had no chance of recovery or return.

'Cruelly, Oliver was reassured that this would not happen, and his voice was not heard and it cost him his life.'

At the age of 18, Oliver died in Bristol, England, due to a combination of pneumonia and hypoxic brain injury.

The commission heard there were 177,000 reports of unauthorised use of chemical restraints on NDIS participants in 2019–2020.

Oliver's death sparked a review by the National Health Service.

Ms McGowan told the commission she had made ground through a campaign overseas, with the UK Government last year committing to introducing mandatory training in learning disability and autism for healthcare workers.

She is pushing for a similar program to be adopted in Australia.

6 years old, autumn

Your last day at the beach, Spider, but you don't know that yet.

Your mother expects a friend from work. Vic.

And now she's run out of beach butter. *Bugger!*

Marjorie says not to worry, that there's plenty in the glovebox. Billy and Marjorie think of everything.

The verandah railings are still so much taller than six-year-old you. Through them, Billy's blue car. Through them, Billy.

Marjorie tells your mother there is a new system for returns at the shop, that things aren't going to be quite so easy anymore. She gives your mother three orange notes. Twenty-dollar bills! Three times what she spends on her weekly shop.

'I ought-a be giving you two money, Marj, for taking her off my hands.'

'We just want you to get yourself something nice.' Marjorie grasps the hand of your mother's that grasps the money. All this grasping taking place at the same level as your head, right before your very green eyes.

Then your mother hears your grandfather at the kitchen door, and she says, 'Righto,' with a hand behind your neck and, 'Better not hold you up,' her other hand behind Marjorie, riches already in her pocket, steering you both down the stairs.

'Seen and not heard,' warns Mother, her lips a hiss in your ear. 'Good girls are seen and not heard.'

Then she turns very quickly and goes inside, doesn't wait to wave you off.

And you're away.

In the car, Marjorie says it's getting too cool for the beach. 'Jay's a little frog. She feels the cold. A movie might be better. A bike ride.'

'Bull,' is Billy's reply.

Marjorie lies on a towel, her back to the sun. Soon she will be asleep. You and Billy climb the dunes, a race to the top, a tumble to the bottom, Billy a boisterous clown. He takes the Coppertone from his pocket, holds it aloft, like a prize. Kneeling behind you, his hands are slow, not like Mother's, trying to be gentle, wanting you to like it. But the sand has worked its way into the lotion, spoiling it, everything spoiled, and the lotion no longer smells pink and sweet. It is bottled burrs, a red rubbing.

'I bet that feels nice,' says Billy, and you, seen and not heard, nod only, Yes.

Because now you're with me, *Spider*, no longer with him.

Your hand in mine, made of paper, we are, lunch-bag balloons.

Swooshing, popping.

Up. Away. Gone.

At night you play games – Twister, old maid, hide-and-seek. Billy never loses at Battleship.

'He's a navy man, that's why,' says Marjorie proudly. 'Hello, *sailor.*' She paints your nails and gives you a 'do, combing and pinning your long hair into a fancy knot, pigtail twirls springing about your ears. She asks if you know how pretty you are, says she'd do anything to have your blonde hair.

'Dirty blonde,' Billy corrects her. 'You're a dirty little blonde, aren't you, Jay Bird?'

Marjorie rolls her eyes but does not look at him, sip sipping her drink.

Your 'do is set in place with long blasts of hairspray that dry like glue at the back of your neck, at the edge of your face, and it itches, but Billy tells you dogs scratch, young ladies do not.

You wear some of Marjorie's lipstick and rouge and a nightie, though not one of hers – one they've bought specially for your visits. Short and wide, like a glamorous poncho, your sleepover nightie is made of fine black lace and a fluffy hem of silver-white fur. The pyjamas your mother packed stay folded in their crinkly bag. You will take the bag home and your mother will use it for something else, waste-notting, want-notting.

'Black is your colour,' Billy tells you.

'Can't go wrong with wide'n'black,' agrees Marjorie, sip sipping. 'You're a lil' Magpie, are'n-cha, Jay? Go the mighdy Maggies!'

You hide as you are told to, on your side on the top of a wardrobe, high enough to almost touch the ceiling.

Billy lifts you up there. 'Something special about you, isn't there, Jay?' he coos as you lie in his arms. 'Billy's sweet Baby Jay.'

Marjorie, the seeker, giggles, hiccups. 'Whadever happ'nd to Baby Jay?' She looks for you inside the refrigerator, at the bottom of a vase. 'Bill? *Bill!* Do *you* know what happ'n't Baby Jay?'

She stumbles, refilling her glass as she walks. '*Hi-yo*, Marjie to the rescue! I'll save you, Jay Jay.'

Billy's lips go flat and his big knuckles crack. You think Billy hates Marjorie sometimes. He delivers you to the bedroom floor. 'Photo time,' he says sharply, a little annoyed with you too.

A lot of photos are taken during your visits. Billy has you lower your head, put one leg out in front, bend your knees, hold your nightie out to the sides. 'Like you're meeting the Queen,' he says, snapping away, 'and giving her a curtsy.'

For your sixth birthday, Marjorie made you a new dress on her sewing machine. Sleeveless, thick stripes, yellow and white. A blue skirt that fans out like the blades of a helicopter as you spin.

'A sweet little mini with a trumpet hem,' Marjorie had cried. Marjorie loves clothes and make-up and hairdos and perfume. She says she loves you too. She made a bow for your hair, jumbo-sized in matching cornflower blue. 'Happy birthday, Mini Marjorie!' Clapping her hands and raising her glass of Mateus Rosé in celebration.

'Get her your slippers, Marj,' calls Billy. 'The ones with the heels and pompoms.'

Marjorie objects. 'She mi-topple over. Break a-ankle. Huh! You wanna 'splain that to *L'NORE?*'

'Just get the heels, Marj.'

You pose with a giant panda in your arms, a beach ball, holding Marjorie's drink. Billy tells you to have a sip. Billy tells you to have three sips. You peek through your fingers, smiling, not smiling, feet together, feet apart, standing straight, kneeling, waving, hands by your sides then clasped in front, as in prayer, a soft red ribbon wound about your wrists.

'Red'n'black? Boo! *Boo!*' says Marjorie. 'Boo those lousy Bombers.'

When you don't get your pose right, Billy positions your arms and hips as he wants them, with his hands.

We are mannequins now, Spider. The mannequins in Marjorie's shop window. We look so real, but we are not. They could stick us with a pin and we wouldn't feel a thing.

'You might be a model one day,' says the cameraman. 'And I'll be Lord Billy, your official photographer.'

Posing and posing, still as a statue, your cheeks a-wobble with ache. *Click whirr* goes the camera, *click whirr. Flash flash* do this, *flash flash* now that. Small comets blinding your eyes and blanking the world.

Marjorie sometimes models too, singing songs, doing the twist, the jive, twirling a baton like she did in her marching band days. But tonight she is tired.

'Good Ol' Colliwood f'rever ...' Sleepy sleepy at the dining table, her forehead rolling along the tablecloth, an empty glass nestled in her lap like a pup. 'They know how'da play the game ...'

Billy lowers his camera. 'What are we gonna do with her, Baby Jay?'

'Too hot, this town,' Marjorie whimpers. 'Hellhole.'

Behind Billy, a wide, dark doorway. Beyond that another, then a third, each one smaller than the one before, nesting, like the set of Russian dolls Billy and Marjorie once gave you.

'They're real ones, Jay,' Billy said, watching you unwrap them. 'All the way from Moscow. Look at the sticker – that's Russian. No junk for our little lady.'

You look up at him, awaiting instruction, holding out your nightie in case Billy wants to take more pictures. He usually does. You see how big his pupils have become, how this makes him look like a doll himself, though a very different kind – a frightening one, its eyes burnt-out pits.

Billy picks you up, hugs you to him. 'You're so tiny,' he says, the three dark doorways beyond his shoulder. 'Wouldn't want to crush you.' He wraps your legs around his waist. Too tight, but you mustn't complain. Seen and not heard.

'You smell good enough to eat,' pretending to take a bite of your shoulder.

You wish Marjorie would wake up. You cross your fingers, hold your breath. You want to go home.

But we're balloons, Spider! We can go anywhere we want.

In his quietest voice of all, Billy says the lace of your nightie is a bit scratchy and rough, that you'd prefer it, wouldn't you, if he lifted it over your head.

'There, that's better, isn't it?' His hands on your bare back, on your tiny, toy-girl bones, soft feathery kisses around your eyes. This part you like, the kisses on your face. Your mother is not a kisser, not a tickler, not a hand holder.

Billy's lips brush the inside of your arm. 'Little tiger,' he says, a playful growl. 'Sweet little tiger.'

And now you think back to this morning – Billy through the railings, not coming up, you not going down, not till the very last minute.

Marjorie's funny looks, Mother's unfunny ones.

'Mummy,' you begged. 'Please, Mummy, I want to stay—'

All in your head, said your mother, the heel of her clicky-clack slipper grinding your toes. *Whatever it is, it is all in your head.*

6 years old, winter

Bedtime. Saturday tomorrow. More beach, probably, even though it is July. More Billy and Marjorie.

I don't tell my mother that parts of me are still sore from my last sleepover, that I feel as flat as a cardboard sandwich. *Shh.* Seen and not heard.

My fingers skate along my stepped wall of books. I choose one and hop into bed, open *Cows of the Channel Islands* and lay it over my face, over Cookie Monster's too. We breathe in the pages. I am almost asleep when my mother comes to my room.

'I try to be good you know,' she says. 'I do.'

She looks at me, but as I don't know what she wants me to say, it is best to say nothing at all.

'Don't always work out but,' she goes on, 'my good intentions. Things ... take a hold, you know? Ever feel that? Like something just ... takes a hold of you?'

In my room, between the curtain and the wall, behind my books, there is a thin, trick space. It catches the sun, and swallows it, stops the outside from coming in. It is where he pushes through, the corner man with the dangling arms, who watches. 'Maybe it's the tall man, Mummy. Maybe he's the thing that takes a hold?'

'In your bloody head, that bogeyman,' is all she says, and I know I've again disappointed her.

We hear the squeak of the sticky garden gate, its sharp metal scrape.

'That'll be Poppa.' She sighs. 'On the bloody warpath, looking for his rent. You stay here. Got it?'

At night, JG comes down from the house on the hill. He brings fruit from his garden for our breakfast, cold meat Grandma has cooked for our lunches, and torment for my mother, complaining about something she has or hasn't done. Sometimes: *What's this I hear about ...* or, *How many times do I gotta tell ya ...?* or *You got two good feet. Try standin' on 'em for bloody once.*

Tonight, his voice drags low, a maggoty thing looking to spoil: 'I'm gonna say this one last time. Things-a-gotta change ... Too many mugs always sniffin' around ... No better than a bitch in heat ... Need I remind you that this house is still *my bloody property* and if it weren't for me you'd be out on yer arse in the street?'

The voice that keeps us in line.

And now, another row about Billy and Marjorie. JG went to see them after all, like my grandma said he would.

'You've gone round there? *So?*'

'You don't know *anything!*'

My mother's voice is whining and girlish. A thing cornered, pretending it isn't.

'*Leaving?* What do you mean they're leaving? *Ohhh ...* They can't be. They *caaa*n't!'

'Who the hell do you—'

'*Darwin?*'

I know Darwin from the weather report. Another hot place. A Billy place.

'Are they coming back?'

'I can't do this on my own! I *caaa*n't!'

'It was Mumma made me keep her ... I didn't ... I don't ... Ohhh, it's all on her ...'

I picture my grandfather's face, his funny little half-mouth, the shape of a 'D' since the last trip to hospital, twisting, a white fizz of dribble.

'You old bastard! *Baaastard!*'

'*How DARE you!*'

'What bloody right—'

And then, two sounds I know so well. The first, the back of Pop's hand against skin, shocked; the second, the strike of a match.

After the rows it goes quiet. My mother will be in the lounge, watching television. JG will be sitting at the kitchen table, polishing my school shoes. Later he will turn out the light, sit in the almost dark, and roll his thin cigarettes. The *pah ... hwoo* of his lips as he draws in and blows out.

Pah pah ... hwoo.

Tall Man watches me from behind the curtains.

I pull the bedspread up to my neck, lay the book back over my face.

Winter is so much better than summer. Things can't be found in the cold.

—

No more Saturdays at the beach. No more beach butter or sand or posing or Billy or Marjorie. No more dark doorways.

Instead, I am cleaning the back stairs of my mother's house. What the mop won't lift I scratch away with my nails.

Mother finds a spot that I've missed. Not good enough now to scratch that spot away, to re-mop.

'I said clean the stairs, didn't I, Mutt?'

Pressing my face so flat to the wooden step I wait for my nose to pop.

'Yes, Mummy.'

She tries to resist it, she does. But then the mower won't start or it rains and a gutter clogs and *it's the weekend and no-one has called not even Nev that bastard.* That's when the thing takes hold, shaking her between its teeth, all the good spilling. I worry one day there'll be no more to tip out.

'I said *clean* the stairs! Didn't I!'

I try to say, 'I did,' but I can't move my lips, my teeth hard against the wood.

I tried, Mummy. I even made them shiny, just like in the commercials.

... From the table to the chair
And woodwork everywhere
Wax and polish as you dust with Mr Sheen!
Wax and polish as you dust with Mr Sheen!

But she slipped. I made her slip. Too clean now. Too polished. I've tried too hard.

'What idiot'd use *Mr BLOODY Sheen* on the *back BLOODY stairs?*'

All my fault.

On the back stairs of my mother's house, I see a peeping half-moon and hear crickets, the screech of galahs winging in to roost for the night. The chooks in the coop follow one another into their little wooden sleep annex, squishing their pillowy selves through the rough-cut entrance. Grandma and I thought up their names: Helen Hen, Bonnie Hen, Mary Ann, Ginger, Mrs Fowl the Third. The chooks whose coop I am still small enough to walk through, scattering their feed every afternoon as they squawk and fly at me, scuttling and stretching their wings so wide I can see the scrawny featherless parts of them. I don't like looking at those pink frightened parts. Too easy to see them as the slow-turning racks of flesh in Charcoal Charlie's. Brought home in silver bags, dead on their backs, headless and leaking.

Jay-dee-Lou is the tennis whizz, the gold-star girl who comes top of my class and first in my heat on sports day. Missy, I am, when someone says something in my mother's office, contradicts her, looks down their nose.

But it is a Mutt day today.

Mutt, that *dummy*. Mutt is the loser who fails to place, the feeble whose racquet falls from her good-for-nothing hands. Sometimes even Mutt is too good for that *little piece*, her face *enough to turn a mother's stomach*. That little piece is taken straight home, put to bed, and Mum watches Mike on her own.

When the news is finished I am allowed back inside. My mother gives me a bath but no tea.

'What did you do, Mutt?' Scrubbing me so hard I am frightened to look down, worried my knees will have vanished, my elbows, scoured into dots, swirling away. 'What did you say to Bill and Marj?' Shampooing me now, a frenzy of suds.

'Nothing,' I say, voice and head juddering. Her nails score my scalp.

'Well, you must-a said something. Was it your grandmother? Yeah, that'll be it. You said something to Mumma and she's gone and stuck her beak in, stuffed up everything.'

I think again of Darwin, of Marjorie. *I'm sick of moving around, Bill … Always such hot places … Can't you find what you're after in the cold?*

'Saturday nights, over now, thanks to you, Mutt.' I'm a spot on the bath. 'Free babysitters, gone. Nice free dresses, gone with 'em.' A spot punished for being missed. 'All thanks to you, Jay. Everything – thanks to you.' She pulls the plug. 'Well, you'll just

109

have to spend more time up the back now.' Hooking me under one arm, hauling me out of the bath. 'See how far that gets you.'

I keep to myself that one day I'd like to go someplace where Christiane, the weather girl on Mike's news, says it's *chilly*. Where I'd sleep in fleecy pyjamas under waffly quilts every night of the year. Mother says chilly is a stupid word, not very professional, and that the tart on the weather shouldn't use it. Most women are tarts, according to Mother, especially the weather girl, who is blonde and Belgian.

Saturday nights might be very different from now on – up the back with Grandma, me and Paddy on the settee.

Shh. New secrets to keep. Better ones.

Naked, wet, shivery. My hair scuffed and scrunched by a see-through towel. All our towels, thin as cobwebs. *Royal Women's Hospital* is written along one end in crunchy blister-blue letters. Mother is fast and rough, always. Standing behind me, we both face the mirror over the low basin. She picks up the comb but her fingers fumble. It clatters into the sink. Swearing, she snatches it up. *Hurry hurry.* My scalp is a thousand sores, the comb my mother rakes across it stripping off its thousand tender scabs. It has her tonight, the thing that takes hold. It's not her fault, what she does. My eyes water. She pauses briefly, smiles, inspecting my pinched face.

Lifting the comb, she stabs it, little razors, into the nest of knots and rips. And rips again. White-hot needles, pulped flesh. Tears run, yes, but I make no sound. *Shh.* I know better.

Now she spins me, slamming the comb at the mirror. Her long nails hook my ears, her thumbs inside my mouth, pulling my lips wide, too wide. Above me, she is a lava woman, a flow of fire, deadly strong. But the thing that takes hold is stronger. It snares her in its teeth, shakes out the best and leaves only what is here, tonight, in this bathroom.

'*You were never meant to be.*' Her rage-breath, a hot spill on my tongue. 'That's why there's so much *wrong* with you.' Wadding up the wet towel, she throws it hard at my head as she leaves. I slip trying to catch it, my left ear smacking against the basin's edge as I fall. It whistles for hours, *eeeeeeee*, like the scary sound the TV makes when the programs have finished for the night.

I am falling asleep with Cookie Monster when Mummy lifts the big book of paintings off our faces.

'Tomorrow'll be better,' she says, sniffling. She has been crying and she wants me to see. 'We'll both be good, won't we? Let's promise.'

I cross my heart, and hope to die.

Spider?

You hear me from across the room.

Spiii-der.

You look up.

You stare and stare, expecting me to vanish with every blink.

Somehow you manage, 'Are you here to punish me?'

Your little smock, so shabby, unwashed, the colour of rust, as though you are already old. Aren't we a pair! I shall complement you – turn my skin a muddy blue, a weary purple, a skull of trodden stone. You think I am a circus man, though not a clown. I decide we will be the couple in the painting – the harlequin and his amour. We are they! Miserable together, yet unimaginable apart.

'Are you here because … I'm bad? There's something wrong with me, isn't there?'

I sigh.

'You've been watching.'

I have. For some time.

'Ooh,' you gasp as my voice settles inside your head.

'And now you're here,' you say. 'Why?'

Because you need me, Spider.

'Are you the devil?'

Game as a pebble, and I'm impressed, but I offer only a wrinkle of my brow, a finger – scratch-thin and long as the handle of a broom – held to my lips.

'Did Mummy send you?'

Ahhh, there you are, inside *my* head now.

She certainly did not!

'Ooh,' you gasp again, adjusting.

'Did God?' you persist. 'Did God send you? To beat me?' Your head falls to one side and you peer, so curious, into my black eyes. Such faith you have. Such pluck. *We'll be together a long time, Spider.*

'Why do you call me Spider?'

One day you will go on about them. I'm just getting in early.

'Will I? Go on about spiders? That's strange, I don't even like them.'

Only fair. They don't like you either.

'What is your name?' you ask me.

There are piles of books in your room, stacked like mountain peaks the length of the window. So many words, so many people, still with you long after the book is returned to its place. Picture books too, though not the usual kind. *Baby books?* your mother did scorn. *Waste-a money*, agreed the old man. Pictures of maps, instead. And pyramids. Pictures of things with wheels and spools and things with horns and fur and valleys of green you will never see, and paintings of women made from colourful cubes. You sniff them as though they are perfumed, and to you they are. You dream of rooms made of books, not walls. Funny thing. Other hearts, other minds, other countries – they astonish you, what you don't see more real than what you do. No such thing as impossible. Goodly good. There is something about you; I have chosen well. You like to read words, even when you don't know what they mean. You will in time – you will know them all, all the tremendous ones, the ones worth knowing, though you will keep that to yourself. *Shh,* they've taught you. *Shh.*

'What is your name?' you ask again.

So inquisitive. Pity. You are one who will see so little and, at the same time, too much.

I raise my hands, my fingers above the books, above the writers. Here is one. You and she, so alike. Kept to herself, did she. All of herself a secret, kept. She loved hounds too, just like you.

It comes to me.

Keep will do.

'Keep?' you say.

Yes.

'Mister Keep?'

Yes.

6 years old, late summer

Grandma's mutton on the boil. Its greasy stench. I swallow back hard. My eyes snap shut but the greying rags of flesh drift and writhe in the pot on the stove, falling through my thoughts as hour after hour they have fallen away from the bone. I breathe through my mouth but cannot escape it. The smell is as much a part of my grandparents' house as the stiff nylon carpet that nips at my feet, as the yellowing pictures of the dogs, long dead. Tyrone Tommy, his muzzled snout first past the post. JG's only winner. His little champion before he became no good, a dishlicker, gone, like all the rest.

Back to the letter, the letter.

Dear Sir.

Dear—.

Pencil? Or the riskier, more mature pen?

'What're you writin'?' he asks, lighting a cigarette.

Pencil. Safety first.

'A letter to Captain Kent.'

When I started school, I already knew my times tables, one to five. My letters never went over the lines. JG made me practise every day.

'Who's ... (*pah*) Captain Kent ... (*hwoo*)?'

'The President of the All Ireland Irish Terrier Club.'

JG hovers, his thinking eyebrows on, danger eyebrows, twisting his head to read my words. A knuckle tap taps the table. Ash drops onto my page.

'In Ireland,' I add helpfully, trying to ignore it. 'See, Pop, in a few weeks we have to start doing morning talks. My group's turn is on Mondays, and our first topic can be a country, an animal or a person, and I've choosen Padd—'

'*Chosen.*'

'Chosen,' I repeat.

'I choose (tap) now but I *have* (tap) *chosen* (tap).' Danger tapping.

'I have chosen, yes. I have *chosen* Paddy.'

Safety first. Obedience first too.

'*Paddy?*' His face tightens. 'You and that bloody dog!'

Grandma first brought Paddy home on a Tuesday, a strip of mewling orange fur left in a bag outside the Methodist hall. Tuberculosis Tuesday, but a happy, slow stroll home with an all-clear set of lungs and a pup of potluck breeding. That's why she named him Paddy. Paddy Potluck. Just a pet this time, she decided. Something ordinary.

'I'm going to tell the class about the tricks he can do, Pop, and how smart he is.'

Obedience first, always, but hard work can make things safe. Hard work, good marks, tick after tick, ten out of ten.

'But I'm writing to Captain Kent to get more information, more ideas.' I look up at my grandfather. 'Did you know, Pop, that Paddy dogs are so brave they fought in the war?' Irresistible knowledge, surely, even to him?

But snuff goes my question. 'How do you know about this ... club? This Captain Kent?' Tiny arrows, his words, flint-sharp, aimed between my eyes.

'Mrs Barron in the library. She looked things up for me.'

His mouth, so lopsided after the operations. Hard for me to know what's coming – happy and mad look the same now, at the start, erupting from that strange dark puncture in his face.

'How long does a mornin' talk have to be?'

'Five minutes,' I reply. 'But Sister Mary Maeve says it can go a bit longer if we want. I'm hoping Captain Kent might send me a big poster to point to. Or a tea towel.'

'A *tea towel*?'

In his voice, so much scorn. Are tea towels wrong? Wanting a tea towel is stupid.

'We make tea towels for pineapples and kangaroos,' I continue, so earnest, my irresistible knowledge getting the better of me. 'Irish people must make them for their famous things too.'

'You're writin' to someone all the way off in Ireland?'

I blink. *Don't look at me with your big dumb googs*, says Mother. I try not to blink, I try not to look. I try not to be.

'For a five-minute talk?'

My chair is too high and my feet dangle. I'm like a wooden dummy with a hole in its back.

'About a dog?'

Tadpoles under my skin. Sock fleas. Toes grinding in my shoes until they burn.

'And who'll be payin' for postage to Ireland?'

Clunk. Grandma, from the stove. *Clunk clunk.* Her wooden spoon against the pot. 'I will be,' she says cheerily. 'I know all about Rory's letter. And I jolly well expect that Captain Kent to give us *two* tea towels for our trouble.' *Clunk. Clunk clunk.* Each one louder than the one before. The beat of her only drum.

She doesn't turn around, but there's a look on my grandmother's face, I know there is. Her damn-the-torpedoes look, she calls it. I can hear it in her voice, her oh-to-hell-with-it voice. Her bruised eye still waters, and the deep split in her lip shows no sign of coming back together, of meeting again in the middle. Three lips now. Too many to keep quiet.

At the top of the kitchen stairs, my grandfather waits. I can't hear anything but his breathing, see anything but how he hesitates.

Choosing. He'd been fleshy, not so long ago, around his middle, his shoulders. But now his shirt is too big, the legs of his shorts too wide. He wears a belt to keep them up and it *clink clinks* as he walks.

I keep my head and shoulders low over my composition, doing my best writing. From some far-off corner of the yard, Paddy starts to bark. He'll be waiting for me to go outside, play with him. But suddenly I am slumped, a puppet-girl, clackety sticks for legs and arms. *Clackety clack* is the sound I make when I move.

Finally, JG makes his choice – heading down the stairs and out the back door.

I look over at my grandmother who presses a finger to her many lips. *Shh.* I hadn't mentioned a word to her about my letter.

Queensland Ombudsman calls out 'brutalisation' of disabled man, held for six years in Queensland facility

A man with an intellectual disability was 'illegally' secluded for more than six years in a Queensland Government facility, with the full knowledge of the department.

At times staff at the facility called on police, who used dogs to control the man, known only as 'Adrian'.

His ongoing seclusion was authorised more than 18,000 times in what sources have told the ABC is a repeated and systemic breach of the law.

Adrian has been held since 2012 at the Forensic Disability Service (FDS) in the Brisbane suburb of Wacol, a medium-security 10-bed facility designed to detain people who've been found unfit to stand trial because of an intellectual or cognitive disability.

None of the detainees at the FDS have been found guilty of a criminal offence or have been sentenced to a period of detention.

Instead, they are held indefinitely under a forensic disability order.

Adrian has an intellectual and developmental disability and was physically and sexually abused as a child, both at home and by carers.

Adrian's case is detailed in a Queensland Ombudsman's report tabled in the state parliament.

'Adrian's treatment at the FDS has been described to the investigation as "brutalisation",' the report states. 'The use of seclusion [on Adrian] has effectively been permanent ... the length of time that Adrian has been in seclusion may have significantly harmful effects on his wellbeing.'

Monitored by 16 CCTV cameras inside the unit, including the toilet and bathroom, Adrian is only able to communicate with staff through a narrow horizontal slot through which meals are passed to him.

He is rarely allowed out of his unit, while most of his 'seclusion breaks' are for one minute or less.

Staff have called police on more than 25 occasions to deal with Adrian, with officers frequently bringing police dogs.

On one occasion, a police dog entered Adrian's seclusion area, with police having earlier recorded in the Queensland Police Service Database that he 'hates dogs and it works every time'.

FDS records reveal that Adrian was left crying in the 'foetal position' in response.

The report confirms that both the FDS director and the Queensland Department of Communities, Disability Services and Seniors were aware of 'the severity of the issue'.

Tuesday, 2:12 am
To: artseditor@rivercitymag.com.au
Subject: Teen Outsider Artist
From: Jay Gundersen

Dear Quincy

I am writing to introduce my son, Frank Gundersen – an outsider artist and young pioneer of art brut in this country. Frank's unique vision documents his experience with bullying, isolation, life on the autism spectrum, and youth culture.

Still only fifteen, Frank's work has won numerous awards, including an Emerging Artist award at the most recent National Outsider Art Fair. His work is distinctive, already noticed by international gallerists and sold to both local and overseas collectors.

If you think you might be interested, perhaps even feature Frank and his work in *RiverCity Magazine*, we'd love to organise a private viewing for you – let Frank talk you through his work and his story.

Warm regards
Jay Gundersen

—

To: Jay Gundersen
Subject: Teen Outsider Artist
From: artseditor@rivercitymag.com.au

Hi there, Jay

Thanks so much for reaching out to us, here at *RiverCity Magazine*.

Unfortunately, we're so slammed with great feature article ideas, we're not looking for any new ones right now. But we've got your details, so be sure to check your inbox from time to time. You never know when you might hear from us.

PS: Jay, it's Disability Action Week 6–12 September. If you'd like to get in touch closer to that time, we might be able to run something on your son.

All the best
Quincy Wong

—

To: nikkiherz@citysatellite.com.au
Subject: Emerging Outsider Artist
From: Jay Gundersen

Dear Nikki

I am writing to introduce my son, Frank Gundersen – an outsider artist and young pioneer of art brut in this country ...

—

Out of office: Emerging Outsider Artist
To: Jay Gundersen

Thank you for your email but I no longer work at the *City Satellite*.

Please redirect your email to editor@citysatellite.com.au or call the office during business hours on 5787 1187.

—

To: jonahkreis@canvas.com.au
Subject: Breakout Artist
From: Jay Gundersen

Dear Jonah

I am writing to introduce my son, Frank Gundersen – an outsider artist and young pioneer of art brut in this country ...

—

Mail delivery failed. Returning message to sender.

I close the laptop.

Two in the morning and Teddy – again so agitated tonight, so loud – is finally sleep. His low-grade fever is back. Oddly, he keeps asking for food: 'I, want, more, sandwich, please, Mummy', only to spit what he has chewed onto the floor. A new behaviour, one I hope doesn't take hold.

Earlier today: 'Just a virus, like I said,' said the GP.

'You said to come back in three weeks if the fever persists. It's been three weeks and the fever is persisting.'

'Some viruses can hang around.' Shrug. 'Nothing to be done. Only pain relief.'

Andy Warhol's tape recorder would have come in handy given I parrot the same information each time. 'Teddy won't take pain relief.'

'There's a new flavour: Babycino!'

The GP wears vintage spectacles of late, swing-era style, tinted a squeamish lime. I can no longer see his eyes, only our reflections, which look grainy and damaged.

'Teddy won't take Panadol,' I repeated, slowly, enunciating each word.

I don't think our doctor sees us at all. I am certain he doesn't hear us.

'Not even the Babycino kind?'

'No kind! Not once in all the years you've treated him.'

'But it's yummy. Kids love it.'

'Not *my* kid,' I snapped, standing. 'Read his file, why don't you?'

I charged down the corridor, the door flung open behind me. Then I turned around and stormed back, Teddy confused, trying to follow my lead.

'Or maybe you could listen to me! For once, just *listen* to me!'

I slammed the door that time. I slammed and I charged and I stormed.

I managed to get Teddy onto the scales tonight. His jiggling about notwithstanding, he looks to be down six kilos.

I lie awake. My head a whirligig.

Art.

Art trends. The art market.

Frank's art.

He attends two classes a week, Monday and Tuesday nights. His fellow students are mostly older ladies who paint pictures of jacarandas and peacocks and Audrey Hepburn, but they are kind and indulgent. It's fortunate for everyone that they mostly don't recognise Frank's typical subjects: cinematic serial killers and dead drummers. At tonight's class he finished off an acrylic portrait of Freddy Krueger and Jason Voorhees facing off. 'Meg really liked it,' Frank told me when Teddy and I collected him.

'*Meg?*' I queried. 'Meg? Who is possibly ...'

'About ... about ... about ninety.' Frank nodded. 'That's ... that's her. She did ... she did think it was a painting ... a painting of oc- ... a painting of oc- ... of oc-*OCTOPUSES*. And ... and sea ... and seaw-weed. But she said ... she said she ... she said she ... she really liked the c- ... the c-*COLOURS*.'

'So that's a win.' I smiled. 'After all, what does the great David Lynch say of his films?'

'It doesn't matter what I think they're about,' ~~Frank~~ the filmmaker replied in his Missoula-born, ham radio voice. 'It only matters what the audience thinks they're about.'

'Good enough for you, Dave, good enough for us.'

Frank had seemed well pleased.

Sleep beckons, has a change of its fickle heart, and rejects me. Over and over again.

So I get out of bed, go to the pile of media articles on my desk. To the last few empty pages of scrapbook #12, I add the story of the English mother who smothered her three disabled children. Stress, not murder, was the judge's finding. Insupportable, mind-snapping stress. Beyond treatment in a psychiatric facility, no time served. And another about the 'helpful science' being developed overseas, offering expectant mums the ability to terminate embryos based on IQ predictions and other possibly underwhelming attributes. No more Adrians to be 'managed' by dogs in such a clever and top-percentile future. No Teddys or Franks either. No further need for a disability action week.

How much improved would you be, world, truly? Where then would you aim your distaste, your mean little eyes?

Come here, go away. Come here, go away. Come here, *fuck off*, taunts sleep, pixying off into the night. It leaves behind no beddy-bye drowse, no coo-sweet lulling. Only its spit in my face.

So I throw back the bedclothes once and for all, reopen the laptop, google home-based art exhibitions.

Other artists do it. A local collective hires a three-tonne truck to exhibit in. There is street food and a cello. A cul-de-sac becomes an overnight mini-festival. Might the ladies who paint jump in? It could work. I'll make it work. I'll rent a crowd if I must. A crowd and a truck and Colombian street food and a band.

A salt lamp occupies a low corner of the bookcase. In its lunar-glow I see that my little doll is missing. The end of the line. Good for her. I decide to look for her in the morning – she can't be far. The other four stare at me with their gormless eyes, their coquette lashes. I nest them, shove them all into the largest. Lonnie. So hard to open now, her big wooden head dry and appropriately cracked. That'd be right, I hear her say. How come it's *my* head got busted?

Mother.

Freddy and Jason.

You don't always need a machete or a bladed glove to be a devil.

Adrian – is he still in that despicable place? The 'facility'? What does it do to him, all that fear, day after day? For *years*.

Abuse, publicly funded.

Is that how they'd torture Teddy? Lock him in a room full of daffodils to subdue him? Lemons? Raincoats? Simple yellow curtains would do the trick.

He's shit scared of 'em, some monster would laugh. Works every time.

Scrapbook #13

All that is non-viable in nature invariably perishes.

We humans have transgressed the law of natural selection in the last decades.

Not only have we supported inferior life-forms, we have encouraged their propagation.

The offspring of these sick people looked like this ...

Healthy, normal people lived in dark narrow streets and ramshackle hovels.

For idiots and madmen, thought palaces were built. But these people were not even receptive to the beauty that surrounded them.

The German people hardly knew the extent of this blight.

They do not know the oppressive atmosphere in these places, where thousands of drooling imbeciles must be fed and cared for, individuals lower than any beasts.

In the past 70 years, our people have increased by 50%, while the hereditarily ill have increased by 450%!

If this development continues, in 50 years there will be one defective for every four healthy people!

An endless procession of horrors would invade our nation, boundless misery would affect our valuable race, which would march headlong to its doom!

Opfer der Vergangenheit (Victims of the Past)
1937 film produced by the NSDAP Racial and Political Office to garner public support for the Nazi party's proposed Aktion T4 euthanasia program.

Thursday, 3:50 pm

'Boop boop boop,' says Martha, the occupational therapist.

'Boop boop boop,' say I, mother hat off, therapy assistant hat on.

We sit either side of Teddy, an assortment of foods – blueberries, white grapes, brown M&Ms, diced orange, cherry tomatoes (halved) – set before him on a large, compartmented plate. Their colours match a face Martha has drawn with thick coloured markers on a piece of white paper: a blue circle head, green oval eyes, brown ears, an orange nose, a red mouth.

It is Martha's turn. She selects a blueberry – a food Teddy will not eat – and bounces it playfully on the back of his left hand – 'boop' – on the inside of his elbow – 'boop' – against his cheek – 'boop' – along his lips – 'boop boop boop'. She then places it somewhere on the blue circle of the head. 'Boop boop boop boop boop!' she cheers, and Teddy smiles.

My turn.

I select a piece of orange.

'Boop' – Teddy's hand – 'boop' – Teddy's elbow. Cheek, top lip, bottom lip – 'boop boop and boop' – before placing it on the figure's bulb nose. 'Boop boop boop boop boop!'

We are 'redrawing' the face – with the exception of the M&Ms – using aversive foods, foods Teddy cannot tolerate. Foods that cause Teddy to retch and vomit. The blueberries go on the head's blue circle, the white grapes around the pale-green eyes, and so on. This is a playful enactment of the SOS or Sequential Oral Sensory approach to feeding, a six-step process to food desensitisation or, more simply, to learning how to eat. We have moved through steps one to three: tolerates, interacts with, smells. Today we resume our work on step four: touch. Almost twelve years to get this far.

Now it's Teddy's turn.

'Let's draw his mouth, please, Teddy,' says Martha.

This requires Teddy to pick up a piece of tomato. Until recently, even the sight of a cut tomato made Teddy gag.

He hesitates, swallows, hovers a hand over the plate.

'That's right, Ted. You need some tomato.'

Having not yet touched the Tiny Toms, Teddy gives his fingers an anticipatory wipe along his school shorts.

'You're fine, Teddy,' says Martha in a confident but gentle voice. 'Tomato, off you go.'

With a look of disgust, Teddy rubs his thumb and forefinger together, as though limbering up, before pincering a tomato half and skimming it, at warp speed, up Martha's arm: hand – forearm – collarbone – neck (me, responsible for sound effects this round, boop-booping, trying to keep up) – before dropping it onto the drawn mouth.

'Boop boop boop boop boop!' Martha and I cheer. Triumph!

Teddy rocks back hard in his chair, laughing, his fingers flipping this way and that against the fabric of his shorts, a vigorous cleansing.

This long game is being won play by conservative play. In the beginning, sensorially repugnant foods would be placed around the room as Teddy and Martha got on with their usual work – a meat pie one week, pungent and steaming and dolloped with sauce. Sliced raw onion the next, hard-boiled eggs, a box of fried chicken, fresh basil in a pot. Each week the food would be placed incrementally closer to where Teddy sat, no expectation beyond a tolerance of its proximity.

Stage two involved Teddy picking up that serve of odious food and handing it to Martha who would eat it, loudly and rather savagely, her mouth wet and dribblesome, her fingers smeared and licked, her teeth picked with relish as Teddy looked on, appalled. He had to learn that those foods caused him no harm, that he and they and the people eating them could safely coexist. There was overenthusiasm on our part, missteps, and much vomit visited upon us. Teddy still won't eat any of them. That may yet be years off, if it happens at all. But he can at least share a table with almost any food now, and touch them, bear to breathe them in.

The boop game takes up the rest of the session, as we compose our face-collage of fruits, vegetables and sweets.

Through Martha's office window, I see children arriving at Miss Kimberley Fallon's ballet school opposite. Tiny girls, mostly, bursts of electric blue and pink, severe topknots, all of them elegant beyond their years. Their mothers bustle behind, carrying things. I remember driving past Miss Kimberley's when the boys were very little, so long ago; I would dream, as mothers do, about what my children might one day be, all options still falsely on the table. Pilots. Astronauts. Inventors. Horse wranglers, tanned and creased from the sun. Sea-creature scientists. Pale museum people. Footy heroes. Tall men who juggled and sang. Laneway chess players. Dancers.

'Boop boop' go the grapes. 'Boop boop' go the berries. Teddy rocks and we cheer; it's been a good session. No barre work or alignment training on our side of the street, but no vomit either. A different kind of flexibility to master.

6:07 pm
The potatoes begin to boil. Fish fingers, mash and peas for Frank's supper, one of his favourites. In a moment I will retrieve Teddy, already soaped and shampooed, from the bath, help him to dry off.

In the hallway outside the kitchen, Frank, on a dog-eared office chair, spins himself in slow-turning circles.

'Lan- ... lan- ... lan- ... lan-g-*GOU*-stine for dinner ... for dinner, Mum?'

'Langoustine?' I reply, peeling carrots. 'I'm not even sure what that is. Some kind of—'

'But that's what I want!' Frank demands, suddenly English and rude and ranting. 'Langoustine! *Langoustine!*'

'Oh, of course,' I say. 'Though I'm afraid fish fingers are the best I can do this evening, Gordon.'

'What did you call me?'

'I mean *Chef*,' I say, playing along, hands raised in supplication. 'Lord-most-high, Chef.'

~~Frank~~ Gordon Ramsay continues to spin, saying over and over, '*Look at that! Like a bison's penis!*' as though it is the most normal thing in the world to do on a Thursday evening. And I suppose, in our home, it is.

I hear a key in the front door, the crisp *tock tock* of Jerrik's immaculately shod heels. Home a week from his latest 'gig', he appears in the doorway of the kitchen.

'I am home for dinner,' he announces, by way of a greeting.

This means Jerrik expects me to prepare him a meal which, no doubt, he will eat in the comfort and relative quiet of his upstairs suite.

Frank pauses his spinning for a moment to look up at his father. '*Look at that! Like a bison's penis!*' he says again, his mimicry flawless as always. He wants his father to try to guess whose impression it is, but Jerrik only shakes his head and turns towards the stairs.

I peel and chop an extra potato, slide the last three fish fingers from the box and onto an oven tray.

Later, after the boys and I have eaten, I place Jerrik's pot-warmed meal on a tray, along with cutlery, a napkin, a fresh roll and a large glass of red wine, and carry it upstairs. I don't knock, but I don't say anything either as I position the tray on his lap. He sits in his favourite chair – an antique French linen Louis XV replica wingback – watching Kevin McCloud. He regards his meal, and then me.

'And this is?' He sniffs. 'Kiddie fish?'

So I snatch one up from the plate, slap the fish finger against the back of his hand, his shoulder, his mouth. 'Boop boop boop,' I say. 'How was *your* day?' But the effort of speaking is greater than I had anticipated. Suddenly drained, I can barely summon breath, let alone interest in a back and forth. This climb to the top of the house feels like a drop to the bottom of something.

Jerrik is stunned but doesn't move. A speckle of crumbs clings greasily to his top lip.

I toss the fish finger back onto his plate, turn and cross the room.

'You are a strange one, wife,' Jerrik replies, as I close the door behind me, so quietly, no earthly point to a slam or a charge or a storm.

Saturday, 9:30 am

It's Saturday, and I have a thing. I never have a thing, but today and for the next two Saturdays, I do.

Jerrik is in charge and here is how I expect the day to unfold: Jerrik will instruct Frank to clean up his room, empty bins, stop gaming, go outside, come back inside, read a book, put the book down – the very opposite of whatever it is he may notice Frank doing. He will make Frank rake leaves and sort laundry and eat a salad for his lunch. Frank will say, 'I'm not hungry, Far', to which Jerrik will reply, 'Nonsense.' Frank will say, 'No beetroot, Far,' but Jerrik will load it on, tell him it is good for his blood. Frank will say, 'Good for my blood?' and focus intently on vampires and how the *Twilight* series was really, really good before it got really, really bad and not hear what his father is saying to him. This will result in Jerrik getting springy on his feet, dressaging through the ~~arena~~ house, a pompous, proppy kind of stomp. Its performance invariably signals that Jerrik has become stressed and that warm Danish words may soon follow. 'Uh-oh,' Frank will worry. 'Far's gone all elastic-ankles.'

For much of the day, Jerrik will doze, shirtless, and eat cheese in front of lifestyle programs. He won't communicate with Teddy on his iPad because he doesn't know how. The boys will mostly amuse themselves. This is why I have a thing. I am literally going to see a man about a dog. The kind of dog that is attentive and responsible and prides itself on task-completion.

Before I leave, I catch Frank staring into his bowl of baked beans. 'What are you doing?'

He replies, 'What's occur-ren is, I'm try-en to move objects with my mind.'

Frank is a Welsh person today.

So I suggest, 'Well, boyo, could you try with something other than baked beans? Teleporting them—'

'They wouldn't be teleported, Mam. I would be using telekinesis. Or possibly microkinesis, depend-en on how I mooove them.'

Teddy and Siri inform us that: 'Ninety-one per cent of all baked beans are consumed on toast.' Then Teddy walks over to me, tucks my hair behind my ears, inspects my hands. For the third day running, he has again refused breakfast. I feel his forehead. Clammy, but cool.

'Okay,' I say, 'but moving beanos about *today* is not a good idea. We can telekinise the hell out of them tomorrow. But today, being quiet and tidy and under the radar is my advice.' A glance over my shoulder in Jerrik's general direction. 'Copy?'

'Copy that, mothership,' says Frank, who then asks, again, if I'll be bringing a puppy home from the thing.

So I explain, again, it's not that kind of thing. That no puppies are being given away today, that there is a process to go through to get an assistance dog, one that is lengthy and complicated. That today I'm only going to listen, to learn, so that we can all make a decision.

'Have you applied your creams?' I ask him, his hair more than the usual mess.

'Creams applied, mothership,' he says. 'Check.'

But his answer is too quick, and I know my son. 'Is that true?' I ask. 'Franko?'

'True-*adjacent*,' he says, his blue eyes clear and soft and knowingly winsome.

135

Teddy: 'Italian black-market delicacy, Casu Marzu cheese, contains live insect larvae. It requires eye protection while eating.'

I apply the creams to Frank's scalp myself, wash my hands, give Ted a goodbye kiss. I quickly open up today's visual schedule on his iPad, reminding him of where I'm going, why, and when I will be back. I take his temperature for the second time this morning: 36.9. Perfect. By lunchtime though, it could be anything.

'When startled, maggots have been known to leap as high as six inches into a diner's face.'

'Black-market cheese is off the shopping list then, hey, Ted?' I say and laugh. Unconvincing.

I am going to this thing because I need to, not because I want to. Because I am always convinced the thing I don't go to will be 'the thing'. The thing I shouldn't have missed. The thing that will make all the difference.

'And speaking of under the radar,' I say, a look at both boys. 'The Russian dolls next to my bed. One is missing. Have you spotted her by any chance?'

'The *dolls*, is it?' says Frank, airily rolling *dolls* around in his Welsh mouth.

'Laika, a three-year-old stray mongrel found on a Moscow street, was the first animal to orbit Earth.'

'Yes, thanks, Ted,' I say. 'Poor Laika.'

'Russian *dolls*, is it?' Frank says again.

'Yes. The colourful nesting dolls that have been on the bookcase next to my bed the entirety of your lives. Those dolls?'

'Ah, *tho-o-o-ose* dolls, is it?'

'Not seen the tiny one lying about? She kind of ... rattles.'

'Not gonna lie to you, Mam. A doll what rattles, I have not seen.'

'Laika died, terrified, overheated and likely starving, shortly after launch.'

'Teddy.' I sigh, losing patience. 'Can we not do dead dogs, please, darling? Not this morning.'

Just as I am about to walk out the door, the cheery Welsh lad disappears. Frank rushes at me, shaking. He tells me he's bled all over his pillow. What should he do? He's so sorry he didn't tell me sooner. If Far sees he'll get mad. His scalp is so sore, but he'll do anything to keep his hair, anything.

With Frank in such a state, it's a bad day to have a thing. And though Teddy's fever has blipped around the high end of normal for the past week or so, and he seems otherwise okay, he barely picks at his food. He looks chalky, snappable. A bad day to leave Jerrik in charge. The trouble is chancing upon a good one.

9:57 am

I need coffee and collect one on the way. Ground Control is at the end of my street, but it is not my kind of place. Milk crates to sit on, crop tops and *glutes* on display. I can't ever shake the feeling that someone will appear at any moment and tell me to get out. I don't know why I come here. No place is my kind of place.

I am asked for my order and my name. 'Long black, please. Gene.' Even if they hear 'Jean', which they no doubt will, I will avoid being called Jayne or Jade or Fay.

Marc with a 'c' once told me that some in his profession – method actors – empty themselves out, become a shell inhabited by their character. They deliver immersive, celebrated performances. Some keep it up too long, do it too often, only to find that once the curtain comes down there's no actor anymore, just a grasping thing needy for something to say and a paid-for reason to say it. Not many method actors left these days; they tend to burn up. And empty shells aren't generally found in places like Ground Control. Everyone here looks so confident, like they know how to do things, like they've always known. There is a void between me and these other people. Perhaps Gene can fill it.

'Got much on, today, Jen?' asks the man handing me my coffee.

I pause, look over my shoulder, then realise he is talking to me. To *Jen*.

Why not? I think. I wouldn't know where to begin to tell the story of where Jay is going and why, but Jen can manage a breezy smile. 'Just a haircut.'

'Oh no,' says the teenage barista. 'Your hair's amazing. Just a trim?'

'Hmm.' ~~I~~ Jen ~~reply~~ nods. 'A trim.'

10:30 am

Metal chairs are dragged into a circle. Faces reel away from other faces, instinctively, like-poles repelling. Awkward introductions as tea and coffee are vigorously stirred. If I could pay to skip my turn I would. We are being auditioned, trialled. Less a question of does the program suit us than are we worthy of the program. Are we worthy of an elite, four-legged operative – a MacGyver-like golden retriever that can load and unload a washing machine, assist with seizures, deter self-harm, dial triple 0, cover a quadriplegic body with a blanket on a cold night? These aren't dogs, per se, but preparations like jars of pickled vegetables. We are here today to prepare for when we are not here. Preppers, we are. Still spooky, but a kind all our own.

Nineteen of us – sixteen mothers, two fathers (here with their wives) and one sister, aged twenty-seven, named Casey. She writes with a pen that is sparkly and fur-tipped, and when she isn't furiously filling a notepad she holds her mother's hand. Casey's older brother, Shane, has cri du chat syndrome. I have not heard of this one. Shane communicates his needs by biting and kicking and scratching.

When he is very afraid, he runs away, though no-one can work out what it is that frightens him so.

Casey's mother's awkward introduction was all about Shane. We learnt nothing of her, not even her name. And Casey's introduction is all about her mother, who is tiny and pepper-haired, born in the Philippines. Casey tells us her mother has cared for Shane all his life, these past thirty-four years. She recently talked her mother into buying an apartment in a new over-fifties estate, and into going on a trip with friends she has made there – her mother's first holiday since her honeymoon nearly forty years ago. Casey's father lives in Winnipeg and no longer visits. She wants her mother to retire after a long life of service, as other workers do. I see the mother look at her daughter with a respect that floors me. Casey tells the group she is doing a PhD, and that she is in the process of taking over her brother's care. She has heard great things about assistance dogs and wonders if one might bring Shane some comfort and trust. Her mum will be nearby, her backup, as they have agreed that Shane must always be cared for by family. They look at one another again as this is said, their vow witnessed by us. There's no question of ever placing him elsewhere.

The rest of us sit in complicit silence. I wonder if the others think the way I do, see the terrible things I see. We probably have more in common than we'd like to admit. But the kinds of plans people like us might have to make don't tend to be shared over rockmelon wedges and egg sandwiches. We keep them to ourselves, locking them away, little misfits, until they become the shape of us and speak in our voices and barely seem monstrous at all.

The dog had appealed for Teddy's sake. Wordless, handsome Teddy, unable to report a sore throat or a toothache. Unable to report anything, to reliably give his side of any story. Future Teddy, aged thirty-something, like Shane, forty-something. No parent, no guardian, no advocate. There is no Casey waiting to

139

take over from me. Here is where they will put Teddy, then there, as a bed becomes available, in this psych ward, in this dementia unit. But the dogs – I had hoped a canine crusader might offer some protection, ward off *the evil that men do*, especially to the vulnerable. But here I learn that the dog is attached to the carer, not to the Teddys and Shanes of the world. *First* carer, *then* dog. I'm mixed up. The carer must sign up to these three Saturdays, to a twenty-page application with video addenda, to an in-home assessment, and finally a ten-day interstate boot camp with their faithful recruit. Who would do that? Only us, eighteen parents and one saintly sister. Loving and caring – comorbid conditions. You don't sign on for that. You are tapped on the shoulder for that and, even then, some of us still head for the hills. To Winnipeg. To Winnies and Minnies.

Casey is young and clever. Maybe she can power on just as she is, sparkly and beatific, energised by the idea of saving her family. Maybe a magic dog *will* help. Maybe Casey will fall in love, and that person will love her back and so hard that her brother's constant, world-without-end-amen-biting-scratching-hairy-grown-man presence won't ever come between them. Casey won't ever be alone, and her brother will be safe, and her mother can rest in peace, and it will all end happily ever after.

But I won't be back next Saturday.

Teddy doesn't need a dog. I knew that already, and yet I came here anyway, hoping to be wrong. Hoping for this thing to be the thing that would *make all the difference*. The thing that would save us, Teddy and I, from being an entry in someone's scrapbook. What Teddy needs is for me to live a good long while, as long as one of Frank's vampires. A long life for me, or a short one for Teddy.

Together for some version of forever.

4:31 pm

On the way home from the dog thing I stop at the salon. I am their last appointment. 'What are we doing today?' the hairdresser asks me.

She is long-haired and glamorous, all in black.

'It won't take long,' I tell her.

She stands behind me and watches in the mirror as I try to explain, delivering a twenty-five-words-or-less recap.

'My son has to lose his hair and he's scared.' I am too tired to say much more and can think only of apples. Enchanted, appetite-inducing apples. 'I'm not high,' I say to the girl. 'This is my reason and it is sound, to me at least.'

She grips my shoulders, gives them a firm little rub. Thankfully, she doesn't say anything, just gets the clippers, plugs them in, and we get down to it.

'It'll be tender for a while,' she says afterwards, and gives me a tube of cream, no extra cost.

After that I cross the street to the local Beet Bar in search of those apples – all Teddy has a taste for at the moment.

The shop and its odours stir a sickly confection of faces and deeds. Memories a *whump*, catching my breath. Another place where, as soon as I arrive, I wish I hadn't.

Years ago, Frank soldered onto my right leg, his face buried in my hip. That day, I held a bag of beans, an avocado, a large pot of baby tomatoes. Mint. That shitty mint. I've not been able to stomach it since.

'Stink,' Frank said, beginning to gag. 'Stink. *Stink.*'

I should have known better. Laying the mint on the counter, I nudged it towards the cashier serving the customer ahead of us. I asked, 'Could you, perhaps, get rid of that for me?' eye-pointing at Frank, doing my best not to intrude. 'My son doesn't like strong smells.'

The customer in front, a woman – tall and striking in plissé saffron silk, gold bracelet, gold kitten heels. I remember how she straightened her back, sniffing long and loud, intruded upon nonetheless. A giantess, tetchy, all the world her box of snuff.

Clutching the bag of apples, I think of Casey and her mother, holding hands, so unafraid. I miss holding hands with someone.

They have refitted the shop since that day, when Teddy stood just beyond the cashier's counter, waiting for me and that wretched mint. 'Mmmmm … wahhh. Mmmmm … wahhh.' Flicking a straw, sodden with saliva. Spittle flew. A human lawn sprinkler. People arced widely by him as they came and went, some more obviously put upon than others.

The big orange silkmoth paid the cashier, swooped upon her bags of produce.

'Excuse me,' she huffed at Teddy who had his back to her, blocking her path.

Frank whining into my hips. 'Mummy … stink.'

'Excuse *me*,' the woman half-bellowed at Teddy.

'Teddy,' I called, edging towards him. I needed to reach his shoulder, turn him to me. 'Teddy, come here to Mummy.' Gripping the plastic tub of tomatoes too hard, I popped the lid. A tomato fell, then another. I was trying to set everything onto the counter when the tall woman spun back to me, cheeks pulsing.

'Your son over here is completely ignoring me,' she said, incredulous. 'I've asked him to move, repeatedly, but he's simply doing whatever he likes.'

Just as I let go of the tomatoes, Frank's arms shot up to my chest. 'Mummy, *STINK!*'

Midair, two combatant corrosives – the spilling Tiny Toms, Frank's projectile vomit – fused into a pelleted mush, splashing the cashier's counter, the shop floor, my jeans and shoes.

Oh, how breathless was the audience. They risked not a blink.

'Mummy ... *sick*,' Frank pointed out, miserably.

The cashier passed over a roll of paper towel. I got down on my knees, tried to perimeter-off the creeping pond of vomit. In the midst of it, fallen avocado stickers: '*Buy me! I'm ripe!*' A child's lost hairclip, pieces of dry macaroni. A silver ring-pull. And many, many retreating feet.

I looked up into the giant woman's face. 'My son ... he has ...' She loomed over me, orange and petulant as an untended flame. 'Teddy wasn't ignoring you.' I wanted her to understand. 'He didn't engage with what you were saying.' I sloshed the paper towel into a tin bucket that had suddenly appeared beside me. 'That's all it was.'

Up and down went her eyes. Tattoos? Missing teeth? Needle marks? Scanning me for further evidence of inferior breeding mettle. But then she simply turned and strode away, a focaccia sitting high in her stylish bolga basket, a tease of olives and cubed white cheese.

Now my fingers are locked, stiff around the Royal Galas. Perhaps I should have chosen Pink Ladies. I don't know which Teddy will prefer. He must prefer one. He must eat something. The shops are about to close but the queues are still long. I drop out of mine, head back to the apples. The person behind slides forward, takes my place. It doesn't matter. I will start again. Start again at the end of the line. Pink Ladies. Jazz. Fuji. Braeburn. Granny Smiths. I will bag a few of them all.

My shaved head is watched, monitored. They don't know what to make of me. Perhaps I am sick – staring at ill people a favourite pastime the world over. I look up, catch one, stare her down – it isn't hard. I'm not me, not Jen or Jayne or Fay. I'm a cowboy, surrounded, pissed off and with nothing to lose.

Have we met? I say with my look. Or maybe with my mouth.

With six small bags of apples, every variety in the shop, I stride past the queues, drop a twenty dollar note under the nose of one of the cashiers. I figure if it's not enough, they can call the police. I'd be easy to track down. I always seem to stand out in a crowd.

5:52 pm

I arrive home and Jerrik is the first to see me. '*For helvede da også, kvinde!* What the hell have you done now, wife?'

Frank's voice from another room: 'Is it a ... is it a ... is it a puppy, Mum? Did y- ... did y-you bring us a puppy?'

Teddy stops rocking in his computer chair, looks me over, round and round, frozen and open-mouthed. The look on his face is as close to surprise as I have ever seen. He rushes to me, runs his hands over my head, exploring, processing, down over my eyes, my eyelashes, my naked ears. I had told him what I planned to do, asked him to keep it a secret. All secrets are safe with Teddy.

'See, it's still me, love. Still Mummy.'

Bald heads have always fascinated him. He's accosted more than one over the years, swooping on a shiny pate as it has passed by on a footpath or in a shopping centre, the host body spinning in alarm. I knew he would be delighted with my update.

Frank, from the hallway: 'M-m ...' He looks panicked. '*MUM!* Y-you ... y-you ... y-you ... y-*YOU* ...' He shakes his head. I don't think he can stop shaking it. 'It's me ... it's my ... I should ... I should've ...' Tears not done for the day. 'Aw, *Mum.*'

'You know what? The hairdresser said I had the most beautifully shaped pill she's ever seen,' I tell him. 'I told her it runs in the family. We're all this magnificent.'

Teddy's hands sweep backwards and forwards over my baldness, down my neck, up and over again as Frank stoops down, rests his wet cheek against the top of my head. The hairdresser's right – it is tender.

144

'See, it's okay, Franko,' I say, rubbing his back. 'We can grow it back together. Race each other. Better hurry up, I've got the jump.'

Jerrik snatches the bags of apples out of my hand, pivots on his elastic ankles and horsey high-steps to the kitchen.

Brisbane girl, 4, dead for days in cot as father is charged with murder

A little girl found dead at a home in Brisbane on Monday was murdered by her father and left in her cot for days, police allege.

A brand new scrapbook, a same old story.

Horrific new details have emerged about how a little girl with an intellectual disability was left dead in her cot for days as Australia's down syndrome community calls for the country to join a vigil tonight.

Willow Dunn, 4, was found dead at a Cannon Hill address on Monday morning but police allege she was murdered by her father on Saturday and left in her bed.

Too much, this one, Spider.

Keep, from over my shoulder.

I turn, look up into his clay-grey face. His head, knife-thin, is almost to the ceiling. Black teeth, no lips. He is Giacometti-like tonight – a giant joyless stick-toy, whittled and denuded. Is he trying to mock my baldness?

Too ghoulish.

I return to my cutting and pasting. 'So says my resident heebie-jeebie.'

Mark Dunn, 43, has been charged with murder and accused of failing to seek medical help after the little girl's death.

All this beating your fetters of iron. Yet here you are. Here you still surely are, alone and fuming at three in the morning. And that wee child, still surely dead.

The Courier Mail reports the four-year-old had horrific sores on her body after being starved and left to die [...] Willow had sores on her hips so deep the bones were exposed when police found her.

Unpleasantness only tunes them out, sets them at odds.
'Hmm,' I reply. 'Because they're already so tuned in and onboard.'

The Australian reports the little girl's face had been attacked by rats and that when paramedics arrived at his home, New Zealand-born Dunn allegedly asked them: 'I'm in trouble, aren't I?'

What would you have them do, Spider?

Dunn was charged under new child killer laws in Queensland that include an extended definition of murder as showing reckless indifference to human life.

Neighbours of the family told the newspaper they never knew about Willow.

'They've been there for that long and we didn't know a little girl lived there,' one neighbour said. 'I can't believe it.'

'It takes a village, does it?' I say, shaking my head. The skin on my face is hard. I am ugly with rage. 'Some village we turned out to be.'

Bitter little bitie. What is your point, Spider?

'My point, Keep,' I reply, 'is to ask what might happen if all this energy were funnelled into the *before* instead of into the *after*?'

Australia's down syndrome community will hold a virtual vigil for Willow tonight with calls for the hashtag #HerNameIsWillow to trend on social media.

'If instead of people wearing out their thumbs, parading their virtual social conscience on their phones, some "villager" had worn out their shoe leather by popping round, knocking on a door, making a discreet call? Showed some *actual* concern?'

Pangs of hope? A dismal woe, Spider, as you well know.

Teddy snuffles in his sleep.

I close the scrapbook, tidy my desk, switch off my reading lamp.

'Yes, Keep, yes,' I say, returning to my bed. 'As I well know.'

10 years old, autumn

A forest of figs separates the lower playground from the cricket pitch, their tripsome thigh-high roots like the tails of dragons. They curve and wind past the toilet block and swings and trapeze rings where Lizzie Long hung upside down, showing off, not really trying to hide her new black undies, before she fell and broke her collarbone. 'Haughty eyes and a proud heart,' warned Sister Everista as we crowded around the sobbing girl, waiting for the ambulance to arrive, 'the lamp of the wicked, are *sin*.' The most ancient of the Moreton Bays looms over us from behind the old church hall. Towering and watchful, it is witness to all that we do, all that we don't. I envy it its distance.

My tree is the one closest to the school gate, facing the busy road. I wedge myself between its two biggest roots – huge, brown-velvet haunches either side of me, branch-crutches in front like pillars, or like the bars of a cell. Private, all the same. Behind my back and shoulders the tree is firm but obliging. I rest my head against its chest. Princely firm.

At morning tea, I watched the old man who lives across the street get on the bus, as he always does mid-morning on Tuesdays and Fridays. A clean checked shirt tucked tidily into old-man trousers. But on his feet, a young man's boots – tan, soft, purple socks pulled high above them. A belt buckle flashes as he turns, like a lighthouse. I tell myself he would smell of pink soap and Sao biscuits. Now it is lunchtime and I am waiting for the bus to bring

151

him safely home. The old man matters to me. I need to believe he's okay.

A book lies open across my knees. The Lapland book. I've borrowed it so many times that Mrs Barron trills, *Here she is, Miss Scandinavia*, as soon as I walk in the library doors. She doesn't make me check it out officially, not anymore, knowing I will take care of it, that I will return the book by break's end. My magic book. I once asked Mrs Barron if she thought the pictures were real, if she believed the sky could really and truly glow green, become staircases of spiralling air, red as a robin, purple as Palm Sunday. Could this be possible? *You'll have to go there one day, see for yourself.* I turned and walked quickly out of the library when she said that, my dumb face about to cry dumb tears. Why the tears had come I couldn't explain to Mrs Barron or anyone else. *She got my sweet tooth*, Grandma once said. *My sad tooth too.*

While I wait for the old man I rest the book against my face, and it begins. The words, the pictures, the pages themselves, like puffs of cirrus, breathe themselves into me, become me, more than mere knowledge. The book in my hands, the fearsome tree behind – we are part of each other and part of nothing. My face goes slack; I no longer need it. My body becomes altered, becomes *other*, and no longer needs me. I am needle lace-light. A grass seed, the wind's stowaway freight. I slide easier than the sea, quieter than a frost's slow melt, I am unfixed, I am hearsay.

And I am gone.

Not to Lapland, not to any place with coordinates or on a map. To somewhere lightless, unpeopled. Where the cars and trucks and buses barrelling by are there and not there too. The earth below me, yet no earth. No warmth or cold, no sound or silence, only what is supposed to be. All broken through, syrupy and dispersed.

'What're you reading?'

The book drops to my chest.

It's the new girl.

'*Journey Through Lapland*,' she reads.

She arrived only yesterday. Vanessa Quinn and Susan Walters set upon her immediately, followed by all the other cheep cheeping girls who flounce around with them, who stand with their two hands perched on a single thrusty hip, lips heavily glossed. But now the new girl is here, bothering with me.

'Lapland,' she repeats. 'Have you been there? Are you going?'

She has an American accent. Mother's ears hear it, seize upon it. *Yank*, Mother would say. *Bloody Yank*.

'Pff,' I say, not meaning for it to come out the way it does. 'Fat chance.'

I see Vanessa and Susan and the rest of their coven over the new girl's shoulder. They probably put her up to this. *Go and say something to the 'dirty Murphy', we dare you*. Why else would the new girl approach the likes of me?

'So, you *want* to go there?' the American girl persists. 'To Lapland? Some day?'

I say nothing, afraid Mother's mouth is in company with her ears. Eyes on the passing traffic, I watch for the old man's bus, the 126, running late.

'Coz you absolutely should,' the new girl continues. 'If that's what you want to do. My mom says you should always follow your heart.'

I stare at her. I can't tell if she's finished. 'Righto,' I say.

'Anyway, I'm Evie Faith Mayhew,' she announces, holding out her hand for me to shake and I do, warily, expecting to be zapped or stung.

Sister Everista will soon be onto her about those flecks of weekend nail polish.

'Born and raised in Michigan. Not as cold as Lapland, but our winters sure get pretty mean.'

Why is she saying this to me?

'Three high school sisters – Ellen, Prue and Caroline. Baby brother – Joel. Eight months – he's so cute! When I grow up, I'm going to be a photographer. And,' she concludes with great flourish, 'I'm a Gemini!'

I've never known anyone to talk this way. She waits, wanting my life story.

'Jay. Aries, I s'pose.'

'Oh my God!' A small bounce. 'A *ram!*' Another small bounce. 'I love Aries people! You guys shoot straight from the hip, and who doesn't admire that? Aries make *the* best friends, loyal to the end, through thick and thin. But I knew that already, Blue Jay! I knew it the first time I set eyes on you!'

Blue Jay?

'So, it's gotta be your birthday soon, right?'

'Yeah,' I reply. 'Soon.'

But Evie Faith Mayhew from Michigan wants more. 'When? *When?* We'll need time to prepare!'

'Today, actually.'

Confusion sets over her face like a glaze. 'No way. Your birthday is today?'

'Yep.' I shrug it off, more for her sake than mine. 'It's no big deal.'

And it really isn't. Not in my house. Not unless Mum's in a good mood, unless Nev's coming around in his big orange car. *Hey Charger!* she says when he appears at the door. *Hey Charger!* like the glamour girls on the commercials.

'Then why're you here by yourself?'

'Where am I supposed to be?'

She looks around, hands on her narrow hips. 'Well, we're going to at least need some party food.'

'There *is* no party,' I say.

'Then let's make one!' she says, bouncing again, but I only wave my hand. 'Nup. Nah.'

I see how pretty she is. Not a single freckle on her entire face.

'Let's go buy a pop,' says Evie. Tall Evie. 'No, a Sunny Boy!' Eyes as bright and green as the polar lights in my book. I wish mine were half as nice. 'No! A Jelly Tip! Jelly Tips are awesome! Tell me your favourite. Jaffa, right?'

Jitter-legged like a foal, jumping out of its skin with all it might be. So many perfectly white, perfectly shaped teeth. I bet she laughs a lot, she and her big family.

'Can't,' I reply.

'Why not?' she asks, her thumb an arrow over her shoulder. 'The canteen's still open.'

Bloody Yank, says Mother.

'I don't get *tuckshop* money,' I say, calling out her mistake, then wishing I hadn't. Tuckshop is a stupid word. I wish I could say canteen too.

'Not even on your birthday?'

I shake my head, refocus on the road.

'Wait here,' she says. 'I'll be right back.'

And she bounds away, just as the 126 blunders to a stop and the old man alights, resting for a moment against the school fence. He runs a folded handkerchief over his face, behind his neck.

'We don't like hot days, do we?' I say as though he can hear me. I watch his back retreat up the hill, so slowly I wish I could give him a push. A brown bag of groceries sits in the crook of an arm, its top folded over, pressed firm and neat. More Saos inside. When I'm certain no-one is looking, I blow him a kiss.

I've returned the book to the library, set it back in its place by the time the bell goes, just as Evie the Gemini tiptoes up behind me outside the classroom door, a garland of frangipani flowers dropped on my head.

'Ta-da!' she says, so loudly that nearby kids stop what they are doing and turn to look. Susan Walters tugs on Vanessa Quinn's uniform, slack-mouthed.

'What? What're you—'

'It's your birthday tiara.' Evie beams. 'Happy birthday, Blue Jay! Queen for a day.'

Snatching it off my head, I wait for it all to fall to pieces, blacken to ash in my hands. To be a trick.

'The flowers are off the tree near the parking lot,' explains Evie. 'Making one is easy, my mom showed me how. All you need is some thread which I got from the lady in the office. She was happy to help when I told her what it was for.'

I dip my head, inhale the sweetness. Frangipani, for sure. But the best frangipani of all time.

'Don't you like it?' Evie asks. Disappointment short-circuits the gloss-green of her eyes. We've only just met, and already she's broken.

Nothing is safe around me.

The flowers are cool, satin-soft in my hands. I want to tell her I like her tiara, my tiara, my birthday gift, the only one so far, that I really *really* like it, but instead I just fall in line when Sister Everista claps her hands and crumples her face and yells, 'Line up, line up! Lining up at once!' We enter the classroom in single-file silence, and I slip the tiara into my desk.

Post-lunch quiet time. Heads down on our desks as Sister Everista reads today's parable. 'Mark nine,' she says, her Bible held aloft. She won't need to read from it. Sister Everista knows it all by heart. 'Verses fourteen to twenty-nine.'

I am ten years old and I'm hungry. My mother *keeps an eye on* my weight. *You can never be too rich or too thin.* The woman who said this had a king give up his crown for her, and Mother says any woman who can manage that is worth listening to. I don't mind. Every night, JG stocks my lunch box with fruit from his garden, a sandwich with meat Grandma has cooked, and a flask of frozen homemade cordial wrapped in an old pillowcase. I drink the cordial, eat the fruit. The buttered bread is thrown to the sparrows and I shove the meat down my socks – Paddy's after-school secret treat. *Wasting food is a sin*, JG always says, *a deadly one. Worse than pride!* I dread what he would do if he ever found out.

'Teacher,' reads Sister Everista, 'I bring you my son, possessed by a spirit that has robbed him of speech.'

Head down, I see myself alongside the old man, Mr 126, walking in step with him up to his house, carrying the brown bag of groceries. *Such a helpful girl*, he says to me. *Don't know where I'd be without you. But I'm so sorry, my dear, I … I seem to have forgotten your name.*

I look down at his tan boots, their white soles. *So have I*, I say, happy he has things that are clean and new. The half-moons on his purple socks wink their big golden eyes at me.

No matter. He smiles. *We know each other, don't we?*

'… This demon seizes him,' continues Sister Everista, 'and the boy screams. It throws him into convulsions so that he rolls on the ground and foams at the mouth.'

I see the hot cocoa, steaming, that he drinks before bed, the Sao cracker spread with jam (apple and raspberry, my favourite). Nibblings dust his lap.

'… Teacher, take pity. I beg you to look at my son, for he is my only child …'

Head down on the desk, it is him I think of, the nice old man, my friend, not the stupid father whose son isn't possessed by the devil. He's only having fits like Dean Gumbleton in Sister Julian's class.

'… This spirit scarcely ever leaves him …'

Head down, breathing in the gluey wood, its soaked-in boredom.

I breathe in even harder, try to haul up the frangipani scent, but I can't. I suppose I imagined the whole thing. Is it even really my birthday? *All in your head, that tiara*, says Mother.

'… And is destroying him!' wails Sister Everista. My finger drags itself around a compass-carved rocket ship.

'… So Jesus rebuked the evil spirit, healed the boy, and returned him to his father.'

I don't have to look up to know Sister Everista has tears in her eyes.

'And they were all amazed at the greatness of God.' She sniffs, as I dream of trading places with the old man, wanting so badly to be him – unhurried and alone and finished with things.

11 years old, early winter

Two-thirty he arrives, always, even though class doesn't finish until three. Two-thirty he begins his patrol, sitting with Mr Tripp, the school gardener and odd-jobs man. With each year's move to a new classroom, JG finds a nearby place to sit so I can see him and know he is waiting for me. As we rise, he does too, and by the time we have formed two orderly rows by the door, waiting to be dismissed, he is there at the top of the stairs.

'Learn all your lessons?' The first thing he says.

'Yes, Poppa.'

'Paid attention? Didn't talk out-a place?'

'No, Poppa.'

'Sunday night, Blue Jay.' Evie, buzz-full of Friday afternoon fun. 'Six o'clock. There or square!'

'Countdown! Countdown!' That's Gayle and her make-believe microphone, chanting our favourite show's opening theme. 'Count-*duh*-own! *Countdown!*'

'Rick Springfield,' says Evie. 'Live!' Laugh lines frame her movie-star smile.

I have practised smiling until my cheeks ache, trying to get those laugh lines. But it hasn't worked. I don't have the right kind of face.

Slinging a faded-denim satchel over her shoulder – a helter-skelter of iron-on patches, crazed doodles and stickers – Evie pecks the air around my face. *Mwah-mwah-mwah-mwah-mwah.* I look down admiring her tatty sneakers, her shoelaces loose and inked (during social studies class) to look like piano keys. 'I'll call you right after,' she says, at war with a crumple of notebooks and homework handouts. 'Like always.'

Evie's Sunday night phone call is the only one I am allowed all week. My mother times it. I have precisely twenty minutes and no warnings. If I haven't hung up by the time the alarm goes on her little wind-up clock, she snatches the handset and slams it into the cradle of our old phone. This has happened only once. Evie called straight back but I wasn't allowed to pick up. The next day I told her I'd dropped the phone, and that it hadn't worked the rest of the night.

She zips away, trying to catch Gayle who has set off for the school gate. Evie is popular with everyone, but she chose me to be her best friend. 'So who's gonna be number one?' she asks, running back to me, her face so earnest, as though it is the whole week's most critical question.

Evie likes the zany songs, likes making up her own lyrics to make them even sillier. I like Blondie and Pink Floyd, even though Mum says 'Another Brick in the Wall' is *sick*, and Deborah Harry is obviously a *tart*.

Like many of our classmates, Evie and Gayle live east, on the 'posh side'. New shops open after dark, tiny window lights winking, and houses built high to welcome things: breezes, views of the bay, guests.

Evie jogs on the spot, knees comically high, making a hit song all her own: 'When Rick Springfield comes along, you must kiss him ...' She stops, Gayle's microphone held out to me. She wants me to make up the next line like we do at lunchtime, to sing something, anything, the dumber the better, but with JG so close I'd only get into trouble.

She continues, '... Before you make Rick wait too long, you must kiss him ...'

Evie is tanned, lean like a gymnast. A ballerina.

'... Before your mother knows you're gone, you must kiss him ...'

The prettiest girl I've ever seen.

'... Now kiss him, on the lips, take your mark, get set, go for it ...'

The prettiest girl there could ever be.

'... Try to embrace Rick, it's not too late, to kiss him, kiss him good ...'

And more. I've never known her to be mean to anyone, even when they deserved it. On the weekends, Evie Faith Mayhew paints her nails blue, takes photographs with her very own camera – of her three sisters playing 'hats and hairstyles', of her little brother, Joel, chasing the water dragons that live behind her high, 'welcoming' house.

'Dunno why your mother lets you watch that tripe,' says JG opening my case. He always opens my school case right there on the racks outside class – to make sure everything is in its place, that no pen or rubber band or other bought and paid-for possession has been forgotten. I feel like I'm being stripped down and twirled around, a mutant curiosity – half girl, half dumb puppet. 'Not right, that tripe,' he reminds me again. 'And your tables?' Everything is lifted out of the sturdy, sticker-free Globite hard-shell, checked, straightened. He opens and closes my pencil case, peers inside, blows shavings out of the zipper that he tests is still intact. 'What about your mornin' tables?'

I could tell him I got them right. It would be so easy. *Ten out of ten.* I've even practised saying it in front of the mirror. But my dumb puppet mouth drops open and out it comes: 'I got stuck on eight times seven. I don't know why I said fifty-four.'

A dangerous silence.

'Well, that's a shame,' says John Gerald Murphy. 'Lettin' us down by one. Still,' he adds, 'won't happen again. We'll make sure-a that.'

161

Today, as it often does, the gearstick in JG's old Consul jerks and snarls and refuses to move as he wants it. *You mongrel.* The car lurches and bucks. *You mongrel bastard.* Once, I giggled, 'This car has hiccups!' Only once. JG's face had turned steak-red, his sawn-off mouth set hard.

At home in one of my books, there is an etching of a man on his knees, gripping his screaming head. William Blake's *Los howl'd in a dismal stupor.* That man is in hell, I think. An angry hell. He wails in horror, his mouth a blood-black, endless moan. You can't help but feel sorry for him. No matter how mean he gets, JG has that same frightened mouth, half of it anyway.

We turn left, left again, then right. School spirals away behind us. At a stoplight, I look down at my lap, at my hands. They bloat tight and blue like five-fingered balloons, zinging with itch as though stung by so many valiant, dying bees. *Only nerves,* says Doctor Timothy. *All in your head,* says my mother. My eyes flick right – once, twice – scoping the trip-wire between me and JG. I want to pop them, my balloon-hands, watch them bullet through the crack of open window, *whoosh,* itch gone for good. But I know I am better off being still.

Up the long, steep climb of Montpelier Street (The Big Hill) we pass Rachel. She walks home every afternoon and once asked me to walk with her. I told Rachel I asked for permission but my mother said no. 'Why'd you even ask,' Rachel said, 'it's no big deal.' But I hadn't asked at all. There'd have been no point and the question would only have landed me in trouble.

Eight times tables pile up in my head like crashed cars.

I try to think of Paddy, of my stash of secret sausage, his whiskery grin, the whirring stump of his tail. But the car seat is too hot and my shoes too tight, teeming with bugs. Wasps. I lift my feet and cross them under me on the molten vinyl, uncross them, cross them again until I'm told to: 'Sit still, girl, for Christ's sake'.

Out the window, times tables slip and skew across the world, always in words, never numbers.

Eight times three. Twenty-four.

Eight times four. Thirty-two.

Eight times five. Forty.

Eight times six. Forty-eight.

Eight times seven. Fifty-si—

Fifty …

Same age as Paddy, if one dog year truly equals seven human ones.

Fifty-six, Jay. Fifty-six, *dummy*!

Eight sevens. Seven eights.

'A miracle he's made it this far,' said my grandmother only last week.

Eight sevens are fifty-six.

Sitting on my fingers, crushing them, I dare them to pop, to whoosh. To get out while they can.

Seven eights are fifty-six.

Later he will ask me, and I will get it right. He will test me again, again, pulling my puppet strings tight. He will try to trick me, confuse me, trip me up, go as far as times thirteen. Bettering me, he will say, for this is the latest thing, the latest push. I am to be better than everyone else in every way. Brilliantly better. It has been decided. JG has given the dishlickers away, but he still likes a winner, still needs something to train, something to punish when it fails. JG will get to my mother and she will test me too, right up till bedtime, again in the morning first thing.

But I will be prepared – not a single misstep in my queasy doll-dance – and they will be pleased.

11 years old, spring

Henry: *I want you to get out of that bed and walk to the window. I want you to scream out in the street, Leona.*

Leona: *I ... I-I can't move, Henry. I'm too frightened!*

Saturday night and Paddy, unyoked, lies across my lap.

Grandma, Paddy and I had scones for our supper. Homemade jam and cream. 'Shh,' she said, 'our little secret.' We are watching one of her favourite movies – Burt Lancaster and Barbara Stanwyck in *Sorry, Wrong Number.*

'Oh, get out of bed, Barbara,' cries my grandmother, so excited she almost spills her tea. 'Just get up out of that damn bed! Hurry!' She always says this even though she has seen it before, as though this time the film may end differently.

I think of Evie's mother, Marilyn, who sips black coffee all through the day. It boils on the stove in a slim silver pot. Mum let me sleep over at Evie's four times, four heavenly Friday nights, but that stopped when JG found out.

'Not this again,' he warned her and my mother didn't argue the point, didn't tell him this was nothing like those other times, with those other people, nothing at all. I helped Marilyn make pizza, chilli beans, coleslaw with pineapple and tiny marshmallows in it. No boiled mutton for Evie's family. And when Marilyn talked to us, she'd call us 'ladies'. *How was school today, ladies? Tell me something, ladies. Tell me somethin' about nothin'.*

Before I really knew them, knew what to expect, before I understood the wonder of them, I said that nobody would want to hear about nothing, that you can't tell about nothing.

But don't you know, Evie's mother said. *Nothing is ever nothing, sweet girl. There's no such thing as nothing. And if there were – hoo boy! I'd buy it a buttonhole and take it to the dance.*

The other Mayhews would laugh, the joke understood. I didn't understand and that was the great joy of being around them. To know there was more to learn, further to go. Other ways to be.

Leona: *Henry ... Henry ... HENRY! There's somebody coming up the stairs.*

Grandma and I are both yelling at Barbara to get out of her damn bed when Mum cannons up the front steps. She and Nev have had a fight. Grandma asks her if she wants a cuppa, says she needs to calm herself down.

'Leave Rory Jay with me, Lon,' says Grandma. She can see how Mum is, knows how she can get. Too much like JG. 'You go down home. You can still have the night to yourself.'

But my mother's pain must be seen and heard, so I'm to get off my good-for-nothing arse, she says, grabbing me by the shoulders, marching me down Grandma's front stairs, down the hill. The jungle of fruit trees hangs heavy by night with huntsman spiders. I cringe, hold my breath.

'What's going on now, Lonnie?' my grandmother calls after us, but my mother ignores her.

I try to look back at Grandma, standing there on the barely lit porch, but my mother has snatched up my collar, her knuckles against my jaw, shoving my face forward. 'Look where you're going, Mutt.'

When we reach our backyard, my mother turns on the

165

floodlights, goes to the shed and gets my netball. 'Practice time!' she says, a thumping throw at my chest.

It is often practice time when Lonnie's had a bad night.

She had JG construct the ten-foot post, fit it with a steel ring precisely five-eighths of an inch thick and fifteen inches across. All the measurements observed and no excuses since.

From my bedroom window, I used to see the mango trees, the mulberries and figs, José's olive grove high up on the hill. But now it's the goalpost. A scarecrow of sorts, chasing away the fun that playing with a ball used to be. I resent it, its closeness to my window, to where I sleep – always there, a stalker, hands in his pockets where he hides the rope.

I aim, shoot. In my nightie, in the near dark, I aim and shoot.

And miss.

'*Again!*' she barks, fetching the ball.

She runs in her platform heels. In her halter-neck mini. Leopard print.

I aim, shoot.

And miss.

My angle is perfect, she says, chasing the bounding ball. Always perfect. I miss only because the ball needs more height. I need to stop being a lazy little piece. All I need to do is: '*LIFT IT!*'

My grandmother watching from the porch at the top of the hill.

Thirty shots, nine misses. My mother after the ball, hunting it down, sweating, swearing. She is my opponent, her arms up trying to block my shots, trying to put me off. Her mascara trickles. The elegant curls that took her so long in front of the mirror clot and clump now, a desperate mess. I was with her when she bought the halter-neck and the big shoes. 'Wouldn't your daughter like to try them on first?' the lady in the shop asked her.

Thirty-eight shots. Thirty-nine.

'*Lift it!*' she screams when I miss. '*LIFT IT!*'

She is hard up against me, not the regulation distance. An obstruction. No-one could score like this.

'*LIFT IT!*' Forty-three shots. Forty-four. 'It's not that hard!'

Number forty-five, butting the hoop.

'You know what's hard, *Rory Jay?*' How she hates my name. 'My life, that's what's *fucken hard!*'

Forty-six. Forty-seven. In and in.

'Mumma never looked out for me. Always off with the fairies. Nose in a book, arse in front of the box. But she looks out for you, hey? Gotta look after *Rory Jay*, save her from *big bad Lonnie.*'

I can see it tiring now, the thing that takes hold.

'Well, runs in the family, don't it? Bad blood.'

Wringing her dry, its jaws cramping. Soon it will lose interest, and when it does: 'I can be good, daughter,' up the back stairs, heels in her hands, tears coursing. 'Tomorrow. Just you wait and see.'

But for now, her screams, the lights coming on in José and Lucia's house, going off in Grandma's. 'Aim that bloody ball, *Mutt*, and LIFT IT!'

Later, in bed, I wonder if Grandma is still awake, re-reading her Cathy and Heathcliff book. Another of her favourites. Not so long ago I picked up her copy, just to have a look. I returned to it day after day, every afternoon after school. A story about angry, hateful people, hurting and being hurt. Catherine Earnshaw is a brat, spoilt and selfish. She breaks the heart of everyone who loves her. She breaks her own. Heathcliff is cruel like JG; he hurts Isabella's dog. He is called a *frightful thing*, but the truly frightful don't love the way Heathcliff loves Cathy, do they? The truly frightful get away with everything. Heathcliff does not – he suffers. And I both want him to, and I don't want him to. Shouldn't it be easy to decide? The people on the moors are trapped like us, the whole of their world only two houses wide. In the American

Plays, swooning couples are soon undone. Heathcliff and Cathy's love is impossible. Maybe all love is. Henry realises too late that he does care for Leona, but not even that can make her get out of bed, and she ends up dying in it. I think these stories make my grandmother feel less alone. No happy endings for the characters she loves. No happy ending for anyone.

Monday, 11:56 am

'Nothing to worry about, Mrs Gundersen. Frank is fine, always a lovely boy. Quite the new hairdo, have to say. Usually, we don't allow that kind of thing. We might have preferred some advance warning but it's all for the best, of course, his health, so forth, etc. But it's quite a look. Just as well school photos aren't for a few months yet.

'Thing is, Mrs Gundersen, a student in Frank's art class has *accidentally* knocked a bottle of paint onto Frank's schoolbag. It was open, the bag, unzipped. We do encourage the students to re-zip their bags after they've got what they need for their class. However, a bottle has been knocked. A litre bottle, yes. Newly opened, yes. Fluorescent Tangerine, as luck would have it. His school-issue laptop has copped the brunt of it. Destroyed, completely destroyed. Not backed up, apparently. We do encourage the students to back up their laptops every evening. We do encourage the parents to encourage the students to back up their computers every evening.

'Now ... we do have the laptop replacement agreement that you will have signed, Mrs Gundersen, but in this case we're willing to waive those terms given it was, indeed, an accident. So ... just to be clear ... we won't be holding you to that agreement. Another student involved, so forth etc. We're happy to provide a second-hand backpack but all of Frank's other belongings will have to be ... to be, er ... to be replaced, is the case, I'm afraid, Mrs Gundersen. His calculator, blazer etc. All of his workbooks and notes and things are completely unusable, I'm afraid, so there'll be some catching up there to be done. Hmm ... Hmm ... And Frank will have to stay behind after school today with the IT consultant, set up a new machine.

'Yes ... yes of course, Mrs Gundersen. The other student has been duly warned to take more care in the art room. Madison was so dreadfully sorry. In tears, poor lass, yes, she was terribly distressed.'

Wednesday, 10:08 am

Coffee Cabin day at Teddy's school, nine till eleven every Wednesday. A life-skills program for the senior classes. The kids take orders, calculate bills and change, learn to prepare and serve hot drinks and light meals – burgers, raisin toast, fruit salad, muffins – to a sprinkling of parents and staff.

'So, it looks like Jerrik's got a new "project",' I say, setting down my half-empty mug long enough to make an (instantly regretted) air quotes gesture.

Vivienne and Tess belong respectively to Zadie and Dylan, two kids in Teddy's class. The three of us meet here as often as we can, do our bit. We are a forgiving clientele. If things go wrong – a drink tipped in your lap, a salad sneezed over as it makes its way to your table – we know what to do which is, essentially, nothing.

'For an indolent man,' says Vivienne, stunning in an emerald suit, 'he'd beat Usain Bolt in a quick dash to a short skirt.'

'I think that's just it,' I say. 'It takes so little effort on his part. Women just seem to latch on to him, like—'

'Shit to a blanket?' Vivienne stirs her black, sugarless coffee with alarming vigour.

The boy who brought us our drinks lingers by our table, staring at my head. He is not alarmed, though that may have been a possibility. Often, it is not what our kids see that disorients them, it is what they don't see. The gaps – what happens when they aren't looking, when they can't prepare and process. I am familiar to this boy, but my appearance has altered dramatically since he last saw me. There has been no explanation, no time to adjust. So I hold out my palm, and when he takes it I run our hands over my stubble, and I talk to him, so he understands the rest of me hasn't changed. It is the best I can do and it seems enough. To Vivienne's great amusement, three more kids dash over to our table for a turn at touching my head.

'Ah, Satan,' says Tess with a heavy sigh, seemingly apropos of nothing.

Tess recently replaced a little daily Prozac with a 24/7 dose of high-octane Jesus. I listen to her trot out a quote from Saint Matthew about the things of God versus the things of men. Crisps of sleep dangle, distractingly, from an eyelash. She is missing an earring and the collar of her shirt bears the bruise of some past make-up skirmish, though today she wears none. Tess's appearance often suggests a weathering of some minor misfortune.

'James four, verse seven,' she continues. 'Submit yourselves, then, to God. Resist the devil and he will flee from you.'

'It's not us who have to resist anything,' grumbles Vivienne.

As many in this cohort do, Tess leans hard into her fanaticism – a popular entry in the self-medication playbook most parents of a disabled child have thumbed through at least once or twice. Zealotry's sublistings are legion and frequently come with a B side: under-eating/over-eating, ultrarunning/day drinking. School trivia night is generally when the born-agains and swingers tend to reveal themselves. We become militant activists or dilettante shoplifters, CEOs or middle-aged meth heads. For the first group, only total world domination can arrest the loss of control that began one day in a hospital or a doctor's office. The latter want precisely the opposite. For the drinkers and dial-outs, it is all about dropping the clutch and freewheeling around the bends, headlights dimmed.

'Honestly, Jay,' insists Vivienne, the table's only world-domination delegate. 'How much longer can you live like this? He rubs your nose in it. It degrades you.'

'Jerrik and I struck a deal,' I say, tiptoeing around Vivienne's more combative than usual mood. 'Eons ago. I look after the boys my way, no interference, and he pays for it. We play to our strengths. Venal as that sounds, it works. Well, it's success-*adjacent*. And Teddy adores his father, believe it or not.'

Vivienne regards me in set-face silence, so I move us on.

'Anyway, this latest peccadillo is called Minette.'

'Teddy would adjust in time,' says Vivienne. '*Minette?* As in … a French cat?'

'Ha! I knew you'd love it.' I laugh, still on tiptoe. 'He calls her Minnie, of course.' I grimace.

'There's this new hack for people who can't stand each other anymore, Jay,' says Vivienne. 'It's called divorce. Many speak very highly of it. Half the world, in fact.' She rolls a thin sachet of sugar between her fingers. '*Minette.* For God's sake.'

'Marriage is sacred.' Tess says this to her steaming green tea, timidly, as though expecting a rebuke.

'There *is* no marriage, Tess!' snaps Vivienne, giving her one. 'How have you missed this?'

Poor Tess. Her many previous hobbies and diversions had justified themselves with an obvious leavening of her mood. But finding God has delivered her the very opposite. Increasingly withdrawn each time I see her, her caliper cling to The Almighty seems more burden than comfort.

'Mark ten, verse nine,' Tess begins. 'What God has joined togeth—'

'And is this "project",' demands Vivienne, copying my unfortunate digital punctuation, 'blonde and twenty-eight, like the last one? Taylor? Tonya? Tuna? I can't believe he actually tells you their names!'

'Lana,' I say, as Tess shrinks back into her place. 'But I'm sure there's a Taylor around the corner. They don't last long once they get to know him.'

Vivienne shivers, still crushing the little cigarillo of sugar.

'It's Satan, Jay,' Tess explains. 'Satan. Tempting Jerrik, ruining your marriage.'

'Right,' says Vivienne, her knuckles white now around a salt shaker. 'It's all Old Nick's fault, then. Prince Pantless just needs to be *saved*, that right?'

'Exactly.' Tess nods, either missing or choosing to ignore Vivienne's sarcasm. 'And only God can do that. Only God can decide when it's time to cast Satan into the Lake of Fire.'

Vivienne dips her head, looks at me over the rim of her glasses.

'By facing tribulation,' Tess continues, 'you cover yourself in God's glory, Jay. Support your husband through his trial—'

'*His* trial?' Vivienne snorts.

I finish my coffee and order another to go. 'Off to Bunnings,' I say, announcing my plan to sand and paint the living-room walls, to give Frank a home-based exhibition. 'Galleries are few and far between these days, and let's face it – art's not about art anymore. Nothing's about itself anymore. Build your brand and they will come whether they need it or not. Anyway, Frank's work is outsider stuff. Appetite for it overseas, but I don't think anyone's heard of it here.'

'So on top of everything else,' says Vivienne, 'you're trying to revolutionise the domestic art market? Lead a philistine horse to water?'

'And feed it pretzels if I must.'

'But to paint the house yourself, Jay,' says Vivienne, 'that's an e-*NOR*-mous job.' She appears so disturbed I'm tempted to offer her a rub of my head.

'Professionals are too pricey,' I say instead, 'and it's just the front room. I can do it.'

Tess raises a coy finger, says, 'Um,' before offering more biblical ballyhoo. 'Give her the reward she has earnt, and let her works bring her praise at the city gates.'

Vivienne, eyes wide: 'Sure, all that, though I'd add I think a show is a marvellous idea. Zadie and I are a lock. We'll bring things. I'll even buy a painting. Preferably one of his less murdery ones.'

I am only a couple of minutes down the road when the phone rings. 'I've just about had it with Tess,' huffs Vivienne, never one for cordial preliminaries when blunt and to the point stand idly by. She must have left school shortly after I did. 'All that wretched Jesus woi-woi. I thought she'd be over it by now, like all her fads. The skydiving, the dog breeding. All those bloody sad sack Salukis sniffing your crotch. Remember when she tried to sign us up for her flash mob?'

'Viv,' I reply. 'I just shaved off a perfectly good head of hair. I'm not one to judge.'

'Now listen, Jay. I didn't want to get into this in front of Saint Teresa, but you really can't keep going on as you are. I could have a colleague draw up divorce papers by the end of the week.'

'Vivienne, it's okay.'

'It's not, you know. You deserve better.'

'I'm not the first woman to live beyond the light of the silvery moon, Vivienne. Tess's hotelier husband isn't in it for the pay cheque, is he? Thinking only of his family's security? It's so he can live in Dubai most of the year, sorting chefs and menus and laundry contracts, leave everything else up to his depressed wife. Tess gets less rest than I do. Compared to Dylan, Teddy sleeps like Rip Van Winkle.'

But Vivienne, a divorced union lawyer, bangs heads for a living. The prospect of combat puts a spring in her step. 'All I'm saying is, I know you're worried about the money, Jay, how you'll keep your heads above water, but—'

'Those are very real concerns, Vivienne.' Only people who don't have to worry about money can so easily dismiss the prospect of penury.

'Yes, they are. But so is staying in a marriage where you're treated like the paid help. Paid help at least have their own room and get to knock off at some stage.'

Vivienne has paid help. A couple who clean, iron and cook up a week's worth of meals for her and Zadie.

'Things would work themselves out, Jay. People would step up—'

'What people?' I ask Vivienne, a woman from a large family – four brothers, two sisters, in-laws, nieces, nephews. She and Zadie are surrounded by people they can trust and rely on. 'I have no people, Viv. Not everybody has people. Not everybody wants them. That's my point. It's just me and the boys. And I'm doing what I think is best.'

'All I'm saying is …' says Vivienne, who thinks she knows me, who wants to *save* me. And I let her speak, because people like Vivienne, for whom acceptance is not survival but a form of defeat, must fight and they must win.

'All I'm saying is …'

Vivienne says I deserve better. Better than what?

Vivienne is in a rush for my redemption, a neat, rose-ribboned resolution. Vivienne wants to hear me say, I am woman, hear me *roar*! Have me fall in love. Get a PhD. Write a trilogy. Birth the next gangbusters start-up from the modesty of my suburban carport, my 'doddle' and my 'hope wrecker' by my side, hands aloft in triumph, viewers tearing up. They wouldn't have to make a movie about me. I'd *be* the movie. Jay, The Biopic. Happily Ever After.

Would that be better enough?

'All I'm saying is …' says Vivienne, over and over. 'All I'm saying to you is …'

What Vivienne doesn't understand is that I do roar. I roar every day. It is simply that some roars are more listened to than others.

After collecting the paint, I stop for petrol. It is one of those days – in and out of the car, one errand then the next, a thing collected here, delivered there. The motion of mothers. I'm glad of it. Traffic and idling engines. The steering wheel volcanically hot in my hands. My ribs against my shirt, wet with sweat. The compass points of my day.

Behind the counter a cashier, late-thirties, a well-loved Moffs T-shirt under his unbuttoned corporate oil uniform.

In the centre of the store, surrounded by snack-size, on-the-run retail, I spy a small circular rack of black T-shirts. 'Are they band shirts?' I ask the cashier.

A prolonged scratch of his chest. 'Bands, TV shows, video games.'

'T-shirts in a petrol station?'

Moff Man shrugs, his chest scratch a thing of deep and abiding returns.

'Any power metal? No Ronnie James Dio, I don't suppose?'

A shake of his head, marginally more alert.

'Speed metal? Groove metal? Nu? Glam? Thrash? Industrial?'

'Damn, woman,' he says, coolly regarding my bald head. 'Marry me.'

Moff Man goes to the rack, ignoring the three customers lined up behind me. Impatient sighs and coin-heavy pockets. Shuffling boots.

'Nobody ever wants these,' he says, holding aloft two Def Leppards and a TANK T-shirt.

'*TANK!* Are you kidding? Well, I know someone who will.'

When I collect Teddy from school, he is the brightest he has been in ages. He presents me with a box he made in wood shop. For dinner, he eats two small bowls of soup, two white rolls, two Tim Tams. Frank sleeps in the new punk metal T-shirt. He thinks he may be the proud owner of the only piece of TANK merch in the Southern Hemisphere. I tell him he's probably the only TANK fan in the Southern Hemisphere. It's a good night.

But by morning, Teddy is flushed and cranky and won't eat his breakfast. I keep him home. For lunch I make him a sandwich, cut into four equilateral triangles. He barely glances at it and vomits, spends the afternoon in bed, listless, YouTubing. The next day he manages half a dry cracker, two slices of apple.

'Probably nothing,' says the GP from behind his bile-tinted lenses. 'Some viruses can hang around.'

This is our fourth visit in five weeks.

'Let's collect some urine,' he says, handing me a specimen jar. 'Though a blood test would be more helpful, young man,' he tells Teddy, a little sternly, as though the lack of diagnostics is somehow Teddy's fault.

'Then let's get one,' I say. 'He's never had a blood test, and I don't suppose it will be easy. But let's try.'

'Probably not necessary,' says the GP.

'You just said it would be helpful. Shouldn't we at least give it a go?'

'It's probably nothing,' says the GP, silencing me with a finger to his lips, listening to Teddy's chest. 'Most things are.'

Nothing has ever been nothing, I want to say. Not for us.

'Has a dentist had a look? Could be an abscess. Have someone check out his teeth if he still won't eat.'

Teddy is down nine kilos.

12 years old, summer

My last term at St Bernie's. High school next year, somewhere. All high schools aren't created equal, according to Mother. All high schools aren't worthy. She has applied to two, the best two for girls, she says. 'And don't you worry,' she has said more than once, though I am not worried at all. 'I'll get you into one of 'em, by the Christ. You just watch.'

JG's old car still grips its way up The Big Hill, passing Rachel who picks flowers from people's gardens to put in her hair. She stopped asking me to walk home with her a long time ago.

I don't need to run the times tables through my head anymore. I know them all, no more slip-ups. Just like I know the dates and circumstances of the first and second world wars, and when President Kennedy was shot, and the geological timescale, and the different kinds of sedimentary rocks and their properties, and how to conjugate the Italian verbs on Signora Salamone's list.

Everything I have to learn is learnt. Everything I have to do is done.

Something else, now, on our drives to and from school. Extracurricular knowledge just for me, scored on my own secret tests:

Finland – population four point eight million, capital Helsinki, coldest recorded temperature -49.0°C, Sodankylä, Lapland, 1912.

Michigan – population nine million, capital Lansing, coldest recorded temperature -51.0°C, Vanderbilt, 1934.

Facts, not inventions. My *chilly* places, waiting for me to grow up and go find them.

When we arrive home, Paddy runs out to greet us, a circling trot alongside the car all the way up the drive. As always, there is mutton on the boil in Grandma's kitchen. And hard swallows so I don't gag. And JG latching the wire door behind us.

All the week's scraps and peelings are collected in a wide bucket in the corner of the kitchen. It is too full for the lid to close and flies hover, land, rub their legs in their scheming way. By now, my grandmother should have emptied it into the pit under the mango trees, turned it all over with a pitchfork for JG to use in the garden. Instead, she sits close to the television on a fraying fold-up chair, the kind campers take away with them. Grandma sits longer these days, cocooned inside her trusty black cardigan, transported by the twists and turns of her beloved American Plays.

From the kitchen I wave hello.

'Shh!' she replies. 'Shh!' Not really cross.

Sunlight has never favoured this odd little box on the hill, always preferring elsewhere. Inside is airless and still, as though the house has held its breath for so long, no point now in letting it go. Sad as a bug in resin. Grandma watches the screen, tilts her cup and pours a dribble of tea into the saucer, puffing her breath over it, tipping it back into the cup. She says tea cools faster this way.

I go to her room, pick up her copy of *Wuthering Heights* and sit on the floor beside her. The book had once belonged to my mother, her name at the top of its front page. *Mary Lenore Murphy*. Might she have been kinder if she had gone by her first name? A tender name, Mary, a holy name. I run my fingers over my mother's handwriting – so lovely, her fancy 'y's carefully drawn. I imagine my mother as a girl, hard as that is, before the thing first took hold. Who might she have been had it not found her? It is Friday afternoon, and I wonder what my mother's plans might be. If she doesn't come home, I will have to stay here, sleep on the settee. If she comes home and it has been a bad day, anything might happen. I wish Grandma and I could live together. Just us, Paddy and Keep.

'Sad tooth?' says my grandmother, her hand on my shoulder, fingers pressed softly to my cheek. I hadn't realised I was crying.

'Sad tooth,' I answer.

Both of us stare at the television as the last American Play ends.

My grandmother pours, puffs, tips, licks the drips from the edge of the saucer.

And I wish for the weekend to be over.

Even *Countdown* and Sunday nights aren't the same since Evie left.

The minute the show ended she would call, full of fire, wanting to debate how that week's National Top 10 number two was ripped off, how it should have been number one. How a lead guitarist is always better looking than the guy on bass. How her mom felt sad for Rod Stewart having lost all the buttons on his shirts. We'd laugh so hard.

Sometimes during our Sunday night calls I would wrap one of my mother's scarves around my neck, slide a gerbera from the garden behind my ear, or pull on a beanie, the only hats I have. One time, gloves. I never told Evie I did this. My mother's eyes would crunch with scorn, her little alarm clock tick-ticking away in her fist. But by dressing up I felt like a girl with ways and charms, like Evie, if only for twenty minutes a week.

When her father was transferred back to Delaware, Evie and I cried for days. We cried at school. When my mother was in the shower, I'd telephone Evie just to cry and then hang up. Grandma bought me twelve blue *par avion* envelopes, like the one she bought to post my letter to Captain Kent. I wrote my name and address on the front of each one and around the envelopes we tied a piece of thin silver ribbon so they kept together and looked like a present.

'No-one else need know,' Grandma warned. 'It's our little secret. Ours and Evie's.'

'No way,' Evie sobbed when I gave them to her. 'A letter a month? Forget it!'

I didn't understand.

'I'm going to write you a *hundred* letters a month!' We hugged. 'Two hundred!'

'Don't forget to put your new address on the back,' I told her. 'So I know where you live. Then I'll put a pin in the map on my wall. And if you put a pin in a map too, we can talk to each other, look at each other. Kind of.'

But that was almost a year ago.

'She probably lost those envelopes, Missy,' said my mother one night after work.

Grandma was pouring us tea, but hesitated, her hand beginning to shake. I stopped breathing. Our secret, those envelopes. *Ours and Evie's.* How did my mother know about them?

'Or threw 'em out,' my mother continued, matter-of-fact. 'Always struck me as an uppity piece. Got herself a new best friend the second she landed, I bet. Like I always say, Missy. Your best friend is only ever your mother. Isn't that right, Mumma?'

'Lonnie, are … are you sure you—'

'Is that what you think happened, Grandma?' I asked, desperate to believe my friend had been faithful. 'Do you think Evie lost the envelopes?'

My mother looked at her mother, eyebrows arched, the skin on her face shiny and tight, her mouth as round and hard as the end of a pistol, where the bullets come out.

'Perhaps,' Grandma conceded, filling our cups. 'And perhaps chance would be a fine thing,' she added, meeting my mother's stare.

I hear JG using the toilet.

I wish I could go down the hill on my own, talk to Keep in my room until my mother gets home. I wish I didn't have to play tennis all weekend. I wish I had time by myself.

From the stall as he pees, JG calls out to me, tells me to pour myself a glass of his homemade cordial. Lemon juice, sugar, citric acid.

I wish it were Monday already.

'It's okay,' I call back from the living-room floor. 'I'm not thirsty.'

In a moment he is up the stairs. The cordial is made for me, made fresh today, he won't see it wasted.

My grandmother and I share a look before I get up and drink as instructed.

Downstairs, Paddy waits for me by the door. As soon as I got out of the car, he could smell Grandma's Aberdeen sausage in my pocket – monster-thick slabs of it on my sandwich today, as though hacked by a giant with an axe. I had to run inside quickly to save us both. Paddy has already copped it this week. Yesterday he got free of the yoke and escaped the yard. But JG tracked him down, as he always does, bringing the dog home upside down like a pig on a spit – two paws gripped in each of his hands – slamming him onto the ground, beating him with a chain, Grandma rushing out – 'Easy John, easy' – before JG turned the chain on her. I watched all this, my legs and arms useless clackety sticks, my dumb mouth falling open but silent.

As I drink, JG unpacks my things – every brown-papered book flipped and shaken. I don't know what he expects to find in them. The wax paper from my sandwich, wadded up neatly around the peel of a sugar banana, is opened out, inspected. There must always be proof I've eaten my lunch. *Wasting food is a sin*, I've heard all my life. But the meat I hide to give to Paddy isn't a waste – it makes him happy, and I don't like meat. When I grow up, I am going to

183

be a vegetarian like Martina Navratilova and Kate Bush. But I keep all that to myself.

JG wipes out my school case with a damp cloth, dries it again before placing everything back inside. Tonight, at our kitchen table, he will conclude the ritual by cleaning my school shoes – a dusting off, a dab of polish, a horsehair buffing that goes on until the brown leather glints in the school day sun. *Lady Muck*, my mother will say, an uncertain look on her face, a soothing Moselle in her hand.

The jacks JG once gave me have found their way to the kitchen. They sit in a bottle on a shelf above the refrigerator. Old bones – real ones, not the bright pieces of plastic the kids at school use. I hadn't really fancied playing with them but I could see my grandfather wanted me to take them, as though giving me something special. The knuckles were big and chunky, greasy too, impossible to trap on the back of my hands. I realised they'd probably been in a stew. My toys – bits of dead cow or sheep, sucked clean of their meat and set aside for play. *Toys are for babies*, JG always says. *Waste-a money*. I remember sliding my fingers under the hem of my shirt, shovelling the jacks back into the bottle, the object of the game ever since being never to touch them again.

A small bag of something dry and crumbly has been stuffed into the bottle on top of the jacks. This place is full of such jars and tins, stacked and crammed and caulked with grime. Old screws, nails, bolts, rings and hooks, washers, eyelets, shoelaces. Broken, stretched, bent, it is all held on to, nothing tossed out. Things are sometimes repaired but rarely replaced. There is never anything new.

I am allowed some time to myself before I must start on my homework. JG tells me he needs to go out, that I am to find something in the garden for afternoon tea. The latest hand of ripe bananas hangs under the house; I can eat my fill. 'Or there's the custard apples. Use the spoon on the tank if—'

'Shh!' Grandma, from her planet in the sitting room. 'Shh!'

JG wipes his moist, mangled mouth on his collar before thundering off. 'Bloody Yank *bullshit*.'

I rinse and dry my glass, skip down the steps from the kitchen. Paddy and I both watch JG start up the hill, disappearing soon enough into the far corner of the property. Cutting through the dead-end lane, he will be on his way to the bookie's, to the pub, to both. Paddy and I make our way down the yard. I reach into my pocket, break off niblets of sausage and slip them to him as we walk. We pass rows of little wooden crucifixes with RADISH, TURNIP, CARROT pencilled on them in JG's heavy hand, sitting down at the bottom of the paddock near the gate to the front house.

'Mine, like ... *bleh!*' calls José from his garden next door, his thumbs and forefingers making small circles. His face is the rubbery droop he knows always makes me laugh. JG calls him Joe the Wog, Joe the Dago. Smiling his gap-toothed grin, José points at the passionfruit vine that blankets the chain wire, sagging with purpling fruit. 'But yous, like ... *ba-boom!*' His fingers are splayed wide.

I gave José some of JG's prized passionfruit once. Only once.

'*See*-cret, *sí?*' He winks, tapping his cloth cap. '*See*-cret? To make grow? One day, I learn it. I grow ba-boom too!' He waves and moves on, tending his own patch. I wave back, '*Hasta luego*,' trying not to think of the 'secret' – the ox hearts and sheep livers JG buries deep in the dirt, blood-feeding his 'trades', the living things he swaps for bets and smokes and bags of severed legs for Grandma's stew.

Paddy nudges my hands. *Here I am! Pat me!* I scratch his chin, stroke his wiry beard, his finely veined ears. I break up the last of the thick sausage and feed it to him, a shake of his paw my reward. He tries to rest his face in my lap, but the yoke, a nasty tangle of wire and rust and rough-cut wood, bangs against my knees.

An overripe persimmon falls to the ground nearby. I take a bite, offer the rest to Paddy. He traps it between his front paws, licks at the sweet-slurping flesh as I run my fingers under the yoke, scarred skin where his hair should be.

I look around. JG is never gone for long.

Evie came home with me one afternoon after school. Only once. She didn't know what the yoke was, only stared at the mean contraption. And though she said nothing, the horror on her face, the distaste, made the ground underneath fall away.

'It stops him running off,' I tried to explain. 'He scrambles under the fences, or tries to jump, mostly at night. Pop says if you have a dog, you can't let it run amok in everyone else's place.'

Evie had looked at Paddy so sadly but pulled back her hand when he offered his nose for a pat. She dared not touch him, the way you wouldn't touch a brain in a bottle, or a chick with two beaks.

I'd been angry at Paddy that day. Why couldn't he be a good dog, not run off all the time and force JG to use the yoke? Why did everything about me, about my family, need to be explained? Why I don't have a father. Why I spend more time with my grandparents – so much older than everyone else's – than with my own mother. Why I can't walk home like the other kids. Why my shoes must always be so shiny, my school case so square and clean. None of it stops Matt Fitzpatrick, the Connolly boys too, calling me a 'dirty Murphy' every chance they get.

I lift the dog's shackled head, hold his face to mine. One of his eyes is sore and closed from yesterday's beating. 'I'm sorry I have bad thoughts, Paddy.'

And I begin working away at the bolts.

Just for a while I want him to be free, to savour the sticky fruit and clean his face with a drag through the grass. 'Buttercup boy, *Te amo*.' I kiss the top of his head. '*Buen chico, buen* Paddy,' I say, the way José has taught me.

The moment the yoke is off, Paddy abandons the fruit and flips onto his back, squirming about in the thick grass, indulging in a long scratch. His rump and shoulders hoist from side to side in a lying-down dance. Next, he circle-eights around me, then cuts loose at full speed, streaking like a rabbit across one garden bed after another. At the fence on José's side, he turns in an almost-somersault, sailing back over the boxed beds, one or two lightning-quick skips in between before launching himself once more into the air. He is showing off, and I cheer him on, quietly: *Pad-dy! Pad-dy!* He darts back to me, drops to a low bow at my feet, panting, stump wagging.

If only Evie could see this. Paddy and me, being ordinary.

Evening edges in, as though the afternoon has thought better of it, drawn its shutters early, left me to my own lookout. From earth to sky, the sound of nothing. (*Nothing is ever nothing, sweet girl.*)

Jumpy, I think I see movement on the porch. *All in your head*, says Mother. Probably only Grandma, no need to worry. We keep each other's secrets.

The pieces of the yoke are heavy as blocks. Despite Paddy's obliging patience, the hinges are difficult to realign.

Be thorough, *dummy*. No mistakes, *Mutt*.

But my heart pounds, trying to kick its way out of me, out of trouble. I'm not certain the yoke is secure. Goosebumps prick my scalp. Even if it doesn't come off, JG will notice. Bees, bull ants, plagues of them under my skin. JG misses nothing. All of me is nettle and sting. Any moment I might burst open, top to tail, my charred insides thrust up and out like a split sausage.

Paddy cannot escape. If he does, JG will be off after him – *bastard mongrel bastard* – the broken-off handle of a rake in one hand, gumboots to protect his feet from the kicking that goes on and on, until a hind leg is held up off the ground for weeks.

'*Buen chico*,' I say to Paddy. '*Buen chico. Te amo*,' I say again, my fingers clumsy sticks, tightening, untightening, testing. '*Te amo. Te amo mucho*,' like a decade of the rosary.

I've taken so long to refasten the yoke Paddy lies down on his side. I pat his tummy. 'Homework time,' I tell him, checking the yoke once more for luck. But the dog stays where he is, weighed down by secret sausage, worn out from his romp, dozing off. I head up the hill alone.

The screen door wheezes open, its routine protest, but the house isn't right. *Quite the imagination*, says Mother. Shadows lounging at the top of the stairs, daring me to come near. The meat simmers on the stove, *plink plink*. But where is the *clink* of the black sauce bottle, the grind and scrape of the cornflour paste, the *clunk clunk* of Grandma's spoon on the pot? JG won't be far off; stew and stout must be ready. Up I go, one step, another, *clackety clack*, deeper into it, into the shadows, their groping cling.

She sits at the end of the kitchen table.

Potato and choko skins, celery leaves and taproot strings, apple cores, peel, pods – so much fester and rot piled on top of her, flung across her meagre chest, the thin rods of her collarbone, pouching in her aproned lap. A prank, a bit of slapstick, except for the bloody film looping from my grandmother's chin, dribbling to the floor. Except for the empty scrap bucket swinging from JG's fist.

'Oh, Rory.' Grandma's voice is tiny and dry, her lips shock-white. 'What have we done?'

Trickle trickle melts the mess. *Plink plink plink*, sobs the dull metal pot, chunks of dead beast begging, trembling inside.

'If a girl tells eight lies every day,' says JG, 'for a whole week, how many lies does she rack up?'

The taste of soft broken spine fills my mouth.

'How many lies, *girl*?'

Surges of sick strike the back of my throat. 'Fifty-six.'

'Oh, darling.' My grandmother shudders, tremors taking over. 'Oh, my poor d—'

'And how many would a girl get, a very *prideful* girl, if she gets eight whacks for every letter of her name?

The bucket in his hand squeaks as it swings.

'J-Jay?' I stammer. 'She … Jay'd get … get twenty-four.'

Swing. *Squeak.*

'Only got given the one name, did she?'

Swing. *Squeak.*

I know what he's doing.

'Just "Jay" is it, this prideful cunt?'

Bettering me.

'Rory Jay Murphy.' The words fire out of me like buckshot. 'Rory Jay Murphy would get one hundred and four. Eight thirteens are one hundred and four.'

'She's quick, this one.' JG smiles. 'A right scholar.'

He goes to the refrigerator, pulls out the Aberdeen sausage.

'Hungry?' he asks, the plate jabbed forward. 'Oh no, that's right,' he says. 'Mumma's sausage isn't good enough for Lady Muck.'

He has always called his wife Mumma.

Mumma? I said once, so little JG still carried me on his hip. *That not Mumma! Gram-ma!*

Only once.

If she were coming home, my mother would be here by now. But it's Friday, and Vic says, *Happy hour, Lonnie? Nev's got a new car. How 'bout a spin?*

The rolled and crumbed meat drops to the table. My grandmother shivers.

JG holds a cleaver above the cut end, pauses. 'Whoops,' he says. 'Don't want none-a that bad bit.'

I watch him hack away at the uncut end, a monster indeed, just as he'd torn at it this morning, or late last night, at the *bad bit,* knowing it would find its way, as my lunch always does, to our potluck pup.

'So, scholar,' he says, chewing, the meat a grey clot jerking and wheeling across his tongue. 'How much-a this stuff d'ya reckon we'd need to kill a rat?' He snatches the bottle of jacks. The jacks he once gave me. The jacks I don't play with anymore, because I am ungrateful. An ungrateful cunt. He opens the bottle, pulls out the crumpled bag. Bait pellets, crushed. Spreadable.

'Say ... a thirty-pound orange *rat*?'

'Let me see to him, John,' pleads my grandmother, trying to get to her feet.

But JG only crunches her shoulder, his slaughterhouse hands cracking her bones like a bird's, the way our chooks' bones crack when JG kills one and tells my grandmother to boil it with barley and carrots for our tea.

Monday, 11:56 am

'All we need is a replacement iPad every three or four years, to stay in touch with the app's updates. But you can't fund that. You won't. The agency only funds what we don't need, though you're suggesting we should take that anyway – goods and services we don't actually require. Correct me if I'm wrong, Rohan?'

It is time for our annual National Disability Insurance Scheme review. This is how it works in theory:

Our government funds agencies, like Rohan's, to collect information on the needs and circumstances of families like mine. Based on this information, a 'care and support' package is calculated.

And here is how it works in practice:

'Mrs Gunnersen, I know it's not ideal. Nothing's perfect.'

'Rohan,' I say calmly, 'I don't expect perfection. Just common sense. It's Gun–DER–sen, by the way. But Jay will do.'

Rohan is our family's local area coordinator. He perches awkwardly at one end of Teddy's workstation – once a dining table – a laptop balanced on his thighs. Rohan has many information leaflets and sheets of paper to find space for amid the coils of thera-tubing and nests of drinking straws, and rain sticks and tambourines and emotion charts, lava timers, puffer balls and jigsaw puzzles. Not to mention my painting gear: Spakfilla and spatulas, scrapers, tape, primer, rollers and tins of Dubious Rubious Red.

I could have straightened things up, but I have been told that the messier your house is when a Rohan visits, the better. Evidence of substance abuse, whisky-breath if nothing else, apparently works in one's favour. Confoundingly, evidence of coping, of *not* being overwhelmed, does not. Just like the prime-time current affairs shows, the National Disability Insurance Agency is interested in us only once we have fallen apart, under a desk clucking like a chicken, our streets a crime scene. Only then, I have been reliably informed, support flows freely. So I weighed up buying a pack of Camel unfiltereds and stuffing it into the top of my bra, but I knew I couldn't be trusted not to smoke them, so I chose instead to run with the ample raw materials already at our disposal.

'Mrs Gunnersen—'

'Let's sum this up, Rohan,' I say, talking over him. 'I have a sick boy to look after and neither of us has time to waste, I imagine. And it's Jay, remember?'

A block tower Teddy built earlier this morning clatters to the floor as I speak. I hope the noise doesn't wake him.

I feel sorry for this young man, I truly do. Rohan is one of many tasked by the NDIA to come into strangers' homes and tick boxes and report data in seemly patterns, however unseemly their discoveries may be. Shove us all into a pair of one-size-fits-all, flesh-toned pantyhose that, in truth, only ever fit the most primly proportioned. But there is little about any disability that is prim.

'Under the old state-based system,' I say, 'such a shambles, apparently, it had to be expunged at great cost to the taxpayer, a non-verbal child in need of a "voice" received a replacement iPad every three to four years. But under this new federal scheme, a non-verbal child is no longer eligible for this purchase.'

Rohan's shoulders sag. I'm *one of those* cases.

'Mrs Gunnersen—'

'Why have a state-run shambles when we could have a federal clusterfuck, right, Rohan?'

'Mrs Gunnersen—'

'Because instead of what we need, the agency would be happier to fund some random person to play mother, to do what I'm already doing, though without my knowledge or experience while I go back to work. Correct?'

'Mrs Gunnersen, the agency prioritises—'

'The agency wants to replace Mrs Gun-*der*-sen with a stranger. Are you aware of what happens to some people in "care", Rohan?'

I am being rude. I am *going too far*. Jerrik says so all the time. *You go too far, wife*. Yes, Jerrik, I do. Because when you are nice to a disability bureaucrat your case gets shuffled to the bottom of the pile to be looked at by ...

Katrina?

Yeah, Trina can have a look at it when she gets back from ...

Sick leave? Her back, wasn't it?

Long service? Parenting?

Or the new guy, let him have a squiz ...

Darren, isn't it?

The acting SO6 from ... Transport?

Mines?

The guy with the Bugatti?

Fisheries? Tourism?

Anyone know where Darren's from? We need him to look at this thing.

Rohan holds one of his many booklets, offers it slow, lazy blinks. He looks tired, possibly hungover. He reminds me of a nurse shark. A tired, bored, hungover one. A creature less interested in food or mating than it is in being motionless and undisturbed on the ocean floor.

'Let me ask you something, Rohan. Do you have a little sister? A niece? Cousin?'

'Lark,' he sighs wearily. 'Niece.'

'How old?'

'Six.'

Poor Rohan, beaten down by *the wife who goes too far*, reduced to monosyllabic responses.

'And can you imagine any circumstances wherein six-year-old Lark would be sent off on an unsupervised outing with a person entirely unknown to her and her family?'

Rohan returns to his booklet.

'But the agency thinks it's a good idea to do just that to children with special needs? To send kids off, adults too for that matter, extremely vulnerable people, with a total stranger?'

Rohan, impatiently. 'Yes. To ... all that.'

He wants to get on with our interview and leave. I didn't want an interview to begin with. But that's what happens when you live in a country so savagely fond of rolling out one monopoly after another.

'Support agencies all thoroughly vet—'

'Their workers, yes. And I can imagine the rigour, Rohan, I can. Though it's likely to be a different person each time, isn't it? It's not like we're assigned a worker or team of workers who might accrete knowledge and understanding of the person they're supporting.'

'Ideally, they'd try to ...' I watch Rohan struggling to gussy up the flyblown truth. 'Yes, it may well be someone new each time. Unless you recruit your own workers. You're more than free to find your own support team, Mrs Gun-*der*-sen.'

'Write a job advertisement, place that job advertisement, interview and recruit applicants, train them? I'm so pleased I'm free to do all those things myself, Rohan. And then do them all over again when the person I've selected changes their uni timetable or decides to go backpacking in New Zealand. I can't wait.'

'Are you a lawyer by any chance, Mrs Gundersen?'

'No, Rohan. Just a mother. The only one of us here with skin in the game.'

194

'Coz I feel like I'm being cross-examined.'

Docile as they are, nurse sharks bite hard when provoked.

'You represent an agency that represents a government whose scheme is about to take five-eighths of the fuck-all we once received but that I could at least spend on stuff my children *actually* needed. How would you have me respond to that, Rohan? With cake and sparklers?'

I don't raise my voice. A stealth missile, Jerrik once described me.

'And these support workers,' I continue, 'they'd be experienced in caring for non-verbal children? Teddy uses Proloquo2go. Almost ten years now. We'd need someone with a thorough knowledge of that app. Trained in AAC, are they, your workers?'

With another sigh, Rohan's glassy pale eyes look up. I fill in the blanks: 'Augmentative and Alternative Communication.'

'Yes, I did … I did know that,' says Rohan. 'So many terms.'

'And those workers would all be trained in the use of Teddy's communication app?'

'No, Mrs Gundersen. They probably would not.'

'So who would be responsible for training them, Rohan?' I ask. 'Oh, I know. *Me.* Even though we may have a different support worker each time? Would you look forward to training someone new to do your job every other day or every other week, Rohan? With no guarantee of an end to it?'

'Mrs Gundersen. I don't make the rules. I—'

'How on earth does Teddy *access* anything if he and his "carer" can't communicate?'

Rohan reaches for the glass of water I offered on his arrival, glugs it to the bottom. 'I see you're doing some home renovation,' he says, a chin-nod at the painting paraphernalia.

'So, you can cover Teddy's speech pathology sessions?' I say, less lawyer now than locomotive. 'And the OT?'

195

'Yes, we sure can,' says Rohan, grateful to land on a tickable box. 'Do the boys have any other therapies?'

Hard to forget the years of Applied Behaviour Analysis I subjected Teddy to. The 'king of therapies' back then that demanded a king's ransom – eighty thousand dollars for eighteen months of drilled cup-stacking and hand-clapping and Pavlovian reinforcement. 'Three more, Teddy, then a break. Two more, Teddy, then a sultana.' Every cent borrowed from the bank; a debt yet outstanding. After that came the three-days-a-week early intervention program – fifty thousand for those two years. At the same time, tackling Frank's anxiety and his speech disfluency – an 'autistic stutter' according to some, a stammer that veers 'off book' to others. A psychologist and speech pathologist working in tandem, two appointments a week for years until we decided, Frank and I, that it was up to us, the rest of the way.

'No,' I reply. 'No other therapies. But about that iPad—'

'Across the board on that one,' says Rohan. 'No iPads for anyone.'

'Even when my son has no voice without it?'

Rohan raises his hands in surrender. 'Out of my hands, I'm afraid.' A willing surrender.

'Teddy's not been well lately, Rohan,' I say. 'He's lying down. Would you like to meet him?'

'Mrs Gundersen. The position on iPads is a lock.' Rohan's lips worm about his face. 'No exceptions.'

'Sure. But seriously, Rohan. Just *listen* to how mad this is. I could go back to work – Lord only knows where, given how long I've been out of paid employment. But let's say I pull on a bullseye T-shirt every day, restock Bangladeshi fast fashion and earn, what? Twenty-five bucks an hour? And while I'm off doing that, the agency will shell out sixty dollars an hour to a support worker – that's about the current rate, isn't it? That's in the ballpark of one hundred thousand dollars a year, Rohan, to a revolving door of unqualified people to babysit my children. If we had a *trained* caring industry it would be different. If our government invested in skilling those workers, mothers like me wouldn't be mothers like me. We'd be dewy of skin and zen of mind. One hundred thousand dollars *every year* as opposed to twelve hundred every three, because that's all we're asking for. Do you hear how arse-clenchingly ridiculous that sounds?'

Rohan makes no reply, only wets his still crawly lips. Those lips want off that face and out of this house.

Teddy slowly emerges from our room. Headphones on, iPad in hand, too unwell for his usual chirrs and trills. His skin is cuttlefish dry and clay-white.

'Hey, bear cub,' I say, 'this is Rohan. Want to say hello?'

Teddy opens his communication app. 'Hello, I am Teddy,' says Liam. Surveying the scattered blocks, Teddy begins rebuilding his tower, Google-searching at the same time.

Rohan's reply is a glum, 'Mate.'

'Your building fell,' I say. 'Teddy fix it?'

'Jump jump.' Teddy sits down in the puddle of blocks – cautious, like an old man. He closes the app, returning to Google.

'The problem with having rectangular pupils,' explains Siri, 'is that goats cannot look up or down without moving their heads.'

'Teddy is quite taken by goats at the moment,' I explain to Rohan. 'He's kind enough to share his knowledge.'

'Just as our accents and inflections vary according to where we come from, a particular goat's bleat will sound different to the bleat of a goat from another country.'

'I certainly did not know that,' I say. 'Thanks, Ted.'

Having repaired his tower, Teddy gets to his feet. He is somehow both flushed and worryingly pale, contrasts that wipe each other out. The colour of cancelled. On his way back to our room, he pauses, inspecting Rohan.

'If he touches your ears,' I tell the government man, 'don't spook. Teddy's always very gentle.'

Rohan flinches nonetheless as Teddy runs his fingertips down and around the pinna of his ear, the lobe, his fingers circling lightly, pressing, examining. He reopens the communication app before turning away.

'February,' says Liam, he and Teddy disappearing down the hallway. 'February. February. February.'

I get up, begin gathering Rohan's papers and leaflets and brochures, wedging them into a not very neat pile.

'February?' says Rohan, getting the message and shutting down his laptop. 'February means …?'

'That you're an Aquarius. Or a Pisces.'

Rohan stops his packing away. 'Ye-ah. February 9. But how …? Did he just …?'

'Teddy's a mind-reader. A soothsayer, Rohan. Clairvoyant. The police even call upon his sixth sense sometimes. You haven't seen him on the news?'

'Whoa. That's amazing!'

I thank Rohan for his time and close the door behind him, wishing I had at least one of those Camel unfiltered to see me through the bin-fire remains of this day.

5:36 pm

Early evening, post Rohan.

Teddy and I, nose-to-nose on his slim bed. I hope it's contagious. I hope I catch its eye, this bastard sickness, and that it wants me more.

There is a fog. Impenetrable. Through the windows we can see precisely nothing, blindfolded by a meaty ghost-grey felt. We're specimens, a giant mournful face pressed to our glass jar.

Jerrik calls. Everyone is stranded at the office, too dangerous to be on the roads. Not that anyone is doing much. All eyes are glued to it, tongues tuned to it – rarer, all agree, than an eclipse. This city of tropical monotony sees no such fogs. Jerrik will have to stay put.

'*Jeg er ked af det.* Sorry,' he says.

'It's fine,' I say. 'Don't apologise.'

Teddy's mystery, on-again off-again illness has been more an inconvenience than a concern for Jerrik. His recent short fuse we can all do without. 'Don't worry about it. See you after the fog.'

'No,' says Jerrik. 'You won't, Queenie.'

The tone in his voice, a long time coming. 'I see.'

'I'm moving in with Minnie.'

When the boys arrived, I had work to do, hammers to swing, things to slay. Head down, all-in kind of work, what I'm good at. No time for anything else. That was me.

'I see,' I say again. And I do.

And he stuck at it, Jerrik, he did. For as long as a man such as he possibly could – a faithless voluptuary, easily distracted. That was him.

And that was us.

'*Jeg er en skiderik,*' he says. 'I'm a bastard. You know this.'

'You're certainly something,' I say.

'Why didn't you do something, Jay?'

And I ask, 'About what?'

'About me,' he replies. 'Why didn't you do something about me?'

'Should we run outside?' I ask Teddy when I end the call. 'Hold out our arms, watch them disappear? Fall backwards into the warm grey glug?'

Teddy looks from me to the window.

'Tag along when it ships out?'

He sits up, amazed, perhaps afraid.

'Just kidding, kiddo.' I wave to the fog, blow it a kiss. 'Hello, fog. Thanks for stopping by.'

Teddy, still following my lead, waves at the fog, blows a kiss. Nobody blows kisses like Teddy.

Lying down again, he sets his chin delicately in the whorl of my ear, holds it there for minutes on end. Our fingers lace, he squeezes, I squeeze, back and forth we go. I have never known if this brings him some kind of sensory relief or feedback, or if it is simply something we have always done. Our ritual. His body simmers, his temperature back up, his skin the colour of sucked-over bones. He smells hollow. I open a story, but he closes the book at once, puts it back on the pile by his bed, resettles his chin in my ear.

Teddy and I both sleep a little, until something kicks open my eyes, drags its brown breath down my face. It does its job so well, they all do, the Other Things – feeding fear, starving rest. When you are little and alone, they know where to tickle and prod. They know just where to land in the hallway, on its loosest board, to cause the creak that wakes you. And when you are older, they know what to whisper and when – the right hour, the right day. The very pitch, the very tone, the just-right register in your ear to make your guts run.

I lie with Teddy all night. Frank sleeps on my bed. The three of us in the same room, as we were for so long.

Close enough to save each other? Close enough to all perish at once? Keep, from above us.

The corner man again – yet nothing like a man. Immense, both terrible and exquisite, the wings of no possible bird, the crushing limbs of a beast. A box of madness, unlocked, and a vigil kept for my children, as it was so often for me.

Still more powerful than a god, Spider?

We look at one another for a long while.

'You sure pick your moments, Keeper. But yes, I am. Of course

I am. Mothers can kill their children in their sleep or serve them cake for breakfast. What god can do that?'

I hear them, the Other Things, stirring, a red rustle. They can't help themselves, their scaled tongues thirsty for any lick of sorrow. One a slither behind the drawers. Another retracts its mutant wing, but not before I see it (it *wants* to be seen), a scrum of tattered membrane. It brays and grunts beneath the bed. The whole room their lair. Some serpent their way back to the pile, to my scrapbooks, where I collect their stories.

Is that your plan?

'I have a plan, Keeper?' I scoff. Bitter.

To kill your children in their sleep.

Teddy, a faraway bubble, turns to face the wall, his thin knees drawing up to his chest.

'If I have to.'

In the early morning half-light, Teddy sits on the toilet for an hour. Purple with straining, he produces only a dribble of urine and a bowl full of blood.

Twelve kilos gone, and we're off to hospital.

12 years old | After Paddy – Day 1

Grandma's pills – one, two, three.

Like three bowls of porridge.

Too hot, too cold, just right, says Mother, placing them

so gently

onto the big metal spoon

the big dipper

so cared for, these pills

swimming in honey.

Day 2

Mother and JG outside my room. My back to them.

'I had to knock her out,' says Mother. 'Couldn't have her going to school and saying things.'

He walks to my bed. 'About what?' *Pah … hwoo.*

'About Paddy.'

'A dead bloody dog?'

'I got applications in with schools,' Mother says. Whisper whisper. 'Posh schools. What if one of 'em calls St Bernie's, does one of them, you know, check-up type things, gets wind of—'

'Gets wind-a what?'

The maggoty voice. Mr Slappy.

'Dog ate somethin' it shouldn't. End of.'

Anyone, *please*, but Mr Magoo.

My eyelids, so heavy they won't hold up. My tongue, a nasty crust.

'No fear-a this one sayin' much,' he says. 'Sookin' baby.'

Bill! BILL?

Marjorie?

Bill, what happened to Baby Jay?

My mind a jigsaw, pieces wet, a jellyfish squish. Nothing fits.

'But I reckon she'll do as she's told from now on,' says my grandfather. 'Won't ya, sook?'

Day 3

'Get her arse back to school, Lon.'

School. My Lapland book. I gave it to Evie when she left, when her family went back home. Mrs Barron said I could.

My magic book, Evie. It's yours.

It'll help us find each other, Blue Jay, she said. *One day.*

I don't care if they shake me again.

Day 4

Night. All night. Every night.

The smoke gives him away. I don't need to look to see him sitting in the greyed-out blear of the kitchen, his head against the wall. No body, just a half-face, a flicker as he inhales, the side that no longer has a mouth.

Pah ... hwoo.

The sound enters my body – a warning, running me through.

Day 5

Another day, not sure which one. Another night.

The garden gate squeaks. JG with fruit for our breakfast, sliced poison for our lunch.

Day 6

And another.

'Open up,' says the dainty 'o' of her mouth. 'I've gotta go to work. So you gotta go to sleep.' The big dipper held to my lips. 'Too hot, too cold, just right,' she says.

Day 7

Keep has horns. A pane of luminous purple, like a window, cuts through him, and in it are his hundred pairs of eyes. They dazzle, so bright my insides show, like a glass frog. His arms, flat against the walls, stretch around the room like branches, ancient and strong. I curl up inside him, my frightful thing. Friend, before I even knew him.

The day he arrived, he told me his name was Keep. I knew what *keep* meant, I wasn't a baby. Among other things, it is the stronghold of a castle, its beating heart, princely safe. Where everyone runs when enemies attack. Still, I checked up on *keeper*, just in case I'd missed something, in Doubleday Dennis's A–L hostage.

Keeper—noun
(say keepuh)
1. someone who keeps or guards.
2. a gamekeeper.
3. a wicketkeeper.
4. a shopkeeper.
5. a goalkeeper.
6. a person in charge of something valuable, as the custodian of a museum, zoo, or any section thereof.
7. something that keeps, or serves to guard etc.

Here, hold my hands. Don't let go, Spider.
'I won't, Keep,' I say. 'Together forever.'

Day 8

Every morning, every evening, three more pills. All our nerves, sorted.

'If you say anything,' she says, 'I'll deny it. We all will and you'll be taken away. Put in a home. A workhouse for bad girls. You'll go mad, good and proper.'

Day 9

She leaves for work. I wobble to the window, drag books back to bed with me. I can't read, the words a blur, but I open *Picasso: Idolised and Isolated* – one of Book Brian's dump finds. I turn to my favourite painting.

Les deux saltimbanques. I looked up what this means. Harlequin and his companion. The two acrobats.

Damaged by water, this book, bled through with stain. But no amount of warping could make this picture less perfect to me, its story more alive with detail every time I look. Catching her before she falls is his job; trusting he will deliver her safely is hers. Takings are poor and they are tired, but their work high above the crowds is breathtaking, dangerous. They are symmetry, no point of one without the other.

'Dunno what you see in it,' said Mother before I stopped showing it to her, trying to make her love it too. 'Most art's garbage.'

But there's something about these beautiful two, this couple in their spill-sticky booth. Yes, they look sad, as though they've never known a day of happiness, but the way her shoulder leans, so weary, into his, their misery is their bond. They wouldn't be them without it. They will leave together, and the next night they will be back with the few coins they have, their warming little drinks, listening to the crooner in the corner, the lonely strumming. I press the book to my face, I breathe.

206

Day 10

Mother, home again. Her tread up the front stairs lighter than yesterday's. Happy Mother. Someone must have paid her a compliment.

She pauses by the door of my room, but leaves again without a word, fries some eggs, and talks to Mike as he reads her all his news.

Day 11

On the wall, Captain Kent's poster. Irish Terriers, red-gold like Paddy, standing in streams or running in wintry fields, muzzles of snow. Captain Kent had delivered after all, many weeks too late for my morning talk. But no tea towel for my grandmother, who paid dearly for the postage, as she knew she would.

Next to the terriers, a map of the world. A pin in northern Finland, Lapland, and two in the United States – Wilmington, Delaware, where Mr Mayhew returned to work, and the other in Ann Arbor, Michigan, where Evie was born. I've been talking to the first pin since grade three, when Sister Ernestine told us all about the northern lights in geography class. And I've been talking to the other two every day for the past year.

I cry, but no tears come.

Day 12

Now when she arrives home from the office, she doesn't even come to my room. I think it's easier for my mother, this new way for us to be.

I wonder where my grandmother is, why she hasn't come down the hill to see me? My grandma-bird, with the broken wing.

Day 13

The next day, a rush up the front steps, a torn envelope in her hand. 'I got you in! I got you in! We're going to Mercy Grammar! I got you in, Missy!'

One Saturday morning, months ago, I sat in a room to be tested, glad to miss tennis. Three hours, rows and rows of girls behind desks. Some knew each other, but no-one talked to me except the nuns who gave out the tests – maths, English, science, logic. I'd never heard of logic. Mother outside all the while, pacing by the windows. It seems I passed, and have been offered a scholarship.

We are going to Mercy Grammar.

Day 14

Another Monday, I think.

The underside of her car scrapes the driveway. Her approach up the stairs, like the dropping of small bombs. Cyclone Lonnie.

She says one day I'll leave her. 'That's your plan, isn't it? *Isn't it?*'

I have a plan?

Screaming until she can no longer scream.

'You'll leave me to rot, won't you?'

She starts to cry and comes to sit on the edge of my bed. I don't move a muscle. So thirsty.

'Well, that'll never happen, got it? Not so long as there's breath in my body.'

Cry-screaming. Scream-crying.

'You'd have nothing if it weren't for me. *Nothing!*'

This is one of those ideas that come to her, a mischief that adds to itself, that pecks and pecks at her like a thing's pin-sharp beak. But so real, to my mother.

'And you're going nowhere, you hear me, Missy? Not without my say-so! Not without *me!*'

Heaped over now, sobbing, struggling to breathe.

I am pretending I am dead. Poisoned.

She reaches over, grips my hand, not kindly. Her weight lifts from the mattress. Almost six o'clock, after all. Mike will be waiting.

More pills and honey.

Department of Emergency Medicine

Here's a request for …

  A request for …

  And we're going to need …

  Scans, scopes, bloods and dyes.

  'I suppose a rectal contrast would be out of the question?'

  I can't tell if this is hospital humour or a genuine ask.

  They start out with: 'Hi, Teddy, I'm Doctor—'

  And end with: 'I suppose this must be Teddy.'

  'Are you guys still here?' asks a nurse at the end of her twelve-hour shift. 'Poor you. They shouldn't be much longer.'

  Security, ward staff, even car-park personnel are summoned for the first blood test. 'Are we all here?' one laughs. Shoulder-strapped walkie-talkies crackle. Three wall-off the cubicle, preventing some imagined escape. One of them brags about the good old days of Goulburn, how easy it was to 'subdue'.

  Those not part of the wonderwall pin Teddy down as he screams and fights, as his senses overload and catch fire. It takes two of them to hold down a single leg. One restrains Teddy's right arm, another hauls his bulk across his chest and middle. The last of them helps a female nurse to steady the hand to be cannulated. Eight people needed to hold down my son, sick as he is. Eight strangers and one shaky doctor. Hands fly from nowhere, my own, fumbling at my face, stopping my lips, controlling what can be controlled.

209

Last term, three weeks, it'll pass. Wrong, wrong. *Get someone to look at his teeth.* Wrong. Wrong floor, wrong building, wrong call. I wait for someone to look up: *Can we help you?* they'll ask.

Yes, no, I don't know.

What do you *want, Jay?*

A cannula is inserted into the back of Teddy's left hand. Twenty-one hours and fifty-four minutes to get us to here.

Two security personnel stay on to 'guard the site' until the sedation takes over.

They lift Teddy from the gurney, slump him into a weigh chair.

Fourteen kilograms gone.

There's nothing about a child that its mother can't fuck up.

'Biopsies will tell us more,' says someone, hair as black as a crow's feathers, arms too thin to be wings – they look like oars. A hopeless half-bird in scrubs.

'Is my son dying?'

'We don't think so,' says someone else, Doctor Someone Else. 'But he *is* in trouble.'

We are transferred to a ward.

A week lost in this whirlpooling place, its trapdoor treatment rooms. We've crossed a river, Teddy and I, the price of passage not our pennies, but our surrender.

An intravenous dose of diazepam every eight hours. Wrist restraints to protect the cannula.

General anaesthesia daily.

Tiny capsuled eyes trawl the sly verticils of my son's failing body. What is hard to see is harder to fix, they all caution.

Another three heads appear at our door, conjoined in the corner of my eye. 'Gut-related?' says the first.

'Immuno?' posits the second, stroking a beard that hangs from his face like a bat hangs dead from a powerline. Residual lunch festers in that dead-bat beard. It has its own breath.

'The brain? The pituitary?' queries the third, twisting her crane's neck.

'Those lymph nodes? Suspicious?' asks a fourth, late to the conference, tiny toenails painted bog-green.

'*Clinically insignificant!*' snarl the three, erupting at her like junkyard dogs.

'But the electrolytes!' The half-bird, her territory under attack. 'Anyone heard of *REFEEDING SYNDROME*?'

Nineteen kilos – almost a third of tall Teddy – gone.

~~A coma~~ Immediate intubation – their only point of agreement. Exclusive enteral nutrition via a ~~feeding tube~~ percutaneous endoscopic gastrostomy.

'Nourish him, at least.' A synchronised nod. 'Doing nothing takes time.' Another pod-nod. 'Deciding nothing takes longer.' The heads don't like to be hurried.

'In the meantime, the boy needs to be fed.'

'But,' I challenge. 'His sensory issues …? A feeding tube …? When he wakes up, he'll fight it. What if he pulls it out? Teddy won't understand.'

'Let us tell you how hospitals work,' roars one of the dogs. I feel like a sheep, bucking between its jaws.

'~~His therapists~~ Baaaaa,' I say. I don't think they can hear me. '~~You need to talk to them~~ Baaaaa. ~~They know Teddy. They can~~ Baaaaa ~~help us help him~~.'

Eyes blink. The beard twitches. The crane pecks at her lunch of berries. 'Did she say something?' the crane asks her colleagues. I am Schenck's anguished ewe, grieving, surrounded. How do I make them understand?

'This is so extreme,' I cry, hands still raised in surrender, shoulders welded by ache. 'Shouldn't diagnosis be the priority?'

'It's care *our* way, or care withdrawn, Mrs ..., Mrs ...' Scanning forms for my name. Do they even know who we are? 'Without it, he DIES!'

The heads weave and whir around me, so close they knot into one. 'Up to you, you're the mother! You're the MOTHER!'

I see myself reflected in their many eyes, a grotesque of mirrors that diminish me – ever older and smaller – until I disappear, leaving Teddy behind, alone, his hand held out to no-one, fingers squeezing the empty air, squeezing, squeezing.

'Up to you, you're the mother!'

Above us, a wooden sculpture – giant parrots, heads eyeless and tumescent.

'You're the mother!'

I can't see. I can't breathe. I wish Teddy and I had run away with the fog when we had the chance. I don't know what to do.

Everything falls silent as the half-bird emerges from the rear, a clipboard thrust in my face.

'Sign here,' she caws.

Ward 9

Another week of saline solutions and investigations. If they can find the cause, intubation may yet be avoided.

When you don't know where to start, you start at the top and work down, on the outside and work in. Brain and neck scans, organ MRIs, everything requiring general anaesthesia because Teddy, terrified, can't lie still for long enough as the metal plates close in on him, clicking and spinning. On some occasions, two GAs in one day.

'She's a *peach* that one, room 37,' I hear the nurse complain. 'How was I supposed to know an ID band was gonna freak her kid out!'

I don't know. She might have asked.

212

She might have borne in mind she works in a paediatric hospital.

She might have noticed that Teddy isn't quite like other children. The ever-present headphones? The flapping? The hovering mother with her iPad communiqués?

A peach, am I? Better than a common pigeon, I suppose, which is all I see when I look at them. Tiny heads peck pecking, beaks open in their little nest-stations – rosters, meal breaks, parking – eyes dull with alarm-ennui.

Haircuts, coffee cups, Birkenstocks, Insta.

Less focus, though, on the care of my son.

Peachy enough, I am, to minister to my own. To watch Teddy around the clock, motes of sleep on a two-inch foam window seat. His vomit dealt with, though they swiftly show me where to dispose of it, give generously of their stocks of disinfectant and towelettes but never their assistance. Show me too where to find clean sheets so I can change his bed myself, fetch extra blankets once the self-help linen trolley empties out. Soap and shampoo when I ask for them, notwithstanding a two- or three-day response window. I brush Teddy's teeth and his hair and shower him every evening, the pigeons generously winging in to 'see if I need anything'. Every drop relinquished by Teddy's bladder, every peristaltic crinkle of his bowel – the under-surveillance bowel – recorded, spreadsheeted on my laptop: time, volume, colour, blood: Y/N, mucus: Y/N, a scale of discomfort.

The nurses take temperatures, change IV bags, but the daily cares of my son, their patient, and the upkeep of his room in their hospital are not, apparently, a Ward 9 pigeon's purview.

Let us tell you how hospitals work.

A place where it is better – for the sake of your child – to be a prickly parent who does the donkey work than a charmer with her feet up.

Hold-ups. Reschedulings.

Imaging equipment broken, offline.

A bed shortage. Only thirty-six in all of paediatric intensive care. Thirty-six beds for an entire state's children. All occupied.

Teddy's refusal to drink contrast dyes.

Teddy's refusal to be fed through a tube down his throat.

Teddy's falling away.

Jerrik and I called to a meeting with all departments thus far involved in Teddy's case – General Paediatrics, Immunology, Gastroenterology and Hepatology, Infectious Diseases. The half-bird, the beard, the crane, Doctor Someone Else, and respective attendant registrars. Youth Mental Health because at some stage someone scribbled somewhere the word *anorexia* and the word *Munchausen* and two question marks. Consultants about to become involved in Teddy's case add to the pile-on – intensive care, surgical, stoma services. Nurse liaison, occupational therapy (at long last), pharmacists. Around a large conference table, Jerrik and I on Team Teddy, eighteen medical staff on the other.

We discuss results: nothing diagnostically conclusive.

I ask again: 'Is my son dying?'

Thirty-six eyes drop from my face. The carpet is scrutinised, dry lips soundlessly moistened. Pens pawed, set down, turned in half-circles.

Doctor Someone Else: 'We don't know.'

But the feeding tube must be inserted without further delay. Day after tomorrow, Teddy goes into a coma.

Paediatric Intensive Care Unit (PICU)

In the room next to Teddy's is a newborn. A boy. Frail, it goes without saying. He lies on his chest in a clear box. Tubes run through him, sticky sensors measle him, as they do Teddy, but miniature versions. I hear one of the many doctors declare that the

214

baby is diabetic, 'among other things'. When these Other Things are discussed, voices in that room dial down. The mother is asked, at least once a day, if her pregnancy had been routine. 'Yes,' she answers, less shocked than offended. 'This is the first I've heard about anything.' Her husband arrives, well groomed. Husband and wife wear rings that cannot be unnoticed. The newborn has a sister, aged four or five. Indie. Billboard-pretty, his family.

I wish I knew the child's name; I never hear it spoken, but I know he will have a surgery tomorrow, more in the coming weeks. The couple is worried about the effects of the general anaesthetic. The surgeon tries to reassure them, but says something like, 'That's the least of our worries at present,' and then leaves. With a laugh. A doctor's laugh – one quite relaxed in its own company, even as it rips through the chill-blue belly of the ward. He clip-clops away down the corridor, his glossy black clogs like hooves.

Six o'clock and the parents turn on the evening news in their son's room. The volume is absurd, unnerving, the faux-fawning voices – *Back to you, Ray. Thanks so much, Tamsin* – gonging along the floor. The percussive clang of the Bunnings and banking commercials pitch me to my feet. Kissing Teddy's forehead – the only part of his comatose face not vandalised by clamps and valves and tape – I tell the nurse I'm going for a walk. He nods. The room is tight and mechanised, grimly purposed. His job is to patrol and refill and adjust. Mine is to watch and wait. I know it is a relief to be free of me.

Paediatric intensive care is all light, all white, all glass. A whole floor of frostbite. I glance into the baby's room as I slide closed Teddy's door. In his box, the infant is panting, doing his best to breathe, but the faces of his mother and father tilt up at the television, reverential, as though heeding a prophet. Their eyes never turn from the leering screen, even as words jab and ping between them: protest, highway, hamburger, ute. Indie sits on the floor with her father's big phone, ensorcelled as a kitten with a ball of yarn.

The Other Things are newborn too. I see them nestling close to the tiny boy, their breath butcher-red.

I sit on a bench in the walkway, just inside the doors of the secured ward. On the walls, fairy lights and children's art. A welcome change from the panels of pork-grey electrical sockets in Teddy's room. Twenty-three in all. Twenty-three pinched little socket-faces.

Greenland – population fifty-six thousand, capital Nuuk, coldest recorded temperature …

I can't think about temperatures.

Inside Teddy's room, time is like a high-speed train, rocketing, as it does, from AM doctors' rounds, to blood test, to nasogastric feed, to alarm, to bed-bath, to urine sample, to alarm, to test results, to the next blood test, to PM doctors' rounds, to refills, to tube changes, to nurse handovers, to another exhausted vein, another cannulation.

Out here it is a bastard trickle, lugging about on its heels, pleasing only itself. I sit until parts of me become numb, then I stand. I stand until I can no longer ignore myself, until I feel too conspicuous, a hallway hazard, and then I sit again. I long for something to hold. An ugly throw cushion, a cigarette I may or may not smoke, a hand. I think of Teddy's game of squeeze. Perhaps it has been for my sake, all along.

Frank texts me often, all through the day. Late at night: *Good night Mummy Bear sweet dreams*, and in the morning: *Good morning Mummy Bear I hope you slept well.* Complaints about the porridge Jerrik (whose flight to Minnie's failed to launch as a result of me rushing Teddy to hospital) made him eat for breakfast, how it looked like backed-up toilet paper. And countless more, minutes apart, no context provided though clearly clipped from a show or a footballer's interview. *If you can't find the ball find a man*, read one. Another: *His name was Jason … Jason was my son, and today is his birthday.* And: *So be it, Jedi* seems to be a preferred way of answering any question at all in the affirmative.

Me: *Make sure you eat an apple.*

Frank: *So be it, Jedi.*

Me: *Trimming your toenails? Using deodorant?*

Frank: *So be it, Jedi.*

I doubt these things are being done, and as good as force-persuasion is, I doubt it works on sweat glands.

In a single text Frank tells me that a stranger tried to lure a year eight boy waiting for the bus into his car, and of the release of a long-anticipated anime. He tells me Madison Fox is now talking to him, being friendly, laughing at his jokes. A text about how she has apparently invited him to sit with her and her *crew* at lunchtime. Such reports about such a girl concern me. I know too much not to worry. I need Jerrik to be aware of this. I know he will not be. Over the phone I apprise him, tell him about the fluoro-tangerine incident in the art room, how it was all staged, all of it to humiliate our son. Jerrik tells me it's great that the boy is finally making friends and that I should stop smothering him. I remind Jerrik to make sure Frank is applying his creams. Jerrik says he is. I ask if he's *actually* witnessing Frank *actually* doing it, if he's making *sure* those creams are being applied and Jerrik hangs up.

A recent scan detected a mass in Teddy's right hip. An MRI is being organised; awkward with an intubated patient, but not impossible. They don't know what they'll find. It could be nothing. It could be something.

Eighty-nine per cent of these are completely benign, offered one in the procession of doctors.

A less than ten per cent chance of ...

Nine-hundred and ninety-five children out of every thousand aren't affected by ...

Meaning:

Eleven per cent are malignant.

One in every ten will have this.

Five children are.

So: you either have it, or you don't. It is, or it isn't. He will; he won't.

All odds are fifty–fifty.

The gastrostomy was inserted three days ago. It can't be used for the first week, and then the surgical team wants to test it for a day or two, with formula feeds every three hours, to make sure all is well. They want to be able to do all that, they make it clear, without 'interference'. By that they mean interference from Teddy. So he must remain in the coma for at least another six days. A nine-day coma because Teddy can't cope with a feeding tube, and because a whole hospital can't cope with him. Six more days for bandit germs to claim his dazed body as their own.

And I agreed to this. I consented. *Sign here,* said General Paediatrics. *Without it he dies. Sign here,* or you're welcome to *take him to another state.* Try your luck elsewhere. Their words. If I hadn't consented to the gastrostomy, and so to the coma, they'd have *withdrawn care. Let nature take its course.*

'Let him die, you mean.'

Doctor General Paediatrics, her white half-bird eyes. Me, weeping like a fool. Doctor General Paediatrics, her oars passing me the Kleenex.

Fuck nature and its course. The coma has kept him alive, allowed

218

him to be fed. It has done that, so far. And on the other side of the coma, I will keep him alive. Me and his gastrostomy.

Is that your plan? To kill your children in their sleep? Keep in my head.

Yes, no, I don't know.

I only meant … I won't leave him behind. To be in someone's scrapbook. Some journalist's headline, filed before their evening blood-orange gin. What kind of mother would I be, to leave him all alone? He is a thing of this world, but it won't make a place for him. It is too small.

Is that your plan? To kill your children in their sleep?

No. Yes. Tell me why it shouldn't be.

I can't be certain. No-one will let me. Certainty is too hard. People would stop for a fallen baby bird, a flying fox, dig in for days to help a stranded whale. That's pretty certain. But for Teddy? Not so much. For Frank?

Guarantee me. I'll wait.

'Better off dead than disabled!' I hear the cries, the shrill outrage. 'She thought her children were better off dead than disabled!'

Not so, know-it-alls.

Better dead than abused, a variant hypothesis. Better dead than routinely raped, than 'managed' by dogs. Starved. Beaten. Better dead than to stew in his own shit until he dies of sepsis. Open a scrapbook, have a read. Until his cankered flesh is snacked on by vermin. Better dead than degraded.

Go ahead, guarantee me. A risk you'd be willing to take with your own child? Get down off your high horse and go and visit a 'facility'. Swear it, and I'll swear too. *Quid pro quo*. Swear he will be looked after, and you have a deal.

Alaska – population seven hundred and thirty-three thousand, capital Juneau, coldest recorded temperature -62°C, Camp Prospect Creek, 1971.

Uranus – population unknown, capital not applicable, coldest recorded temperature -223°C—

'Jay.'

It's Ryker Shulmans, Teddy's PICU consultant. He seems nice. He seems German. He seems to be offering me a handkerchief.

'Jay, let's have a talk.'

We have our talk, and I dry the tears I hadn't realised I'd cried.

Here and there he touches my shoulder. And then Ryker Shulmans goes on his break, and I am on my own again, time creep creeping, a weaselling thing behind my stooping back.

As with many intubated patients, Teddy has developed a chest infection. Pseudomonas is present in the surgical site. He has more to contend with now than ever before. Over the past week, spots of pink on his testes and neck indicate nascent vitiligo.

'Does he have any others?' asked the skin specialist called in to have a look.

Other whats? Necks? Pink spots?

'Rare to get only one.' He meant autoimmune diseases which, I have learnt, tend to hunt in packs.

The small patches of molluscum contagiosum that appeared a couple of months ago are out of control, growths the size of garden peas sprouting all over Teddy's face and thighs. I drown them in Doctor Wheatgrass several times a day. By the hour I watch them bloat, purple. Suffocate. It feels good to annihilate something.

Small bowel and bone marrow biopsies are next. And his neutrophil count is dropping, so another IV medication must be administered. Another vein to be cannulated. The neutropenia has triggered tests for aplastic anaemia, Evans syndrome, liver cancer, rheumatoid arthritis, tuberculosis. The alphabet of diseases.

According to my phone, it is still news time. I remain on my bench in the corridor, praying for Teddy to stay strong, for his veins to galvanise, for nothing else to grow on him, in him, willing his neutrophils to level out before the next round of blood tests. For the sports update to be done, the All Ords index, the weather report and anything else the newborn's noisy parents might have a mind to watch.

A large window looks over the northern reaches of the river. From where I sit I can see the river bridge, a city landmark. A function-first ugly duckling as bridges go, though a pretty lit thing by night.

Left of the bridge, Mercy Grammar. Its imposing, rampart-like retaining walls bestowed it a nickname: The Fortress. Born 1863, it was home to long draughty corridors, powdery Mothers Superior and staircases darkly stained – so wide, six girls abreast could climb them without touching. The last boarder left her dormitory only two years before I arrived. How I envied those girls, characters in all that history, bunking in with its ghosts and stories.

It was intimidating and exhilarating. And I belonged. I passed their tests and I belonged. My fortress, the last to be *my kind of place*.

From around a corner, two women, new mothers, one sobbing. I can't help but hear the young mother's tears, and the silence of the other who cannot possibly know what to say.

'They reckon she'll walk, one day, probably. But she's definitely vision impaired. As for all the other things … too early to tell.'

But I know she won't have long to wait. Other Things grow unfairly fast.

This is her first baby, her only baby, the baby who won't see but who might walk, might not. As the new mother speaks, her hands skim her belly – an exhausted post-partum sag. A voided, liminal place no longer shared yet not quite her own, its reputation blemished early, and forfeited for good. It will always shoulder the blame.

And I wish I could talk her through it: that day when she finally takes her child home and notices the leak in her ceiling. It will be in a room far down the hall, a spare room for storage, overnighters. She will place a bucket under the leak to catch the drips.

In the next downpour the leak will become urgent, the drips have more heft. The bucket fills quickly. She will buy one that is bigger, then another, many more. Her baby's father will try to patch it, but only makes it worse. The carpet is ruined. Crusty brown mould cankers the ceiling. It leaks even when it's not raining.

One night during a storm, the young mother will get up on a stepladder, hold a baby's blanket to the leak. Quickly sodden, it will be thrown to the floor, replaced by another, one that is thicker, then a towel, a blanket. Soon she'll have emptied the linen cupboard. She tapes plastic to the ceiling, but the tape won't hold. The whole roof sways with damp.

Before long the house is flooded, water ankle-deep. Furniture floats, table legs ooze and pulp.

One day, desperate, she will hold her mouth to the leak, and swallow.

With her lips to the ceiling she won't know if it is day or night. She will decide it doesn't matter. Nothing else will be done – no cakes baked, no play dates, everything stamped overdue. No time for more children; the mother dares not leave the drip. Her jaw will ache, and her child will cry, but she will stay focused, her mouth open, swallowing, swallowing. It is the only thing that works, more or less. The only thing that stops them being swept away. The leak will be all she consumes, other appetites gone. Her husband and the years will scatter.

People will check on her, from time to time, in the room far along the hall. They will praise her, her composure and strength. They will see she's no longer unmoored, as once she had been, her bloated blue lips now fused with the ceiling, her feet with the rusted tiers below. They will see she no longer frets about fixing the leak, no longer waits for the day when she will climb down from the ladder.

We'll see ourselves out, her visitors wave, *cheery bye*. Everyone so relieved, none will notice the Other Things, their flickering, pinprick eyes hunting the halls, deciding who may leave and who may not, claiming the house as their own. *Cheery bye*, call the visitors who glide by the rippling pelts, wet and slick against the walls, mistaking them for ulcered paint. Hearing not the red roars of triumph, only the skirling screams of a bird.

I go back to Teddy. The news is over, the newborn's family gone. Quiet restored.

The baby boy sleeps in his box. As expected, the litter has grown since I left. They are sitting up now, little claw-buds blooming. One licks the child's ear, getting a taste of him. The others cast long shadows along his butter-soft body, waiting for the parents, whom they've come for, after all, to return.

Doctors consult outside Teddy's room. Heads huddle over monitors, scanning results, straightening up to talk, hushed, furtive. I track the skin on their faces – how it moves, where their eyes rest – count the clicks of their pens, how long their knuckles squirm in airless pockets, grappling with their godliness revoked.

They don't know. They truly don't know.

I spend days this way, and I can't say what frightens me more – a hospital confounded, or the Other Things born alongside my own babies, here with us, waiting at home too, watching us always, day and night, as we lie nose-to-nose, chin-to-ear. So monstrous, a flick of a tail once cracked me like an egg. So cruel, they've patched me back together. *Cheery bye*, call my visitors. *Doesn't she look well?*

Teddy's cheek is soft, cooling, his fever finally outplayed.

Scrapbook #13

Carer accused of filming and abusing disabled children. *The Sydney Morning Herald*, 2 May 2020

1 in 2 adults with disability have experienced violence after the age of 15. *People with disability in Australia – Web Report*, 2 October 2020

Disability royal commission hears children made to sit in own urine, 'belittled' for needing to go to the bathroom. abc.net.au, 5 November 2019

'The names that don't get spoken': Senator breaks down listing deaths in disability care. abc.net.au, 18 September 2018

Group homes were meant to fix the problem of 'barbaric' institutions. Have they? abc.net.au, 7 December 2019

'Crooks are skimming $2bn from the NDIS': Shorten. skynews.com.au, 17 February 2020

Hospital dismissed Rachel's son as a 'grizzly child with Down syndrome' months before his death. abc.net.au, 19 February 2020

Intellectually disabled people 'unsafe' in hospitals, royal commission hears. abc.net.au, 25 February 2020

PM rejects suggestions he 'ran down the clock' to avoid disability vote. abc.net.au, 16 February 2019

12 years old, summer

My first day at Mercy Grammar. First assembly. First break.

Nearby, a girl with large spectacles and wide white teeth. Matilda (Tillie) Tan. Every time a group of girls bustles by her, she leans towards them, no, tilts herself at them, a gushing giggle, as though they've spoken to her, said 'Hi,' said something witty. But they haven't. No-one is speaking to Tillie Tan. And just like Evie did when she and I first met, I know Tillie and I are going to get along.

Then Prim, all six-feet-plus of her, ruins of something chocolate rimming her mouth, bursts through the doors of my life, thus:

'My aunty just had a baby, right? That kid did not have a name for nineteen days. My aunty wanted to get to know him first, see, take in all his little expressions, how he reacted to things. Find the right match. After a few days, Aunty Cath decided ... *Harry.* He bawled like a Harry, sneezed like a Harry, spewed up like a Harry. So he's Harry. Now, *that's* how you name a baby. But *my* parents, not so smart. The second my mum knew she was preggers, she was like, "If it's a girl I'm calling her Primrose."'

She gives her mother a guinea pig's voice.

'Too bad what I slopped out looking like, hey? CHECK. ME. OUT. Do I look like a Primrose?'

I don't know if she is speaking to me or to Tillie Tan, tilting herself towards us at a perilous angle.

'Um?' I reply.

'So it's *Prim*, right? Only ever Prim.'

And then we tell her our names, which Prim instantly makes her own.

'Come on, Kid,' she says to me, and I am Kid from that day forth. Something to do with how tiny I am compared to her.

'You too, Sweet Tillie Sauce,' says Prim, who talks often, and rapturously, about food. 'Let's check out the tuckshop.'

And we follow her, as instructed, Tillie still tilting until the three of us kind of fuse.

14 years old, autumn

On the day of JG's funeral, I miss school.

'Geez, Kid,' says Prim on the phone. 'I'm so sorry. What happened?'

I tell her what my mother told me. That while I was sleeping, JG brought us the usual bananas, passionfruit, persimmons for our breakfast, but it was night, and he fell down the back stairs.

'How awful,' says Prim. 'He sounds so nice, bringing you fruit and stuff.'

I have never told her or Tillie about my grandfather. About Paddy. I rarely mention even my grandmother, my life in the front house folded neat like a blanket in a box. I go to say things sometimes, but I worry that if I do, if I open my mouth and say the words, tell those tales, all the dirty Murphys will fly out, and all the sorry names they have for me, and I will be one of them all over again.

I surely don't mention how my mother went on and on about the steps, always so slippery after they've been washed. How those stairs have never been the same since 'some *idiot*' used wood polish on them.

'I'll collect any handouts for you,' says Prim. 'Hang in there, Kid.'

The night of JG's funeral, my mother wants to go to the drive-in.

228

I think I need to point out Poppa just died. I need to say: *Shouldn't we be … sad? Is this something we should do on the night of a funeral?*

Instead, I say, 'But it's Thursday night, Mum. A school night,' because I'm not sad. I don't feel anything, especially when Mother feeds me the pills, crushed on her big spoon and drizzled with honey. The pills she started giving me after Paddy, that she still gives me when she plans to go out, stay overnight, or when she brings home a friend and 'needs privacy'. She gets them from a new doctor – we don't see Doctor Timothy anymore. She told this new one, Doctor Hocking, that I'm a moody piece, that I see and hear things that aren't there, that I believe there's a man in my room. I was embarrassed, and my mother didn't tell it to him right, she didn't explain things properly, but I knew better than to interrupt.

'So what if it's a Thursday night?' says Mother. 'Let's live a little for once.'

Generally disapproving of any fleck of food I put into my mouth – *How many calories in that? How many calories so far today?* – she buys us hot chips and ice creams at the drive-in as we watch a James Bond double. Two ice creams each. All the way home she talks about Nev, her boyfriend, her favourite again. He gave us our two-door Datsun Sunny, second-hand but in ripper shape, says my mother. Nev who sticks by her, who's 'gonna leave that bitch wife-a his any day now,' she assures me, eyes glistening. 'Any old tick-a the clock.'

I don't think I've ever seen her so happy.

15 years old, winter

It is the state Catholic netball titles, and Mercy Grammar has made the final for the first time in over thirty years. We are up against Laurel Hill – athletically invincible at everything. Over the weekend-long tournament, Laurel Hill has slaughtered every opponent, holding Holy Cross to nil in the semi. I watched that match, their girls made to look like infants. Some cried all through the last quarter.

But with barely a minute to go in the second half of extra time, the seesawing score is locked: twenty-eight all. It's been a wild game, intense. And this season, we have a secret weapon. A national basketball representative, Prim is usually away this time of year playing point guard for the under-eighteen side. But a timetable change has allowed her to step in, be our six-feet-three-inches-and-still-growing goal keeper. She has kept their shooter quiet, worn her like a glove.

I have missed only a handful of shots, bagging twenty of our total score. 'She's playing out of her brain,' I hear someone say.

We are in front of the largest crowd of my life – players and families and teachers from other schools. Most of them paused, intending to have a quick look before heading home – it is a wintry Sunday afternoon after all, school tomorrow – but they have stayed, wedged into the demountable stands, herded around the entire court, both sides, both ends, huddled against the bullying westerly wind. Almost everyone is cheering for us. '*Mer-cies! Mer-cies!*' With the exception of their teachers and parents, everyone hates the Hillers.

Amy, our centre, hurls a long ball of hope.

It's mine, just inside the circle. My less preferred side, as far from the goalpost as it is possible to be.

Veronica, our shooter, being monstered. The Hill's goalkeeper is an Amazon with the eyes and arms of a sloth.

Carla, our wing attack, on the edge of the circle. A tiny tornado, trying to get free. 'Jay. *Jay!*' she calls.

I think about it – a flick pass back to her, trying to work my way in, closer to the hoop. Risky. Not sure I can improve anything.

Mrs Harvey, our coach, frantically tapping her watch: Time! Time's almost up. When in doubt, take the shot, Mrs Harvey always says.

So I eyeball the post, and ready to shoot. I have three seconds.

I think of my grandmother, that damn-the-torpedoes look she would get in her eye when she decided to have her say in her to-hell-with-it voice. The come-what-may tilt of her chin at JG. Come the bruised eye that usually did.

Laurel Hill's goal defence, a red-freckled bag of bones, her ropey plait flaying me in the face all match, has her fingertips almost on the ball. The shortest three feet I've ever seen.

Two seconds.

And it's so windy. I will have to aim well left, that's if I can clear the stick insect mauling my view.

I feign to shoot and my defender leaps, lands almost on top of me. She and her whip-switch of hair.

Whistle. Contact.

She comes to stand beside me, so close I can feel the prickling heat of her body. 'Buckley's,' she snipes, hands on her knees, sucking in breath. 'You got Buckley's.'

I have a clear shot, and three more seconds.

Everyone but the dry winter wind falls silent. If I miss and our girls lose possession, the other side will haul a Hail Mary deep into the centre of the court, pray their goal attack or shooter might free up. Two passes – *zip zip* – might get it done.

All eyes are on me, the hopes of my teammates, the buck, stopping.

The girls deserve this. Mrs Harvey and The Fortress deserve this.

I take the shot, and damn the torpedoes.

Then it happens.

'*Lift it*, MUTT! LIFT IT!'

The umpire's whistle drops from her mouth. All the eyes that had been on me zero in on my mother. Faces in the crowd lock in her direction. It was always going to be this way.

As the ball sails through the air, I begin to laugh, hysterically. Unable to stop, I try to restrain my face with my hands. I don't need to look to see my mother's clenching fists, the way her eyes bulge, her doll-head becoming an old cartoon's round black bomb, fuse lit. I feel sorry for her because this isn't the thing that takes hold, that comes and goes. This is just her. This is what stays.

I hear the umpire blow her whistle. Game over.

This is it for you and me, I tell the netball, Prim having delivered it back to my hands. Mercy Grammar's year eleven and twelve students participate in only rowing, hockey and tennis. This is the last time, ball, I am ever going to hoick you at a metal ring nailed to a lump of timber and hope you cut through it as though it is rimless.

My shot was never going to miss.

Mrs Harvey is cry-laughing, and the girls are ecstatic – so am I; I will never have to go through this again. I see a way forward – the closing-off of things, a sealing-down of myself like a dead-letter envelope. A coward but irresistible relief in that.

My girls are over-joyed too. Jay-dee-Lou, world-beater, has saved all their good-for-nothing arses – Mutt's, Missy's, the *little piece*. Heading home in the car, listening to 'our' mother relive all twenty-one of the gold-star girl's glories. 'You should-a seen the look on … You ought-a heard what … And that last goal, stuck it right up the lot of 'em.' Because that is life for Lonnie – a war, the imperative to find someone to stick it up before they can stick it up you. Only in a fight does the world wilt to her shape, its neck cricked, thrillingly, under the heel of her shoe.

'All you had to do was *lift it*, see? What I been sayin'.'

Supper tonight, and a bath. It has been a good day for my mother, a good day for me. I can only hope today's reprieve is like a spore, hitching itself to the hem of tomorrow, the day after that, the rest of the week.

Buckley's, said the girl with the ropey hair, trying to hex me. *Buckley's*, as though she knew me.

16 years old, spring

My grandmother takes all her clothes off and walks naked around the vestiges of JG's overgrown garden. She whistles, calling Paddy, and sets a big bowl of stew and rice by the door every evening. After school, I sometimes find her sitting on the end of her bed and waving her hands about like she's conducting an orchestra, only there isn't any music. One day she gets into the bath but doesn't get out. Lucia from next door finds her, calls an ambulance, and goes with her to the hospital.

I am in maths class when a message from the office is delivered. Mr Fletcher reads it, calls me to his desk, rests his hand on my shoulder. Tillie, Prim and I connect in a glance.

Lonnie arrives to collect me. 'Fat Lucy should have called me,' she says. 'It was my place beside Mumma in the ambulance, not hers.'

My grandmother's mouth lies open and I look away. Her arms reach out from the hospital bed – white eels steering their heads this way and that, blindly. Perhaps she's missing her trusty black cardigan. I wish I had thought to bring it.

Grandma dies that night. My mother gets a call from the hospital and she crunches her eyes and throws back her head, but she doesn't shed a single tear and we watch the news as usual.

Only I don't watch or listen. Instead, I observe my mother, how she seems to think of only one thing at a time, see only one thing at a time. Right now, she sees only Mike, the television, the advertisement for Arnott's Assorted Creams. How simple it must keep things for her, that clarity. And while I always think of too much at once, one thought knocking heads with the next and the next, everything piling up, compacting down, I am glad I am not like her. I put my hands around my face, pretend I am fussing with my hair, an earring, because I don't want my mother to see my sad tooth. She would head straight for the spoon and honey.

Now that our home is no longer the front house but the only house, the back gate's squeak silenced for good, I wonder if Lonnie might take her chances, find another way to be? She could sell up the back, her plan for some time. She would have money, be free – to have, to do, to let loose her softer self, no longer a need to be so gun-metal hard. Someone who might travel and see the things I have shown her in my books, who has guests around a table, pinching noses and singing along with the radio.

But then Christiane the weather girl on Mike's news says this: 'And today's maxi-mom, *oof* ... so *'ot*! Sirty-nine d'gray in Clonn-corr-*ay*.'

And my mother says this: 'Why they gotta have a French tart doing *our* weather beats the hell out-a me. Clonn-corr-*ay*? What rot!'

And I see that the woman across from me is the only woman there will ever be, and the night my grandmother dies is just like any other.

5 days till extubation

'Mum ... Mum ... Mum ... We need C- ... We need C- ... C- ... We need C-*COMMANDER* Noah Hay. Remember how ... remember how bef- ... how bef- ... how bef-*BEFORE* he was in *Dimension Unknown* he w- ... he w- ... he w-*WAS* that doctor ... that doctor in that hospital show and he ... he c- ... he c- ... he c-*COULD* always w-work out ... wh-what w-was ... w-was wrong with a person, even ... even when all the other doctors c-couldn't, but then he c- ... then he c-couldn't ... he c-*COULDN'T* ... w-work out w-what was wrong with his own g-girlfriend, and then he did w-work it out, but by then ... but by then ... but by then it w-was too late and his g-girlfriend ... she died. Well, really, she had ... she had ... she had to die because the actress w- ... w- ... the actress w- ... needed to leave the show and become The Impossible W-Woman in the new Marvel movie, but ... but ... but anyway, she died and then C- ... C-*COMMANDER* Hay, well Doctor Lucien "Lucky" Dahl he w-was c-called in the hospital ... in the hospital show. Doctor Lucky had to become an alcoholic bec- ... bec- ... bec-*BECAUSE* he lost his epic love, and he w- ... he w- ... he g-got so sad.'

'Ah, yes,' I say, dabbing Tazarotene onto Frank's prickly scalp. 'Yes, he had to become an alcoholic.' The head-shave strategy has worked – Frank's scalp is vastly improved though his stammer is as bad as it gets. 'But then he forgot about being an alcoholic a couple of episodes later and got on with being Doctor Lucky again. He even found a new "epic love", didn't he?'

'Netw- ... netw-work television, Mum,' says Frank, shaking his head. 'Network television.'

'So lame,' I concur.

'Anyw-way, we need ... we need ... we need him. We need Doctor Lucky to w- ... to w- ... to w- ... to diagnose w-what's wrong with Teddy.'

I take Frank's face in my hands, my thumbs stroking his brows and eyelids, trying to tame the hard blinks. 'Yes, darling. It would be lovely to have Doctor Lucky around. Tell me, everything alright at home?'

'Yup,' he says, a little too quickly. Possibly a truth-adjacent reply.

'Jerrik doing ... what he's supposed to be doing?'

The volume is muted but Frank uses the remote to flick through the stations on the television above Teddy's bed. 'Yup.'

Jamie Oliver at a cheese festival.

I smile at Teddy, reminded of his black-market maggots.

A woman weeping on Kevin McCloud's show. Her husband looking sheepishly at the camera, his hand dutifully on her back. They are sitting in their futuristic, moated, eight-bedroomed, three-hundred-year-old 'mouth-watering' barn conversion. But a 'dreadful miscalculation' has been made concerning the depth of their knife drawers.

'*They are too shallow!*' wails the weeper.

The drawers, that is.

'Okay, so how long have I got you? What time is Jerrik due?'

I don't know when I stopped referring to Jerrik as 'Far'. Here in the hospital he has become known only as 'Teddy's father'. I know I haven't said the words 'my husband' for years. But for Frank's sake I should probably stop with the Jerriking.

'He said he might ... he might be a bit ... a bit late. His fr- ... his fr- ... his fr-friend from w- ... from w- ... from w- ... from the off-office had to go to the doctor's, and she's a bit … she's a bit … a bit sad.'

'His friend Minnie?' I ask.

'Yup.'

Frank resumes the silent channel surf. *MacGyver. In the Night Garden. My Kitchen Rules.*

'She had to go to the doctor's?'

'Yup.'

Seinfeld. Weather. *John Wick 2.*

'And she's a bit sad?'

'Uh-huh.'

'I see,' I say. I would require no digits to finger-count the number of times Jerrik has accompanied any of us to a doctor's appointment. 'Have you met Minnie?'

'Nope. Far takes … Far takes … Far takes me to school in the morning and then I c- … and then I c-catch the bus home—'

'You're catching the *bus*?' I have cut Frank off. I never do this. 'By yourself?' It is my golden rule. 'Since when?'

'It's … it's … it's oke- … it's oke- … it's alright, Mum.'

'It most certainly is not. Your father has not discussed this with me. And nor have you, Franko.'

'F-Far says … F-Far … F-Far says—'

'I don't care what Far says.'

Jerrik agreed to step up while I am in here with Teddy. Not re-engineer the wheel. Frank has never caught public transport on his own.

'He c- … he c- … he c- … c-*CAN'T* … g- … g- … g-get away from w-work to c- … to c- … to c-*COLLECT* me at three, so I'm ca- … so I'm ca- … so I'm c-*CATCH*ing the bus. It's oke- … it's all g-good, Mum.'

'Did he show you *how* to catch the bus?'

'No, but—'

'Did you have a trial run first? Did you have six trial runs first?'

'No, but ...'

Hands over my face. Oh, *Jerrik*.

'Madison ... Madison ... Madison showed me the travel app, and I ... I downloaded it.'

'*Madison?*'

'And she ca-catches her bus from the same ... the same ... the same stop as me.'

'Madison?'

'Mum, I like ... I like ... I like ca-catching the bus on my own.'

Frank tells me that Madison has changed, that she likes his shaved head, thinks he looks cool.

'And catching the bus on your own makes you feel grown up, I suppose?'

'Yes,' he answers.

I soothe my own brows for a moment. 'So, when does Far get home? What time? How long are you at home on your own?'

'Look, Mum! Look! It's *Dimension-* ... It's *Dimension-* ... It's *Dimension Unknown*. Season one. It's ... it's ... it's the very f- ... the very f- ... the very f-first ep! Look at how young Comm—'

'*Frank!*' I can't stop myself. 'When does your father get *home*? How long are you left on your *own*?'

Teddy's nurse looks up from his monitor. I know Gabriel has been listening. How could he not?

'He ... he brings home dinner.'

'At what time?'

'Eight or ... eight or nine or ...'

'Right.'

Frank and I sit for some time in silence. He watches our show, an episode we must have seen a good six years ago. I watch Teddy's beeping monitors, veiny peaks and valleys of red and blue and green across their screens. Teddy's fairy-blond hair has sunk a shade; it needs a proper wash. He has been so long in that bed – its apparatus breathing for him, tensing his muscles for him, feeding him – he is beginning to look like a part of its design. A hospital-human hybrid. I want Teddy back, but even this version of Teddy, this hybrid-Teddy, is better than none. Even if that meant staying in this room forever, its twenty-three socket-faces, mean and pinched. Would I become number twenty-four? Am I not this already?

An alarm sounds on Teddy's infusion pump blasting through my morbid thoughts. I hear them scatter, my cruel imaginings, see their snouts and claws and lizard tongues retreat, blink-quick, into the room's shadowy seams. Gabriel immediately sets off for the medication room. None of Ward 9's 'alarm fatigue' in paediatric intensive care. He will return with a replacement syringe and a colleague to double-check Teddy's details, that the medication is correct, its dosage and flow rate. My job is to sit here, triple-checking in stealth.

Before I cut him off, Frank was trying to say how much younger Commander Noah Hay looks in this early season. And, of course, he does. At our age, six years show. Still handsome, though, as he was when I knew him, the actor, a very long time ago.

As though reading my mind, Frank asks, 'Do you still like him as much, Mum? Commander Noah Hay?' He sounds so miserable now. So miserable, even though he got through a whole sentence in his own voice, no stutter.

'You bet,' I reply. 'I'd be Jay Hay any day.'

'Hey, Jay Hay,' he says.

'Hey, Frank Hay.'

But no-one laughs.

Jerrik arrives just after ten to collect Frank. Too late for a school night. He pulls into the set-down zone outside Emergency, texts Frank to let him know he is waiting. He doesn't come up to see Teddy.

17 years old, autumn

This one, straight down the line.

But I drag on the head of the racquet instead of following through. The ball smacks the top of the tape, kicks back my side.

A basket of balls at my feet. I pluck another. Straight down the line, I tell myself.

Now the toss is off. I let the ball bounce.

Exhaling, I try to breathe away both frustration and the cleaver deep between my shoulder blades.

Straight down the line.

I'm serving to the ad box – always my Achilles heel according to Mother.

Tape. Fault.

Torpedo into the net. Double fault.

Fault. Fault. *Lift it, MUTT!*

We are playing St Hilary's this Saturday. Or, rather, we are playing Judy Nixon. 'Nikko' needs neither introduction nor teammates. National age champion four years running and state age champion since forever, Nikko could easily play a doubles match solo, and still hold most high school pairings to love. Lean and relentlessly springy, Judy Nixon's thighs should be up on a wall chart to illustrate textbook human musculature. She made it to Junior Wimbledon last year, bundled out not by an opponent, but a burst appendix. Two years before that I drew her in the first round of the only national comp I ever qualified for. I barely won a point.

I thought Lonnie was going to kill me. Everyone at the courts that day thought Lonnie was going to kill me.

Instead, she tried to Nikko-size me, adding diet pills to my usual trail mix of meds. The team has had before- and after-school practice all week. So, of course, I have to have before-before- and after-after-school practice. Worse, she's booked a private lesson every night this week.

I am tired of tennis. Tired of having to win every match, every game, every rally, every point. More specifically, I am just plain tired.

'Can't wait for you to have another crack at that skinny bitch,' said Lonnie. 'Get your revenge.'

Revenge? We were fourteen. She won, I lost, end of story.

'Mum,' I snapped, 'there'd be no *revenge* if I played her this Saturday or the Saturday after that. Not even if I had a private lesson every night for the rest of my life! Judy Nixon will hand me my backside on the strings of her racquet every time. Things can't always be the way you want them.'

She was so silent, as though I'd smacked her. I apologised, blamed the diet pills; she has doubled my dose.

'They're making me snarky,' I said, hoping she might consider a pull-back. She didn't.

So here I am on a Thursday afternoon at almost five-thirty, over a hundred practice serves later, my right hand raw and sticky with torn skin – every finger taped, two more private lessons to go.

The old Georgian convent is at rest behind me and, for a moment, there is only me and the river, the bridge, the whole school and its autumn shadows all to myself. Its high block walls, more than a century old, wrap around me, princely firm. For the next minute or two, I'm a boarder left behind, forgotten, staying on, living here at the school in secret. Surviving on what I find in the tuckshop, taking just enough so as not to raise suspicion.

Doing my homework in the library, reading all night every night, every book, starting at Aisle A and working my way through. I sleep on the day bed in sick bay. Dawn laps around the campus before a quick dip and shower at the pool. Everything I need, right here.

Tape. Double fault.

Net. A likely foot fault anyway.

Double. Double.

Not enough light to see the form of my strokes, where the ball lands.

Five in a row, I bargain with myself, and you can stop. Five in the box and you're done.

But as I bounce the ball, I am worried about Metternich and the Austrian Empire and the chapters I need to read and summarise before tomorrow's history class. It will be close to nine o'clock by the time I get home from the courts.

Thwump. Net.

I will be fried by then. It will have to be another five am start.

Thwump. Tramlines.

Tackle the old Prince of Metternich-Winneburg in the morning. Will five be early enough?

Thwump. 'Arrh!'

The racquet clatters to the ground. A blister eyes me from the webbing of my thumb, not just weeping, bleeding. Impossible spot to bind and protect.

Blowing on my palm, I head to the other end of the court to collect balls.

'Jay. The rest of the team left ages ago. Shouldn't you be heading home too?'

Sybella Moorcroft. A heckle of assignment papers perched on

her hip. She appears on the steps of the nearby staffroom, turns to lock the door. I hadn't realised anyone was still here.

'Did Mr Gillon ask you to keep practising?'

'No, Miss,' I reply, hooking my fingers through the court's wire fencing. I once overheard Miss Moorcroft call Mr Gillon the *Bone*Head of Health and PE. 'I've got a six-thirty lesson at the club so Mum's collecting me after work. She said to keep on my serve while I wait.'

'More tennis? Tonight?' asks Miss Moorcroft. 'I don't like leaving you here on your own. It's getting quite dark.'

'I'll pack up and wait by the chapel then,' I say, happy for an excuse to quit the court. 'My mother won't be far off. Anyway, some of the sisters are already prowling about.'

Sybella Moorcroft smiles.

'Oh God!' I yelp. 'I didn't mean *prowl*. I meant ... You know, vespers. I didn't mean—'

'Relax, Jay,' she says. 'I know what you meant. You know, Mrs James showed me your exam paper on the October Revolution this afternoon. It was excellent. Outstanding, in fact.'

'Thank you, Miss.'

'It's the truth. And I'm starting on the Steinbeck assignments tonight.' Her hip shifts under the burdensome folder. 'Yours will be the first one I mark because I always like to eat the icing first. I expect to be gratified and enlightened.'

Praise still feels like the prelude to a gag, a set-up. 'Thank you, Miss.'

'It's a gift you have, Jay. With words. I hope you intend to use it? What do you think you'll do, when you leave here?'

I never want to leave here.

'Mum says law.'

What my mother actually says is that doctors and lawyers are posh and make a lot of money, but that since I'm no good at maths, it has to be law. I once mentioned journalism to Lonnie. Sportswriting. 'What rot,' she replied. 'Who the hell'd wanna hear what some bloody woman thinks about football?'

Miss Moorcroft hesitates. 'Is that … *your* first choice?'

I know Miss Moorcroft is single, that she lives alone with a cat called Rolf. What a wonderful life, it seems to me, to be Miss Moorcroft. To be Rolf. And suddenly the throbbing in my hand feels like the bite of a bear and my eyes start to water, and I can see myself sitting in her flat or in the dark beetle of her car, my sad tooth telling her things never confessed to anyone. I pack it all down – I do, I'm good at it, deep and neat – but right now there's more of it than there is of me, using my mouth, my face.

So I say only, 'Mum wants law, so …' just to stop myself saying anything else. I'm tired, not thinking properly.

Norway – population four point two million, capital Oslo, coldest recorded temperature -51.4°C, Karasjok, 1886.

'At least promise me you'll sit by the convent to wait for your mother, Jay.' Miss Moorcroft plucks her car keys from her shoulder bag. 'And go inside to use the phone if she's not here soon. I know you'll be sensible.'

I think, *Please don't go just yet*, but I say, 'Goodnight, Miss.'

'Goodnight, Jay.'

As instructed, I wait for Lonnie outside the convent. She is late. I hope she is stuck in the worst traffic jam of all time, come what may, even the foul mood that surely would. Damn the torpedoes.

Emerging from the chapel is Sister Agatha, or Aggie-a-GaGa as she is known around the school. She carries her rosary beads in her two hands like she is cupping water or ferrying an injured bird. With surprising dart she proceeds to volleyball court two, her pale-grey habit like the fluting train of a bride. Head down, she follows the court's chalk outline, reciting the psalms and canticles, turning sharply, robotically, at the corners. I guess she has been doing this a long time and has her way of going about it. Sister Aggie's groove.

Tiny and Irish-born, the nun is notoriously impossible to converse with given she talks only to herself, most of that talk being prayer. She once served as a relief teacher (religion classes only), arriving stooped and mumbling, wafting her thurible about, its mysterious whiff, the first twenty minutes of each lesson given to exorcising the devil, casting out his evil spirit, sprinkling holy water on everyone and everything, bestowing sacred power. But parents complained. Sister Aggie has rarely surfaced since.

But here, on the soft green lawns of the terrace, in the dimming light of a May evening, Sister Agatha looks anything but bonkers. She looks serene, possessed only of an enviable peace.

After vespers, Sister Aggie will return to the convent. I go through her steps: she will bathe quickly and have her dinner with the other nuns. I see her in a thin iron bed. On a cross above her head is Christ – pale, lashed, but soon to rise and ever-listening. On the nightstand is a lamp to light the pages of her Bible, and a glass of water, a little crocheted doily over it, weights sewn into its edges, keeping out the dust and bugs. In the nightstand's single drawer, she places her glasses just before going to sleep. I imagine Sister Aggie is a sound sleeper, but that even when she does wake, on a hot night, she would see it as simply another blessed opportunity to pray.

Lonnie still hasn't arrived. I close my eyes and will her to have forgotten tonight's booking.

'Wake up, dearie.'

Sister Agatha, standing directly in front of me. I thought I'd only closed my eyes for a second, but perhaps I fell asleep.

'There's something about you. God put it there. Don't let them take it away.'

I have never seen Sister Aggie address another living soul. Not a student, not even another nun. Not in any way that makes sense.

'When the Lord lays His hands over your ears, and He will, dearie, you must listen. And when He puts them over your eyes, pay attention to what it is He shows you.'

'I ... I will, Sister.' What else can I say?

'Walk while you have the light. John twelve, thirty-six. Walk while you have the light, before the darkness overtakes you.'

Headlights swing around the chapel. Lonnie.

'Stay the darkness at your heels, *Spider.*'

And I cry the strangest tears.

'What?' says my mother in the car on the way to the courts. '*What?*'

'Nothing,' I say. 'Just a pain.'

'Oh, Jay,' My mother, exasperated. 'You're like a broken bloody record.'

'I know,' I say. 'All in my head.'

'I just died in there.'

Prim agrees. 'Those last three motion equations were tough, I'll admit. And that differential field felt like it was frying a part of my brain I don't actually possess. I got it in the end, I think.'

'I just died in there,' I say again.

Morning tea time, and my maths class is filing out of a squinty-bright classroom. Limping out. For the past two hours and thirty minutes we've been locked inside a chastened silence, heads down over exam papers erupting with batty symbols and diagrams and equals signs adding up to very few of my calculations. As the shock and grind of it slowly retreat, all Prim and Tillie want to do is eat. All I want to do is cry.

'I couldn't get *near* the antiderivatives,' says Tillie. 'I've never been good at those. Didn't even know where to start. So I just left them, went back over everything else. Hopefully most of that was right. I'll pass. Do you think I'll pass? I'll pass.' Tillie often asks and answers her own questions.

'I just died in there.'

'Stop saying that, Kid,' says Prim. 'You'll be fine. You're always fine.'

'God, Prim, you sound like my mother.'

Prim stops unwrapping her jam rollette. 'Geez, low blow, friend.'

'You don't get it,' I say, trying to breathe away the burn of banking tears. 'I'm not exaggerating. I hate that everyone thinks I always exaggerate.'

Tillie swallows a mouthful of boiled egg. 'We don't think you always exagg—'

'I couldn't even do the first block – the geometric sequences, the function values. The easy ones! I've only done, like, a million of them with Lloyd.'

Tillie blinks thoughtfully. 'Who's Lloyd again?'

Prim mouths, *maths tutor*, over my head.

'I can do them in my sleep,' I say. My hands are shaky. 'But not today. God, I'm so dead. There's no point going home. I should just take off. You know what? I've finally worked out what I want to be when I grow up. A missing person.'

Prim and Tillie look at each other, helpless chewing.

'We've met your mum, Jay,' says Prim. 'We know you're not exaggerating.'

My throat is dry and I feel shivery. 'It was like … Remember when we made jam in grade eight home ec?'

'Strawberry!' shouts Prim, loudly and quickly, still in quiz mode.

'And remember the set test? You spoon some onto a cold saucer and run your finger through it, to make a path down the middle. If the jam doesn't wrinkle up, and floods back into the gap straightaway, you know it isn't done.'

The girls nod.

'Well, every single question was like that. I'd look at it, and in that first second, I knew exactly how to nail it. The solution would be right there, clean and clear like the white strip of saucer you can see through the jam. And then ... *glurp!*'

'All the jam flooded back in?' asks Tillie.

'All the jam flooded back in.'

Tillie and Prim decide to eat *all* their food – both morning tea and lunch. They agree that the stress of the maths exam warrants it. By second break they are both ravenous again. At the tuckshop, Prim orders two hot dogs with sauce, a Summer Roll and a Diet Coke. She gives one hot dog to Tillie, along with half the Summer Roll.

'Thanks, Primsy,' says Tillie, making an enthusiastic start on her sausage and bun. 'I owe you.'

'You owe my dad,' Prim replies. 'And don't worry about it. Mr Fat Cat lawyer can afford it.' She hands me the Diet Coke. 'Your usual, Kid.'

'Thanks, P.'

We head in the direction of our home room, the bell not far away. Prim stops to have a drink from a bubbler. She says the water is a hot dribble and tastes like hair.

'Do you think Summer Rolls have got shorter?' asks Tillie. 'I think Summer Rolls are definitely shorter.'

'One good bite shorter,' agrees Prim.

'So, we're being ripped off?' says Tillie, talking to the chocolate-covered nougat. 'Not good enough Europe food bar company.'

'Still,' ponders Prim, 'you're probably saving a bunch of calories. One bite would be ... How many calories in a bite of Summer Roll, Kid?'

''Bout fifty,' I say.

'I knew you'd know,' says Prim. 'So, Tills, you're saving yourself at least fifty calories. Multiply that out over five days a week over the course of a school year ...'

'What's that?' muses Tilly. 'Forty weeks, give or take?'

'By forty weeks, give or take,' repeats Prim. 'And you're about ...' Prim does finger calculations. 'Ten thousand calories in arrears. Girl, you got some serious pigging out to catch up on. You risk wasting away.'

I lie down on the warm grass, inching myself under the wooden bench I've been sitting on, my forearm across my face, shading my eyes from the sun.

As they chatter, Tillie and Prim watch me.

'Er, Kid?' says Prim. 'What are you doing?'

'Well, I appear to be lying on the ground,' I reply. 'Shading my eyes from the sun. William of Ockham's principle, ladies. No need to theorise beyond necessity.'

The girls seem satisfied with this, turning their attention to last night's episode of *Falcon Crest*.

The truth is I'm too tired to hold myself up. This morning's exam has run my batteries too low. I feel like paint not yet applied to anything, just a wet, loose swirl in a can, spillable. While Prim was at the bubbler and Tillie devoured her hotdog, I downed another of Lonnie's *slayers* with my zero-calorie drink. That is what I call the diet pills she gives me, her uppers. Just one, to get me through this afternoon.

As I lie in wait for the pill to kick in, for that yo-yoing moment of feeling dropped and then suddenly caught and suitably adjusted, I listen to Prim and Tillie. I don't tell the girls this, but I love our conversations, their idling chat. As pointless as a half-pair of shoes; also, the most important voices I hear all week, buoying me above the brinks. On the ground, under my fingers, small stones. Without looking, I let one choose me, no more than a pebble, hot and dusty but smooth enough. I roll it between my fingers, a rough pearl, a tiny underworld, then slip it into the pocket of my tunic. Prim's and Tillie's words follow the stone as though it is a piper, their words enchanted children. But the enchanter is mine and so are their voices now, darlings humming sweetly against my hip. I will wrap my hand around the word stone, around the girls, when the night comes and with it the thing that takes hold of my mother. The thing she long ago stopped trying to resist. Already I feel the stone's tender twinkle. *Walk while you have the light*, said Sister Aggie. Prim and Tillie and this place, they are my light. But like Paddy and Evie, their radiance can only go so far, and we must keep moving. We have no say in this – we are moved on, no matter how much we would like to stay where and when we are. Only so many lanterns strung to guide our way, from the beginning of us to the end. A happy life is one where the distance between each is short, always just enough light to keep the darkness at your heels and not at your throat.

'Hey, chickos,' I say to the girls. 'Have you spied Sister Agatha lately?'

The *Falcon Crest* discussion seizes up, mid-word.

Tillie, quietly to Prim: 'Does she mean Aggie-a-GaGa? I think she means Sister Aggie.'

Prim, in her lovingly no-nonsense way: 'That's probably enough sun for you today, Kid. Sister Aggie died when we were in year nine.'

Were my back not hard against the ground, I am not sure I would feel it, just as my left arm over my eyelids, like a ballast, loans mass and form to my head. The whereabouts of the rest of me, at this very moment, I cannot with certainty verify. Still falling off the edge of somewhere, waiting for the diet pill to catch me by a bootstrap. Prim once told us that before she had Harry, her Aunty Cath was pregnant with another baby, but that baby had had a condition. *Incompatible with life*, the doctor said, and that baby died inside her.

I sometimes feel like that, like I am incompatible with life. It is all around me, a twilit space, I see it, I hear it. My fingers press in on its hothouse surface because I've heard that is what fingers like mine and people like me are supposed to do. But, somehow, I just can't find my way in, no entrance stays open, not long enough anyway for more than a toehold, and life remains unconvinced of me. Inside, the hothouse people mingle in the fecund green, their tables laid with white linen, barely time to breathe for all their charm and chatter. So I turn and walk away. *Oh, shame*, they say, the hothouse types, looking out at the back of my head. *Won't she be lonely?*

'Do you think she just … forgot?' Tillie asks of Prim, trying not to move her lips as she speaks. 'I think, you know, exams and all. I think she just forgot.'

Tillie is half right – I do forget things. My name, sometimes, my other one, and I wake in the night to say it, over and over, lending it a body, a mouth, remembering what it sounds like.

'We all went to her funeral in the chapel,' adds Prim. 'The whole school. Remember, Kid?'

The bell sounds. I unbury myself from under the bench, relocate my left foot, my right.

'Well,' says Prim, 'I'm off to geography. What have you guys got this afternoon?'

'Religion, then double spare,' says Tillie. 'So, basically, a triple spare. Praise Jesus.'

I am light-headed. Might the pills, or a lack of sleep, explain what took place at vespers – what I would Holy-Bible swear was real? 'French exam,' I murmur.

'Damn, Kid. You've got a day,' says Prim. 'But that's gonna be okay, yeah? I mean, *oui*? You can blitz a French test, any *jour* of the week.'

252

'Yeah. French should be alright.'

'Anyway, that's not what I meant,' Prim continues. 'I meant *after* school. Tillie, can you hang around for a while? Kid, have you got tennis squad? Deportment? Maths tutoring? Chem tutoring?'

'Oh, yeah,' says Tillie. 'Deportment. How's that going, Jay?'

'Done. Over. Thank God,' I reply, rubbing my eyes. 'Finished last week. Lloyd is coming for chem tonight, but not till six. Why?'

'I thought he was your maths tutor,' says Tillie.

'He is,' I clarify, 'on Monday nights. Maths on Monday, chemistry Tuesday.'

I press my palm against my pocket, feel the warmth of the stone, enchantment in action.

'I can stay,' says Tillie, looking up, way up, at Prim. 'What's the plan? Stealing the history test? *Please* let's be stealing the history test?'

'Not quite,' replies Prim. 'Though there may be a small element of criminality involved. Meet me at the Kemp Place gates. Don't be late.'

At 3:45 pm, we are a line of three along a bench at the northern end of Brunswick Street station, Platform 1.

On Prim's lap is a cream-coloured box large enough to contain a wide-brimmed hat, but which holds instead eighteen dollars' worth of raspberry madeleines, éclairs au café, tartes aux fraises, mini croquembouches, mille-feuilles, tartes tatin, and two rum babas – Prim's favourite.

'I cannot believe we stole the mission money,' I say, halfway through the finest vanilla slice I am ever likely to eat. I feel revived. 'Even though I am so glad we did because I love sugar. And fat. Honeymooned together, fried and crusty and squelching full of more sugar and fat. Totally worth the plunge into moral ambiguity.'

'*We* didn't steal the mission money,' Prim reminds us. '*I* did.'

'I cannot believe *you* stole mission money to buy cakes,' I restate.

Tillie corrects me. 'These aren't cakes, mademoiselle.' She is eating a gâteau opéra from the top down, one layer at a time. One lick at a time. I smile, reminded of Paddy with a persimmon. 'These are gifts from God and all His angels, who got up early to make them for us by the agency of their own heavenly hands. And if God, being the all-powerful being we know He is, didn't want us to be sitting here eating His wondrous creations, well, we wouldn't be, would we? We'd be off doing something else, because that something else would be His Divine Will. So, who are we to question?'

'If only the Olympics had a rationalisation event,' says Prim.

'Gold medallist, you reckon?' Tillie replies.

'My mother is going to know, you know,' I say, swallowing. 'She's going to know I've eaten these.'

'Coz that's the worst thing, isn't it,' says Prim, 'according to your mum? Stealing mission money to buy patisserie cakes is one thing. But actually *eating* the cakes would be a capital offence.'

'You know it. I'll have gained ten pounds by the time I get home, and she'll be able to see it, I swear. She'd rather I come home drunk on gin than ten pounds heavier. Now there's a thought. Next time we steal mission money we should just go to the pub. Martinis would have fewer calories I bet.'

'You aren't going to gain ten pounds in one pig-out,' says Prim. 'So relax and enjoy it. Just make up for this splurge by not eating tomorrow. Oh wait, you'll do that anyway.'

'So, tell me,' Tillie asks, 'what goes on at charm school? Got any tips?'

'Well, sure,' I say.

I set my pastry on Tillie's lap, stand side-on to the girls, a catwalk pose, arrange my plait over my shoulder, one hand on my hip, a thigh thrust out in front.

'I could teach you how to not just *walk* into a room, ladies,' I say, lips pouting, eyelids flickering, '... but *commandeer* it, with nothing more than your –' I lean into their faces, my voice a purr '– *bearing*.'

'Bearing?' says Tillie, her voice low, her eyebrows high. 'Bear-ing.'

I resume my seat, my vanilla slice, and my regular voice. 'I could I also teach you how to clench your bum in a way that makes your waist look thinner, or your neck longer, or your booberinis bigger. Something like that. Or I could help you sort out, once and for all, every girl's most pressing dilemma: where to put her napkin – table or seat – when she goes to the bog. Point out the egregious offence of using the salt and pepper *before* tasting your hostess's food, and whether cutlery at eleven o'clock indicates resting or finished position. What to look for when choosing a palate cleanser, and criteria for selecting living-room furniture to optimise posture potential. You know, all of life's essentials.'

Prim's mouth is slightly ajar, but Tillie asks, 'So, which is it? With the napkin? Table or chair when you go to the toilet?'

'Dunny break – chair. Table – specifically *left* of the dinner plate, only once you've finished your meal.'

Another short silence before Prim asks, 'So, who is it your mum wants you to be? Martina Navratilova, Marie Curie or Jackie Onassis?'

'She's hedging her bets,' I say. 'But no doubt expecting the trifecta.'

'Jesus,' says Prim, shaking her head.

'So, you're just going to ask your dad for twenty bucks?' I ask Prim.

'Yeah. I'll say it's for an excursion or something. Put the money back in the box in the morning. I'm on collection this week, so it's sweet.'

'Pardon the pun,' I say, selecting a strawberry and custard tarte from Prim's lap. 'Thanks, P.'

Prim picks up her second rum baba. 'We're only blowing off a little steam. With cake, for God's sake. Harmless. I mean, check them out.' Prim looks over at a group from St Joseph's, the Terrace boys, huddled against a wall on the disused side of the platform. 'Here's us and our pastries, and there's them, Terrace turds, smoking. We're hardly renegades.'

'Except I'll bet they paid for their fags with their own money,' says Tillie, without looking up from her slice. 'Not like us, stealing it from starving people, from the homeless. Do you think we'll go to hell? We're probably going to hell.'

We laugh, eat, lick our fingers, discuss feeling slightly ill and debate how to dispose of the gigantic cake box.

As peak hour looms, the platform wriggles with commuters. I need to catch the 4:40 pm train and pray there's no hold-up on the line. If I am not home before Mother, in plenty of time to make my bed, get the washing off the line and start dinner, I won't be asking for trouble, I'll be on my knees begging for it. Last month, she came home from work early with a headache, found my bed unmade. She went ahead and made it herself, pulled the sheets up nice and tight, classic hospital corners, then emptied three cans of tomato soup over the whole thing. 'That'll teach you to do as you're told, Mutt. Looks like you've got laundry to do.'

A jockey-sized Terrace boy begins a slow swagger our way, cigarette propped proudly between his fingers. Long strands of fine, fungus-white hair fall across one eye.

'Uh-oh,' I say to the other two. 'It's Mr Benson and Hedges.'

Tillie looks up. 'Jay, he goes to Terrace. A Willem II man, if you don't mind?'

The boy comes to stand in front of us, takes in the box on Prim's lap, then me, before setting his sharp blue eyes on Tillie – on her face, buried in the ever-diminishing striae of her opera cake.

'Well,' he begins, his mouth peeling open to reveal small square teeth. Everything about this kid is bonsaied, except his ego. 'And we ask ourselves why Mercy girls are such *fat dogs*.' The rest of his puffing stooges look on, buckling with amusement.

Tillie looks up, a tiny tuft of coffee buttercream clinging to the edge of a nostril.

'Do you?' asks Prim, her voice theatrically loud. She straightens her long back against the wooden slats of the bench, stretches out her impressively long legs. 'Coz we never have to ask ourselves why Terrace boys have such *small dicks*.'

She sets the box of cakes on Tillie's lap and stands up, unfurling her lean Amazonian frame. Taking a few steps forward, she looks down at him, inviting his next move. He flicks his blond bang to the side, sucks deeply on the cigarette, angles up his chin and blows a lungful of smoke into her face. But the smoke recoils into his own eyes. They water and he does his heroic best not to blink.

'*Freak*,' he says, strutting back to the huddle of boys.

'*Barbie*,' Prim yells after him, her voice tunnelling through the concrete underground.

Tillie almost chokes. I give Prim a raised fist salute.

Looking up, I see a boy on Platform 2, directly across the tracks. Not a boy – a young man – early twenties. He wears jeans, a T-shirt and thin jacket, a booted foot raised against the wall behind him. I have seen him before and I know he has been listening to us, to our rumble with the Terrace boy – who knows how long before that? He looks over, smiling.

And shining.

4 days till extubation

The latest test results have ruled out almost all of the capital 'S' syndromes and capital 'F' fevers, and most of the queried illnesses ending in -*osis*.

We are still waiting on biopsies: the bone marrow and samples taken from suspect lymph nodes in Teddy's small intestine. The lump in his hip is considered of 'improbable clinical significance'. However, the gastroenterology consultant on Teddy's case has warned that one radiographer's 'clinically insignificant' is another's 'collection of note'. I am not sure how she expected me to react to this revelation, but I responded with wordless tears – my go-to response to almost every piece of news and no-news for the past four weeks.

In two days, Teddy's gastrostomy will be used for the first time. Jerrik can't even pronounce it.

In all the dictionaries I have pored over in my life, never once has my eye fallen on this word.

Gastrostomy. Noun (say gas'trostuhmee).

Teddy has a gastrostomy now.

A feeding tube inserted into his stomach accessed via a silicone button positioned in his left lower midriff. The button looks much like a bung in a beach ball or a baby floatie. Flip to open, press to close. Through it, he will be fed a 'complete food' formula. When the formula is the only source of nourishment, it is called exclusive enteral nutrition. EEN.

Teddy's gastrostomy – a thing of many parts. We will adjust, he and I. I will learn how to use it, care for it. The whole routine of it. He will learn to respect it despite his horror of adhesives.

For the coming while I will have to feed him every three hours, like a baby, around the clock. It is hoped EEN will bring his inflammatory markers back down to earth. A faecal calprotectin level under 50 micrograms per gram is considered normal; between 50 micrograms per gram and 200 micrograms per gram is borderline.

Teddy's is almost 21,000.

A provisional diagnosis has thus been made, mostly by eliminating other possible causes than by identifying hard and fast evidence: inflammatory bowel disease, another thing of many parts. For if this diagnosis is correct, they don't yet know exactly where in his digestive tract the disease is active. It certainly isn't where they have looked, where they can see. They must keep looking, then wait awhile, and look again.

'You'll get to know this hospital very well,' says PICU consultant Ryker Shulmans. 'Lucky you live so close.'

'Gotta get lucky sometime, Doc,' I reply.

'I had ... I had ... I had the dream again last night, Mum.'

Frank is back. He caught the bus to the transit centre opposite the hospital. He is coming here to Teddy's room, now, after school. I think it is a fair compromise. Jerrik will collect him after work, meaning: Jerrik will collect Frank and take him home when it suits Jerrik. We are having a late lunch, Subway sandwiches, Frank's favourite.

'Did you, lovely? And was the dream the same as the other times? Just as wonderful?'

'Pretty ... pretty much.'

'Tell me again.'

'Oke … oke-okay. So … so … so we're on the big … the big boat.'

'Daniel's boat.'

'Y- … y-yes, Mum,' says Frank, eyes rolling. 'Daniel's … Daniel's boat.'

I butt my shoulder against Frank's. 'Daniel's boat.'

'Yes, ex- … ex- … only no. We're sinking. And everyone's running … running around, panicking.'

Frank's stammer has settled.

'Is Daniel there?' I ask.

'Yes, yes, I c- … I see … I see his back. He's dashing about, sort of organising things.'

'Saving people?' I suggest.

'I … I think so. Maybe.'

'I'm sure that's what Daniel would do on a sinking ship. Selflessly save others.'

'If you say … if you say so, Mum. Though, you know he's not … he's not … he's not really James Bond. He's just an actor.'

'Righto,' I say. 'So, being just an actor, he's probably lying facedown sucking his thumb.'

Frank laughs.

'Okay. What comes next?'

'W- … w- … w-well … oke-okay … I'm running around too. I'm not sure … I'm not sure what I'm doing, but I'm … I'm scared.'

'Poor baby.'

'And then … then I hear people start to say, "Look at that boy. That boy, over there, on the rails. Look at that boy!"'

'And it's Teddy?'

'Mum!'

'Skipping ahead. Sorry, babes.'

'So … so people are pointing and y-yelling, and I look, and … I look … and I look and I see Teddy standing right … right on the rail of the ship, and he's g- … he's g- … has his arms out in front,

261

his hands pressed together, you know, in a diving ... in a diving pose.'

'What balance!' I say.

'I know. He's ... he's amazing.'

'He is.'

'And the sun ... the sun ... the sun ... it's setting. And it turns Teddy kind of ... g- ... go- ... go- ... g-golden. And everyone's ... everyone's ga- ... ga- ... g-gathering around, really excited. Watching Teddy k- ... watching Teddy k- ... makes them forg- forget the boat is sinking.'

I smile.

'And then ... and then he jumps.'

And then he jumps.

'Jump jump,' says Teddy, says Liam. When the answer is yes, when Teddy is happy. 'Jump jump. Jump jump.' When Teddy is saving us.

'And he turns ... he turns into a dolphin, and swims awa-away. We can all see him gl- ... gl- ... we can all see him gliding through the water, skim-skimming along, and it's like he's smiling, we see his little ... his little pointy dolphin teeth, and he's g- ... he's g- ... and he's g-grinning back at us as he swims away. Like ... like he w-wants ... like he w-wants us to f-follow. Like if w- ... if we'd all just jump, w-we'd turn into dolphins too. Or something.'

I'm looking at Teddy, his pale chest rising and falling, his nostrils clogged with tubes – yellow and thin in his right, clear and painfully thick in his left – his mouth open. I can't say anything.

'And that's ... that's about it, really. Everyone ... everyone on deck is cheering and jumping up and down. Because he's ... because he's saved us all, somehow. I don't know how we know, but by turning into a dolphin, he's ... he saved us. And it feels *really* ... it feels really g-good. I'm so happy standing on that deck. I don't ... I don't ... I don't know how he does it, but the boat ... the boat ... the boat doesn't sink anymore.'

'What a wonderful dream.'

'It is, Mum. It's a … it's a … it's a fan-fantastic dream. I w- … I w-wish there was a multi- … a multi- … a multi-version of it, like a PS g-game. We c- … c- … we could have it together.'

'And where's Daniel Craig? Is he calling out, "Where is she? The love of my life, has anyone seen her? Has anyone seen my darling Jay?"'

'I think … I think that's your dream, Mum.'

'Could be. Silly me.'

Jerrik arrives to collect Frank, again too late for a school night. But at least he comes up to PICU, visits a few minutes with Teddy.

Frank and I take a wander along the corridor.

'Do … do you … do you like my new … my new k- … k- … my new k-kicks, Mum?'

I look down, see a new pair of leather boots. 'Very sharp,' I say, surprised I hadn't noticed them earlier. 'Where did you get them?'

'Far.'

'Your father bought them for you? Your father bought you new shoes?' A Jerrik first. Perhaps as some kind of compensation for prioritising his girlfriend over his son. *Sons.*

'W-well, Far … Far bought … Far bought them for himself … on- … online. But they … but they … only they didn't f-fit. So they … so they … they're mine now.'

I think, *That sounds more like it,* but I say, 'Cool. They look awesome.'

But more than that, they look familiar.

Back in Teddy's room, Frank slings his backpack over his shoulder. 'Oh … Mum! Mum! I … I … I meant to tell y-you. I … I've been looking for that … that little doll you lost, and I … I f-found her!'

'Frank, you beauty! Where was she?'

Jerrik – awkward, bored – listens in on our conversation. 'What is lost?' he asks. 'What little doll?'

'She … she … she'd f- … she'd f- … fallen onto the fl- … onto the fl- … behind … behind your bookcase. Got all mixed up with the elec- … p-power cords. Why … why does she rattle? The others … the others, the oth- … none of them rattle.'

'A rattling doll?' says Jerrik. 'A broken doll, sounds to me. *Ødelagt?*' he mutters under his breath. *'Ligesom alt andet.'* Wrecked, like everything else.

'There's a stone inside,' I explain. 'A special one, from long ago.'

'A stone?' asks Frank.

'Like us.' Jerrik grins, amused, as always, by himself. 'Rolling stones.'

I dip my head towards Frank. 'Funny-adjacent, your father.'

'C-can … c-can you tell … tell me about it, Mum? About … about the special stone?'

'I will,' I assure him, pressing the back of his hand to my cheek. 'I'll tell you about all of it.'

'ALL of it?' says Frank, intrigued.

'Kom nu, lad os gå,' Jerrik tells Frank. Come on, let's get out of here.

When they leave, I take Teddy's iPad out of my bag, power it up. In four days' time he will wake up and it will be the first thing he will want. His devices, his headphones, Liam and Siri. He will need them to tell me something random and fun and strange, quite possibly at the least appropriate moment in the least appropriate place. Just something that occurred to him while he was sleeping. Something he overheard in some thin corner of the wayside. In four days' time, Teddy's groove will be back.

Jump jump, I think. Jump jump.

17 years old, winter

As soon as he arrives on the platform and settles in the usual place, he looks across the tracks at me. At first, I pretend to read my old copy of *Wuthering Heights*, glancing up every half-minute to make sure he is still looking. He is.

It is like a play, a two-hander. Our little show has been going a month now.

But today – suddenly brave, suddenly reckless – I decide to go off script. Setting the book on my lap, I look back at him.

His train arrives, idles on the opposite platform for no apparent reason, as trains do.

My train arrives.

He sits on the right-hand side of his carriage, facing south, the direction he is travelling, and he watches me as I board. I take a seat also on the right, facing north. Different trains, separated by layers of glazed glass, but closer than we have ever been.

With our trains lazing side by side, I can see the bronze-brown of his eyes, the stubble on only the tip of his chin. He watches; I watch. We seem to be skimming over early scenes in our story – embarrassment, self-consciousness – as though time is already running out. His expression isn't cheap, isn't vain. Nothing like the Terrace boys who patrol the platforms for victims, giving their *What's up you?* look. It isn't a dare, not even particularly flirtatious. Only like I've been telling him something and he is waiting for me to finish.

My train starts to pull away and I can't believe I do this, but I press my hand to the dirty glass and he raises an index finger, gives me a little salute. *See ya.* His lips a half-smile. And then the smile says, *Oh, what the hell,* and kicks off its shoes and becomes a laugh and a bit bottom lip and a run of his fingers through his hair.

And I keep looking until his train is long gone and all I see are railway buildings and corrugated siding and tracks and late-afternoon sky.

I did that, didn't I?

But those skipped scenes are catching up to me now, all that risk and gamble steaming up my face, my ears booming with heat. I must look a fright. I must look a fool.

I will never do that again.

I will never go back to Brunswick Street station as long as I live. I will start catching the bus. Or walking home.

Damn the torpedoes.

I can't wait for tomorrow afternoon.

On my way home from the station, I need to talk myself down – elation too close to the surface. There is undoing in having my own experience – it never stays mine for long, my mother, I am convinced, all but able to read my mind. I will take the washing off the line, fold it all away, make my bed, make a start on our ~~dinner~~ tea. Obedient again, servile again, I will do my homework, stop thinking about the boy on Platform 2, and all will be right for tonight.

But nothing is right. My mother is home early, her car in the garage. Has it been a look-down-their-nose day, the usual grief? I am up the front stairs, two at a time, through the front door.

I can't see her, hear her. I can always hear her. I'm scared.

Nothing is ever nothing. Not ever.

Through the kitchen window, a backyard blaze. The old goalpost burns like a stake, absent its witch.

I go to my room. My bed unmade, as I left it.

But under the window, my great wall of books is gone.

Punishment, for not making my bed.

Punishment, for the washing still on the line.

Punishment, for once again being thrashed by Judy Nixon.

Punishment, for not being all my mother wants me to be.

Or just for the hell of it.

She looks up, sees me watching on from my bedroom window, the horror that is my face. The heat of the fire has fouled the graceful smooth of her curls. From where I stand, her eyes are holes, black notes of nothing, ringed a burnt orange. They roll from the fumes to me and back again like sated animals, sure of themselves. My mother and I, we don't have much between us. Very little to show for our time here. But I had my books. They were my friends, my faith, my flight, and she knew it.

JG's crude carpentry burns, page after page fed to its flames.

Almost four-thirty, and he's not here.

But I can wait – no rush today. It's Friday. Happy hour. She'll be off to the pub with whomever asks her. She'll be off to the pub even if nobody does, the little overnight bag she keeps packed in the boot of her car, always hopeful. I will be home in plenty of time to make my bed – that's if Keep hasn't made it already. He has been doing that since she took our books away.

The station hustle begins. I flit along the platform, all the way to its farthest end, my eyes cast across the tracks again and again, scanning, hoping. I turn around, weave my way back through the bottleneck of business suits and briefcases and stockinged legs. He has caught the train for the past many weeks, but perhaps this was a change in routine for him? Maybe his car was broken down and is now repaired. He might never catch the train again. All that has taken place between us, which is nothing in truth, only a game to pass the time.

I am back at the northern end of the platform, my usual spot. He isn't coming. With all the benches occupied, I sit on the old side, the discontinued line, cross-legged on the concrete. I get out my copy of Heathcliff and Cathy, safe in my bag at the time of the fire. An ancient hardback, its moss-green cloth cracked, its brittling pages the colour of over-brewed tea. Read so many times, whole scenes known by heart. My dead grandmother's book, yes. But more than that, Emily Brontë's story is dear to me in ways hard to define. Its rawness, the bleakness. Where some of us reside, like it or not. Where we do our mournful best, feel at home, think our pale brightest. My *sad tooth*, I suppose.

'Did you wait for me?' he asks, breathless.

I look up. 'No,' I say, defensive. 'M-maybe.' I am almost sick with joy.

'It was supposed to be one quick pint, for luck.' He drops to his knees in front of me, panting. 'But then the boys at work wanted to carry it on. I knew you'd be here, and I had to catch you.'

He is flushed, but I think that's because he's been running.

'You did?'

An assertive nod. 'I decided it was about time you and I actually met.'

Brunswick Street, grimy and cavernous. But not anymore. It's a quaint old train station now, treasured. The best train station of all time.

'First of all,' he says. 'Hello.'

'Hello.'

'I'm Marc. With a "c".'

'Jay. No "c".'

He grins. 'Jay? As in … the little bird?'

'I guess. I don't really know too much about birds.'

'Me neither. It was just something to say. You make me nervous!'

'I do?'

We both look away for a moment – study the concrete, the tracks, the rubbish on the tracks.

The 4:40 train arrives.

'This is yours,' he says. 'Damn it.'

'Don't worry,' I say. 'I'll get the next one.'

'Really?'

'So, why do you need luck?'

'Sorry?'

'The pint? For luck?'

'Oh, yeah. Well, I'm going for a job next week, and the boys at work were giving me a shout, for luck.'

'I'm confused.' I press past the hot fluttering in my ears. 'You have a job, but you're going for a different job and your colleagues know about it? I mean, I'm a school kid, so no expert. But aren't you supposed to keep that kind of thing to yourself?'

The train pulls out of the station and a platform bench becomes free.

'Let's grab it,' he says, offering his hand to help me to stand.

I take it. My hand in his.

'Right now, I'm a French polisher. Just a fancy way of saying I muck around with wood to make furniture. But really I'm … well …' He looks over his shoulder, over my head. 'I'm a …' He can't seem to finish the sentence.

'A parolee?' I offer.

He pulls a face, mock-offended.

'I'm …' he tries again. 'What I'm good at is …'

'Denying all charges?'

He drops his head, chuckling.

'Let's see,' I say. 'You're a Mr Whippy? No … a singing telegram? Yes, that's it! *Elvis!* Flame jumpsuit. Brocade. A cape!'

His lips roll inward and he slowly shakes his head, but his eyes still laugh.

'Shoe stretcher? Scarf model?'

'Close, but no cigar for you, wise guy,' he grins. 'Seriously, you have to promise not to send me up. Or I'll be crushed.'

I cross my heart, stone-faced.

'I ... want to be an actor. I'm *trying* to be an actor. And I've got an audition next Tuesday in Melbourne. With Crawfords.'

Stone-faced.

'You're not saying anything.'

'I was close,' I say solemnly. 'With the ... brocade and ... scarves and ...'

'Not so much a school kid but a comedian! Ha-ha!'

'Joking apart,' I say, 'that's fantastic. Crawfords? Wow! *Cop Shop*, right? *The Sullivans?* Just about everything that's ever been on television? Oh my God.'

'Yeah, I'm pretty excited.'

'And Melbourne? I envy you.'

'Oh, you've been there?'

'No. Never,' I say, feeling like an idiot. 'It's just that ... it's a cold place. I love cold places. Even though I've ... never been to one.'

A confused smile. 'I do too,' he says.

'Well, break a leg then! And ... it's been nice knowin' ya.' I do my best to sound whimsical. 'Marc.' I've been wanting to say it ever since he told me his name. *Marc.*

'Aw, don't say that,' he says. 'I mean, it might not lead to anything. Not right away.'

'But we should hope it does,' I say. 'I mean that, I do, even though it feels like ...' I look at my feet. Down the platform, a man drops coins into a soft drink vending machine.

'Like we're saying goodbye,' he says, 'right after we've just said hello.'

I feel like the can, cracked open. 'Hmm.'

'Well, this is not *at all* how it played out in my head,' he says, leaning forward to rest his elbows on his knees. 'Us meeting.'

Us.

'Look, I'm flying down for two days, and then I'll be back – back to work, back on the train every afternoon. They're casting for a new pilot, and even if they like me, shows take ages to get up. Or so I've heard. Besides, I'll probably stink up the audition and they'll burn my headshots and I'll sand French oak for the term of my natural life and we can live happily ever after.'

'I'm not really smiling,' I say, smiling. 'It's a condition.'

He looks at my face, top to bottom, side to side. I'm probably doing the same to him. I'm still having trouble accepting that I'm here, that this conversation is taking place. That Marc with a 'c' is real and looking right at me with his bronze-brown eyes.

'You're one funny chick,' he says. 'But I knew that already.'

'You did? How's that?'

'The same way I know I'll never be able to look at a serviette ever again without thinking of you. "Dunny break – chair."'

'Oh my God. You heard that?'

'"Table – specifically *left* of the dinner plate, only once you've finished your meal."'

'Oh my God,' I say again, my hands over my face.

'How could I ignore a girl with such *bearing*?'

'Ah, you're horrible!' I groan, still covering my face. 'A horrible horrible scarf actor.'

Gently, he peels away my fingers. 'Anyway, the good news is – I'm not gone yet, and I'd like to ask you out.'

I'm no longer sick with joy. I'm dying of it.

'Are you allowed? To go on dates?'

'No,' I say. 'I mean, I wouldn't know. I've never been on one.'

Marc looks pleased. 'How about tomorrow then?'

'Tomorrow?'

271

'Well, I'd rather it was tonight, right now, but then you'd think I was a pushover.'

My turn to look pleased.

'So ... tomorrow?' he says.

'Saturday,' I say.

'Saturday. Often comes after Friday?'

'Yes, that's also been my experience, Marc. We have so much in common.'

'So ... are you free?' he asks again, brushing my fingers. I imagine him touching my jaw, his arms around me, what that would feel like. I imagine standing behind him and slipping my hands into the pockets of his jacket, the side of my face against his back. You don't have to look at me, I'd say. You don't even have to like me, not for long anyway. Only, just take me with you, into the hothouse, or whatever your version is of the world. I don't think mine is quite right.

But you won't do any of that, will you, Spider?

Saturday means tennis. Saturday has meant tennis for as long as I can remember.

Instead, you will do what you always do.

Mother is secretary of the junior association. So Mother will be at the courts. So I will be at the courts. She, the main event; me, her support act. She has been shopping me around of late, cherry-picking boys from the richest families collected by fathers in the fanciest of cars. Angling me in front of them.

Platform 2 has asked you out. Isn't he one of your little lanterns, lighting the way as you walk?

Marc's knuckles slide across the top of mine. If he holds my hand, I realise, he will be the first. The first person to do so because he wants to, because he likes me.

You've a mouth, Spider – use it. Bind up that hole in your back, move your own arms about.

I look up at Marc. Marc with a 'c'.

Speak! Be!

'Am I free?'

Your mother's livestock otherwise.

'Free as a blue jay,' I say, in a voice I hope is my own.

3 days till extubation

'Well, I'm officially corrupted, Ted,' I tell him, Q-tip in hand, dive-bombing his mollusca with dollops of whipped wheatgrass. 'I've signed up to Facebook. This jedi has gone to the dark side.'

Reapplying Vaseline to his lips. 'The Oley Foundation, Crohn's and Colitis Australia, Crohn's and Colitis UK, the Fecal Transplant Foundation, the New England Journal of Medicine, World Gastroenterology Organisation. Only getting warmed up, Teddy boy.'

I have thrown myself into a crash course in inflammatory bowel disease – its treatment, current research and clinical trials. And in the *Proper Care and Maintenance of your MIC-KEY Low Profile Feeding Device.*

'Cracking my old library-lady knuckles,' I joke to him.

It is Saturday. No visit from Frank today. We talk on the phone instead. He says he has lots of homework to do, two reports to write. He will need help with them, but he says he is okay. I know he is staying at home because Jerrik doesn't want to bring him to the hospital where Jerrik might be expected to stay awhile.

'I don't like hospitals,' Jerrik sulked, day one.

'Don't you?' I replied. '*Truly?* How extraordinary, because, you know, everyone else just loves them!'

Jerrik – Bartleby reborn – the man who never got the memo advising that sometimes, often, life involves doing things you would really prefer not to.

In the early evening, I am stooped over the laptop reading about why, despite its apparent efficacy in flushing car radiators, Coca-Cola should *not* be used to clear blocked feeding tubes when my first 'friend request' appears.

Tess, from Teddy's school. I realise I have not spoken to her, nor to anyone outside this hospital, in weeks.

I can't face attempting a connection on the networking site's jammy interface – its boxes within boxes and exhortations to like, comment, share, add to this, edit that. Make 'friends' with the click of a button like adding water to a packet of sea monkeys. I have signed up to this time-wasting cyber-fidget in the hope of learning things, of educating myself and helping my son. It is for others to pimp their opinions, overshare their emotions and turn the minutiae of their self-infatuated everyday into *ME – The Musical!*

Another place that is not my kind of place.

Giving Teddy a kiss, I tell Gwen the nurse I'm going to stretch my legs. I take my phone and head to the inpatients-only garden on the eighth floor. It is almost always empty on weekends and the views are not too shabby, especially at almost five pm, with the sky crushing dark and the lights of the city just beginning to do their thing.

Tess and I talk for more than thirty minutes. Her husband, David, has met someone in Dubai. A fish chef. He won't be returning any time soon. I tell her I am sorry (though I'm hardly surprised). What does surprise me is Tess, who sounds remarkably sanguine. She and Dylan and their new 'just-right'-sized dog (no more snivelling crotch-sniffers) have moved into a townhouse in a new complex near school. Vivienne has set her up with an associate to handle the divorce, meaning that David and his *poissonier* are about to be made penniless. There is no mention of Jesus or hardcore hobbies. No longer needing to distract herself from a moribund marriage, Tess seems to be largely woi-woi free.

She scolds me, gently, for not being in touch. Everyone's been so worried, she says, though not wanting to intrude. I tell her I haven't felt up to talking to anyone about what has been going on. Too much, too complex. Still coming to grips with it myself. 'Suffice to say Teddy won't be back to school for quite some time.'

I do mention that Teddy's illness thwarted Jerrik's plans to move in with Minnie. 'I think our separation lasted, officially, for about six hours and twenty-two minutes.'

'Well, depending on how you look at it, Jay, Teddy either saved the day or wrecked a marvellous opportunity for you.' Then she asks, 'How are you finding the new hospital, anyway? I've heard mixed reports.'

'Mixed about covers it. The good here is very good. The bad is unforgivable.'

'At least it's modern,' she says. 'Does it feel nautical inside?'

'Nautical?'

'Hmm. You know, like it is on the outside? How they designed it to look like an ocean liner?'

'An *ocean liner*?'

Tess laughs. 'You really don't get out much, do you, Jay? Those four big coppery stacks are meant to be funnels and the pointy city end is like the bow. Have you never noticed, driving by?'

I look up at the now-obvious seafaring motifs. 'I had no idea.'

'Why a cruise ship,' says Tess, 'is anyone's guess.'

We hang up, but Tess's comment brings to mind Frank's dream, starring his brother, the day-saving dolphin.

And the sun is setting. And it turns Teddy kind of golden. And everyone's gathering around. Watching Teddy makes them forget the boat is sinking.

Frank's dream makes me think about Heathcliff and Cathy, how her dreams fell through her *like wine through water*, changing her, altering the colour of her mind. And Cathy's dreams dredge up thoughts of my own. Then I realise how like Teddy I am – connecting things.

No. Instead, I decide that dreams are complete bastards, scammers, nothing but sewage of the subconscious, and I head back to paediatric intensive care. On the way, I pass Ryker Shulmans.

'Is this hospital meant to resemble a cruise ship?' I ask him.

'I believe so,' he replies, a contemplative nod. 'And when you consider … the overcrowding, the poor air quality, the abhorrent sleeping conditions, the high rates of cabin fever and virus transmission, I would argue it's a largely congruous design, wouldn't you?'

We both smile and continue on our respective ways.

Almost midnight. Eyes blurring. I can read no more of intestines. My next actions I put down to mind-altering exhaustion and the diminished discretion that invariably comes with it.

I accept Tess's friend request on Facebook.

I attempt a request of my own, to the P & C Association's page at Teddy's school. I think it worked.

I look up Madison Fox, find nothing of any great interest except for mild esotropia in her left eye.

I look up Jerrik. Nothing.

I look up the firm Jerrik works for. In its many pages, I find Minnie.

Minnie Rollo. A Nordic surname, just like Jerrik. Tall, like Jerrik. Slim, like Jerrik. Not horsey, unlike Jerrik.

Minnie Rollo wears sunglasses a great deal, even at her desk it would seem. Perhaps she is cross-eyed like Madison? Or a cyborg – Jerrik's type.

Apart from that, I have a surprising lack of interest in the Minnie Rollo who requires an escort to her doctor's appointments and who is sleeping with ~~my husband~~ the boys' father.

I think of Tillie and Prim. To find them, I would need to type their names on a keyboard for the very first time. No. I decide to leave them be, perfect as they always were, further along the river where they belong. In a century that is gone.

But I look up Evie. Evie Mayhew. I find several, though none who look anything like I remember her. I try Evie Faith Mayhew. She may have changed her name by now, as I have. She may have changed a lot more. She might also be a social-networking conscientious objector, though I consider that unlikely. I recall her many sisters whose names evade me, though I remember her toddler brother, Joel, and scout about for him. Again, there are more than one Joel Mayhew. However, one of the Joels has a 'timeline' (I can't believe I am using this term) with many pictures. A recent one is of a middle-aged man at the birthday celebration of an elderly woman. Marilyn, Evie's mother. I recognise her instantly. I adored her.

I look her up. Marilyn has her own page, with recent posts and many photographs. Evie's sisters, their families I assume. Pictures of Evie too – young Evie, my Evie, a stunning Evie graduating high school. No recent pictures, however.

DO YOU KNOW MARILYN? asks the robot behind the screen. *If you know Marilyn, send her a message.*

It's 12:08 am, and I do.

17 years old, winter

Marc takes me ice-skating. He says he chose that because I like to be cold. He remembered what I said at the station.

I buckle and topple and slip. He picks me up, does his best to break my slapstick falls. Twice I knock him off his own feet. I panic and squeal and I am breathless, my clothes wet from the ice. I laugh, eyes watering, and he teases me without mercy. By the end of the session, I skate – upright, jerky, listing, my hand in his. Why is there no word for the magic of hand-holding? I could fly if I wanted to, circle the world, never come down, only I don't. Right here, mostly on my backside, is the best place I've ever been.

I told Lonnie I wasn't well, felt fluey, that I wasn't up to a day at the courts.

All in your head, she said, but let me stay home anyway.

She will be there all day, right to the end to phone in the results to the Sunday paper. I arranged to meet Marc in the city.

He had wanted to drive over and collect me, but I hadn't given him my home address or our telephone number. I won't, not ever. He might try looking us up but there are a million Murphys in the White Pages and he won't know my mother's first initial. And I lied about where I lived, naming a suburb two over from mine. I need to protect us both, and to do that is to make certain Marc and Lonnie never cross paths.

I have an explanation worked out for every possible contingency. If Lonnie says she called, I will say I took the honey pills (as instructed) and was in a deep sleep, didn't hear the phone ring. And if Lonnie leaves the tennis centre early and gets home before me, I will tell her that I walked to the pharmacy to buy more flu tablets but that it was closed, and I had to keep walking until I found one that was open. Codral Day & Nights in my pocket just in case.

After skating, Marc drives me back to the city so I can catch a train home. I tell him enough about Lonnie so he understands the need for subterfuge.

'So, your mum wouldn't like me because I'm not a Terrace boy, or a tennis jock? Some rich kid?'

'She wouldn't like you because she didn't pick you.'

We kissed. Well, he kissed me while I trembled.

I was still shaking on the train, all the way home. Not only because of Marc, but because of me. I put my hand up to the glass. I decided something for myself and, so far, I have lived to tell the tale. A story of my own making, for once. About love.

Spring

He pulls away.

'But I want to,' I say, my hand on his bare back. 'With you.'

'You're only saying that because you think that's what I want.'

'And you don't?'

'*Hell yes!*' He picks up his T-shirt from the edge of his sofa bed. 'But I don't want you to think that's all I want. You're more to me than that. You're my girl.'

'Aww,' I say.

'And I hate having to sneak around. I want to see you whenever I want. Whenever you want. You won't even let me call you.'

We've been to see *Paris, Texas* at the Metro. We go there nearly every Sunday afternoon, and afterwards we have fried rice and dumplings in Chinatown. 'Hey, slow down,' he laughed the first time he took me there. 'It's like you've never eaten cheap Chinese before.' I hadn't, and it was magnificent. Now we are back at his flat. Lonnie thinks I am at Tillie's, studying – my cover story for spending time with Marc. If he and I meet after school, I tell her I am staying late to work on a group assignment; on Sundays, I am either at Tillie's or Prim's.

'You know that ancient Celtic thing,' I say, changing the subject. 'The idea that heaven and earth are only three feet apart?'

Earlier, I'd pulled off his T-shirt. He sits scrunching it up, idly passing it from one hand to the other. I don't want him to put it back on, and I know he doesn't want to either.

He shakes his head. 'No, Einstein. I don't know about this ancient Celtic thing. But clearly you do.'

'And in *thin places*, heaven and earth are even closer than that.'

He smiles. 'I'm listening, Professor. But keep it simple for me. An actor over here, remember? Nothing but a pretty face.'

I punch him on the arm, and he kisses me on the jaw.

'Anywhere can be a thin space – indoors, outdoors. Not everyone finds one, and you can't go looking. They either take you completely by surprise, or you never know them at all.'

I think of the Moreton Bay fig I used to hide in at primary school while I waited for the old man, Mr 126. A thin place, some days, the veil to the other side pinned back. Other days, just a tree, a girl and a book, the pinning not up to me.

'So … what you're telling me is,' he says, folding and unfolding his fingers around mine, 'that you've experienced this? A thin place?'

I love his hands. If only I could photograph them, then I could hold them whenever I need to. But I won't dare take a picture of us, just as I'll never give him my address or phone number. It isn't safe.

'Actually, yes. There used to be this book—'

'A *book*?'

'Yeah, you know, a thing with words on paper pages? You might still be reading the pretty plastic ones that float in the bath?'

He licks my face.

'It was an old travelogue kind of book, about Lapland and the northern lights. I would open the book and lay it over my face, like I was having a nap. And then it would start. I know it sounds nuts, but I could hear it breathe, the book – I swear. And then it was like everything just fell away. In a thin place, there's only room for … the essence of you – whatever it was that jumped in to take you from a cell division to the person you are. And suddenly, everything becomes … perfect. What we're all supposed to believe a heaven would be like. You don't *do* anything, you don't even see, you just *are*, held close in a kind of ecstasy. Maybe it *is* heaven and some of us for some reason manage to sneak a look.'

Marc's face is difficult to read.

'That sounds mental, doesn't it?'

'No more mental than love at first sight,' he says, serious. 'Do you believe in that?'

'Do you?'

'Dunno.' He shrugs. 'Maybe.'

'People swear it's a thing,' I say. 'So, I guess I do. But to be so real it has to *be* something, right, made of some substance? Chemicals? Neurons, electrical impulses, past lives, future lives? God? For that random person, chanced upon only once, to stay locked inside you? That can't be nothing, so which is it? Science, or just plain occult?'

'*Occult?*'

'Let's imagine this girl,' I say. 'For the purposes of our experiment, we will call her Rory.'

'Is this Rory anything like my girlfriend Rory who didn't even tell me her name was Rory until we'd been going out for three months?'

'Yes,' I say, my insides still a beehive every time he calls me his girlfriend. 'This Rory is just like that Rory.'

'Got it,' he says.

'And she sees this bloke, this … *hunk*, a perfect ten, like … hmm, let me see …'

He waggles his head expectantly.

'Boris Becker.'

'Oi,' he yells, tossing his T-shirt at my head.

'Okay, okay. So, this girl, Rory, sees this bloke, Marc, just one time, and in that moment she feels something … lock in … between them. A connection so *real*, so palpable, it could be a rope tying them together. Marc might not feel it, he might not even notice her. She sees him, and that's all that matters – once, briefly – but never forgets him. The details of him, his face, all as clear as a picture to her. She'll think of him, on and off, all of her life, hope he's okay and happy, even though she has no right to wish anything for him. No right even to think of him, really. She will always be able to find him, even when he is nowhere to be found.'

'But I did see you,' Marc says. 'As I remember it, I saw you first. And we're here, together. We made it. You don't need a picture – you've got me.'

'Then I guess I'll always be able to find you.'

He kisses my palm as I add, 'Even when you're nowhere to be found.'

'I'm not getting lost, Ror. I'm not going anywhere. I love you.'

We look at each other and I steady for a burst of laughter, for his words to be a wind-up, but instead his cheeks and ears colour.

'Don't know about the palpable, chemical, at-first-sight ropey occult thing. Only know how I feel. In love, I'd say.'

No-one has ever said this to me. Not Grandma, though I know she cared deeply for me. Not even Keep. I have read these words in books and I have spoken them aloud in my room using other voices, pretending those voices are speaking to me. But then I'd catch my reflection in the bedroom window, the look on my face, the idiot hope, and shut would be the book, and off would go the light, as fast as the idiot reflected could do so.

My turn to throw a shirt at him. 'You also, I do.' And this is the way it comes out, silly and half-formed and bashful.

'*You also, I do!*' He flops backwards onto the mattress, knees up, laughter finally catching its cue. 'What's *that?*'

'I don't know!' I wail, my embarrassment a part of the game that sweeps us along. 'You just said the L-word and I briefly lost the power of speech. Stop laughing. I bet Boris Becker wouldn't laugh at me.'

'Stuff Boris,' Marc says, sitting up, grabbing my waist. 'Come here, Yoda. Let's make out.'

2 days till extubation

Ryker Shulmans opens Teddy's door. 'Teddy's mum, how goes it?'

'Two days to go, Doc, but who's counting?' I stand up, take the opportunity to have a stretch.

'Now, you know how much we love having you here,' he begins.

'But?'

'You need a night off, Jay,' he says. 'I can easily put you in touch with the right people to get you some accommodation. The hospital owns half those towers you can see over there.' He points to the wall of windows behind Teddy's bed. 'You only have to say the word. Teddy's going to be in the wards for some weeks yet and I know you have your other son to care for.'

'But we live so close,' I remind him.

'And yet you haven't been home in weeks, Jay, isn't that so?'

'The boys' father has brought me things. Change of clothes, et cetera.'

But Ryker Shulmans is going hard this round. 'Nothing beats a real bed or a real shower. Hospital bathrooms are like campground amenities, I'm afraid.' A shiver of mock disgust. 'You feel grubbier coming out than you did going in.'

He almost persuades me.

'I'll have a think about it,' I say. 'Let you know.'

'Go home, Jay,' he says, his hands cupping my shoulders. 'Get a couple of hours in your own bed. Trust me – it makes a difference. I'm on tonight, so you know Teddy is in safe hands.'

'But what if—'

'Teddy's going to be extubated in a couple of days and he's going to need you, especially if you end up back on Nine.' Ryker Shulmans leans in. 'Actually, I'm trying to get you onto another floor. I know what Ward Nine is like. I've had parents begging to bring their kids back to PICU.'

At least I know it isn't just me.

I collect a few things, then attempt a goodbye snuggle with Teddy, mindful of the cannulas and sensors and tubes. I press his palms gently to my ears. In fairytales, graveside tears open dead eyes, bring back to beating life a still, princely heart. My tears fall now onto Teddy's face, and I let them.

'I'm here if you want to sing, big Ted. I haven't heard your beautiful voice in far too long. And even if I'm not here, I will be tuning in. We've got a bandwidth all our own, you and me.'

It's been a month since I have been outside this building. And I feel like I have grown.

I decide against a cab, that the exercise will do me good. But as I make my way, something changes. I feel as though I could scale walls unaided, step over the entire hospital precinct in a single stride. The traffic lights seem no bigger than pieces from a Brio set. I imagine them between my fingers, grinding them to dust if I cared to. I do care to. To think I used to stop for them, obey them, like they mattered. Like traffic mattered. Or getting somewhere on time.

That day in the walkway, on the bench, having fled the noisy news bulletin in the room next to Teddy's, Ryker Shulmans stopped to talk to me. He talked about time. And chemistry, my weakest subject.

'I know General Paediatrics are concerned about RFS,' he said. 'The risk of refeeding syndrome.'

'Yes,' I said, thinking of the horrible half-bird. 'It was one of the biggest guns she put to my head. It was either intubation or the trigger pulled.'

'Let me explain how much chance Teddy has of developing RFS,' said Ryker Shulmans, making a circle with his thumb and index finger. 'Zero.'

The hospital is behind me now, and I am passing the famous cricket ground. Only I am above it, looking down on the looping yellow-and-maroon stadium seats. But where are all the players who chase the tiny ball, who bowl and bat it? They need me on their teams tonight. Tonight, I am Captain. I am oracle and steel and doom-dragon and Queen.

'We take blood from Teddy every two hours,' Ryker Shulmans explained as we sat on that bench. 'And if his magnesium gets a little low, or his phosphate, I top it up. And if his salt starts to climb, I give him something to bring it down. His heart is steady, his organs all functioning as well as anyone's. He was never at risk of a refeed. I don't know why they mentioned it. It only scared you.'

Another few strides and I will be home. But I am enjoying the view. The stream near our house is barely a puddle now, given the size of me. But just when I forget everything else, my mother appears, all around. Her false teeth drip from her head, one by one. They become the thin white line I follow down the centre of the road. Her hair is the leaves on the ghost gums, lifting and falling in the sooty night air; her voice, the bats feasting and feuding.

Tomorrow, on my way back to the hospital, I will take a detour to the care home and drop off that clean dressing-gown. Make the most of the state I am in. My child is ill. A disease is suspected that cannot be cured; a disease that will almost certainly, if not rigorously monitored and treated, shorten his life. Not all test results are yet known. He may have comorbid conditions, on top of existing comorbid conditions. He is being kept alive. A machine breathes for him. A gastrostomy eats for him. I'm a calamity other calamities pretend they don't see. I am a Titan of fucking calamities. I have never been safer, more certain.

'In a way,' said Ryker Shulmans beside me that day, 'the human body is a walking, talking chemical experiment – our bodies the flasks warm and bubbling over a burner – little collisions occurring inside. Each experiment – a mysterious new compound, the elements around it forever altered. Soon enough, of course, all our experiments come to a stop – some not as routine as we think, while others simply run their course. Not so the mystery that was inside it, not at all. When someone dies, I think of it as more an *interruption*. All those random collisions inside the flask – they still happened, didn't they? And all those elements – the people who knew them, who loved them – remain altered. Duration doesn't change that. So death is only the death of time, when you think about it. And with it, perhaps, expectation. Take away the pain of not having what we *expected* to have and, I think, we see things very differently.'

Duration. A concept Teddy has always found so challenging. Why should it mean anything?

12:02 am

I stand outside our home, the dip-down, a Titan astride two frowning hills. I bend down, unlock the door, and turn on a light. The Other Things scatter – claws in all directions, running for cover. But I know they'll be back. When I am small again, stopping at traffic lights, they will be back. And small again I must become; how else to fit into this less-than world?

I see now why Frank hasn't been coming to the hospital. The repainting of the front room, a job I'd barely begun two months ago, is nearly finished. Frank has taken over where I left off, and he has done a spectacular job. *Oh, Frank.*

I open the door to his room. He is lost to sleep, and I kiss his head, touch my lips to the fine prickling of hair. He stirs, rolls over, but doesn't wake. I will surprise him at breakfast time. The hallway light pools across the floor of his room, becomes a kind of spotlight. In it are the new boots, their cream laces loose, shoved-in socks inside out. I pick them up. New boots, new-boot smell. They are starting to eat away at me, these light brown boots. No doubt I know them from somewhere.

I head upstairs. The door to Jerrik's ~~suite~~ room is closed. I wonder who I might find in there. Minnie Rollo of the formidable fringe and sunglasses? Someone else? A threesome? Jerrik needs to know I am here, that I can take care of Frank in the morning, get him to school before I return to the hospital. I knock lightly, but there is no response – no scrabbling of sheets, no shushing panic.

The room is empty. Worse than empty, abandoned. I wonder how long it has been since Jerrik has slept here? How long Frank has survived on his own, fifteen years old, covering for his father, cleaning up the Dubious Rubious chaos I left behind? Catching the bus on his own, ready or not. Doing for himself at an age when no child should, especially not a boy like Frank. Sensitive Frank, already so wearied, understanding the tension in this house, living in dread of setting it off, of tripping its thin white beams stretched sly and mean across the doorways, never knowing what to say and so saying nothing, which is how things go from bad to worse, from a dilemma to an emergency, no-one safe, all my promises nulled.

Gum wrappers on Jerrik's floor. Luggage tags, cufflinks, junk mail, belts, Panadol boxes, discarded tissues (stiff and drying to dust), paperclips, bulldog clips, pens, at least thirty ties, used envelopes and possibly hundreds of receipts. I stopped cleaning this room years ago, believing my threat to do so would prompt more regular upkeep. An anti-snoring nasal spray lies on the floor, crushed against a chest of gaping drawers, mostly cleared out. Funny, I had no idea Jerrik snored.

I look around this large space – too big a room for the archiving of rubbish and a not-quite marriage. Instead, I see walls of dramatic red, and paint pots, brushes, sketchbooks, charcoals and inks. I see Frank behind an easel. I see a painter's studio. I see myself, looking on, small again in this house. But a smallness altered.

Joy as Canberra disco for people with disabilities returns after coronavirus shutdown

After months of coronavirus social restrictions, Darren Tait was getting itchy feet.

'I love dancing,' he said.

Darren lives with an intellectual disability and was a regular at the Northside Recreation Group (NRG) disco until COVID-19 put dancing on the social-distancing 'blacklist' back in March.

Like many others who attend the disco nights, it was a highlight of Darren's week – a chance to not only dance it out but also socialise with friends.

He usually attended with his friend Gary Comerford, with whom he has shared a home for 30 years.

The pair are known as Daz and Gaz.

The NRG disco was conceived in 2018 as a safe place to go for people with special needs, where they could socialise in a nightclub atmosphere.

Organiser Karen Champion, who works in disability support, said she wanted to give her clients the same fun night out that other adults enjoyed.

'You just see a light switch on, and they come alive,' she said.

Every Tuesday night, volunteers would transform the Palmerston Community Centre hall into the NRG disco, complete with dozens of swirling lights and a pumping sound system.

But in March the hall fell silent, as the disco was forced to shut its doors due to social distancing requirements.

'It's very difficult with individuals with a disability to understand the change. The whole shutting of the doors ... [they'd say], "Why can't we go?"'

But with Canberra's coronavirus restrictions beginning to lift, the disco is now back up and running, providing a vital social outlet – and a chance for Daz and Gaz to blow out the cobwebs after three months of self-isolation.

The pair have become as close as any family – living, holidaying, and socialising together.

17 years old, late spring

He tries kissing my neck.

'I have to read,' I say, not really resisting.

'But you've read it already. You only just finished reading it.'

'Yes. But I need to read it again.'

'Why? Why, for the love of God, would you read that thing twice? I can't get beyond the third page.'

'To really, you know, get it stuck in my head. Dig so deep into it I'll be able to shake the life out of any exam question that gets thrown at me.'

'Ror, why are top marks so important? What's wrong with a B?'

'We don't get Bs. We get sevens and sixes, down to threes. At least, I think it goes down to threes.'

'So what would be wrong with a six? Or a five?'

'I do get sixes. In stuff I'm not good at.'

'So … what would be wrong with a six in English?'

I blink at him.

'You see? You're looking at me like I just said, what's wrong with a kitten omelette. Like a six or a five in English or French would mean a firing squad.'

'For me, it would.'

I am being reckless. Being Saturday, Lonnie is at the courts, and I have claimed to have yet another sick headache. As soon as she left, I caught a train to Marc's flat. I will run with the trip to the pharmacy story if need be.

'That's bananas,' says Marc, bringing me back to him, to the here and now. 'It's just high school.'

'Says the wise old man who quit school four years ago.'

'Seriously. The day you walk out those Kemp Place gates nobody's going to ask you what grade you got in high school English. No-one. It won't matter.'

'But if my grades aren't the best they can be ...'

He looks at me, eyebrows raised.

Even if I get the law school offer, I plan to change my course to arts, a journalism major. I know I will get into their honours stream because of my humanities grades – straight sevens so far in English, French, German, history. There are masters programs in England I've already looked into. Lonnie will never know. I will find part-time work while I study, get to know people, then move into a share house. I will run away if she won't let me go. I just need that law offer to get me through the Christmas break, keep her off my back.

'It's just what I'm supposed to do, Marc. What's always been expected. If I don't do well ... if Lonnie doesn't get what she wants ... I have to get out of that house. Find my own way to be.'

I can't seem to sleep anymore. Can't seem to put the pen down, to stop rewriting every essay, re-reading what I've already committed to memory. What is happening to me?

'You will,' he says.

I shake my head. 'You don't know my mother.' My body stiffens and my breath stops; I think I can hear her outside Marc's front door, about to burst through. My brain works so fast that my thoughts bottleneck – what to do, what to say, where to hide. But it's only dread. It has been circling all day, testing the locks. 'Lonnie's like quicksand. The more you struggle, the surer it is that she'll get you.'

'You *will* get out of that house, Ror. Right after graduation, yeah? Even if I have to come and carry you out myself.'

'Promise?' I say, with a cheeriness I don't feel.

'Promise,' he says, a quick kiss. 'Though you'd have to give me your address first. I'm fiercely intelligent. And a handsome rooster. But I'm not a mind-reader.'

'Sure,' I say, returning to the voyage of the *Pequod* and its crew. 'But until then, I'm not blowing my seven in English. Not even for you, Cocky Locky.'

Marc grabs the Melville, tosses it over his head. 'I've got a better idea,' he says. 'Let's have a nap.'

But my eye is on the clock. I've always got an eye on the clock and an ear listening out. Every passing car is Lonnie's bright-green Gemini. Quieter than her old one. Sneakier. 'Oh. *A nap* is what we're calling it now?'

'No, I mean it. An honest-to-goodness snooze. You look wiped.'

He goes to his record player, selects 'I Put a Spell on You'.

'Okay. Come on, lie down with me.'

'Now what?' I say, humouring him.

'We just kind of ... love up.' He wraps me in his arms.

'Love up?'

'Yeah. We lie here, hold hands, make cow eyes at each other. I can breathe on you, if you want? Like a book.'

The next afternoon we see an Akira Kurosawa double at the Metro – *Throne of Blood* and *Rashomon*. We arrive back at his flat as his phone rings. It is his agent calling.

Marc has an agent now because, apparently, Marc Stringer, actor, is really very good.

'No, I'm not sitting down,' he says with a laugh. 'Just tell me already.'

Less laughing now. More listening.

'Uh-huh,' he says, looking over me. 'Uh-huh. Yeah, it's current. Oh, c'mon. You're killing me, Trish.'

Trish. Marc's agent who is at least fifty, I was happy to learn.

Then, 'You're kidding,' he says. 'You have *got* to be kidding. You're *kidding*?' Two or three more times.

He turns away from me, his hand to his forehead, shaking.

When he hangs up the phone, Marc, in fits and starts, tells me that though he wasn't picked up by Crawfords all those months ago, he did impress some people at the casting.

'And one of them was this guy, and he's now an AD on a film shoot in LA.'

'AD?' I ask. 'LA?'

'Assistant Director,' he says, pacing, unable to speak the words as quickly as he wants to. 'Anyway, filming's about to get underway in Los Angeles and it's all been cast, only some guy who plays the lead character's son has got sick or got busted or got sacked or something and has to be replaced. Pronto.'

'And …?'

'And … apparently, I look a lot like him. Same complexion, build. So wardrobe wouldn't be an issue.'

'And …?'

I can see where this is going, but I want him to tell me.

'And … this AD thought of me. Showed the director and the EP my audition tape.'

'EP?'

'Executive Producer. And they liked what they saw, Ror. They really liked what they saw. But, Rory old thing. Guess who the EP is?'

'No idea,' I say, palms up, a plus-size look of expectation.

'The EP who is *also* the film's *lead*?'

'Still no idea,' I say, maintaining my pose.

'None other than … Hold me down, Rory, *hold me down*.'

I grip him by the forearms.

'Jack FREAKING Nicholson!'

We jump up and down, forearms still locked.

OhMyGod!OhMyGod!OhMyGod!

Marc grabs a pair of underpants from a basket of washing and snaps them onto his head, galloping around his flat yelling, 'I'm in a movie with Jack Nicholson! I'm in a movie with Jack Nicholson!'

And I jump up and down on the spot yelling, 'Are those undies even clean?'

And he yells back, 'Let's hope not!' and we laugh and fall down and jump and holler some more.

He is still shaking when he walks me to the station a couple of hours later.

He has to be on set in three weeks' time, he says as we amble along. For a month-long shoot. And Trish has organised a *bunch* of auditions while he is there.

'A whole bunch of them, Ror.' His voice quivers with disbelief. 'Trish says I should probably stay on for a bit, after the shoot. It's pilot season soon. I'm going to work in Hollywood, Ror. Hollywood, California.'

We kiss before I take my seat on the red rattler – one of the old wooden trains they run on weekends, muck-brown not red, sash windows and tough, tussocky bench seats. As the poorly lit carriage creaks into motion, Marc turns, walks a little way along the platform, then spins back, shoves his head through the window and grabs me by the collar. 'You, I love, Rory Jay. *Hrrmmm*,' he says in Yoda's voice, and kisses me again. Then he mock-stumbles as he runs alongside, clutching his chest and falling to the platform like Omar Sharif at the end of *Doctor Zhivago*.

As the rattler heaves away, the station's lamps grow smaller and closer together, brilliant as tiny moons. Marc frog-hops backwards up the steps of the overhead bridge. His T-shirt, whipped off in a blink, whirls aloft like a lasso. He is pure energy, each pratfall and antic a surge of his own current.

The stone begins to warm my pocket. My fingers test for tears, loose stitches, but there are none. The little stone is safe. So is this afternoon, and this train, Marc's kiss, still on my lips. All of it, pocketed, easy to lay my hand on when this night is long gone and nowhere to be found.

1 day till extubation, 12:41 am

I take a shower, possibly the greatest shower of my life. Ryker Shulmans was right. I get into bed, try unsuccessfully to sleep. Teddy's salt lamp is a blanching green. Across the room, his empty bed is slablike, a menace. All my little misfits run riot in my head, their lumpen forms and cloven hooves and trough-breath, snuffling and snouting their favourite what if game.

What if this?

And *what if* that?

What then, *Warrior Mother*?

So I get up, sit at my desk and call Teddy's hospital room. 'All okay since I left?'

'It's barely been two hours,' laughs the night nurse. 'Everything's fine.'

'Call me. For any reason.'

I have started reading print newspapers again, buying them each morning from the hospital kiosk. Opening scrapbook #13, I add a story from yesterday's edition, all about a man in Albury who shot his wife, his two autistic children and the family poodle. Keep finally arrives.

'I was half-expecting you'd come to the hospital,' I say. 'It's been my room too, as well as Teddy's.'

Squalid places, he says.

'I missed you.'

Miserable together, he says, *yet unimaginable apart.*

I try to recall which of us first said this, and when.

Besides, you didn't need me, Spider.

'Rubbish,' I say. 'I always need you.'

His hands hover over my desk. *No moving on from all this business? I would have thought you have enough to worry about.*

I look up at him. 'Who are you and how did you get into my house?'

Silence.

'Move on? It's moving on and getting out of the way that's part of the problem, Keep. I'm the one who remembers. Remember?' I reach down, haul up years of scrapbooks, drop them onto the desk. 'A lot of names here. Babies and children. A lot of people who lived their whole lives without a single kind word. Where are their marchers? Their protesters, hmm? Even the young, who claim to care so much about everything and everyone, where is their energy for this? Disgrace after disgrace, one indignity after another and nobody cares. It's up to half-dead mothers like me, isn't it? We brought them into this world, so we must do, we must be. That's being a good mother. A warrior. So long as we *do* and *be* quietly, without fuss, keep our *roaring* to ourselves. We bring them into this world where nobody wants them, but we mustn't take them out of it – that's being a bad mother. Evil. Even Lonnie didn't actually *kill* me. If I don't remember their names, Keeper, their stories, what other bastard will? Hard to see the woods sometimes, for all the self-righteous trees.'

And then? he asks. *How does it all end?*

'End?' I say, my hands on the top of the scrapbook pile. A thick dust has gathered in my absence. I try sweeping it away with the back of my hand, watch as it resettles quickly. 'As if it will ever end.'

Before leaving the hospital, I told Ryker I would take up his offer of hospital accommodation. He texts me now to let me know a welfare officer has already confirmed a vacancy – Frank and I can move in immediately, details to follow. Once Teddy is back in the ward, I won't be able to leave his side, but at least Frank will be only across the street. Hospital accommodation – hollow and sterile, perhaps. But also tripwire-free.

When he wakes in a few hours' time, Frank will see the note I have pinned to the back of his bedroom door:

I'm home.
How about brunch?
Just us, anywhere you like.
Bacon permitted!
We can talk about your solo show – postponed, but not forgotten. We'll make plans.
The living room looks amazing – thank you, my wonder.
Love, Mum xx

17 years old, late spring

She stabs at their yolks, bullying them around the pan, hating those eggs, their ferocious scrambling like a penance long overdue.

She asks, again, how yesterday's study session went at Tillie's.

'Fine.'

'No more sick headaches?'

'No.'

She instructs me to take a shower while she fixes dinner. *Dinner.* I tell her I will have one later.

'*Now*,' she says in such a tone I do it at once.

Marc flies out in two days. I want all his dreams to come true, I do, I swear it. I want him to 'have it all'. I just wish he could have it here, with me.

The tennis club AGM was held last night. Lonnie got home late, white as a sheet and eerily quiet. My mother is not a quiet woman. She sat in the lounge all night, watching television, the sound muted, drinking an entire bottle of Moselle. I don't think she went to bed.

When I am done showering, she tells me she has made custard for pudding. 'Your favourite, isn't that right? A treat for all your hard work.'

Dinner. Pudding. *Treat.* My mother is not herself. I wonder if she has invited someone over. It has been some time since Lonnie has had a gentleman caller.

'Just us tonight, is it, Mum?'

'Who you expecting? Charles and bloody Diana?'

There she is, my mother. I feel a little more relaxed.

We eat while watching Mike. Lonnie rushes through her meal, angry eating, still furious with the food. I offer to wash up.

'You haven't eaten your custard. Not that I suppose mine could ever hold a candle to your grandmother's, but wasting food is a—'

'*Sin*. Yes, Mother.' Pretty certain I have learnt that lesson.

And with that, Paddy is destroyed all over again. I cannot remember him with love. JG scourges all memory of the dog. Sometimes I swear I can hear the squeak of the garden gate. I hate this house. I am sure the old man haunts it.

After I eat the pudding, Lonnie insists I take some honey pills.

'Why?' I ask. 'My headache's gone.'

'Don't want it coming back,' she insists.

A robust crushing of white pills, a vigorous whipping with honey – creamed honey tonight, a special touch. A sour, gritty, drug sorbet, every last scrape transferred to the tip of a metal dessert spoon. The big dipper.

'Mum, I'm almost eighteen. I can swallow tablets. Anyway, they make me drowsy and I still have study to do.'

She spins around, her face and neck streaked red. 'But you study *so hard*, don't you, Missy? *All* Saturday and *all* Sunday. Hours and *hours* at Tillie Tan's, isn't that right?'

Oh God. She knows. Somehow she knows.

Those black eyes are back, my books burning at their edges.

She thrusts the spoon at my face, a gauntlet bearing ill gifts. I am afraid to open my mouth, afraid she will shove it in so hard it will punch through the back of my neck. I wonder if she is about to poison me, if I am to go the same way as Paddy.

I surrender. I supplicate. It is what people like my mother rely on. I have been reading about them. Lonnie is straight out of a case study.

My mouth falls open and I lick her trusty old spoon like a beat-down dog. I survive.

I could be a case study too.

She retreats to the lounge and another bottle of drive-thru Blue Nun.

On my way to my room, I stand for a moment in the kitchen.

Just because I can see JG in his chair, and just because I can smell his tobacco, and hear the *pah pah* of his twisting half-mouth, doesn't mean he is there.

Hwoo.

—

Book open on my desk, pen in my hand. I start to feel like lead. Hot lead. Spinning hot lead. My head hangs, a stalk, trodden.

Words blur. Pen drops. Head sinks to the desk. Cool desk. Solid. Princely.

Knees sway, slide. Too much, even to sit. My stomach heaves.

The pills – she crushed only two. I saw them.

Why is it so hot?

The eggs? Something in the eggs?

The custard. She was right, not a patch on Grandma's. Artificial sweetener, she said, so it might not taste so good. Lousy Sugarine, she said, but better than lousy calories.

Can't breathe. Call Marc. Can't walk. Crawl. Can't.

Lonnie, pacing. My eyes too swollen to see. I've been sick.

Lonnie, at the end of my bed.

Lonnie, no longer the tennis club secretary. Voted out at last night's AGM. Off the committee entirely. Not one vote in her corner. Complaints from families.

Lonnie, humiliated. The world no longer wilting her way.

'My *nasty attitude* they said. What fucken attitude?'

I try to speak. Retch.

'Feeling sick, are you, Mutt? Feeling sick in the guts?'

I moan.

Now she's behind me, wrenching my hair, her fingers a small machine, pulling, threshing.

'Let *me* tell *you* about feeling sick in the guts.'

My head snaps back. A comb? Is she combing my hair? It cuts, hurts.

'Sick in the guts is how *I felt*, Mutt. How *I felt* when Wendy Coleman, nice as pie before the meeting started, asked after you, Lady Jay, Queen-a the courts.'

My hair, she is ripping it out. 'Mum … plea—'

'"Not seen much-a Jay lately," said Wendy the bitch.'

'*Mum!* You're hurting—'

'"Must be too busy with that handsome new beau of hers," said Wendy the la-di-da *cunt.*'

'Please, Mum …'

I see it, spilling out.

'Turns out, Wendy's son, *Dion* … that fucken name … *Dion* works at the pictures in town.'

The last of the good. Gone. No more to tip out.

'Remember him, Mutt? *Dion?* Shit player. Had a crush on you, turns out. Doesn't everybody?'

Lonnie, savage. I try to twist from her grip, but she pulls me back, too easy. I am soft as a baby.

'Well …' she spits.

Metal tractoring over my head.

'*Dion* sees *you* almost every Sunday.'

The room is on the boil like Grandma's stew. A black simmer. *Plink plink.* Marrow in my mouth.

'At the *movies*, apparently.'

Her face, too close. Her forehead hot and *hard hard hard* against mine.

Hard as hate.

My eyes fix on my mother's pert little mouth, those lips – two plump berries.

'But you never notice poor old Dion, do you, Mutt?' They part and close, those two little swellings, blown with venom. 'Too busy with your new *boyfriend*. Too busy opening your legs for your new BOYFRIEND!'

Inside my pocket, my fingers find it, the word stone. I carry it always. My fingers find Tillie and Prim, they find Miss Moorcroft and Sister Aggie and the boring old Prince of Metternich-Winneburg.

'*SLUT!*'

Something warm huddles against my chest.

'Druggie good-for-nothing *SLUT!*'

Paddy! Paddy's home!

'Gonna run off with him? Is that the plan?'

Paddy blinks at me, eyes so trusting, stumpy tail whirring. I catch it in my fingers.

'That it? Gonna run off, like I always knew you would?'

The yoke is gone. Wretched thing. Don't worry, red boy. I'll never let them put it back on.

Lonnie's lava hands grip the sides of my neck. I vomit onto the floor.

'Ungrateful little *bitch!*'

Teeth clenched. Fist knock slap.

My throat, splitting like a busted zip.

Ireland, Paddy. Let's go! Spain, where José and Lucia used to live.

'After all I done ...'

There's a place called Lapland, Paddy, did you know? All the snow we could ever want, skies that glow alien-green.

'... Slutting around, making a fool of me! Of *ME*?'

Free now, Paddy. Free to be.

—

She has left long strands, like streamers from some macabre parade. Between them, craters of bleeding baldness. He peels the beanie off my head without saying anything.

He doesn't say it doesn't matter. Doesn't say he will always love me no matter how I look. He kisses my forehead, my cheek, my lips. Firm kisses, not romantic. No prince's kiss. Like his lips on my skin might take it all away, turn back time. He holds me. I can't see his face, but his body shakes. I have never seen him angry.

He does say, 'It'll be long again soon, if that's what you want. Or wear it like Mia Farrow—'

'Except this isn't how I *wear* my hair. This is how I woke up and *found* my hair. What's ... what's left of it.'

Luggage by his front door. On his way to a whole other world.

'I told you, didn't I tell you? Didn't I say you can't win with her. She's probably parked outside. She's probably got me bugged and I'm too stupid to know it. Wait till she finds out I'm wagging school.'

'She's the one who should be worried. It's assault, what she's done.'

My head pounds, still so groggy. I don't know how many pills she managed to get into me. I threw up three times before I left the house, again at the train station. The station guard shooshed me away, made me wait at the very end of the platform, like a danger. Like a bad person, a girl who is mad.

'Ror, we're going to the police. Even if you won't, I am. This is ending, right now.'

'Marc, no.'

'This is INSANE!'

'I've got four more exams, and I'm done. Am I going to let her cost me all that work? And where am I supposed to go? Where am I supposed to live? You're going to America tomorrow. You might never come back.'

'I'm coming back.'

'You might never come back.'

'Come with me.'

'I have … to finish … my exams.'

'After.'

'I don't have a passport!'

'Get one!'

I didn't know he could be angry, didn't know he could yell. Here I am, a dirty Murphy, infecting him with our sickness.

'Am I supposed to live with Prim? Her father is a lawyer. He'd probably want to involve the police too. Tillie? Her parents are really strict – they already don't like her hanging around with me. They think I'm weird. Wait till they get a load of me now.'

He tries to hold me, but I pull away.

'I'm a freak.'

'I'm going over there. I'm gonna tell that fucking bitch to lay off you, or else.'

'As if she'd listen to you. You'd only make things worse for me.'

He stands. Fists clenching, knuckles cracking. He sits. 'So … what?' Now he links his fingers over his head, knee bouncing. 'I'm supposed to just let you go back there? Let her do whatever she fucking feels like doing to you?'

The wheels of the train in my brain – *thunk thunk* at the back of my skull. Where my hair used to be – tufts, spiky. I can't stop touching them. The floor spins like a roulette wheel, stops, spins again.

Nothing is said for a while.

In my quietest voice: 'I got you a going-away present.' I barely mouth the words, every pulse of my blood an axing through my head. I still can't swallow properly, as though her hands are still around my throat. I know I will be sick again. 'Kerouac. *On the Road*. But I forgot it.'

Behind me he says, 'Hang on to it. I'll read it when I get back.'

I manage an almost-nod, cradling my forehead. I don't turn around, I don't think I can. I feel him staring at the back of my stricken, blood-hot head. He must think I'm crazy. As crazy as Lonnie. I look it now. He must be glad he is getting away from me.

'Because I am coming back.'

Day of extubation

I have given Frank the day off school. It's a big moment, and he wants to be there for his brother when Teddy finally wakes up. After we have the special breakfast I promised him, Frank and I drive to the hospital apartment.

'Wh- ... wh- ... wh-what's in the big ... in the big bag?' Frank asks, gesturing towards the back seat.

'Just some things I'm off-loading. Donating, you know.'

'To Teddy's hospital?'

'Hmm,' I reply. 'Among other places.'

The apartment turns out to be an older-style unit but spacious and nicely redone – air conditioned, a massive television, and a darkly elegant indigo entry hall.

'Purple,' Frank insists. 'It's deep ... it's deep purple, Mum.' He loves it and wants to know how long we can stay.

'You can settle in if you like,' I suggest. 'Test out the telly, pick which bedroom you want.' Frank is keen. 'But keep the front door locked. I'll drop those donations off, and text you when it's time to come over. Agreed?'

I pull into a ten-minute set-down zone outside the Gardens of Holy Marian, wrench the dressing-gown out of the plastic shopping bag.

'Where the bloody hell have you been!' Lonnie spits, her mouth full of yoghurt. 'Come to watch me *rot*?'

'I've had things to do,' I say, handing her the robe, and turning to leave.

Her words skitter after me down the corridor, little ghosts whose spooking grows weaker with every step. 'Get back here, Missy, or you've *had it*!'

When I was little, I waited for my mother to turn into my mother; that is, into what I imagined a mother was supposed to be. She would look like Carol Brady and love like Marilyn Mayhew. When that didn't happen, I waited instead for her to turn into a monster, fanged and gilled, for that was what she surely was, no? Not so different to the thing that took hold? It was only later I realised that the screamer, the schemer, that terrified, unstable thing – who worked in an office and stood on the sidelines, on committees, in pantyhose unladdered, driving cars bright green and new – whose hands too often took hold of me was far more frightening. Some keepers ought not to be keepers. Some keepers get away with too much. Too late once we're in the headlines, on the news. Too late for anything to be done.

'Don't you walk away from me!'

There is a view that we are forever bound to our mothers, a psychic, imperishable weaving. Cyclone Lonnie is forever in my head. There is no word for the power of her, nor for the power of mothers generally – an agency of terrifying magnitude, entrusted by chance, unpredictably carried to effect. We cannot be spared it; even early dead mothers have their own signature of aftershocks.

'Get back here, I said. *Right now!*'

I stop, turn, walk back to her room, and wait.

'You're all I got. You're all I ever had. When you leave, I worry you won't come back.' She lunges, skewers my arm with her nails. Digging them in, she watches my face as I allow her to hurt me. She would rather be despised than ignored. 'Why do you come back? Give me an answer.'

Her skin, thinned to crepe and mottle.

'Say it to me, just once. Why do you come back, all these visits, all these years? For the love-a God, daughter, don't let me die without hearing somebody say it to me.'

I know the words she wants me to say. Fairweather friends, those little words. I have never needed them.

'I come back for you because you wouldn't for me,' I say, with a mouth I hope isn't round and hard like the end of a pistol.

Jay, 17, Harriet House, summer

Hey? Kid? How ya doin'? It's us.

Do you think she can hear us? I don't think she can hear us.

She can hear us, can't you, Kid? It's Prim. It's ... talk to her, Tillie. She won't bite.

I can't stay much longer. If my parents knew I was here—

Well, they don't, so get over it.

Mum went spare when I told her. I'm basically grounded—

Tillie!

'That's it for today, girls. Rory needs her rest.'

Her name's Jay.

I've got to go, Primmy.

We gotta go, Kid. But we'll be back, okay? We're coming back.

Jay, 18, Harriet House, autumn

Nearly died when I found those pills, Sister. Couldn't believe it. Not my daughter, I said to myself. So full of promise.

Made sense, but, those pills. Up and down, such a moody piece. Worse and worse, she got. Telling me a pack of lies.

A 'secret' movie-star boyfriend. All in her head, he was. Just like everything else.

No, no, don't mind me, Sister. I'll be alright. Not the first time I've cried my heart out over this one. Won't be the last.

I should-a seen it coming, but. She's got a history. Sniffing books, bogeymen behind the curtains, talking to dead dogs. She's always been so highly strung.

I blame myself, but I don't mind saying it, she scared me that night. All those pills, throttling herself, the Stanley knife taken to her lovely hair. Here, here's a picture of what she used to look like. It could just as easy have been me, hacked to bits.

I'm doing the right thing here, aren't I, Sister? It won't hurt her, now, will it? I just want my daughter back. The girl she was. The girl she's supposed to be.

—

Oh, no.

The French exam? Biology?

Aren't they today?

What time is it? What if I've missed them?

I've gone mad. How could I miss my exams?

Think! Think!

Must get up, get dressed, get to school. Thursday? Yes. Sports uniform. Cool and light.

But my head ... can't lift it, can't *feel* it. I don't think it's there. My hands are all tied up, ropes around them.

No, not ropes.

Ropes poking through them.

No, not ropes.

I can't think of the thing I'm trying to remember.

Will it hurt? I ask the nurse. Sticky pads on my forehead. What you're going to do, will it hurt?

You ask this every time, she replies. And, no, you'll be fine. A reset, that's all.

Where are my friends? Where did they go? Are they coming back?

Friends? replies the nurse, so white. White upon white. White hat white tunic white watch white eyes white walls white ceiling.

Clock on the wall, white. It tells me the time, not the day. All in crosses, her white white face. Her face like a tired road.

On the Road. Is somebody.

It will reset you, is all, says the nurse.

Reset me?

What about my exams? I insist. I have to finish my exams.

Not sure about those, says the nurse, checking gadgets, the drip in my arm. You might have to miss those.

Miss my exams? I am horrified. I don't think she's listening to me. Not hearing me right.

She is ridiculous.

Plenty of time to make them up, she says, patting my arm. The arm I cannot raise. My restrained arm.

But it's November, and these are my finals. I won't graduate unless—

It's April now, dear, says the nurse.

April?

April. A whole new year. You had your birthday not so long ago, don't you remember? Your mum dropped off a cake. Not to worry, says the nurse. We're here to look after you.

April?

I remember now. School.

I arrived late. Airport, I'd stood there for hours, long after Marc's plane had disappeared. Silly daydreams of him suddenly popping up behind me. *As if I could leave you, Ror.*

My English exam was on in the building we call Nazareth. Third floor. But they'd only want to know what happened. To my hair. It used to be nice. Scratches around my neck, I could hardly speak. Wrong uniform, too; it wasn't even sports day. *A right scholar, this one,* JG used to say.

So I lay on the terrace instead, on the ground, under the wooden bench Tillie and Prim and I sat on to eat our lunch. Eat my pills. Shading my eyes from the sun.

Jay?

Miss Moorcroft. My friend.

Jay? Oh my God. Jay! What's happened to you?

William of Ockham's principle, Miss, I told her. No need to theorise beyond necessity.

Jay, I'm right here, love. I'm right here.

A mask walks in. A mask with an ear and an eyebrow. A big rubbery drooping ear and a falling black frown.

All ready to go, doctor, says the nurse.

Reset me? *Reset me?*

But no-one responds. It's like I'm not even here.

Reset me to what? I'm not a clock.

Kerouac o'clock, Spider. Time for us to go.

Keep? Thank goodness! Now … *shh.* They're not real people here, Keeper. They've gone strange, their heads—

Nothing to fear then. It's only people who do the harm.

You're so right.

Come along, now. Hands in mine.

I don't like people, Keep. They get away with everything.

Do you remember how?

Remember?

Together on the count of three.

Oh, yes, I remember.

One.

I won't ever forget.

Two—

One two together, Keep. Together forever.

Day of extubation

On my way up to PICU, I stop off in emergency, leave one of Teddy's old train sets and the four Russian dolls in the waiting area. I remember our first day in this place – kids' play areas marked off with foam puzzle flooring and alphabet mats but nothing to play with. Little hands will twist the dolls open, give them new names, cast them in soft silly stories. Inquisitive fingers will press on Mother's cracked head; she may be in pieces before long. Only she won't be Mother anymore. She'll be no more than a lump of wood, painted and pursed and hollow.

I am back on my bench in the corridor.

The extubation is taking place and family may not be present. 'Not a pretty procedure,' Doctor Ryker Shulmans told me. 'It takes time, and the room will be crowded, all hands at the ready.'

North Dakota – home to three of the five coldest cities in the United States: Williston, Fargo, Grand Forks. Capital, Bismarck. Coldest recorded temperature -51.1°C, Parshall, 1936.

I text Frank, tell him it is time to make his way across the street. *Remember to lock up*, then, clarifying, *FIRST, put the key into your pocket. THEN close the door. Tell me you will cross at the lights.*

So be it, Jedi, he replies.

As I wait, I open my laptop. Marilyn Mayhew has responded to my message:

Oh, Jay, honey. Evie passed on July 30, 1992, a little over a month after her nineteenth birthday. She died in her sleep, in her dorm room. She was at Dartmouth, doing so well. No cause was ever settled on. I think today it would be called Sudden Adult Death Syndrome.

She wrote you, Jay. I don't know what happened, maybe those letters never arrived?

You gave her a book when we left, a picture book. Norway? Snow dogs? She took care of that book, said a Blue Jay would come looking for it one of these fine days, that it kept you connected. I think she said it was magic, that was Evie. And maybe she was right, because here you are.

I'm so happy to hear you're okay, Jay. Would you like the book back, honey, because I kept it for her, for you both, I guess? I would happily send it to you.

Tonight, I will write back, tell Marilyn many things, and that, yes, I would love to have the book returned. I will tear out the pages, carefully of course, laminate its pictures and pin them under the desk in the laundry. Meerkats have had their day. I will tell the boys about Evie, and about the northern lights, the places where the sky glows alien-green. And when he is well, when every test result is known and Teddy has recovered or is in remission and the use of his gastrostomy is second nature to us, we will get passports, buy three plane tickets, damning what torpedoes we have left, and go see them for ourselves.

Of all days, Minnie Rollo somehow discovers my number. And uses it. She can't find Jerrik.

'I see,' I say. Her voice has a colour. Yellow. Bright, gaudy, run-screaming-from-the-room yellow. I imagine her dressed in pleated linen and smelling glorious.

'I'm pregnant.'

Glorious-smelling and hopefully cross-eyed.

'I see,' I say again. I don't know what she wants from me. 'Well, I'm not hiding him. Jerrik's all yours, Minette. He's *so* all yours that if he had a twin, if he had a clone, if he had a factory full of fucking replicants, they'd *all* be all yours.'

'I've checked his work schedule,' she says, teary. 'He's not where he's supposed to be.'

'Of course he isn't,' I say. 'He's Jerrik.' And then I tell Minnie Rollo I'm very busy and hang up.

I hear the television playing to itself in the parent lounge. Not a Marc show, though any television anywhere, on or off, almost always brings him to mind.

He never did come back.

'How would you know?' asked Doctor Crasno at one of our visits. 'You were in hospital for months after he left. Your mother authorised an involuntary treatment order. God only knows what "therapies" you might have endured back then.'

Truth was, when I woke up, when they let Lonnie take me home, I hadn't been *reset* at all. I'd been *unmade* into something unbothered. By anything. For years.

'Marc may have come back, but even if he'd called every Murphy in the book, do you think your mother would have passed along a message? Perhaps you owe *him* a letter,' she suggested. 'You wouldn't have to send it.'

And I suppose I could do that, try to contact him through an agent or a studio.

Dear Marc. ~~Remember me?~~
An email, or the riskier, more mature pen?
~~Dear Marc.~~
If I went ahead and did that, and if Marc actually got back in touch, Frank would flip. *If I was a magician, Mummy, I'd make Commander Hay come around, hold your hand, whenever you are sad. I know how much you like him.*

'Hey, Mum,' says Frank, planting himself on the bench beside me. 'K- ... k- ... the key's in-in my pocket.'

My magician, I think. 'Great job,' I tell him.

A nurse appears. 'Doctor Shulmans says you can come through now.'

We pick our way through the too-bright wing, boxed babies left and right. Infants with their tiny mouths rammed open, nostrils stretched and bogged, their every breath, every blink, such toil. All the while, the Other Things, thriving, don't even try to hide themselves. There's a pack for every parent present, making the most of the time they have, feasting on the wellspring of worry.

Teddy's eyes are still closed, but there are no more tubes or tape. His face shines, pink and featherless, tired and lovely. He breathes steadily.

'All went well,' says Ryker Shulmans. The various staff, still gathered in the room, still at the ready, look softer, loosed by relief.

I am told Teddy will stay another day or two in intensive care, before being moved to a ward.

'Ward Eight, as it happens,' notes Ryker Shulmans. 'You owe me a beer.'

Teddy's gastro consultant has a word, tells me they want to

commence him on an infusion regime. Crohn's disease is his official diagnosis.

My mouth falls slightly open, and she takes in my surprise.

'Have you not heard? Have Gen Paed not updated you? Teddy's bone marrow has come back all clear. Same with those lymph nodes. We'll monitor them, but we've ruled out any kind of malignancy. Dear me, dear me,' she says, full of apology. 'The communication in this place. We'd be better off with carrier pigeons.'

Frank looks at me; I'm not sure which of us will cry first. We fist-bump.

Infusions will occur at regular intervals – every two weeks at first, then every four weeks or six, depending on his body's response. Our first goal is to get Teddy into remission. I ask how long this might take.

'About as long as a piece of string,' says the consultant, a wry smile. 'Remission is a shifting beast and Crohn's a tricky disease. We will discuss a treatment plan in the coming days. Nothing is certain, we will adjust our response as we go, learn as we go.'

Of course we will. An approach uniquely suited to my skill set. Nothing so certain in my life as uncertainty. Rory Jay's groove.

It will be a couple of hours before Teddy is fully awake. Frank and I sit either side of his bed. The three of us, as we have always been. Close enough to save each other, the darkness stayed at our heels. Our duration uninterrupted, for now.

I pick up Teddy's hand, lace our fingers, and wait.

Ward 8

John Carpenter's *Halloween*. My alarm. Teddy's 1:00 am feed.

I need a moment, just one, to chisel my bones from a too-thin recliner chair, and to run through the list: wash, flush, prepare, measure – hands, syringes, dressing, formula. Careful, I don't want to wake him. Dim light, all I need. I know what I'm doing – been doing it every three hours for five weeks. Remove bandage. Unclamp. A thirty-minute bolus feed. Clamp. Re-dress, rinse, dry, finish. Watch him breathe – the rising, falling, rising. Such simple mechanics able to save two lives at once – Teddy's and mine.

I sit down again, rub my puffed-up feet, set the alarm for 4:00 am.

Across the room, the light above the basin flickers – comes on, stays on. A dusty, gentle light. The one I'd have chosen.

It's been almost six weeks since I've been home. The longest we have ever been apart.

'Hello, my Keeper.'

He is formless and shaggy. A beast, unclassified. I love him this way.

I tell him about Teddy, his diagnosis, what the doctors have advised, his current blood results, our treatment plan. I tell him everything. I know he would want to know.

'We're allowed to go home tomorrow.'

Then you need to sleep, Rory Jay.

'Hey. That's the first time you've ever used my name.'

I think not.

'It is. In forty years. Believe me, I'd know.'

You need to sleep.

'Why? What's going on?'

You need to see.

'See what?'

The rest of the way.

And though he doesn't move, though he is still across the room, hands cover my eyes.

'I will, Keeper. I will.'

What else can I say?

I wait for him at the bus stop. The 126 rolls in.

'There she is,' the old man says, smiling at me, brown bag of groceries in the crook of an arm.

'Let me carry them,' I insist.

'What a g- … a g-good … a good girl, you are,' he says. 'Oh no, here I go again. I seem to have f- … forgot- … f-forgotten your name, my dear.'

'So have I.'

'Doesn't matter. We know … we know each other, don't we?'

Up the hill to his house. A big house, shared. All the big houses are shared now. He lives in one half of it – the smaller half. The owners live in the other.

'Been here a long time,' says the old man, unlocking his front door. 'But you … you know that, don't you? You've been w-watching.'

The old man has few possessions, but everything is lined up, neat and clean.

'They're very good to me, Rollo and Pearce. Make sure I've always g-got what I need.' Two bedrooms, a living room and kitchen. 'Make sure I don't f- … f-forget things,' he says, tapping a temple. Coffee mugs on a wooden tree. A toaster, a small bench oven, a tea towel threaded through its handle. Books. A television and two armchairs. Sao crumbs.

A paved area out the back, and a patchwork of stones hopscotching to a large shed.

'That's w- ... w- ... w-where I ... that's where I do my w-work,' he says. 'W-want to have a look?'

'*Do I?*' I say, a little skip.

I follow him and his tan boots, purple socks pulled high, little half-moons.

'I'm very lucky,' he says. 'It's an old boat shed, so it's roomy. Not ... not too many boats around these days.'

He presses his palm to a panel in a wall, and a small light flashes. Inside is pretty, like another small house. Pastel greens and blues. A wink of lilac on its high ceiling, and a big Tahitian-style fan. Workbenches run along its sides, an organised clutter of pots, brushes, tubes, spray bottles, palettes. Two easels, one larger than the other. And paintings – hung, leaning, stacked, framed, unframed, pegged to lengths of string – everywhere.

'*Oh,*' I say. 'I just knew I'd love them.'

'I sell qu- ... qu- ... I sell a lot, overseas mostly. My kind of thing never found a market here. Rollo, my half-brother, he does the f-framing, and his partner, Pearce, helps me run the business side of things. I couldn't manage w-without them.'

The old man holds his cluster of keys. In a small see-through case threaded onto the key ring is a tiny wooden doll. I lean in, inspecting her.

'She w-was ... she w-was ... my mother's,' he says. 'The only one left. They w-were nesting dolls, you see, dear? A set. But Mum said, *She's the important one, Franko. She's the only one that matters.*'

I look up into his face, and we remember together. 'She drilled a ... a little hole in the bottom, see?' He holds it up for me to look.

'Hid a ma- ... hid a ma-magic pebble inside, sealed it up with wood g- ... g- ... with wood glue. It's held all these years. *When you need to hear our voices, Franko,* she said to me. *Just hold the little doll. We'll be inside.*' He smiles. 'My twin, he ... he had a lovely voice, an angel's voice. My mother, she had a nice voice too. I do ... I do listen sometimes. It is the sound ... the music ... of time apart, ending.'

I follow him back to his half-house; we're going to have afternoon tea. His boots. A young man's boots. As the old man reaches up, retrieving a teapot, the curls of yellow on his socks, I see, aren't half-moons at all. They are dolphins, jumping and spinning out of the waves. Golden and perfect.

I wake. It is 3:16 am.

'Pretty thoughts,' I say aloud. 'Sometimes dreams are just dreams, though, aren't they? Bastard dreams.'

Keep, his back turned, a blur in the corner. *Perhaps,* he says. *And perhaps, in our world, dreams are something else.*

'Oh, Frank,' I say, my fingers pressed to my eyelids. I am so tired. 'I suppose I should say thanks, Keep. That was you, right? Giving me ... what? Hope? A counter argument?'

It can all be from me if you like.

'I don't understand,' I say, my head heavy. 'But I'm not meant to, am I? I'm not allowed.'

It begins to rain. Wilful, belligerent, drenching rain. Through the window, the city is a slip-down straggle of golds and silvers, ember-reds and whale-belly blues. Ghost lights in the empty theatre of night, left on for those of us who need them.

'So, if that's Frank,' I say, 'where's Teddy? My sick Teddy, over there, in that bed? Needing me more than ever. Where does that leave him? Because the only way he will ever be safe is for this world to be rebuilt, bottom up, and the human design re-engineered – eyes, ears and mouth phased out, all the levers of judgement dismantled. Until that happy day, Keeper, where does that leave Teddy?'

Keep turns, comes sharply into view. A harlequin of sorts, diamonds of light and dark blue, ruffs worn from travelling, from gruelling endless performance. A face, gaunt and powder-white, tired too from the things it has seen, black slots and slits to see and hear. A painting. A man from a painting.

I demand again: 'Where does that leave Teddy?'

A man from a painting in a book that burned. A paper man, just as he was when I first saw him. Perhaps as he has always been.

Why, with us, Spider, he replies. *Where else but with us?*

NOTES

The epigraph is an excerpt from *Siddhartha: An Indian Tale* by Hermann Hesse, translated by Joachim Neugroschel, translation copyright © 1999 by Joachim Neugroschel. Used by permission of Penguin Books, an imprint of Penguin Publishing Group, a division of Penguin Random House LLC. All rights reserved.

The articles 'Special needs group pays tribute to 11yo Sydney boy with autism killed by train after escaping from respite care', 'SA Police investigating death of woman in "disgusting and degrading circumstances"', 'Disability Royal Commission hears teenager was left with severe disability after being given psychotropic medication', 'Queensland Ombudsman calls out "brutalisation" of disabled man, held for six years in Queensland facility' and 'Joy as Canberra disco for people with disabilities returns after coronavirus shutdown' were published by abc.net.au. Reproduced with the permission of the Australian Broadcasting Corporation.

The lines 'The only people for me are the mad ones. Who burn, burn, burn, like fabulous yellow Roman candles exploding like spiders across the stars' are taken from *On the Road* by Jack Kerouac, copyright © 1955, 1957, by John Sampas, Literary Representative, the Estate of Stella Sampas Kerouac; John Lash, Executor of the Estate of Jan Kerouac; Nancy Bump; and Anthony M. Sampas. Used by permission of Viking Books, an imprint of Penguin Publishing Group, a division of Penguin Random House LLC. All rights reserved.

The article 'Brisbane girl, 4, dead for days in cot as father is charged with murder' was published by news.com.au on 27 May 2020. The use of this work has been licensed by the Copyright Agency except as permitted by the Copyright Act, you must not re-use this work without the permission of the copyright owner or Copyright Agency.

The extract of Henry and Leona is taken from *Sorry Wrong Number* © Paramount Pictures Corp. Reproduced with the permission of Paramount Pictures Corp.

The definition of 'Keeper' on page 205 is from *Macquarie Dictionary Online*, Macquarie Dictionary Publishers, an imprint of Pan Macmillan Australia Pty Ltd, Sydney, 2020. Reprinted with permission.

The line 'His name was Jason … Jason was my son, and today is his birthday' is taken from the film *Friday the 13th* © Paramount Pictures Corp. Reproduced with the permission of Paramount Pictures Corp.

ACKNOWLEDGEMENTS

My sincerest thanks to:

Aviva Tuffield, for reading my manuscript in the first place, for her guidance and expertise and willingness to take on a raw and unschooled voice. And to all at UQP, especially Felicity Dunning and Lou Cornegé. Thank you for this dream come true.

The Australian Writers' Centre – tutors and classmates. There for me when no-one else was.

Debbie Guertin, Jane McGown and Bernadette Foley for bravely confronting very early drafts.

Angela Slatter – sensei and friend. No Angela, no book.

Candice Fox and her generous Write Club Q&As.

Nikki Gemmell for her words, columns and kindness.

Dr Sarah Sasson – writer, doctor, editor and friend – for guidance on all things medical and for giving me my first-ever writerly acceptance.

Sophie Pitt, Institute for Marine and Antarctic Studies, University of Tasmania; Giselle Bramwell, Meteorological Service of Canada, Vancouver; Trausti Jónsson, Icelandic Meteorological Office; Eve at the Meteorological Office, Devon; Ville Siisonke, Finnish Meteorological Institute; Angel Corona, National Weather Service, Alaska; Inger Marie Nordin, Norwegian Meteorological Institute, Oslo; National Weather Service, Bismarck, North Dakota and Michigan.

Tanya Darl, for lending her artistic brilliance to our front cover.

Danish chums Tatiana Larsen, Pia Blak and Charlotte Hansen for translation assistance. (Danish best wishes to all at Heimdal!)

Veronica, my darling sister and co-survivor. Always in my corner, especially when I can't be there myself.

Scott Richard, for all the parts he has played.

The past fifty-plus years – I hate you and love you in equal measure. Mean as you've often been, you've taught me some stuff I'm definitely better off knowing.

The many writers whose books I have read. The best how-to-write tuition of all.

And, of course, Boy Wonder 1 and Boy Wonder 2. All and everything, because of you, my darlings, because of what you have shown me – so much more than I ever would have discovered for myself.

BOOK CLUB QUESTIONS

1. *The Keepers* is essentially a love story – a story of a love so ferocious it bares its teeth. But it is also a story of people who cannot love, and the lifelong consequences of that. How successfully does the novel balance these light and dark themes?

2. Jay has a close and unique relationship with her boys. What is your favourite moment between her and Frank or Teddy (or both)?

3. Abuse and neglect is a central concern of *The Keepers*. However, in surveys conducted both in Australia and around the world, the care and welfare of people with a disability routinely ranks last as the social issue of most concern to respondents. Why do you think this is?

4. Jay has a complex relationship with Jerrik yet, no matter how poorly he treats her, she remains in their loveless marriage. Why does she choose to stay with him?

5. Some parents come to realise that raising children with special needs requires skills and endurance they simply do not, and will never, possess. Given this, what do you make of the character of Jerrik?

6. How did you respond to the character of Lonnie as a mother who is so unstable, violent and manipulative? Did you feel any sympathy for her, given what her own upbringing must have been like at the hands of JG?

7. Who or what is Keep? What role does he play in Jay's life?

8. The author intersperses real-life media stories about the mistreatment and suffering of people with a disability in the form of Jay's scrapbook entries, alongside the fictionalised chapters. How did these add to or change your perspective on Jay's story?

9. What do you make of Jay's relationship with Marc? How does this story arc add to the development of Jay's character?

10. At the end of the novel, Jay meets an elderly Frank but Teddy is not mentioned. What do you think happened to Teddy, and what do you think we need to do as a society to make sure people like him have a future?

Full notes available at www.uqp.com.au